I0823770

Praise for Elizabeth Anne Martins and *Dry Lands*

"A testament to the power of hope and motherhood in the worst of situations."

Kirkus

"Liv's daily battle against starvation and predators, human and otherwise, is visceral, and – thanks to Martins' gift for characterization – her evolution feels earned as she gradually adapts her ethics to keep Milo alive at all costs. The tenacious, well-shaded heroine elevates this above many similar efforts."

Publishers Weekly

ELIZABETH ANNE MARTINS

OPPOSITE WORLD

This is a **FLAME TREE PRESS** book

FLAME TREE PRESS
6 Melbray Mews, London, SW6 3NS, UK
flametreepress.com

US sales, distribution and warehouse:
Simon & Schuster
simonandschuster.biz

UK distribution and warehouse:
Hachette UK Distribution
hukdcustomerservice@hachette.co.uk

The font families used are Avenir and Bembo.

Flame Tree Press is an imprint of Flame Tree Publishing Ltd
flametreepublishing.com

A copy of the CIP data for this book is available from the British Library and the Library of Congress.

1 3 5 7 9 8 6 4 2

HB ISBN: 978-1-78758-960-5
ebook ISBN: 978-1-78758-961-2

Printed and bound in the UK by CPI Group (UK) Ltd, Croydon, CR0 4YY

Represented in the EU for product safety and compliance by Authorised Rep Compliance Ltd., Ground Floor, 71 Lower Baggot Street, Dublin, D02 P593, Ireland. Contact at www.arccompliance.com

ELIZABETH ANNE MARTINS

OPPOSITE WORLD

FLAME TREE PRESS
London & New York

For those piecing together the past,
to have a piece of the present,
and peace for the future.

'Please assume, then, for the sake of argument, that there is in our souls a block of wax. In one case, larger; in another, smaller; in one case, the wax is purer; in another, more impure and harder; in some cases, softer. Let us, then, say that this is the gift of Memory, the mother of the Muses, and that whenever we wish to remember anything we see or hear or think of in our own minds, we hold this wax under the perceptions and thoughts and imprint them upon it, just as we make impressions from seal rings; and whatever is imprinted we remember and know as long as its image lasts...'

Plato, *Theaetetus c.* 360 BCE

Part One

Twilight

Chapter One

I once heard my voice ring out loud as church bells.

It was mine, but it was also beyond me. It was sharp and raw, like metal thwacking stone. It punched past the deepest barriers of my brain, rattling through nerves and roots – places nobody's supposed to touch. I was on the floor, convulsing – another episode. They came and went like storms, but this one hit different. It was angry, more savage, like it had fangs sinking into my cerebrum. Like it wanted something from me.

Through the delirium, another voice surfaced – my mother's – passing through me like an electric jolt. *Pip. Pip!* Her voice withered and warped. I writhed in the chaos, twisting, trying to pinpoint her face, spine arching, limbs locking, eyes fluttering. There she was – frantic, turbulent, in and out of my vision, her cheek pressed against the wooden floor amid a tangle of wires. She reached for my hand. My father hovered close, his boots pinning my head in place like an anchor. Colors burst behind my eyes – grays and whites with smears of ruby red and parrot green, a jumbled mess of pigments that didn't belong together.

Then the world ripped apart. Mechanical buzzing, shouting, something tearing from the seams inside me. My skull felt like it shattered – the edifice of time breaking into scattered potsherds, my memories smashing to the ground like crushed ceramics, pieces I'd never get back. When the convulsing subsided, there was nothing. No sound. No light. Just thick, infinite darkness. I plunged into a dense, obsidian slumber that seemed to swallow me whole.

But just before I slipped away, something stirred in the void. A voice, soft and close, seeping through the cracks: *I'm going to hurt you, but it's the only way.*

Chapter Two

My father hauled us out of Seattle after the episode the way a hunter might drag a dead boar – rough, wordless, not looking back.

I was nine, maybe ten – it didn't matter much. Time was slippery. I sensed us moving, the long bumpy truck ride, the sway of each turn. But I was too tired to piece it all together. My eyelids remained fastened even when I felt my body land on a strange bed. I was a loose lump of bones, drifting in and out of sleep, bedridden, weak. Every now and then, something hot or cold slipped between my lips – soup, water. At times, I'd stir, aware only of the fleeting current of scents – burnt wood, damp leaves, garlic and dirt, sweet maple syrup, the faded trace of jasmine – my mother's scent.

And then I'd slip back into a long, dark sleep.

One morning, my eyes peeled open like stubborn pages fused together. The light stung, and it took a minute to recognize the hands on my chest were my own. I brought them into view – pale and thin. They trembled when I moved them, like they hadn't seen sunlight in months. I ran my fingers over my neck – damp with sweat, strands of cedar-brown hair clinging to my skin like matted vines. The strawberry-blond flecks from my mother's side were gone, swallowed by darker strands.

The room was foreign to me. Wooden beams stretched above, coated in dust, brittle and aged. Toys I no longer played with sat scattered in strange places, as if someone had plucked them blind from our Seattle home. My mother's clothes lay draped about like wild weeds, unkempt and forgotten. I tried to call for her, but my words wouldn't come, stuck like stones in my throat.

Then, he stirred.

At the edge of the room, slumped in a chair woven from branches, my father jolted awake at the sound of my finger bones cracking. His sunken eyes swept the room before settling on me. For a long moment, he just stared – like he couldn't remember who I was or why I was there – then he sank back into himself, as if battling some inner war. Finally, he stood, jittery yet mechanical, shuffling toward a small table beside me where an old whisky jug rested. His rough knuckles wiped the drool from my mouth before he lifted the jug.

"Drink," he muttered, his voice clotted with spit as though he hadn't spoken in days.

I turned my head away.

"It's water," he said.

He tipped the bottle to my lips. The water hit my teeth like ice but didn't clear the stones away.

"Rest," he whispered. As though sleep was the only gift he had left to offer. His face hovered close right before he peeled away. But his eyes gave him away. There was something splintered there, some remorseful sign in the oak of his eyes – I was waking up from something more than sleep. Something during that last episode had clawed inside me, taken something special, and scraped me hollow. And I knew, deep in my marrow, whatever it stole wasn't returning.

Chapter Three

The day came when I found the strength to ask questions.

I called out for my father. My voice exploded in the cabin room like shrapnel. It burst everywhere, dripping off the log-plaited walls and falling onto the flimsy blanket covering my body. I lay in bed as my father shuffled in, hunched and red-eyed, a carving tool tight in his grip. Flames from a fireplace crackled and popped in the pockets of silence. Was this my bedroom?

"What happened to me?" I asked.

He went to dab my drool, but I beat him to it.

"You were sick," he said, the words clumsy in his mouth. "But you're getting better."

I searched his face for grounding, but something told me his beard had grown like his lies. Feral and out of control. "What is this place?"

"Our new home in Snoqualmie Pass, by the mountains."

I let his words settle.

"Are we close to Seattle?"

"About an hour away. We took you camping here once. Do you remember? The time I was a storm tamer…"

I watched him fidget.

"Where's Mom?"

He paused. "She's…not here," he mumbled, each syllable oozing out like a paste.

"Where is she?"

"She's gone to Heaven, Pip."

"*Heaven?*"

"Yes."

My eyes watered. My lungs constricted. I couldn't breathe. I tried to get out of bed, but he wouldn't let me. Said I was too weak. "But I just saw her." My words trembled. "She was on the floor next to me. She was holding my hand—"

He lowered his head. "She got sick too."

Rain tapped at the windows, an incessant hammer that seemed to get louder and more agitated with each passing second.

I turned my head to the pane, gulping for air. I couldn't stomach his face. I blamed him for allowing this to happen. But his reflection met me in the glass anyway. I couldn't escape him.

His face strained with something worse than guilt.

Like he was sorry I woke up at all.

Like maybe the truth was something I was better off not knowing.

Chapter Four

Nobody likes to think about their mother dying.

For me, it became an obsession – a knot I couldn't undo. I kept returning to it, trying to untangle the threads. The timeline of my life blurred, and I searched for scraps to make sense of the last time I saw her: her jasmine scent, her final words, a hazy glimpse of wires. My mind, still reeling from the episode, refused to let go of the flashes I saw behind my eyes. What did those colors mean? And whose voice spoke to me at the end? Did she die while I was having an episode? How long was I out, anyway?

My father offered nothing. "She had health problems," he said, his voice clamping shut like a steel door anytime I asked. "These things happen."

But shame covered his face. He could hardly meet my eyes.

Instead, he threw himself into the woods surrounding our new cabin, hunting sticks to whittle into knives, pressing his bare feet into the soil to test the earth's foundation for beets and onions and other things he could bury. He mushed berries into measly excuses of watery jam and carved obscure trinkets out of maple.

School wasn't allowed anymore. Not at this place. But I held on to what I could from the city – bits of math, wonders of science, the serenity of art. And screens. God, I missed them. Computers, TVs, tablets – hell, even a crackling old walkie-talkie would've felt like a treat. That was before he destroyed every sign of technology, calling them all poison. But my craving for learning stayed. I made do. I collected pinecones, arranging them into perfect mandalas on the floorboards – tiny acts of order to keep my mind from gnawing at its own roots for entertainment. My designs became my only reliable truth. But no matter how carefully I tried to soothe my inner world, the images kept returning to me.

Her. Tangled in wires.
The voice. *I'm going to hurt you.*
I wanted answers.
I would have killed for them.

Chapter Five

One year passed.

I found my father in the shed at dusk. It was just across a path of wild grass from our cabin, his makeshift woodcarving studio. August heat was pressing in, thick as tar. His refurbished oil lamp flickered when I twisted the knob, splattering crooked shadows across the wooden floorboards. He was perched on a stool, a headlamp wrapped around his forehead like a miner's tool. He didn't look up from the chest he'd been hollowing out for weeks. The room reeked of sawdust and sweat.

His bare feet pressed into the grimy, dust-covered floor. I noticed, with a pang of frustration, that he hadn't bathed – again. I crossed my arms as I watched his knife peel thin spirals of wood, each curl shedding like dead skin. He looked like a grizzled woodsman there in the dim shed, his meshwork beard fraying at the edges and his sullied shirt clinging to him like wet felt. But I knew better. This was the same man who once built algorithms and codes to change the world. Dr. Richard Screed, the genius who'd left it all behind to hide out in the woods.

He finally noticed me and switched off his headlamp. Blond shavings flitted from his ragged sideburns. He tapped the wooden chest and gave me a tired smile.

"Almost done," he said. "What do you think?"

What did I think? I thought I wanted answers. I wanted friends, school, a chance at something beyond these woods. I wanted a life. My mother. But he couldn't see that. All he saw was his hollow chest – a distraction, another project to keep the world away. I wondered if I could leave him behind. If I did, would I forgive myself? Would I regret abandoning the only person who cared for me, even if that care felt like a chokehold?

I stared at him, the words curdling in my mouth. "I think I need to go to school, Dad. I'm almost eleven. I should be in fifth grade by now. Maybe sixth. I don't know."

"Nah," he said, air trembling past his lips. "I'm your teacher."

As much as my father's reclusive antics annoyed me, he was my everything. I loved him. But love didn't mean we understood each other.

"You won't even give me a pencil," I said.

"I gave you a whittling knife." He turned back to his chest, his own knife gliding through the wood. "I teach you about foraging. The woods. Cooking."

I stood there in the wood dust, trying to reason with him. "Why don't we have computers anymore?"

His blade slowed, but he didn't look up. "We've talked about this, Pip. Computers are...mind suckers. I prefer a simple life." Finally, he met my eyes and sighed, resting his knuckles on the worktable. "I want the same for you."

"Okay, but why is our mailbox boarded up? Why aren't we allowed to say our names when we go to town...if we even go at all? Why can't I have friends? Why do you shut us away? Ever since Mom—"

"Stop." His voice cracked like a whip. He got back to carving, his strokes growing quicker and sharper. "There are some things you don't understand yet, Piper. It's better this way. Trust me."

I kicked at the dust. "Then explain it to me!"

He slammed the knife down, cutting his finger. He didn't even flinch. "You're being too loud. Someone could hear us."

"Who, Dad? The chipmunks?"

He was paranoid to a fault. Our closest neighbor was up a steep hill we never trekked, and there were maybe one or two others scattered miles and miles down the road – off-grid no-names we never saw. The forest dirt could have opened and swallowed us whole, and no one would've blinked.

He stared at me, stiff-jawed, blood welling at his cut. When he finally spoke, his voice was hoarse, almost a whisper. "We're safe here, Pip." He paused, like he wasn't sure whether to say more. "There are people out there. If they find me…" His eyes shot toward the narrow slit in the door, then back to me, his words dissolving on his tongue. "Forget it."

I gritted my teeth. "Tell me."

His cement face softened. "It means they're looking for you too."

It was the most information he'd given me in the year since my mother's passing, but it felt like a weight. It sat heavy on my chest, paralyzing me. I didn't know what to say back.

He flicked his headlamp back on, pressing his wound to his mouth, and I became invisible again. I left, slamming the door so hard the frame shook. I stomped off, but something made me stop. The door hadn't latched right. I paused with a quiet sigh and retraced my steps to ensure his clumsy door clicked shut. Before I left, I eased the door open, just a sliver, and watched him carve, sweat dripping from his brow, wondering what he meant. His blade scored harder, like it was cutting through something denser than wood. I shut the door quietly, but the carving sounds scraped deeper. More aggressive. I slipped away, back to my room. I curled up beside my pinecone mandala and cried until my throat burned. It took me two years to find a friend. By then, speaking felt like forcing words through rusted pipes.

Chapter Six

I met Farley Renner in the creek.

He was a tall, wiry kid with a bushy head of golden-brown hair that couldn't be tamed. He was fourteen; I was twelve. He lived on the other side of the creek, tucked up a steep trail that dried the breath from your lungs by the time you reached the top. But I never minded the climb. Farley was the closest sign of life to me, and soon enough, he became the only link to anything that felt real.

He would fish in the creek in warm months, sometimes cold, and often his aunt Vera would let me sit with him on their enclosed porch and play video games. I'd sink into their cushioned rocking chair, gripping a video game controller, the electric fuzz melting into my palms, feeling so connected to the world it made my skin buzz.

Their cabin was colossal, inhaling you the moment you stepped inside. It used to be a vacation rental before Farley's parents died in a tragic crash, before his aunt turned it into their home, rebranding grief with rebirth. She became his guardian, though most of the time she treated him like a roommate. On the far end of their driveway was an in-law suite no one touched. It just sat there, awaiting purpose. An unflashy, quiet force – much like my and Farley's nascent relationship. Visiting Farley felt like my one shot at normalcy, like I could slip into the skin of a regular kid. I never told my father about him. If he found out, I knew he'd find a way to destroy it.

"Pip, maybe some time I can come to your house," Farley said with a video game controller between thumbs.

I guided my avatar into a new room, tapping rhythmically. "My dad doesn't let anyone come over. So probably not."

"Does he know about me?"

"No," I said, shifting in the rocker. "He thinks I'm out foraging right now. I'm not allowed to go out too far or see anyone."

"Why's he like that?"

"Probably because I had problems when I was younger."

"Like what?"

I didn't want to say, but I didn't want to lose my only friend.

"I would shake until I fainted."

He paused our game and steadied his eyes on me. "Do you still?"

"No. Not anymore."

"What's different?"

"My mom died." The words felt like a punch. "That's when I got better. But ever since, my dad has us locked up from the world. I'm not even allowed to go to school."

"Sorry. That's not right."

"It's okay."

"Losing your parents sucks."

Farley sighed, releasing a part of himself. I was quick to understand the weight of his breath.

"Yeah," I said, unpausing the game for the both of us.

I didn't know what else to say, and suddenly, an image of my mother on the floor with wires flashed through my mind like a faulty light. I worried an episode might come on, so I changed the subject back to the game. "I think you can teleport through this door. Follow me."

He was quiet for a while. Then: "If you marry me, you don't have to be locked up anymore. Plus, you can always play my video games."

I tried to hide my smile as I looked at him.

He leaned forward, grinning. "I'm serious."

I felt my cheeks warm. "All right."

He leaned back, confident, clicking his controller. "For real. You can always count on me."

I couldn't stop smiling. "All right," I said again.

Vera was behind us, sipping tea. I didn't know she was there until I said everything I said. After we were done playing, Farley was going to walk me halfway home, but she stopped us. She looked down at me like I was a sickly possum caught in a snare. After her eyes scanned my gaunt face, she said, "Pip, some kids go to school online. You can come here at eight and I'll make sure our computer room is open. I'll set everything up."

My tongue froze. The offer stunned me. For a second, I thought about what my dad would say – what he'd *do* – if he found out. I should've felt grateful, but something twisted in my chest. It felt like betrayal.

Farley leaned in and whispered, "You don't have to tell him, you know."

I nodded, not trusting myself to answer. Like he might hear me. His aunt sipped her tea, and Farley gave me one of his charming, clumsy smiles. I tried to smile back, but the image of my mother, tangled in wires, flashed in my mind again. This time, something about it felt different, like there was a message buried in the memory, something I hadn't noticed before. What if she wasn't just holding my hand? What if she was trying to tell me something? A warning.

Chapter Seven

When my father found out about Farley, it was like setting off a flare in a sleeping bear's den.

The first time he caught us together, he came barreling through the brush with his shotgun cocked, shouting loud enough to scatter birds from low-hanging branches. Farley took off, boots tripping on roots, mud shooting up behind him. It was rough. I figured that was the end of it – that no kid would be stupid enough to stick it out. But Farley was stubborn. Like a hook sunk deep around the bone, he reeled me in with patience, even though my father tried to snap the line.

Vera was the one who cooled the flames. One afternoon, we were walking in the woods on our side of the creek when my father stumbled across the three of us. I'd told them we were too close, that this was his turf. But they didn't feel the same danger I did – they couldn't. The moment I saw his haggard form through the trees, gun in hand, my heart dropped. I knew what came next. The gun. The shouting. The threats to keep me caged. But when he saw Vera with us, the fire in him dimmed. The grip on his gun slackened, and all he said was, "Get on home, Pip."

That night, Vera showed up at our place with a big bag of chocolates and fruit. She was a bright, bold meteor slamming down on his planet. I knew what she was doing though – taking stock, trying to figure out if the kid she was helping get an education was in danger or just being raised by an off-grid woodsman with a grudge against society. It was gracious of her to give me an education. Truly. I wouldn't have stayed informed about culture or technology without her. I appreciated her in that regard, but in other areas, she felt like a threat. She moved quickly, almost too naturally, into spaces that still belonged to my mother.

That night, she stayed extra-long and sat at the table like it was her roost, peeling an orange, her cinnamon-streaked hair catching the kitchen light, and I swear, every time she brushed her hair over her shoulder, my father flushed red. It rattled me, and I couldn't help it. I should've been happy for him. For us. At some point, she reached for my sweater and held the fibers between her fingers as though I were her pet, and she was making a mental note to take me to the groomer. Most of what I wore came from my mother's old wardrobe, whatever my father managed to salvage. None of it fit right. Her clothes were well-worn and loose on me, but comfortable. Vera's touch, whether coded or not, signaled it was time for me to move on. My clothes didn't fit me. And neither did my grief. Not anymore. I was almost afraid to wear my mother's clothes around her. If I left something behind at her cabin, like a scarf or jacket, she'd wash it immediately. She didn't mean harm, I'm sure, but every rinse felt like another piece of my mother's jasmine scent – whether real or imagined – was disappearing, leaving nothing but the fumes of store-brand detergent behind.

Three years came and went. I finished all my online courses under the watch of Vera, and still, my father didn't know. My feelings toward her continued to sway back and forth. Most days, I appreciated her kindness and how she tried to forge me a future. Other days, every gesture felt like a small step toward the deletion of my mother's memory. In the end, my feelings stayed the same: grateful but guarded.

And even after all that time, no visit with Farley or Vera ended without a lecture from my father.

"I know I can't keep you in my pocket," he said. His hands clasped shut at our crooked wooden table one day. "You're a teenager now. I get it. Just be careful who you trust. Nothing—" his voice tightened, "—nothing can come back to me or the Screed name."

"I know. I wish you'd just tell me why." I met his eyes. "But I know."

He gave me a haunting look. "Consider me a ghost."

"*I know.* Anyway, Farley proposed. Soon, I'll marry him, and then you can be done with me."

He clicked his tongue. "Stop."

"You won't have to worry about me anymore," I continued. "The Screed name will disappear for good. I'll be Piper Renner."

"You're fifteen," he said flatly.

"So, when can I get married, then?"

"When my beard has gone all gray."

"That'll take forever."

The corner of his mouth twitched, just a hair, but it was the closest sign of a smile I'd seen in him in years. "It always seems so," he said.

It took my father a long time to tolerate Farley. Acceptance didn't come naturally to him. But the more freedom I claimed, the more he slipped away from me. Some weeks, I didn't see him at all. When it was warm, he stockpiled supplies. In the cold months, he locked himself in the shed, carving until his fingers chapped like bark. His constant scraping, his boots clopping from the cabin to the shed, became the drumbeat of my winters. He closed himself off from everything – even me.

Years blurred. By the time his beard turned the color of smoke-covered snow, Farley had become my whole universe. We were in the creek one summer when I was eighteen – his arms around my waist, kissing, laughing – when I slipped on a mossy stone.

Farley caught me, reeling me in. "God, I love you, Piper Screed. I can't wait for our wedding day."

He was the only one who knew my name.

He was the only one who knew *me*.

He was also the only one who proposed to me on an annual basis.

I whispered, "I love you right back, Farley Renner."

He cupped my face with his palms, his olive-green eyes looking into mine. "Through thorns and through darkness, I love you."

I smiled. "I hope we get roses and light too."

He grinned and then kissed me. "All of it."

With every step I took toward Farley, my father drifted deeper into the woods – into whatever madness was waiting to infect him. But I knew the truth; he wasn't just running from his past. He was burying it. And sooner or later, I was going to dig it up.

Chapter Eight

Three years later, Farley's real proposal came like a worn and welcome path through the woods.

A few days before our wedding, I sat on a stone by the creek alone. Farley came beside me, slipping his hand across my waist. I should have felt comforted by his presence. Instead, I felt...scared. Like I was stepping into a foreign life with a past that wasn't fully pieced together. A past I still wanted answers on.

"You're quiet," he said.

I shrugged, feeling like I was wearing new skin. "It's just change. You know."

He stiffened, like the word *change* had reprogrammed him. He stared ahead at the rushing water. "Don't overthink it. Whatever it is. Just keep moving. Everything will fall into place."

I hesitated. "So don't talk about things. Just ignore them?"

"That's not what I said, Pip." He exhaled, his hand slipping away from me. "Can't we just enjoy this moment?"

My father's voice drifted through my mind for some reason: *Be careful who you trust.*

Our wedding ceremony was small, held at Vera's house, our vows exchanged by the tallest fir. My father refused to show up, and to be honest, I was relieved. By then, Farley had been living in his aunt's in-law suite for years, and after the buttercream cake, I moved in with him.

The suite sat tucked behind Vera's fortress of timber and stone – a cozy outpost just far enough to feel separate but close enough that if I screamed, she'd hear me. I got used to making the reverse trek down the hill to check on my father, but every time I passed his boarded-up mailbox, my stomach churned. It pulled me back to when I lived alone with him, cut off from the world, caught in his web of paranoia and secrets. Visiting him kept me on edge, worried his irrational distrust of others was only getting worse. He hobbled around his cankered cabin, peeking through slatted blinds as though the trees were spying on him, carving endless projects until his fingers bled. But if I voiced my concerns, Farley would shrug and say, "Really, Pip? I'd kill for a dad like yours. So the man's a little skittish. At least he's still standing."

A year into our marriage, I began to understand my thoughts were better off caged. Farley didn't want to lounge in the muck with me. He wanted to fix things, patch them up and move on like nothing ever happened. He'd grown quick to snuff out my fires before he could ever feel the heat.

He'd caught his fish and plopped it in the tank. What else was there to do?

Husband Farley wasn't Creek Farley. I'd missed the warning signs that things were going to change. Marriage had made us strangers sharing bedsheets and bar soap. It happened quietly, without panoply – the way faces changes over time, the differences invisible until you step back and look at the photo album in its entirety.

Living with my father was isolating, but marriage brought a different brand of solitude. Our suite was a silent refuge, interrupted only by birdsong outside our A-frame windows. It was smaller than Vera's house but sculpted from the same bones – pine and limestone, dark beams running the length of the ceiling. It should've felt like a dream, but instead, the walls pressed in. Outside, the trees resembled bars. The air, pinched.

Meanwhile, Farley found freedom in everything. He threw himself into his landscaping jobs, lighting up every time a new project came in. It was his escape. If he wasn't on a job, he was in the woods with his rifle, shooting targets, or off drinking with his work buddies. The boy I fell for – the one who fished with me in the creek – started drifting farther and farther away. It was like losing my mother all over again, only this time I was watching it happen, slow and deliberate. But Farley was right about one thing: I could always play his video games. And on nights it was just me and the stink bugs, that's what I did – played until the screen bleared. Until I wasn't sure which reality suited me.

Vera came by often enough to eat dinner with us, but work was her real home. When she wasn't at the office, she was thick in emails or on the phone, pacing the gravel stretch between her home and our suite, buttering up her clients. One morning, I caught her on her way to work. I could tell she was buzzed on coffee already. If I was going to ask her for help, now was my chance. I needed an excuse to get dressed. A reason to leave the woods. Something to open my lungs.

Vera had a connection. She worked at Nyxyn, a sleek tech company in Issaquah, about seventeen miles east of Seattle, where she did app development. I didn't care what kind of work it was. All that mattered was that it got me out of Snoqualmie Pass, even for a little while.

I caught up to her just before she got in her car at the driveway's edge. I opened my mouth before I had time to think, letting an old habit slip out. "Miss Renner," I called, coming off stiffer than I intended.

She turned around with a snort. "Miss Renner!? After all this time? Come on, Pip. We're family." She paused, eyes softening. "You look pale. You okay? Sleeping all right?"

I glanced down at myself and noticed how disheveled I must've appeared to her – my oversized sweater slouched awkwardly off my shoulder. Plus, I'd forgotten to do something about my dark tangled hair. Instinctively, I ran my hands over my baggy jeans as though I might suddenly fall together. But Vera was right – I hadn't been sleeping. I couldn't. Images of my mother had begun haunting me again. Maybe the isolation was inviting room for it. The frantic wires, her expression just before everything went dark – I couldn't stop replaying it. I measured my life in two parts: before her death and after it. I'm sure Vera couldn't tell where my brown eyes ended and the dark circles beneath them began.

Vera was good to me. Maybe better than I deserved.

But still, my brain struggled to let her in completely.

"Yeah, I'm fine," I mumbled. "Sorry. Vera. *Aunt* Vera – do you think Nyxyn's hiring? Anything, really. I know I don't have a degree, but I've done some pruning work for Farley. His boss didn't know, but still, I did it." My voice weakened. Sweat dripped between breasts. "I'm a quick learner," I added, my words toppling out. "I could sweep the floors if that's all they need."

Her brow creased like she was trying to decipher some hidden message in my pupils. "You don't need to sweep floors, Pip. I'll see what I can do."

Relief flooded my chest, but it didn't last. As she climbed into the car, she grinned through the glass. That same satisfied smile she gave whenever she fixed one of my problems. I watched her tires scuff over the gravel as she left, but then something prickled at the back of my neck. There was a flash of a figure in the corner of my vision. I went still. My ribcage squeezed tight.

Someone was out there, between the trees hemming our land. Watching. Listening.

Then – nothing. Whatever I'd seen was gone, swallowed by the woods.

My father's voice came to me: *They're looking for you too.*

For years, his ominous threat had seemed to vanish. My father never mentioned it again, and I was too nervous to bring it up. I convinced myself it had just been another one of his paranoid fears, something that had dissolved over time.

But what if the threat was actually real?

Maybe it was nothing – a stray hiker, a hunter.

Or maybe, the warnings my father tried to bury were done hiding in the dark.

Chapter Nine

Down in his gut, my father must've known this day would come.

A wife. A job. The final erosions of his control. An eerie silence settled over him the day I crossed the creek and told him I'd found work. I didn't dare mention it involved computers – that would've set off a bomb. So, I lied. "It's a curtain company," I said. "My only job is letting customers feel fabric swatches. Just a nameless clerk, Dad."

His response: he brought me into his dark woodshed and asked me to sit cross-legged in the far corner, where varnish and resin clung to the air. I did as he asked. As I moved, a thought consumed me – what would he do if I told him about the strange figure I saw on Vera's land the other day? The sense that someone was out there, watching? He'd probably flee the country on the spot, no questions asked. I kept that part to myself. It was easier to believe it was just a weird feeling, a hiker, and nothing more.

"I want you to be happy in your life," he said quietly, sitting across from me. "I can't expect you to be like me. I knew this would happen. Can you…humor me with an exercise?"

I couldn't even see him.

"Dad, what is this? Are you about to murder me?" I joked.

"Shh. Close your eyes. Hold out your palms. Do you remember comfort carvings? They helped you when you were a kid. They'd bring you back to center."

It was night, and the darkness closed in, suffocating. The wind blew through the slats, causing the beams to creak and the outdoor rain barrel to shift against the cabin. I started to see shapes and lines in my imagination to make up for the lack of sight. The scent of rum and honey wafted from his breath.

"Yes, but I don't need help anymore. I'm fine now."

"Here," he said, placing an object in my hand. "A refresher."

The small trinket was made of wood, cube-shaped, smooth.

"It's a simple carving. Feel it. Describe it."

I laughed.

"Come on, Pip. I'm serious. Pay attention to the details."

"Why do we have to do this in the dark?"

"Because darkness sharpens our other senses."

"This feels…silly."

His voice cut through the night. "If not for me, do it for your mother."

I paused and swallowed a lump. "Okay. It feels like a cube. Sanded edges."

"Describe it better. I can't see a thing. How can I know what it looks like?"

"Okay…it's very smooth, like a baby's heel. Soft, like satin. Two inches in height. The edges feel slightly curved…like a solid creamy cube of butter."

"Good. Smell it. Describe it."

I smirked and brought the object to my nose. "It smells like you. Like something you carved a while ago, and it's been sitting in a room, waiting for someone to come in and appreciate it. And once they do, it's all they can notice anymore. Like new construction. New beginnings. It smells warm and familiar. Like a family is here, and everything is okay."

"Very good."

He took the object from me and gave me something else to hold. The piece was more complex than the first and had ridges and grooves all around it.

"Feel it. Describe it."

"Sudden dips that come and go, like a choppy sea or the moon in my hand if I were a giant."

We continued this exercise for four more pieces. The third smelled like pine – sharp, fresh, balsamic. The fourth was sleek and small, no bigger than a bullet. The fifth fit snug in my palm, solid and square, heavy as an anchor with no rounded edges to lighten the load. The sixth felt warmer – a buoy to the anchor I'd just held – shaped like an eye, its center bulging, watching.

An hour must have passed.

Time fizzled away.

The six shapes were clear as day in my mind's eye.

"Open your eyes now," my father said. "How do you feel?"

"Calm."

"Good. Where is your mind?"

"Here."

"Good," he said again. He gave me a long look that settled like sediment in the shadows, and then he stood. He clapped the dust off his hands and said, "One day, the darkness may not ask permission first. But you'll know what to do."

Chapter Ten

A few nights later, the scent of smoke jerked me from sleep.

I shot upright, heart pounding. My first thought was of my father. I knew something was wrong in the woods. I fumbled for my shoes but gave up. I tried to wake Farley, but he was dead to the world beside me. I bolted from our bedroom, my mother's wool cardigan whipping like a foxtail as I followed the smoke trail through the trees. My feet hammered into the earth, cold with frost, but I staggered on, determined to make sure my father was safe. Breathless, I tore down the path, across the creek's footbridge that Farley had built, past familiar trunks painted black by night, wind rasping at my skin, until I found him swaying in a mound of leaves. He stood bare-chested, his face white with shock, as he watched his cabin ablaze in front of him. Flames roared like waves, feasting on wood. Once he saw me, he tried to shoo me away. But I ran to him and pulled him back from the smoke. The night moved on in a blur. I can't recall how firefighters were summoned, but the memory of a truck dousing flames remains. While they tamed the fire, we scurried off into the woods before any questions arose.

In the woods by a tree, we spoke quietly.

"Someone did this," my father said, his voice unstable. "I didn't do it."

"I didn't say you did."

He shook. "I didn't do this."

I rubbed his arms, trying to warm him. "How did it happen then?"

He mumbled a single word under his breath, so soft I almost missed it: "Evadere."

The following night, my father was settled into Vera's spare bedroom. I could still smell remnants of smoke drifting through the vents, and I imagined what would have happened if my father hadn't made it out in time. I left the house with a flashlight while everyone slept. It must have been four or five in the morning. I still couldn't find my shoes and didn't want to wake anyone looking for them. Leaves were spears of ice against my toes as I moved sinuously through the desolate woods. I faced my father's burnt home, the place I could never really call *my* home; the place I was almost glad to see gone but wanted closure on, nonetheless. When the wind blew, I thought I heard my father mumble, but it was just the mailbox down the gravel road, the one we were never allowed to touch. No one knew the address. But now it squeaked and swayed in the wind, half-burnt from the fire that snaked its way through the brush, ending here, its red flag pointing upwards like a raised hand. I went to it.

With naked and sore feet, I hobbled over stones to get to the gray letterbox that was always boarded up. The boards that had sealed it shut were gone, discarded nearby. I reached inside to find an envelope. It was addressed to my father, Dr. Richard Screed, from a company called The Reverie Cloud. I was about to open it when someone grabbed my arm. My father appeared behind me like a ghost, shaking the spirit out of my body. His presence made me tremble. His eyes were wide and white in the moonlight as he snatched the letter from me and ripped it in half. An unhinged voice rose from the hollow of his throat.

"Close your eyes, Pip," he breathed. "Quiet your thoughts. Can you see the six shapes of wood in your mind?"

I closed them, trying to tame my rapid breath.

Yes, I could see them.

Part Two

Plunge

Chapter Eleven

It was snowing the morning I started at Nyxyn.

Then it rained. I swore Aunt Vera drove like weather didn't exist, like turn signals were folklore. She shot me a smile when we slid into a parking spot. Nerves filled my chest, but I smiled back. I owed her everything for this job. I would've gone over the guardrail with her, shaking her hand on the way down, thanking her for getting me out of Snoqualmie Pass after all these years. Though my father had kept me and my name hidden from the world, Vera had quietly ensured I had everything I needed to be paid and start a job like anyone else. Despite my gratitude, I still kept her at an emotional arm's length, clinging to the stubborn belief that honoring her meant erasing my mother. Part of me wished I could flip a switch and let her in – after all, she did so much for me – but old patterns are hard to break.

I tumbled out of her cramped blue hybrid, glad to have my feet on solid ground. The building loomed above me. Its sharp brown edges and polished glass caught the drifting clouds in its façade. It was sleek and unapologetically corporate, yet mountains in the backdrop gave it a sense of vitality. It reminded me of places my parents used to take me to when I was little, in the *before* days. Now, as I stood there in my twenties, those memories felt far away, foreign even, like they belonged to a different person entirely – a version of myself I was still trying to understand.

I tried slipping into Vera's shoes, imagining how she did this every day – making the daily pilgrimage out of the woods and into this stoic, impenetrable world. It was admirable. I wondered if I could carve a niche in tech too. Of course I could. No, I *knew* I could. Screed blood ran thick in me. I just had to make sure no one ever found that out.

Vera ran her hands through her rain-soaked hair and turned to me.

"It's prettier inside," she said. "Ready?"

She was right. The interior was dazzling. Immaculate egg-white walls. Polished concrete floors. Modern art draped just right. Everywhere, screens blinked with flashy loops of Nyxyn's latest digital creations. Everything was clean, sleek, and cool. "Nyxyn builds digital ecosystems," Vera had said in the car, but I knew what that really meant. It was a fancy phrase for *apps*. Digital experiences. Tiny pixels that make real life feel digestible. I didn't care what it was called. It felt like the opposite of my father's world, and I wanted in. Thanks to courses I'd taken at Vera's house as a teenager, I wasn't a complete novice to apps or tech. And when I married Farley, I got my first phone right away and spent hours tinkering with it, exploring programs – a silent riot against my father's ban.

The receptionist didn't look up as we crossed the lobby. "Badge or retinal?" she asked, her words spilling like mousse from a can.

I froze, unsure how to answer.

"Badge," Vera replied for me, reaching into her bag and handing me a slim card. "I had this made for you yesterday," she said, placing it in my palm.

The badge was smooth and had a golden chip beneath its sheen of plastic. It felt like a key to another world. I tapped it over the scanner at the gate. A soft *ding* confirmed my access, and a glass door slid open with a *whoosh* as though the building itself had exhaled.

Vera gave me a quick pat on the shoulder right before I went through.

I smiled, but something gnarled inside me. A feeling I wasn't supposed to be here, a force pushing me away. But I pressed on. This wasn't my world. Not yet. But it would be soon enough. I just needed to relax. Just as quick as I settled my thoughts, I sensed the bitter sting of someone staring at me from across the lobby. I looked up. A slender guy with chiseled cheekbones, arms coiled tight as copper wire, had his eyes locked on me through thick, black-framed glasses. He appeared callous and unblinking, as if my presence was a crime. As though his only job was to wait for someone to cross his path and screw up his day, and I was right on time.

"Hey, Wyatt!" Vera called, far too chipper, coming up from behind me. She guided us over to him. "This is Pip Renner. It's her first day. Pip, this is Wyatt Fink."

Wyatt offered a terse nod, dissecting me with his eyes. It looked like he was figuring out how quickly he could snap me in half. My chest burned.

"Pip Renner, huh," he said slowly.

Vera tilted her head. "Wait, do you two know each other?" She glanced between us.

"No," I said quickly.

Wyatt's eyes stayed on me longer than I would have liked, his expression strange, like he was trying to read something in the meat of my eyes. "Doesn't look like it," he said, oddly detached.

"Oh," Vera said, brushing it off with a laugh. "My mistake. Anyway, yeah. We've got a few new names around here. Pip, and—"

"Andrew," Wyatt interrupted. "Yeah. Heard. Interesting choice." He looked back at me, scanning me up and down. "Well. Welcome to Nyxyn...Pip. Watch your step."

"Huh?"

He gestured toward a yellow caution sign near the elevator. Wet floors.

"Wouldn't want you to fall," he added, striding off, but not before his brooding eyes sliced into me – a pointed message I couldn't place.

Vera placed a hand on my back, herding me toward the elevators. "Don't mind him. Wyatt can be intense, but he's brilliant."

"Got it," I said, but my mind was spinning. Wyatt's greeting felt less like a welcome and more like a bad omen. As I walked toward the silver elevator, I wondered if life beyond Snoqualmie Pass was worth chasing, or if I was sinking into the same sea that drowned my father.

Chapter Twelve

We rode the elevator to the second level; Vera called it the *idea floor.* Walking through the office felt like entering a futuristic universe.

Overhead, industrial pipes twined across the ceiling and dangling pendant lights cast a cool gleam over the expansive open space. Long communal desks speckled the expanse, stacked with massive monitors and glossy keyboards. Labyrinthine corridors branched off into private offices, giving the floor an organized yet topsy-turvy feel. The air buzzed with some sort of caffeine-fueled energy that practically seeped into my skin.

The floor was filled with two types: seasoned pros like Vera, who carried coffee-stained mugs like they were relics of war, and sharp-eyed creatives who seemed miles ahead of me, untouchable in a world I was only just beginning to dip my toe into. They looked at me like I must be the new janitor. In my oversized black suit, oak-brown ponytail, and mouselike demeanor, I practically invited their stares. They looked ready to hand me their trash.

I wondered if they could sense fear in me as I passed. Could they smell smoke from the cabin fire? Could they feel the anguish that twisted in my chest over my father? Could they sense the puzzle I carried in my heart over my mother?

All eyes followed Vera Renner, Nyxyn's top rep, as she walked the vast space like she owned it. Her knack for snagging clients kept the company swimming in bonuses and high-end restaurant reservations. She wasn't just my savior – she was everyone's fat paycheck. I thought, *what would it be like to belong here?* To make ideas breathe with life. To have purpose. But Vera had other plans and led me to a glass-walled cubicle down a corridor tucked away in a quiet corner, removed from the bustle of the open floor.

"We call this the fishbowl," she said with a smirk. "But don't let the name get to your head."

I mumbled, "I'll try not to splash."

"What?"

"Nothing."

The copy machine just outside the fishbowl hummed to life. Vera looked behind her at the young man making copies, a glass wall between us. "Hey, Ray."

"Hey, Vere."

Vere.

"Working on the app contest?" she called.

Ray chuckled, gliding a hand over his light pomade hair, his voice muffled behind the glass. "Haven't slept. It's all I think about."

"Come on in. Tell Pip here about it."

Ray sauntered past the glass divide as Vera continued. "Pip is our new quality assurance assistant. Pip, this is Ray Cleary, one of our best app designers."

Ray ambled in, lithe and lanky, with an Icelandic sweater that made him look effortlessly cool. Clear-framed glasses rested on his nose like a statement. But what struck me most was where his eyes went – right to Vera. Like a gnat tracking the light. I couldn't blame him. She wore a white blouse that draped like silk over her chest and chestnut pants that wrapped her legs just right. People didn't just look at Vera; they orbited her. I always thought she was beautiful, but seeing how others reacted to her made me realize just how stunning she really was.

I tried to say something – anything – but nerves pinned my tongue like a dead beetle under forensic glass. I was out of practice speaking to people, let alone being around them. Aunt Vera was the only person I really talked to. My father didn't do conversations, and Farley only talked when he wanted something. Lately, those conversations ended with me in a red-laced bra and thin, ribbon-sized thong. Despite our gradual rift, we were trying for a baby, and he had a very specific way he liked things. I always thought this part of my life would feel romantic. Instead, I felt like a doll tossed to the rug when the fun was over.

Vera talked for the both of us. "Ray is in the process of designing an app for an eco-conscious apparel company called Fazzle."

Ray nodded proudly.

She continued. "We're offering the company our top designs, and the design that's selected by the client, that developer-designer team gets a bonus! It's the buzz around the office these days. Just a little something fun we're trying out."

"I'm going bold, Vere." Ray spoke with his hands. He was sincere but lofty. A naïve charm to him. "I'm thinking fun, bright colors you wouldn't expect. Like, disgustingly bright."

Vera chuckled. "Tropical colors *are* in these days."

"Exactly!" He flashed us the printout of his concept – a vivid explosion of color, like a kaleidoscopic rainbow had melted on the page. I blinked, disoriented. The colors reminded me of my episode – the bad one. An image of my mother came into view, her terrified face covered in webs. I shivered without warning. Ray looked at me. I breathed, calming myself. *Please, no episode. Not here*, I begged myself.

Vera grinned, oblivious to my struggle.

"And imagine if it's customized," Ray went on prudently, "where you upload a picture of yourself and see the clothes on your own image first. How slick would that be?"

"What do you think, Pip?" Vera said. "You're going to have the honor of testing out each app."

A flash. My mother. Tangled wires. Eyes wide. Lips cracked, mouthing something I couldn't hear. Shadows behind her. Cold. Dark.

She was trying to talk to me just then. *Run.* I could *feel* her. Hear her. My heart pumped.

Vera took notice of my silence. She leaned in, talking lower. "Don't sweat it. Own it."

Ray skirted his eyes between us. I'm sure I appeared like a real piece of work.

I exhaled and cleared my throat. "Sorry. Yeah. I really like it." I realized talking kept the visions at bay. I hadn't had a shaking episode since I was a child, but I was always wary of them returning. I forced my mind into work mode. I felt ideas rising. Brainstorming, I realized, was no different than arranging pinecone shucks into beautiful mandalas. All you had to do was take it piece by piece, until the tiny flecks added up to something orderly.

"What if you really leaned into the eco part of it," I said, offering more than what was asked. "You could show the carbon footprint of every item in real-time – like hey, here's the life story of your cardigan! And – oh! What if each designer had their own profile with quirky facts, like their favorite sandwich or something? It'd make everything feel more human. Might be neat?"

I don't know where this came from, but it gushed out like a sudden downpour.

I couldn't control it, but I liked it. A new spark.

They both stared at me.

Ray lifted his eyebrows with a slow nod. "Favorite sandwich. That is...*quirky*." He snapped his eyes back on *Vere*. "I should get back to work. Me and the Nyxynauts are heading out early for Joey's birthday today."

"The Nyxynauts are one of our core app design-developer teams," Vera said, leaning into me. "You'll work closest with them."

"Nice meeting you, Pip," Ray said, saluting before he left the fishbowl.

I felt my face exploding red. Something told me app testers were supposed to keep quiet in this place, that hierarchy was everything, and that I'd just broken some unspoken rule.

When Vera finally floated out of my fishbowl, I flitted through my new space. Like a fish testing out a new pebble, I tapped my hands around the dusty desk, uncovering a note folded just beneath the keyboard. I opened it up and read: *Watch your step.* I quickly crumpled it, my breath hitching in my skull. I looked through the glass divide and caught Wyatt sailing down the hall just outside my office, his eyes trailing me like he knew something I didn't.

Chapter Thirteen

Back home, I sensed something was wrong.

Upstairs, I crept toward Aunt Vera's spare bedroom, where my father was staying while he figured out his next steps. I pressed my ear to the door, hearing the scrape of his boots, the clonk of objects hitting the floor. My hand palmed the knob just as it twisted quickly from the other side. Before I could react, the door flung open. My father yanked me inside.

"You lied to me," he snapped, bolting the lock behind us.

"What are you talking about?"

He held up an envelope with Vera's name scrawled across the front, the Nyxyn logo stamped in the corner. Vera and I had kept her job vague on purpose. She knew what he was like. Probably once, years ago, she or I told him she worked in retail. I can't remember who spun the lie. If he'd known the truth – that she worked in tech – he never would've let her near me. "You knew she worked with computers. And in Issaquah, no less. You kept this from me."

"Dad, please calm down. And what's wrong with Issaquah?"

"We have to leave. Now." He paced, frantic. "She's a plant. A spy. We're in the lion's den."

"A plant!? *What?*"

He dropped down on the bed, muttering to himself. "I knew letting you go was a mistake. But what could I do? I couldn't keep a lid on you. Your mother wouldn't want that. You're a grown woman, for god's sake." His hands fumbled over wooden carvings, remnants he saved from the cabin fire. I tried to get a good look at them, but he snatched them up. He crammed the shapes into a black satchel, bundling the sack like he was hiding sacred jewels.

He turned to me. "That cabin fire was intentional. It was a warning. They're coming for me. *For us.*"

My throat burned. "Who!?"

He ignored me, looking out the window. "We need darkness. Darkness keeps us safe. Keeps us strong. It's too light in here."

He stood and paced again.

I looked out the window, spotting Farley's truck sliding into the driveway of our suite across the lot, its tires grinding over gravel. I sighed with relief. Maybe he could help. But the sound of his truck spooked my father. He jerked me away from the window, his hand on my arm. "*You* don't work there, right?" he said. He didn't give me time to answer, not like I would have. His mind was a live wire.

I thrashed away from him. "Stop. Just stop!" I said, cutting off his questions and rants. "You're not dragging me back into this...into your... paranoia. I've built a life – *my own life* – and I'm not running away from it just because you think the world is out to get you."

He exhaled. "I know you don't understand my caution. It's for your safety. But I have to tell you something."

"I've been waiting half my life for you to tell me *anything*, Dad."

"I did something wrong. Years ago."

My stomach dropped. "What did you do?"

I glanced back at the window, hoping for another glimpse of Farley, but he was gone. All I saw was his red rake propped against the wall – a quiet promise he'd return to sweep the leaves.

"The woodshed back at the cabin is still intact. Let's go there. It's dark there."

I crossed my arms. "No. Not until you tell me what's going on. Right now."

His eyes were bloodshot. He was on the verge of a breakdown. "This is life and death, Pip. You have to trust me."

"What do you mean life and death?"

"I made a mistake. We're paying for it now. They want something from me. Something that could hurt people. They're ruthless."

I watched him sweat.

My heart pounded. "Does this have anything to do with Mom?"

His arms sealed his sack like he was cradling a newborn. The wood pieces clunked around as he shuffled back and forth. He peeked out the window. "Sun is setting," he said.

"Dad, please. Talk to me."

He shook his head. "Too many words," he whispered. "They'll find me. They'll find my words. They'll use it as a pinpoint to get to the timeline they need. To get what they want. We have to keep our minds strong right now. Our senses."

I felt my eyes blearing, my chest twisting. "What the hell are you talking about!?"

He stared past me, his eyes widening like he was seeing someone – or something – standing right behind me. "There's nothing for you here!" he shouted. "Do you hear me!?"

I stood back, horrified. He was talking to someone else in the room, not me.

He looked at me, breathing heavily. He dropped to the bed and held back tears with calloused fingers.

I sat next to him and rubbed his back. I remembered a conversation I had with Vera recently; she said my father was showing signs of early dementia. There was a documentary I watched once, back when Farley and I were teens. In the documentary, the caregiver went along with the patient's visions. Maybe Vera was right. She usually was.

"Dad, I'll go to the woodshed with you."

Chapter Fourteen

We reached the shed after dark, the scent of woodsmoke still lingering in the air.

Beforehand, I had stopped by the suite to let Farley know my father and I were taking a walk through the woods. I wasn't ready to explain his mania was more medical than quirk – not yet. First, I wanted to understand what was really going on with him.

"It's darkest in the back," my father said. "Hold my hand. Watch your step."

A harsh, acrid odor permeated the shed. We found a spot past his worktable and sat on the cold ground. I sensed my father settle across from me. He opened his sack, letting his wood pieces clatter out, syncopated. He picked up a piece. Tears welled in my eyes and slipped silently down my cheeks. He reached for my hand, turning my palm upward.

"Dad," I whispered. "Why are you doing this?"

"Here."

He placed a wood carving in my hand, and I clasped it, rubbing both hands over the structure.

"You know what to do. Feel it. Describe it."

"Dad, please tell me why you make me do this. I beg you."

"Comfort carvings," he grunted.

"I don't need them anymore. I've grown up. I'm fine now."

"Pip, do you remember that envelope you saw in the mailbox?"

I talked through tears. "Yes, I remember. The Rev—"

"Shh," he said. "Don't say it. Don't give it power. But yes, you know what I'm referring to. If you ever come across anyone from there, run the opposite way. Even if it's Vera."

"Vera...she...wouldn't..."

"Feel the piece," my father said. "Describe it."

"It feels like a figure. A person. There's a long braid in the back. It feels like…Mom."

I brought it to my nose, whiffing the jasmine perfume she used to wear. My father had lathered it with her trademark scent. The memory of her sweet smiling face came to me. Still, I wondered. Why would he do this? Why would he do this to me?

Chapter Fifteen

The next night, my father was gone.

He had driven off in his truck, leaving nothing but a note in the mailbox. He promised he'd be back soon. But days passed, and he didn't return. Aunt Vera suggested calling the police. Farley recommended the lumberyard. I assured them both he'd be back and not to worry. I didn't tell them exactly what his note said.

Pip, my distance from you is the only thing that will keep you safe. It's me they want. Do your exercises in the woodshed. I left items for you there. Trust no one. Remember, senses open doors. I'll be back soon. You're stronger than you know. Love, Dad.

He always told me never to call the police. "They just make things worse," he'd said. His warnings, irrational as they seemed, had a way of sticking in my head. Plus, I wanted to believe in my father's note. I wanted to believe he was safe. In control. I convinced myself he had a good reason to leave and a solid plan for coming back. But when I stared at his letter, the messy, shambolic handwriting, each stroke appeared like stone, like it might slip off the page and fall right through the nightstand. I left it there anyway, staring at it until dawn arrived, rude and punctual. Life was moving on, with or without him. But still, his warnings swarmed my head like a virus.

Chapter Sixteen

The next night, I thought of my mother.

A gentle memory dangled in my mind's eye. My tooth was hanging on by a thread when I was seven on my mother's lap. We were on the soft rocker as milky snow fell just outside our window. I was too big to be rocked, but she never minded, especially not when a tooth was ready to tumble out. I leaned my head against her chest and smoothed my hand over the single chunky braid that rested like velvet on her shoulder. She grazed my arm tenderly.

"Will I have you forever?" I asked.

I'm sure the question came out of nowhere, but it had been circling my head all day at school.

She paused as the rocker creaked to a stop. "Of course, sweetie," she said with a light chuckle to show her surprise at my question. But then, as if she couldn't hide the truth, she added, "I'm here as long as you need me."

It was her way of telling me she would try, that she would be there for me within the physical limits that life allows. Her honesty was meant to assure, not sugarcoat. She always told the truth, even when I couldn't understand its full weight.

The room was soft and still, the snowflakes thick against the windowpane.

"What made you ask?"

The day's events poured out of me. "I didn't like a story my teacher read today," I admitted. "It was about a dragon. He ate anyone who stepped inside his cave. I don't want a dragon to eat you or me." The gruesome details of some fairytale dragon had burrowed into me, far too much for my seven-year-old brain. The shadows of its teeth and claws bled onto my bedroom walls.

Sensing my nerves, my mother brought my head to her chest and began rocking us gently again. “Do you remember Grandma’s story?” she asked. “The one about the warrior princess?”

I nodded.

“Princesses don’t run from dragons,” she said, kissing my head. “They wield their swords. And then, dragons disappear.”

“Okay, Mom.”

The snowflakes on the windowpane grew heavier, obscuring the world outside, plus any dragons that might be lurking. In that moment, the world beyond us ceased to matter.

I could have rocked silently with my mother for eternity.

I might have.

Chapter Seventeen

Imposter syndrome is hell.

I tore through my closet trying to find anything that didn't scream rookie, like the letter beneath my keyboard implied. *Watch your step*. In the end, Vera showed up with a suit that hung on me like a parachute. Perfect. She didn't say anything, but the way she clicked her nails against the steering wheel, I knew her frustration was simmering. I'd made us late. Not a good look for the inexperienced app tester she pulled strings to get hired.

But my mind had been muddled. Sleep never came. I stayed up late replaying my father's note, replacing it with thoughts of Nyxyn. Like Ray Cleary, I couldn't stop thinking about the Frazzle app contest. I saw it so clearly – the design, the interface, even the brand colors. For the first time in a while, I felt like I'd stumbled onto something I might be good at.

At lunch, I drifted toward the Nyxynauts' table, hoping to slip into their conversation. Work was the only dam holding back the floodwaters. It made it easier to believe in my father's note – that somehow, he was okay. Maybe we both were.

The lunchroom was painted a glacial blue, crisp enough to make your teeth chatter. I spotted Ray Cleary first. He was wearing another crisp, cool sweater that looked like he snatched it from a Norwegian fisherman. He leaned against a metalwork chair, eyes tracking a woman named Lyra Pierce beside him. There was an obvious spark between them. Across from them, Joey Swifton and Wyatt Fink huddled together, their closed conversation moving quick as keyboard clicks. My stomach plunged at the sight of Wyatt, but I pressed on. I wouldn't let some stranger I barely knew saw the planks off my ladder so fast.

I approached the group. "Mind if I sit here?"

Joey turned first. "Sure, but we're just talking about super lame stuff." Joey Swifton, with his flustered khaki hair, plaid button-up, and easy smirk, looked like someone who always had code running in the back of his head. Vera said he was smart as a machine but kind as an alpaca, which made me think the Nyxynauts might be approachable. But as their eyes scanned me like a computer bug, I wasn't so sure anymore.

Ray Cleary pulled out the seat beside him, and I sat down. The chair legs screeched against the concrete floor as I pulled myself in. Wyatt winced like the sound had stabbed him. With his deep, black hair and slate collared shirt, he reminded me of a shadow. A shadow I should stay away from. And yet, a part of me wondered what I'd done so soon to get on his bad side.

"Like what?" I asked, moving past my brusque entry.

"Oh, you know," Joey said, shrugging. "Backend infrastructures, network protocols. Really exciting stuff."

Lyra Pierce smirked. She was the only woman among them, and I looked up to her like she was a rare book on a shelf I couldn't quite reach. I felt like a grubby toddler around her. She wore all black, her jewelry loud and bold – bracelets and earrings from boutiques with names that could've been sound effects: Zap. Sizzle. Bling. Her straight white hair sat perfectly in place, unmoving, as if her head were protected by armor. "Don't bore her, Joey," she said, without missing a beat. "Sometimes I think the only people impressed by the Nyxynauts...are the Nyxynauts."

Joey gave a mocking laugh, letting her jab flit like snow to wet pavement. She rolled her eyes. From what I'd picked up since I started, Lyra was sharper than she let on, but she kept it hidden. I stared at her, hoping I might break through to her someday.

"He's not," I said, smiling politely, "boring me."

"Anyway," Wyatt said, steering the conversation elsewhere. "I need to troubleshoot my app before we go out tonight."

As the conversation continued, I felt increasingly like an outsider. They spoke in a language that felt deliberately exclusionary, tossing around technical terms and inside jokes with a casualness that made me feel even more invisible. Still, I idolized each one of them. They were creators. Artists. They were gods to me. Free in ways I'd never been. But in the pockets of their banter, I noticed Wyatt watching me, his disgust stewing. *Why*, I wondered. I averted my eyes.

Finally, Ray realized I was still at the table.

He turned to me with a crooked grin. "So, Pip, how's your app testing going? Any bugs yet?"

I could feel the weight of everyone's eyes shift to me.

I knew Wyatt was just waiting for me to stumble. "A few."

"Like what?" Wyatt said, folding his hands.

I shifted uncomfortably. "Oh, well. I noticed there was an issue with the CharmSynx game app."

Wyatt's brow raised. "Ah, my baby, you mean?"

Despite Wyatt's ominous disdain for me, he was Nyxyn royalty. He'd risen in the ranks in just a few short years and had won multiple awards, or so I'd heard. His face plastered magazine covers. He had an online group that fawned over his work. He was legendary in the tech world and his dark dreamy looks were an extra bow on the gift he gave to the world. However, I had heard he got the last app tester fired because she criticized his work too much. I didn't know Wyatt was behind the CharmSynx app. The apps came to me anonymously so that I would never show bias.

"Well, I noticed an issue with the *X* button," I said, feeling myself shrink. "Doesn't close right."

Wyatt squinted. "Sorry, the *X* button?"

"Yeah." I made an *X* with my hands. "You know, it closes the browser out. It's only an issue on computers, not mobile devices."

"Sorry…I don't know what you mean," Wyatt said, syncopated.

"She means the dismissible *X*, Wyatt," Lyra explained, touching his forearm.

Wyatt burst with laughter. "Ah, okay. Very good." He raised his hands in an *X*, ninja-like. "Got it. I'll work on that," he said sarcastically. He got up, chuckling. The others followed suit, their laughter mingling with his. They pushed their chairs in, still talking, as I sat still. Just before Wyatt turned to leave, he crossed to my side of the table and whispered into my ear. I could feel his hot breath on my skin. He arched over me, smushing his fist into my half-eaten sandwich. "If you're going to provide feedback, learn the right fucking words. And it closes just fine. Dust your trackpad."

As Wyatt left, I felt myself evaporating. I couldn't move. Couldn't even look up.

I heard the fridge squeak open behind me and realized Ray was still there, topping off his tumbler, last to leave. Had he heard what Wyatt said? Did he care? He was on his way out the door. I don't know what possessed me, especially after such a painful sting of humiliation, but I chased after him. I was compelled to find connection, even where it hurt.

"Ray, you mentioned you guys are going out after work."

Ray paused at the door and scratched the back of his neck. "Oh, yeah. Hey, look, I don't think it would be your scene."

"Oh." I pulled my ponytail in front of me. "No, of course not."

"I mean, no offense," he said, lowering his voice, "it's just we're going to a *strip club* after work. Lyra isn't even going. You know, guy stuff."

"Of course."

"Yeah."

He offered his fist for me to pump, which I did.

"Plus, we're all kind of going out in solidarity. Not sure if you know, but we're getting a new development director. Andrew Janess starts tomorrow. None of us were promoted. Vera is awesome and all, but she recommended his hire out of the blue. It kind of stings they didn't hire from within. It would have been sweet to be director, but I've made peace with it. Wyatt, not so much."

"Oh. Jeez. Sorry."

"It's okay. Some people think he was hired because he brings a pretty big client with him. Kinda cushions the blow, if you know what I mean."

"Yeah, sure," I said. Vera never talked about Nyxyn's management side with me, although I remembered Wyatt mentioning Andrew's name when I first started. Still, I was in the dark about most things beyond my fishbowl. But maybe knowing more would make me seem less like a helpless guppy. "What's the client he brings?"

"They're called The Reverie Cloud."

Chapter Eighteen

The day before the last time I saw my mother, a thunderstorm tore through Seattle.

We had lost power. It was night. No light. I was skittish of the howling wind and thunder. My father came into the room, reminding me that he was a storm tamer. Nothing could ever hurt us. Not with him around. It was a silly joke, something from a camping trip we took once when he claimed he scared off a storm. Meanwhile, my mother unloaded her mesh craft basket. Threads and yarn and knitting needles crashed to the floor. She lit the room with a beeswax candle. The crafting fibers came to life with color.

A fuzzy, chunky blanket was our project. We used two thick skeins – gray and white. As we looped the chunky yarn between our fingers, she said quietly, "Maybe this can be a gift for someone who really needs it. Someone who's feeling sad." The memory is murky after that, our full conversation lost to time. I only remember feeling warm and useful in the faint light with her, as she taught me how to knit using just our fingers.

When the power returned, we hooted like we'd won some prize, and I flipped the television on. Our blanket sat unfinished and abandoned. I caught a glimpse of my mother's broken smile as I lounged on the couch, the remote dangling off my fingers like a large black wart. I didn't like seeing her like that, so I zapped the television off. Turned the lights off too. Went to the floor. The candle was still wavering from before. We finished the blanket until our eyes misted from the dim glow, until our fingers were tired. We curled into bed, blankets up to our chins. I slept all night in bed with her, lost in dreams, naïvely peaceful.

My mother's name was Cove.

Cove Screed.

And she was.

She was my cove.

I often thought about the night we lost power. If things had gone differently, if the power had stayed on, if we hadn't knitted a gray-and-white blanket, would she still be here? But things don't work like that. You can't go back and rearrange things like clay. You can't repaint, resculpt, or redraw the past. Otherwise, I wouldn't have lost everything the following day.

I had woken up alone in my parents' bed, the sheet clinging to my drool-stained lips. I blinked against the window sun and rubbed the sleep off my eyes. The faint murmur of my parents talking came from the computer room down the hall. It was Dad's sanctuary. I rarely went in there. I wish I hadn't that day. If I'd just stayed where I was, maybe things would be different. Maybe I'd still have her.

The memory is cloudy, then it freezes, stuck like a glitch I can't clear. I remember rising from the bed and walking straight to the computer room. But that's when everything cuts off, where the memory block kicks in. All I know is that it happened right then – the bad episode, the fall, the vision of my mother tangled in wires. Her frantic face, fading from view. The last time I ever saw her.

Chapter Nineteen

In the afternoon Andrew Janess passed by my fishbowl surrounded by Nyxyn's most elite.

Vera Renner, among them. The swarm of execs whirred by my glass as Andrew was given a tour. I caught a glimpse of him. Firm build in a tight white button-up. Short, dark, wavy hair cascaded over his forehead, each strand impeccably placed. Peacock-blue eyes. I was messing around with Fazzle ideas when I should've been app testing. I leaned my cheek into my fist, resting my elbow on the sketches, and watched Andrew interact with his groupies. From a distance, I caught snapshots of him, the trail of his cologne, the flash of his perfect smile; he was magnetic. I instantly understood Vera's decision to recommend him. He was a celebrity.

Andrew and company stopped where I could still see them, some lively conversation keeping them all suspended at the far end of the corridor just beyond my bowl. I couldn't peel my eyes off him. Something about him. Almost familiar. In my indiscretion, I didn't notice Wyatt Fink move past them and waltz into my office. The light above my desk started flickering like a warning. It was just a bad bulb, but I took it as a sign.

Wyatt waited until the brigade outside my fishbowl was in full conversation, blocking the volume of his voice. Although handsome, he had a downward-sloping face, as though smiling might take extra effort. His glasses were straight out of the 1950s, like some doo-wop singer. He pulled up his dark gray sleeves before he leaned down and swiped the Fazzle design I'd been working on, giving me a paper cut in the process.

He inspected my sketch, drawn with colored pencils I'd found in a drawer.

Then he looked down at me with a curved eyebrow.

"Whose concept is this?" he asked. "Can't be Ray's. It's not Lyra's. Guessing another department. Thought you were only testing Nyxynaut concepts."

I twiddled my fingers. "Well, I finished all my testing and notes for the day."

"Congratulations. But that doesn't answer my question."

Wyatt made my skin crawl. I looked out at the Andrew platoon and wished Vera would notice the distress signal in my eyes.

"It's my design," I said under my breath. "I'm just messing around until I get more work to do. It's nothing."

Wyatt laughed, a snooty squeak escaping. "Cute."

I looked through my glass and could have sworn Andrew Janess's eyes drifted into my fishbowl. Ray Cleary's words resurfaced – his link to The Reverie Cloud, the company my father saw as some satanic mark. I wondered if I should stay away from him. Guessing by his popularity – execs fawning all over him, people clinging to him like epoxy – I assumed it would be easy.

"Seems like an exciting day," I said, trying to change the subject. "With Andrew starting and all."

"Oh please," Wyatt said, rolling his eyes. "Just another wannabe."

Wyatt said this in a way to imply that I was the *first* wannabe.

"Oh. I guess I thought he was a big deal."

"Andrew Janess is a nepo baby. He's only some big shot because his dad works in tech."

"Nepo baby?"

"Oh, you don't know that term. You know when you get a job because of some family connection?" He snapped his fingers at me like he'd had an epiphany. "Like how your husband's aunt got you a job here."

Now I understood. Wyatt didn't like that I got a job because of Aunt Vera. He didn't like that *anyone* got anywhere due to a handout. Although worlds apart, he put me and Andrew into the same box. And some part of me allowed his cruelty, knowing that his frustration toward me was really about Andrew. It was pure vindictiveness, and I was an easy target.

I didn't know what to say. He wasn't wrong. I wanted to tell him to back off, that this job was the only thing keeping my brains inside my head, that I loved it here despite his poison, and that for the first time in my life I felt useful. I felt a connection to something besides pinecones. Besides grief.

He smiled to the side and turned to leave.

"Wait, you still have my sketch."

"And?"

"Are you gonna give it back?"

"No." He looked it over. "It's quite good. I think I'll keep it."

Wyatt left. I was burning inside, seething. My father warned me about getting too close to people. About the fine line of trust. Yet, he didn't warn me about people like Wyatt. People who don't hide their brutality. He didn't warn me about myself; what I might do if Wyatt made me angry one more time. Pressure tensed in my fists, my teeth grinding hard enough to shatter. I caught Andrew Janess looking at me from down the hall.

Chapter Twenty

At night, my brain wouldn't power down.

Thoughts of Wyatt looped. His sharp, dismissive voice needled at my skull. I tried to shift my focus to something else, anything else. My father's carvings surfaced. No matter how odd they were, I knew their purpose. They were meant to ground me. I could vaguely remember holding them as a child, the smooth cool wood against my palms, bringing me back from the edge when the shaking episodes overtook me. I wished I had something to hold now, something concrete to pull me out of my mind.

Farley was in bed beside me, gripping his phone between fingers. I longed for his touch. I reached for him, but he turned over just in time.

"Farley?"

I waited.

"Farley."

"Hmm," he said, slightly turning his head.

"Do you want to talk?"

The glow from his phone created a blue glow in the room.

"Tired," he said.

I stared at our dark maroon walls until he clicked the lamp off. Images of my father offering me his woodcarvings flashed through my consciousness. Sleep was not coming. I thought of my mother, of my husband turning his shoulder.

Chapter Twenty-One

It took over a month for the Fazzle app concept winner to be announced.

The company had wavered so many times that we started to believe they might back out of Nyxyn altogether. When the decision was finally made, it called for a company-wide meeting, the kind with champagne and an oversized check to mark the bonus. I wasn't given a seat at the glistening oval table, but I was invited – and that was something.

I stood quietly in the corner, gripping my elbows. Andrew Janess had been elusive for weeks, meeting with clients, but he showed up for this one – relaxed, refined – seated at the executive side of the table. I caught the whiff of his vanilla cologne from across the room.

Vera stepped to the front, where a rectangular easel stood draped in white cloth, the glossy check propped off to the side on another stand. Her presence alone hushed the room. She cleared her throat to speak. "I'll get right to it. We've waited long enough. The past few weeks have been an exciting time filled with creativity, grit, and a little more caffeine than I'd like to admit," she said, smirking. The room rustled with quiet laughter. "And I couldn't be prouder of everyone's hard work." She paused, building up the momentum.

I noticed Lyra and Ray holding hands beneath the table. They really wanted this win.

"It wasn't an easy decision," Vera continued, "but today, I'm thrilled to announce the winning Fazzle app design and all its exciting features."

With a theatrical sweep, she pulled the white cloth away, unveiling the design mounted on a large board beneath. Wyatt Fink's name was plastered beneath it in bold, black letters. The room erupted with applause.

But all I saw was my concept – my sketch, navigation flow, style, colors, aesthetic choices, button layouts, notes in the margins no one was supposed to ever see, even the snappy tagline I'd scrawled at the top – all of it, blown up for everyone to admire. It was the blueprint Wyatt had yanked from me. Acid rose in my throat. I slipped out of the room and found the nearest bathroom, heaving up crackers and cheese.

On the commute home, I wondered if I should bring it up to Vera.

I stared out the car window. My father's voice rattled in my mind. *She's a plant. Lion's den.*

"You okay, Pip?" Vera asked. "You're quiet."

Maybe my father was just paranoid. Or maybe he wasn't. A knife twisted in my chest, emptying my heart onto my lap. How long had it been since I'd seen him? He said he'd come back. He promised. He wouldn't have left me with a *plant*, would he?

I exhaled. "I was thinking about Wyatt's concept."

"It's sleek but beautifully understated, don't you think?"

"Yeah…um…" I hesitated. "Vera—"

"Speaking of sleek." She cut me off, eyes glazing over my clothes. "We really need to head to the department store. Those are *still* your mother's clothes, right? It's been years, Pip. Maybe this weekend?"

"Watch out!"

She swerved the car, almost mowing over a bicyclist. I reached for the door handle, my heart ricocheting. I caught my breath, eyes wide, panting, wishing I had my own car to get around in. God, if I didn't know better, I'd think she was trying to kill me. Vera made sure the doors were locked. Then, she reached for the radio and put on soupy jazz.

"What were you saying about Wyatt's concept?" she asked, as if nothing had just happened.

I steadied myself. I couldn't lose my nerve now. "I think Wyatt's concept might be…borrowed. I think he— "

Her knuckles tightened on the wheel. "You're getting comfortable at Nyxyn I noticed." Her tone carried the slightest edge. "That's fine. But just remember, I pulled a lot of strings for you. Most employees have experience, not just online courses from my computer room."

There it was.

She'd made me. If not for her, I'd be nothing. She knew exactly who I was – some mountain bumpkin she'd pulled from my father's madness. I was her project. Maybe she wanted to replace my mother, or maybe she just wanted me close, like my father warned. Either way, I kept my mouth sealed the rest of the ride home.

When we parked, Vera released a long sigh and said, "Pip, what are your favorite flowers?"

I stared ahead. I breathed out. "Zinnias." And then, I left.

Chapter Twenty-Two

When Andrew Janess came into my fishbowl the next day, I thought he might be lost.

I was halfway through testing one of Ray Cleary's apps on a mobile device, trying to tune out the constant drone of keyboard clicks from down the hall and the drifting murmurs about Wyatt's brilliant prototype. Around the bend, executive suite doors slammed shut like tiny bombs. And to top it off, a stray hair kept tickling my cheek, refusing to budge no matter how many times I tried to swipe it away, catching on some trace of breakfast syrup. The blinking lightbulb above my desk wasn't helping either – the likely culprit behind my headache and sudden sensitivity to noise. I dropped the test phone the moment I saw him standing in the doorway, his frost-blue eyes cutting right through me. He ran his fingers through his walnut-brown hair – some unconscious tic – and laughed, almost sheepishly, seemingly embarrassed for the both of us.

"Sorry, didn't mean to scare you," he said.

It was the first time being so close to him. My cheeks felt microwaved. I wondered if he noticed.

"I saw you needed a new bulb," he said, twisting one in his hands. He looked up at my strobe light. "Mind if I fix it?"

"No. Not at all. Thank you."

Andrew came in, eyes meeting mine with quiet kindness. With his free hand, he grabbed the edge of my desk and eased himself on top. I quickly slid aside to give him room, my knees knocking against the wood. He reached for the busted bulb overhead, tapping it to test its heat, then he swiveled it free. The hem of his shirt lifted from his camel-colored slacks, revealing a tantalizing hint of hair. Dark stubble accentuated his jawline, and his tongue slipped out in a moment of concentration as he screwed in the new bulb.

"There," he said, hopping down. He strode to the door and flipped the switch a couple times. "Better?"

"So much. I think I just got used to the blinking."

"Enough to make someone go crazy, right?" he said, flashing a smile that seemed almost too friendly, like he was taking on too much and might soon crack.

"Yes," I said, a nervous laugh escaping.

"I don't want anyone uncomfortable here. If there's anything you ever need, you know where to find me."

"Thank you, Mr. Janess."

"Call me Andrew. And you're Piper Renner."

"Yes," I said, shocked he knew my name. "Everyone calls me Pip though."

"Pip. I like that!" He smiled with his whole face.

Just then, Vera walked by my office, peeking in, glancing from Andrew to me. She opened her mouth to say something when someone grabbed her with some urgent news. She gave an apologetic wave as she hurried off down the hall. I was glad for it. For some reason, I felt guilty that Andrew was in my office. Like I wasn't allowed to communicate with anyone besides her.

Andrew lingered in the doorway, surveying the new bulb, arms crossed proudly, when he dropped his gaze and caught my eye again. I smiled, though I'm sure it came off awkward.

"Quick question for you," he said, drifting in, stopping just short of my desk. "You wouldn't have some time after work today to look at this client I need help with, would you?"

"*After* work?"

"Yeah," he said, stroking his jaw, like he wasn't sure how the invitation might land. "It's off-site – kind of in the woods. They keep late hours. I thought maybe you'd want to help test the app for our new client."

"Oh. I don't normally go off-site for app testing."

"But developers and designers do, right?"

"Yes. Sometimes. But I'm just an app tester. I don't think app testers leave."

"Pip," Andrew said with gravity. "I know you had input on the Fazzle concept."

I felt my face flush. "What do you mean?"

"I'm a stay-late kind of guy. During the day, I'm swamped with meetings, but once everyone clears out, that's when I can actually get things done. One night a while back, I stopped by to swap your lightbulb – didn't have the right one, though. While I was here, I happened to see some sketches on your desk."

My heart fluttered. "I was just doodling."

Andrew's smile was infectious. "Doodling? Pip, those sketches were brilliant." He puffed air from his lips. "I wish I had that kind of talent." He smiled, his cheek dimpling. "Anyway, I'm sorry it took me so long to replace the bulb. Like I said, meetings."

I shrugged, trying to appear nonchalant. "Oh no, it's okay. I should have gotten to it, but I – um..."

"I'm guessing you didn't want to rock the boat. Keep your head down, do your job, avoid making waves, right?"

His words hit a nerve. I felt exposed.

After a second, he said, "Sorry, I'm probably getting too personal. It's just, I've been there. But I have a vision for this company. There's so much hierarchy in the corporate world, but I believe in giving everyone a fair shot. We all come from different backgrounds, and we shouldn't let our privileges or lack of them dictate our future. Differences make us stronger, right? I know. It's a bit cheesy."

I hadn't expected Andrew Janess to be so insightful. "I appreciate that, Mr. Janess. Andrew."

"All I'm saying is, I think I'd like to have an app tester – *as well as* someone with a knack for good ideas – accompany me to visit the client. I don't believe in boxing people into specific roles."

"I really appreciate that. But I commute with Vera."

"Oh, well, I don't mind giving you a ride home afterwards."

"I'm not sure. I'd have to talk to her."

"Of course," Andrew said. "Just buzz me or knock on my door when you make up your mind. I'm on the third floor. It won't take more than an hour, I'm sure."

"What's the company?"

"It's called The Reverie Cloud," he said.

My chest tightened.

"They do incredible work," he continued. "It's a sleep therapy program, mixed with virtual reality, designed to help people boost their confidence and overcome trauma. Remarkable stuff."

He sat lightly on the edge of my desk beside me, the bulb cupped in his lap, his tone playfully conspiratorial. "You must've heard of it."

My shoulders tensed. "Can't say I have."

Despite Andrew being slightly older and much more experienced than me, his demeanor was unexpectedly relatable. From afar, he seemed like a distinguished business figure, but up close in my confined fishbowl, holding a dead bulb, he appeared almost like a potential friend. And I desperately needed a friend in this place. But…The Reverie Cloud?

"Overcome trauma?" I asked.

Andrew nodded. "Yes, they're doing amazing work to help people get through emotional distress. Very helpful for those who might be grieving, suffering, or just need a shot of confidence, really."

Grieving. Thoughts of my father filled my mind. Had he ever sought help from this therapy program after my mother's passing? Perhaps the letter we received in the mailbox was merely a bill and my father simply had a bad experience with them and refused to pay. Wouldn't be the first time he was stubborn over money. My mind raced to his disappearance. How could I have been so naïve to believe his note, to let him go without taking any action? Of course he was suffering from some cognitive impairment; what else could it be? I felt a wave of sickness wash over me at the realization of my carelessness in letting him go without a fight.

Andrew held the bulb over my head a moment and chuckled. "I've got a feeling you've got some good ideas in there." He pulled the bulb away but stayed perched on my desk like a paperweight. "Anyway, think it over. I better get back. You let me know. Okay, Pip?"

"I will."

He leaned toward me from where he sat, like he'd discovered some secret on my face. I arched back, unsure why he was coming so close, his vanilla cologne climbing up my nose.

He shifted closer, raising a hand. "May I?"

I nodded, my heart hammering, although I didn't know what he meant.

His fingers brushed against my cheek, slow and careful, moving the syrupy strand off my face, tucking it behind my ear. In that moment, every nerve surrendered, and my lungs took a full breath.

He finally peeled himself away and stopped at the door. "Hey, Pip?"

"Yes."

"You never have to wait until another bulb goes out. Just let me know right away."

I smiled as he left, my cheek tingling where his fingers had been. The warmth stayed with me the rest of the afternoon.

Vera visited me around 4:45 p.m., ready to take me home. She had attempted to approach me earlier in the day, but I spotted her heading my way and swiftly changed course. Ever since our awkward conversation in the car, where she refused to listen to me, I'd been craving some distance from her.

"Pip, if I didn't know better, I'd say you were avoiding me earlier," she said bluntly.

I traced a knot in the wood of my desk, unable to look up. "No, of course not. I just got swamped today." I finally met her eyes.

A suspicious look crawled across her face. I knew she must've been curious why Andrew was in my office earlier. I bet she couldn't wait to squeeze the information out of me.

"So, are you ready to go?"

I didn't want to give her that satisfaction. I wanted to keep something from her.

"I actually have plans."

She angled her head. "Oh?" A condescending smile followed. "What kind of plans, Pip?"

"I'm going out with Lyra. Lyra Pierce. She'll drive me home, or I'll rideshare."

She shrugged. "Girls' night. Have fun. Should I tell Farley you'll be home late?"

I felt my face twitching. I wasn't used to lying to her. "Sure," I said. When she left my office, I watched her car pull out of the parking lot. I went up to the third floor of Nyxyn, ready to knock on Andrew Janess's door. My heart was pounding through my blouse.

Chapter Twenty-Three

The Reverie Cloud building was tucked away in the woods of Issaquah, nestled amongst a horde of evergreens.

It felt more like a stone temple than a tech hub. With its intricate stonework and domed top, perhaps it had once been just that. A wide, sloping entrance curved downward into the building's stone façade, like the stem of a brain, large enough for trucks to descend and vanish inside. We parked out front, moving briskly past finely landscaped bushes, up a flight of stone steps, and toward the building's massive entrance. Carved into the leviathan wooden doors were mazelike coils of a brain; the patterns on the left panel flowed into matching designs on the right, symbolizing both hemispheres. Andrew pushed one open, detaching hemispheres as we stepped inside.

We walked in rhythm, stepping into the expansive building. Its smooth stone walls were washed with marbled colors of afternoon blue, sunrise orange, and muted honey. A huge skylight let in dappled light and mingled with amber wall sconces, sending fractured light across the slate-tiled floor. Tan minimalist furniture and pallid-blue floor pillows were scattered throughout like scraps of driftwood on a barren shoreline. We moved toward the steel elevator at the far end of the foyer; it whispered us up to the top floor.

Andrew guided me into a meeting room showered in the same soft light that filled the rest of the building. A woman named Everly Noon was already there waiting for us. She stood cool in a delicate gray jumpsuit. Her flowing light hair framed her elegant face and steel-blue eyes. She was all business, but the way her hair bounced so whimsically, I could have imagined her having a second life as a lifeguard or swimsuit model.

"Welcome back, Andrew. And you must be Pip," Everly said, her voice landing soft on my ears. "Andrew speaks highly of you. I'm glad you're both here to discuss next steps for The Reverie Cloud. Please take a seat."

"Thanks, it's nice to meet you," I said, stunned she knew my name, no, my *nickname*, ahead of time. I was even more shocked that Andrew had mentioned me, let alone complimented me.

Everly grabbed a slim remote from the table and pressed a button. A seamless panel in the stone wall slid aside, revealing a pristine white screen beneath. As we both took a seat at the boldly oblong honey-grained table paired with plush white Scandinavian chairs, Andrew raised his eyebrows, as if to say, *wait until you get a load of this*.

"I'm not sure how much you know about The Reverie Cloud," said Everly. "I know Andrew is up to date, but I'm curious if you've seen any ads or promotions for our brand."

An image of the burnt mailbox, a letter ripped in half, my father's maddened eyes came to my mind.

"No, I'm not familiar."

"A clean slate! I like that."

Everly and Andrew shared a laugh. I forced a chuckle.

"The Reverie Cloud can best be described as a playground for your mind. It's a mixture of sleep therapy and virtual reality."

Everly seemed to understand the confused look on my face.

"I know what you might be thinking: how does one experience both rejuvenating sleep and virtual reality all in one beautiful package?"

"Yes," I said, fidgeting in my seat, catching Andrew's eyes on me.

"This video I'm about to play will explain in detail, but first, think of your dreams. You know how when you are dreaming, you don't always have control?"

Dreams? I barely had control of my thoughts.

Flashes of my father in front of his burning cabin.

My mother on the wire-tangled floor.

Farley turning his shoulder.

"Yes," I said.

"In The Reverie Cloud, you have control of your dreams," she said. "I mentioned a playground. That is truly the core of The Reverie Cloud. Think of it like an interactive jungle gym for your mind. Imagine being able to control your dreams as if you were fully awake. Imagine fulfilling fantasies, confronting fears..."

"Exploring desires," Andrew added.

Everly smiled. "Yes, brilliant. Something our clients enjoy very much. Remember, this is all in the privacy and safety of your mind. It's a virtual reality program where your own life is the backdrop, and *you* are the main star."

"How does that work, exactly?" I asked, my interest piqued. "How can you have control if you're technically asleep?"

Everly beamed. "I am so glad you asked, Pip. When clients are connected to our Reverie Cloud BCI – that's short for brain-computer interface – our team can stimulate the brain's region that is responsible for self-awareness, giving the dreamer agency to manipulate, enhance, or control their own dream content. Internally, we sometimes just call the BCI the *halo*."

I stared at her.

"Since it goes over the head," she explained. "I know, it's a lot. This video will explain further."

Everly used her remote to dim the lights. Using the same remote, she pushed play.

The large white screen swished to life.

The video featured a woman overwhelmed with anxiety – trouble with her boss, her mother, her own self-image, her self-worth. I couldn't help but feel a connection to her, embarrassingly so. It seemed this company had their marketing strategy well in hand – slick graphics, impeccably calm aesthetics, attractive actors. I felt out of place, like I had nothing to contribute. Maybe they were seeking to connect with a new audience, which made me wonder if that's what Andrew saw in me – some sad yokel who knew how to get more sad yokels interested in this program.

In her dreamscape, the woman was confronting a virtual version of her boss, his image born from the depths of her own memory. She practiced speaking to his likeness, using talk therapy to build confidence in the safety of this imagined, digital world. She moved forward, facing her fear of flying and learning how to communicate with her stubborn mother too. As the video played out, the woman emerged on the other side – confident, refreshed, reborn. The montage that followed showed her returning home, landing the promotion, flying confidently on a plane, and speaking with her mother as if all their old arguments had melted away. The camera zoomed in as they walked down a sunlit path together, framed by gorgeous orchards. The scene unfolded in slow motion – peaceful, serene, almost too perfect. Upbeat piano music played as a smile stretched across the woman's face. The final shot pulled back, revealing clouds drifting placidly overhead, as if the world had changed just because she imagined what it would be like to pull all the strings herself. The video faded to white. My thoughts circled back to my father. Had he been through this same program? If he had, what did the program show him? What was so unbearable that it broke him to the point of no return?

Chapter Twenty-Four

The mother in the video reminded me of my own.

Once, when I was a kid and strapped into a booster seat in the back of our car, she drove us down a quiet, empty road. I don't remember where we were going, only that we passed a sprawling horse ranch and rustic barn, majestic horses grazing in the tall, wild grass. I was going through a very serious horse phase. I wanted her to stop there, but she wouldn't. A thunderstorm was on the horizon; she wanted to rush us home, naturally. At the time, I couldn't understand her point of view. I remember pointing toward the brown-and-white horses, pleading for her to stop. I kicked at the back of the seat.

"Yes, it's so lovely," she said calmly. "It *would* make a lovely experience, wouldn't it? We'll visit someday."

There was something so strange about her response, like she was some tour guide penciling me in for a later date. The windows were open, the hot wind gushing in, and I cried into it. All I wanted was to see horses up close. And she wouldn't stop. I swallowed my salty tears, but beneath the surface there was something else bubbling. I missed my father. He'd been gone on a business trip for what seemed like an eternity.

"We'll visit soon," my mother repeated, zipping the windows up.

"Okay," I said, rubbing my eyes. After a pause: "Mom, when is Daddy coming home?"

She didn't answer. Or maybe she didn't know. His work always felt like this enormous stigma – some behemoth beast lurking in the shadows. They both worked at the same computer company, partners in the same demanding world. But somehow, my mother never made it seem as dire as he did. Her job was just as critical, yet she always found a way to put me first. I don't know how she managed it. Tears welled again. My mother's eyes peered at me through the rearview mirror. I looked out the glass. We passed a creek. My mother reached a hand back and gripped my fingers. I looked ahead. I held on to her. We drove on, hands clenched. She clutched the wheel tightly with her left hand, while her right anchored me in the back seat diagonal to her. At some point, I was hot, and the windows came down again. The wind blew. The sun shone. A song we both loved came on. The bass drum hit one beat, then a pause, then two quick beats – a beating heart. The lyrics: *Let's take a joyride, darling, past the county line, where clocks are broke, and no one talks 'bout getting back in time.* I stayed clinging on to my mother's hand, singing off-key out the window. All my questions flew out with the breeze. My melancholy vanished. She didn't let go, and neither did I.

Chapter Twenty-Five

Everly swiveled to me and took a stylus pen and tablet from the table, ready to take notes.

"So, what did you think?" she said.

There were words scratching the perimeter of my brain, but I couldn't let them out.

Do you know a Dr. Richard Screed?

Was he a patient here?

Was he a disgruntled customer?

What happened to him?

Where is he now?

What does he know about my mother's death?

Is he responsible for it?

"Incredible," was all I said.

Everly smiled, her stylus hovering. She glanced toward Andrew, who met my eyes with a look that said everything: *This is it, Pip. This is the reason you were hired. This is the future. The Reverie Cloud is where you want to be. Forget the Nyxynaut amateurs. Come with me. I am your lifeboat.*

We left the meeting room, our hour ticking down. Everly motioned us toward another wing of the building. "Let me show you the dream hub," she said. A patient shuffled past us in the low-lit hallway, wiping sweat from his brow like he'd just walked out of a deep-tissue massage. He caught my eye and whispered, "You're going to love it."

The dream hub was a circular room, airy and vast, with the same marbled stone surrounding the interior of the building. Meditative music hummed through hidden speakers, and soft lights gave the space a relaxing aura. In the center sat a single white desk on a slightly raised platform, minimalist and sterile. Beveled white doors dotted the perimeter like portals, each leading to a private dream room. We entered one.

Inside the comfortably sized room, a sleek beige-gray lounge chair sat waiting. It looked extremely inviting. I ran my hand along the cool leather. Andrew was right behind me. I could smell him. His vanilla smell, intoxicating.

"This is a sleep pod," Everly explained, spilling into the room and shutting the door behind her.

I nodded, moving on to a touchscreen that was built into the wall.

"What is the screen for?" I asked.

"They're multifaceted," Everly explained. "They monitor a sleeper's heart rate and other vitals. They alert the sleeper and Reverie Cloud staff when a sleep cycle is concluding, and they provide the dreamer's menu selection."

"Menu selection?"

"Yes, dreamers have a few setup options before they begin. They can choose from any of Reverie Cloud's core Dreampaths: Terra, Echo, Quest, Restore, or Openfield. Let's start with Terra. Here, dreamers have the option to choose from a couple of Reverie Cloud-generated environments – lush natural landscapes or immersive urban spaces. Dreamers can explore, create, and engage with the world around them in Terra."

I nodded, taking it all in.

"Then we have Echo," she continued. "This option allows the dreamer to visit reconstructed moments or characters from their life, providing opportunities for imagination and introspection. Next, we have Quest. This is what it sounds like – thrilling quests, magical realms, things of that nature. Then there's Restore, designed for dreamers seeking a meditative session. Think tranquil places, flowing water, golden sunsets, gentle breezes, things like that. And finally, my all-time favorite: Openfield. This one is a fusion of all the Dreampaths – a creative space with no boundaries."

I thought instantly about my mother. "The Echo one…"

"Yes!" said Everly.

"Can you…see loved ones who have passed away?"

Her expression softened. "Yes, but just like in real dreams, it is a representation of the person. Imagine your memory of the person intertwined with the wonder of artificial intelligence. We do like to remind dreamers that these visions are influenced by their own subconscious, emotions, and memories, rather than direct communication with the deceased individual."

"How long do people usually stay asleep in the program? Do they stay under all night long?"

Everly chuckled lightly. "Well, the Reverie Cloud team does close shop eventually. We lock our doors at ten. We're looking into nighttime options, but I'm afraid we only offer a session for one sleep cycle. For now."

"How long is one sleep cycle?"

"Ninety minutes."

Andrew's hand landed on my shoulder. My skin tingled.

"I have to tell you, the Quest Dreampath is the most amazing thing I've ever experienced," he said. "There was this one adventure where I had to find a treasure chest in this enchanted forest. I swear to you I was crying happy tears when I woke up. It was life-changing."

"Oh, wow, you've tried it out?" I wondered if this was how Andrew came across so calm, so sure of himself. Maybe The Reverie Cloud played a part.

"Yes, many times," Andrew said.

Everly tapped her tablet. "And when can I pencil you in for a session, Pip?"

Chapter Twenty-Six

There came a day when my mother was finally ready to take me to the horse ranch.

We parked nearby and walked up to the penned-in herd. The wooden fence was rugged beneath my fingers as I climbed the second rail, draping my arms over the edge. The scent of grass, dust, and hay was laced with a leathery musk wafting from the pen. A foal was resting near its mother in a buttery column of light. Her spindly legs folded, as she struggled to stand. Her mother whinnied at her. Then, the mare seemed to notice us; she stood in front of the baby like a massive brown wall. The foal stumbled headfirst into the grass, and something peculiar tightened in my chest – a melancholy I didn't have the words to describe. I had longed to visit the horses, but standing there, a message seemed to inscribe itself along the walls of my heart: *Life is hard, even for horses.* As a child, I was starting to understand the idea of impermanence. For whatever reason, I was an early adopter of this truth. Maybe it was because of the transient nature of the digital world my parents were so engrossed in, where data could be erased or altered in an instant. The spooky dragon story my teacher told didn't help either.

My mother pressed her lips to my forehead, and then she looked at the horses. "You're my little foal."

"The foal can't stand," I said. "Why?"

"Well, that's just right now," said my mother. "She'll get up."

"What if she doesn't?"

"She will."

"How? It looks impossible."

"Look at the mare. Once, she was like that too. Now she stands."

"What if the mare gets bored and leaves?"

She laughed. "No, the mare loves the foal too much."

"What happens when the mare dies. Will the foal be lonely?"

"She'll be sad. But she'll be a strong mare, and if she chooses to, she'll have her own little foal to keep watch of."

"Will she forget the mare?"

My mother was quiet, and then her voice filled the landscape, like it was the only voice in the entire world. "No, love never goes away. Some things change, but love doesn't."

I stood and watched the foal eventually get to her feet.

There was a part of me that always longed to return to that memory with my mother. I remember being encouraged to visit it too.

When the episodes came on, when the convulsions began, my mother would instruct me: "Think about the horses! Think of the mare and foal!" And I'd go there in my mind. This seemed to ground me. Soothe me. Looking back, I know my parents tried their best to help me, to find a cure. The doctors weren't helpful; they never discovered anything wrong. Scans and tests all came back normal. Comfort carvings and horse memories. That's what worked.

Chapter Twenty-Seven

When it was time to leave The Reverie Cloud, Andrew offered to drive me home.

I told him I was fine with a rideshare. I massaged the truth, telling him I needed to make a stop somewhere and didn't want to burden him. Truthfully, I was nervous for Vera to spot him, for her to catch me in a lie. He stood with me on the stone stairs while I waited for my driver.

As we waited, I felt guilty the way my eyes searched his face, noting shades of black bordering the blue of his eyes. He was like a painting I'd been admiring from afar. Now, up close, I had the opportunity to appreciate the nuanced brushstrokes. There were times I caught Farley checking out women, convincing me it was just instinct, embedded into a man's DNA. As if I didn't harbor my own fantasies. As if I couldn't understand. I wondered if I was allowed to walk a similar gray path.

"I don't want to pressure you," Andrew said, "but the experience really is life-changing."

I'd told Everly I needed time to think about scheduling a session.

"How did you learn about The Reverie Cloud in the first place?" I asked, hoping to shift the spotlight.

He watched me carefully, almost like he was trying to decide if my naivety was an act or not. Maybe The Reverie Cloud was better known than I realized. "Targeted ad," he said, shrugging. "Checked it out. Thought, hey, maybe I could help them out with some tech products. Nothing too exciting, really."

Andrew spotted my car winding down the wooded drive, a look of disappointment staining his face.

"Well," I said. "That's me. Thanks again for the invite."

He grabbed my hand before I could leave. "The reason I kept coming back…it opened up repressed memories – things that'd been locked up for years."

His eyes watered. The evening was rolling in deeper, but I wished I could have stayed with him just a bit longer. His hand was so soft and grounding.

"Anyway," Andrew said, releasing me. "Think about it. Again, no pressure. I just think once you experience it, you have a better way of knowing how to market the app."

Ah, business.

"And if rides are an issue," he added, "I have no problem getting you a company car."

I asked my driver to drop me at my father's shed. I wanted a moment. A contemplative walk before heading home. As the car drove off, I couldn't help noticing the mailbox that bore scars of the fire. One half of it was hollowed, blackened by flames. The other side remained untouched. The red flag was on that side, and it was raised. I went to it. There was an envelope inside the mangled mailbox but no return address or stamp. I stuck the envelope in my purse. It was too dark to read it on the spot. I wondered how long the letter had been waiting.

I was out of breath once I crossed Vera's house, headed toward our suite. I saw her bedroom window light up yellow as I passed. I trampled over gravel until I reached our home across the connected lot. I pretended I didn't see her up there.

Inside, a fire was swooshing in the fireplace, but Farley wasn't around. I sat down and watched the flames snap, marveling at the resiliency of wood.

Moments later, Farley burst in. A lit cigarette dangled from his lips. A rifle was slung over his shoulder. Smoking was a habit he'd picked up years ago but had since abandoned. Something about him seemed off.

"Where've you been?" I asked.

"Me?" he asked, crazed. "What about you?"

"I thought your aunt told you I was out with a coworker."

He put his cigarette out in a nearby bowl, smushing it into oblivion. "Nah, she didn't tell me. I've been out."

I stared at him, and then at his rifle.

"Raccoons," he explained, swaying. "Found 'em in the trash. Tried to scare 'em off."

"I didn't hear any shots."

He chuckled, adjusting his weight. "Went out for target practice first. Then saw the raccoons. Didn't shoot – just yelled."

There was something festering beneath the surface. It smelled like he'd been drinking. I didn't like that rifle on him either. He got an impish look in his eye; I knew he wanted us to go up to the bedroom together.

I remembered the envelope in my bag, and I went to it, trying to buy time. He came up from behind me as I opened it. As I read over the letter, the hairs on my neck shivered. Something felt unsettling about Farley, about Vera, about everything. *She's a plant, Pip*. Did that mean Farley was a plant too? My father's paranoia, his madness, was beginning to drill into me. I was starting to feel like him. Unstable, untrusting.

"What's in the envelope?" he slurred.

"Nothing," I lied, folding the paper and tossing it into the fire. "Just coupons."

I watched the letter from The Reverie Cloud, addressed to Dr. Richard Screed, curl in the embers. A bill for millions vanished in the flames. Farley's breath was hot on my neck as he leaned in, his rifle adding weight. I stared at the burning letter and knew there was only one way forward: I had to confront The Reverie Cloud head-on. Whatever connection my father buried there, it was time to unearth it – even if it meant going against his life-or-death warnings.

Chapter Twenty-Eight

By noon the next day I'd seen Andrew a couple times, but he never looked my way.

Yesterday evening I was a bright sapphire in his eyes; today, I was a stone beneath his soles. To make matters worse, I caught Vera laughing with him on the idea floor, her hair flipping like breakers on the shoreline of her shoulders. Jealousy simmered in my chest. Andrew wasn't mine to want. Shame snaked through me. I called Farley at lunch to clear my head.

Yet, as the day wore on, I found myself watching the hall, longing for his return. I contemplated loosening my bulb, prompting my fishbowl to flicker. I wondered if being part of The Reverie Cloud was the only way to earn his respect.

Around four he moved by in a blur. I felt my heart thud against my chest. I hated this. Hated these intrusive thoughts.

When I was a kid, my mother used to explain my father's addiction to me. It came with a warning, as though it might come and snatch me up one day too. "Sometimes Daddy stays at the lab or in the computer room very long," she'd say. "His work is very important, but it's good to know when to take a break. Let me see you take a break from the television now."

She worked with him while I was at school. The two of them spent their days in our home computer room or at their office downtown. They called it the lab. I didn't even know its real name. My mother was careful to separate work from home, always knowing when to unplug. My father, not so much. I wondered now if that's why he banished all our gadgets when we moved to Snoqualmie Pass – maybe he wanted to save me from a similar fate.

But addiction doesn't care what niche you carve. Once it's in your blood, it can manifest in ways you're least expecting. At least, that's how it felt with Andrew. An addiction. And I needed to kill it before it got out of control.

Chapter Twenty-Nine

Wyatt Fink caught me in the hall the next day and cornered me.

His stance was wide, eyes raptorial, as though he'd catch me if I dared to run. He said nothing at first, just stared me down. His presence was feral. A hawk nosediving through my chest, coming out the other side with my heart in its beak. I tried to look away, but he grabbed my chin with force, moving my face back toward him. The movement left me speechless.

"You lost me a client," he said, spit landing on my collarbone. "Your notes on my MountainTrek app were sloppy at best. You missed critical bugs, didn't test the payment gateway, and completely overlooked mobile login issues. Did you even test the damn thing at all?"

I swallowed. I wanted to spit back at him. Not just for the way he touched me, but for robbing my ideas. And now, somehow, I was the one on *his* bad side. "I'm sorry, Wyatt. I'll try better next time," I said, not wanting to get into the weeds with him until I knew exactly how to take him down.

Vera walked by us. She must've overheard him. I thought she would mediate, but she only hummed and kept walking.

Wyatt leaned in, his lips grazing my ear, and he whispered, "You should leave here before things get ugly."

His tone was sinister, dripping like hot wax, meant to scald me. I'd had enough. Why was he so cruel? Sure, I was still finding my footing, but what did he expect? This was a new world to me. I wasn't perfect; no one is in the beginning.

I should have turned the opposite way and gone right to human resources. That was my initial plan: wait, stay steady, take him down. But something in me snapped. I wanted to know what I'd done. Why was I under his skin so much?

My voice rose slow, dragging like a slug. "Why don't you want me here?"

"I'm late for a meeting, Pip*squeak*," Wyatt whispered, jerking away. "But listen to what I said."

"Wait, please. Tell me!"

Wyatt left me standing there, his warning leaving me stunned.

By lunchtime, I found myself in the cold-blue cafeteria, replaying Wyatt's voice over and over. Chatter and laughter came from the hall as the Nyxynauts shuffled past, headed off-site for lunch, honking like geese on the move. "Hold on, forgot something," Wyatt said, last in line, as he peeked into the cafeteria. He slipped in, headed for the fridge. He brushed past me like I was a mote of sand. I felt my heart pump like a wagon over rocks. Leaning on elbows, hunched over yogurt, I wondered whether to stay hidden or interrogate him.

"Back in the day," Wyatt rasped after a beat, our backs turned to one another, "they'd shun the families of criminals – make sure no more bad guys got through the cracks. Now, those same people waltz into jobs they don't deserve, like they've earned it."

My pulse ticked up. My heart drummed. What did he mean by that?

I turned just enough to catch him in my periphery.

He was preparing his iced coffee to go. I wanted to throw my yogurt at the back of his head.

"Funny, right?" he snickered, excusing himself. "Anyway, have a nice day, Pipsqueak."

I sat and stared at my lunch, the particles fizzing into blurry shapes. I hastily crumpled the remnants of my meal into a heap, slamming it into the bin harder than I should have, ready to quit Nyxyn right on the spot. I hadn't quite made it to the door when Andrew breezed in.

"Hey, Pip!" he said, headed for the coffeepot. "I'm sorry I haven't had a chance to speak to you lately. How are you?"

"Fine," I said, my voice barely escaping.

He stood at the counter pouring coffee into his mug, shaking out the sugar, stirring gracefully. As I stood in the center of the barren cafeteria, I imagined him turning around, opening his arms to me, ironing out my nerves. I felt breathless watching him there, his light blue shirt stretching across his back as he shifted. He turned around, leaning his hips against the counter as he swept hair from his eyes. Then he just smiled.

I weighed my options. I could leave. Go home. Blend into the furniture for the rest of my life, waiting for my father to return, for my marriage to reboot, for Vera to accept my ongoing grief. Or I could align myself with Andrew and find my own path, my own voice. I could soar higher than Wyatt, until he was nothing but dust below. But his comment left me unhinged. *Families of criminals.* I needed to find out what that meant. My father's voice came to me – *I did something wrong.* Did Wyatt know something I didn't? How would he even know our relation? Did Vera mention it? Wyatt wouldn't give me the answers I craved, not without suffering first.

But The Reverie Cloud might.

Andrew said it could unlock repressed memories. Maybe the mysteries involving my parents were right inside my own mind. I just needed the right key to unlock them. Plus, I needed to know what grip the program had on my father.

Andrew's voice tethered me back to the moment. "You okay, Pip? You look…upset."

"I think I'm ready to make my Reverie Cloud appointment."

He smiled, his ocean eyes warming the room. "You're going to love it. It really is life-changing."

Chapter Thirty

It was quiet when I arrived at The Reverie Cloud on a Thursday night.

I went alone, following Andrew's advice to explore the program in solitude. "Enjoy every moment," he'd said, offering me keys to a company car. My face flushed when I finally admitted I didn't have a license. Thinking fast, he suggested a rideshare budget instead. "It's only fair," he added. "This is important market research."

When I arrived, my senses were ablaze. How could one ever tire of approaching The Reverie Cloud? I had a feeling each visit would be like my first time. My lips parted in awe as my driver slid down the wooded drive and we approached the building. It was like some massive alien ship dropped right into the woods. Its dome top seemed to symbolize a higher consciousness, a space where dreamers could float to. A temple of dreams. Anything less would crush the illusion. From a branding perspective, it was genius. Everything, from the cloudlike logo to its mystical stone architecture, seemed to hint at transcendence. As I entered the building, I couldn't help but imagine ways to enhance their digital presence – maybe a dream journal, a gallery for dream-inspired art, even a sleep playlist. Ideas rattled on. In fact, I forced them out, convincing myself I was there for work. The truth was different: I was there for answers. I wanted to learn what really happened to my mother. I wanted to unearth my father's crimes. I knew the answers were riddled inside me. I just needed to draw them out myself.

Everly Noon greeted me in the open foyer. She drifted toward me, gliding through a column of muted light. When she met me, she pulled me in close. A tight chest-to-chest hug I felt in my bones.

We rode the elevator together, accompanied by two other customers – a teenage boy who stared blankly into space and an elderly woman who cussed dramatically when the elevator came to a halt. Everly and I followed them into the dream hub. As they disappeared into their individual dream rooms, Everly guided me to the sleek white desk, where she swiveled a screen in front of me and handed me a stylus.

A waiver appeared on screen, its words tiny and packed. I skimmed the lines as best I could. "Is there anything I should be worried about?"

"Nope. These are just standard forms," she said, moving quickly past my question. "We need your initials on each page. Standard protocol."

I nibbled a nail on my free hand. "Does the program come with any side effects?"

She handed me a water bottle. I'm sure I appeared nervous.

"Some mild confusion and brain fog may occur afterwards," she explained, "but that's rare. Our team is here to help you. *I* will be here to help you, Pip."

"And how do I fall asleep?"

"You'll get settled into your sleep pod – think of it like a cozy massage chair. The pod uses soothing sounds and gentle vibrations to guide you to sleep."

"What if I physically can't fall asleep?"

She grinned warmly, tucking pale hair behind her ear. "Trust me, the environment is extremely relaxing. But should we run into any hiccups, we have all-natural patches to quicken the process. It feels very nice."

I shifted in my seat. "What if I don't wake up?"

"You will. It's a single ninety-minute sleep cycle. We'll guide you out of the program during your natural waking window."

I hesitated. "But what if I miss it?"

Everly's smile buckled. "Come on, Pip. Let's get you settled."

The dream room was drenched in waterfall soundscapes and dim lighting. With Everly's cue, I sank into the sleep pod. It purred to life.

Warm nodules swirled against my skin in slow succession, as if it already knew my body and what it needed. My eyelids grew heavy. Everly slipped a remote into my hand, explaining how to use the screen in front of me to adjust my dream settings. The screen, embedded in the wall, displayed a series of windows with various options. I recognized the Dreampaths from our earlier conversation.

"Can I select the Echo Dreampath?" I asked, ready to click.

Everly perched on a leather stool beside me. "We don't recommend Echo right away. It's a little more complicated than the others."

I shifted in my pod. All I could think about was diving straight into my memories, unearthing pockets of childhood blurred by time. I knew I wouldn't see my actual parents – only reflections of them, crafted by my mind – but maybe I could winnow out clues from my subconscious.

I just hoped I could handle whatever my mind showed me.

Everly sensed my concern. "Our dreamers love Echo, but it's better after your first or second visit. You'll want to get a sense of the experience first. Let's try a rudimentary Dreampath first to get oriented. How about Terra or Restore?"

I took a deep breath. "Terra, please."

"Perfect. So, swipe with the remote until you reach the window that says *Terra*."

"How will I know I'm in the program? Won't I just feel…asleep?"

Everly stood and went to a sleek white cabinet by the screen. She pulled out a stretchy band that had nodes all around it, resembling a black spider's web. She presented it like it was a carnival prize I'd just won. "I'm going to place this BCI band around your head, Pip. Remember, we call it the halo? It connects you to the program. This is how our panel of experts who work in the control center know you are ready to be awakened to your consciousness inside your dream."

"Will they be able to *see* my dream?"

"Not quite the way you see it. They have other ways to monitor brain activity." She held the stretchy band between her fingers and wrapped it snugly around my head. Then, she pressed a button on it. Lights flickered on the halo's nodes. "This nifty device will read your neural patterns and let us know when you're in a sleep state. From there, our team will initiate the dream experience and gently wake you up inside your own dream."

I exhaled. "Wow."

She smiled before continuing to adjust my halo. "Because this is your first time, I will meet you inside your dream to help you get started. I'll wear my own halo and connect myself to you, except I'll be awake, dropping into your experience."

I pulled back. "I thought you said dreams were private."

Everly nodded. "They are. I won't see your dream exactly, but I'll be there – like a guide. Just in case things feel confusing at first."

"So, I'll see you in my dream?"

"Yes, but only as a version of me that your brain interprets. As long as you don't see me as a squirrel or something ridiculous, I should appear mostly the same." She grinned, continuing. "My voice will cut through your dream experience, and your perception of me will match my voice."

My eyes shifted; I was feeling a little exposed by having my brain on display.

Everly chuckled. "Don't read too much into it. Just relax and go with the flow. That's the best way to approach this."

I reached for the water on the table beside me and took a swig.

"I'll be there only momentarily to remind you you're in a dream state. As I'm sure you're aware, dreams are tricky. Sometimes we don't realize we're dreaming. It takes a couple times to master The Reverie Cloud, to realize you're in the program. We've seen dreamers literally do nothing once activated, assuming they're having an organic dream. My presence will only serve as a gentle guide to get you going. This ensures a seamless transition between reality and the simulated environment. Once we're inside, I will also explain to you the concept of conjuring."

"Conjuring?"

"Yes. Making things appear in your dream just by thinking about them."

"Like daydreaming."

Everly nodded excitedly. "Exactly, Pip! You're a quick learner."

I blushed. "How do I do that?"

"Well, you already do it all the time, don't you? As humans, we're always conjuring…daydreaming. What are daydreams except electrical impulses and neurotransmitter releases that allow the brain to generate images and scenarios? You can do it in the program too. All you have to do is trust yourself."

I looked at the screen. There was a new prompt.

"Ah," Everly said. "So, Terra offers two options. Nature or Urban."

"Nature."

"Good choice. Go ahead and select."

I clicked and another screen loaded – this time, even more options appeared: *Lagoon Retreat, Mountain Vista, Rocky Canyon, Golden Pasture, Forest Hideaway*, and a few others. I tapped on *Lagoon Retreat.*

The room grew warmer. The scent of lavender and chamomile seeped in, filling my nose. I felt myself getting sleepier. There was a mesmerizing, pulsing noise coming through speakers. The sound was inebriating, making my limbs heavy. My anxiety was melting away, but a quiet voice nagged: What if I wasn't ready for the program? What if the truth might unravel me completely?

"I'm going to put these black patches on your fingertips," Everly said. "It's just some extra monitoring. Do you have any more questions before we begin?"

"You said it's an hour inside the program?" I asked, groggily.

"One hour and thirty minutes."

"And I'll know when to wake up?"

"One last thing," Everly said, layering an adhesive mask across my eyes and the bridge of my nose. "If you wake prematurely, this will prevent lucid dreaming."

My body felt fuzzy, distant, foreign.

I wanted to ask Everly more questions, but sleep was pulling me under.

The program was beginning.

Part Three

Passage

Chapter Thirty-One

I opened my eyes to a green pasture blending into a sandy shoreline.

Beyond it lay a lustrous lake. Silver birds chirped with hauntingly beautiful melodies. A warm wind blew the scent of rain-soaked earth. Utopia.

"Piper," called a familiar and comforting voice. "Welcome to The Reverie Cloud. You've arrived."

I shivered, disoriented, my vision blurred. "Huh? Who is that?"

"It's me, Everly Noon. Look to your right. Slowly, please."

I turned my head, the world lagging, everything coming up double. Her shape wavered before settling into place. Everly posed, stunning in a crimson swimsuit, modish sunglasses, and wide-brimmed beach hat. Her details were bright and saturated, like an overdone model on the walkway. She looked so real, but at the same time fragile, as if blinking might cause her to disappear.

"Lift your fingers to eye level," she said softly.

"Where are we?" My voice echoed in my head.

"Piper, love. Focus on your fingers."

I obeyed, raising my hands.

"Remember when I put black patches on your fingers before you fell asleep? They're gone now because you've entered a dream state. You can move freely here. Do you understand?"

The memory rushed back – me, groggy in my pod, Everly securing a band around my head. Me, selecting my Dreampath.

I gasped. "Yes. I understand."

"Very good. Let's try an exercise. See the sand by the shore?"

I looked ahead at the champagne-colored sand. It looked impossibly soft.

"Join me there and imagine a rake."

I followed her down a slope. The sand was sun-drunk beneath my toes. A golden blaze of warmth draped my shoulders. Nearby willows provided shade. There were birches beyond the shore, cattails like lollipops, poppies like puffs, everything idyllic and serene, perfectly crafted. Then, the harsh hoot of a dove pounded straight into my eardrums. It was too much: unbearable. I clamped my head with my hands.

"Oops. Adjusting the volume," she said.

The sound softened to a gentle coo.

"Better?"

I relaxed my body. "Yes."

"Good. Now, I want you to think about a rake. Sometimes it helps to close your eyes," she said.

I shut my eyes, but instead of a rake, my father's wooden cubes filled my mind – objects I knew only by touch but could see clearly in some hidden section of my brain. I had the strange urge to hide this from Everly, so I cleared my thoughts and focused on a rake. I remembered Farley's rake leaning against the house. When I opened my eyes, there it was, red and vibrant, lying on the sand by Everly's feet.

She beamed. "Nicely done."

"What do I do with it?"

"In this Dreampath, many dreamers like to rake patterns in the sand. A zen garden. It's quite calming. Would you like to try?"

"Sure."

I picked up the rake and drew creamy, mollifying lines into the sand. She was right; the motion was soothing. I almost forgot she was with me. I glanced in her direction, her body fizzling back into place. This time, she wore the gray-and-white blanket my mother and I knitted by hand during a thunderstorm when I was a child. It was wrapped around her like a shawl.

I jumped back, dropping the rake. "Why are you wearing that?"

"Pip, I can't see what outfit you've chosen for me. I'm just a reflection of how you perceive me."

"But you're wearing a blanket my mom and I made."

"Sometimes other memories or images from the subconscious can unexpectedly bleed into dreams," she explained. "We call them *dream leaks*. Our minds and memories are like toolboxes, but sometimes we can accidentally grab the wrong tool. It happens when we lose control – like dreams where your teeth fall out or you're suddenly naked in public. Just relax, focus, and change my outfit. Remember, it's just like daydreaming. You're in control."

I closed my eyes, took a deep breath, and centered my thoughts. When I looked again, she was back in a swimsuit – a purple and yellow dotted pattern, something I wore once as a kid. My toolbox was rusty. I shrugged. It was good enough.

"All better?" she asked.

"Yes."

Everly smiled. "Great. Let's head to the lagoon."

I followed her to the water, a dazzling blue oasis. She sat on the sand at the water's edge, so I did too. I wasn't sure if I made her sit or if she controlled her own actions.

"Did I make you sit down, or did you do that yourself?"

"A bit of both," she said. "My actions are influenced by how you see me and what you remember about me, with a touch of algorithmic intelligence. In The Reverie Cloud, characters are shaped by your thoughts, instincts, and needs, and all for your benefit."

I wanted to test out her theory.

I imagined her drawing a heart in the sand. She did, effortlessly.

"See?" she said. "But remember, I'm different from other characters you'll meet in the program. I'm speaking to you in real-time, directly from the physical world. I'm part memory, part live input. Others will be solely built from your imagination."

I nodded, eager to learn more. "So, what else can we do in this mode?"

"Let's keep practicing," she said. "Look at the lagoon. I want you to reimagine it. Change the colors, make some waves, fill it with life. It's your canvas, Pip. See what you can do."

I concentrated on the water, squeezing my eyes shut. I pictured summer rain, the kind that feels plump, juicy, and warm. When I opened my eyes, fat drops splashed on the surface, creating gossamer waves. A smile tugged at my lips.

For the first time in years, I felt in control.

Powerful.

I looked over to share the moment with Everly.

But she was gone.

Time blurred as I played with the lagoon, changing its form – swirling pastels, ribbony ripples, a pool of diamonds. I felt invincible. I felt like God.

But then, without warning, pinecones erupted from the water like spears, filling and drying the lagoon, their shucks cramming into one another, grating on my nerves. I'd lost control. A dream leak. Everly was gone – no guide to tell me what to do. Panic flared, but then it hit me: this was *my* world. I made the rules here. I decided what stayed and what didn't.

"Stop!" I barked at the army of pinecones.

Instantly, the pinecones crumbled to dust, absorbed by the lagoon floor. Exhaling, I calmed the world back to its glacial-blue state. I stepped into the water, soaking in its cool caress. I swam around, conjuring anything that came to mind – koi fish, clouds, rainbows, snow. Time seemed to unravel. And then, after what felt like an eternity, peaceful music unfurled above in the form of six soothing chimes.

Everly's voice drifted from the ether. "You will be leaving The Reverie Cloud momentarily. We hope you enjoyed your dream experience. Please walk forward to exit your dream. And come back soon."

I emerged from the lagoon and walked toward the horizon, where colors and light turned to mist. I woke up with a gentle start in my sleep pod. A slow and gradual warmth blossomed in my chest. I felt wonderfully restored.

As I stepped out of the dream hub and into the hall, movement caught my eye – a fleeting figure rounded the curve. Wyatt? I followed, but whoever it had been was already gone.

Chapter Thirty-Two

The next day at Nyxyn, Andrew came to see me.

He dragged a spare chair from some other office and plopped it down next to me. He swung the chair around and sank into it, grinning in my direction.

"You need a chair in here," he said. "Consider it a holdover. I'm working on your new office upstairs."

"What?"

"Yep! This office is a little…" He glanced up at the glass wall. Ray Cleary stood on the other side, making infinite photocopies, offering a sideways smile. "A little public. Anyway, how was your dream experience?"

I didn't want to seem vulnerable, but my words came out like a geyser. "Absolutely incredible." I told him about the lagoon, the painted waters, the sandy shore, the peace that came over me. I left out the pinecones and my mother's blanket – those felt too personal, too strange to share.

"You've got to try Quest with me some time," he said. "Or maybe Openfield."

"With you?"

"Yeah, it's a new feature. You can be in The Reverie Cloud *with* a partner."

"Like how Everly assists."

"No, I mean *really* with someone – both of us asleep, sharing the dream."

"That's amazing." I hesitated. "You'd want to do that with me?"

"Of course, Pip. I told you – the program is transformative. Quest and Openfield are my personal favorites. I've been waiting to try them with someone."

I rested my cheek on my fist. "What are they like?"

"In Quest, you go on a mission or defeat some character…nothing too scary. Like a troll or dragon or some mystical wizard."

"Does the program ever win?"

Andrew leaned in, his smile tapering. "It wouldn't be fun if you could always win."

"But Everly said the program always benefits the dreamer."

"Sometimes losing is a benefit. There are lessons in defeat, like how to do better next time."

His eyes hung on me. At some point, Ray had finished his copies and left. Out of the corner of my eye, I caught Wyatt standing at the machine, watching us. Because I'd do anything to stay one step ahead of him, to learn about my family's past, and to make sure Andrew remained on my side, I said: "How about tonight?"

Chapter Thirty-Three

The dream experience was mine to conquer alone.

Andrew got pulled into a last-minute meeting when we were about to head to The Reverie Cloud together. He said I should go anyway. He wanted me to keep learning the program, so I'd know how to market its features. I was keen on trying out Quest and hoped he wouldn't mind if I attempted it solo. In the back of my mind, I couldn't wait to tell him about it.

He said it was life-changing.

I wanted life-changing.

Everly greeted me with a complimentary water bottle and led me to the same sleep pod as the night before.

"I'm glad you're back so soon!"

She seemed genuinely interested to see me. I'd wondered about payment for my appointments. Andrew said sessions went for thousands. He told me not to worry about it though; it was logged under Nyxyn's business account.

"Should we try the Restore Dreampath today?"

"I was thinking Quest."

Her face fell flat. "Pip, are you sure? It's a little more complex than Terra."

"Yes, I'm sure."

I was ready to dive in.

Just before sleep, I selected *Dragon's Treasure Chest* from the Quest menu. The objective: navigate a tangled forest maze and reclaim the treasure chest some sly dragon had snatched. The thumbnail showed a red dragon, not exactly terrifying. The artist had chosen whimsical features, almost endearing. I could take him.

This time, my awareness kicked in quicker; my mind was getting used to syncing to the program. A radiant purple hummingbird appeared, showing me the path to begin. No Everly this time – just me and some speedy bird. I looked down at my outfit. The program had chosen a leather tunic costume for me, fitted with a steel sword in hand.

I pushed through twisted vines and tall, swaying grass. An awning of leaves dampened the light, coating my path in moody shadows. Somewhere nearby, an owl bellowed a sharp hoot, as if it had flown right over my shoulder. Then, a blast of heat brushed my face. I was on the right track. The dragon was ahead, breathing flames I couldn't see. Only feel. That meant I was getting closer. I moved onto a new trail, following a stream of heat.

There were moments I had to lift my fingers into view, just to confirm the black sticky patches were really gone. Everything felt so vivid here. The forest glowed in emerald hues, marbled with bronze and yellow highlights. Leaves swept softly against my cheeks as I wandered past. Whether fabricated or not, the urge to find the dragon and claim the treasure surged through me. It felt real. Personal. Courage broiled in my chest.

Then, a wall. A solid hedge came upon me quickly, too thick to push past. My palms pressed against the thick grassy mass, but it held firm. I swung my sword against it, only to be met with an unsatisfying *thunk*. Frustrated, I dropped into the grass, leaning my back against the hedge. Time was ticking, and all I could think was: how would I tell Andrew I failed my quest?

If I couldn't win, I would improvise. Instead of getting up and continuing my search, I decided to experiment with conjuring – maybe it would spark an idea. I was thirsty too. I closed my eyes, and when I opened them, a goblet of sparkling red liquid shimmered before me. Bubbles spilled over the top of the intricately designed glass. I stared at the labyrinthine glassware, surprised the delicate patterns came straight from the canals of my mind. I lifted the goblet and took a sip. Mango, strawberry: sweet and rich. Exquisite.

I nudged the goblet to the side, half wondering if the scent would lure the dragon from hiding. I knew I was straying from the game, but conjuring was just too much fun.

Then a thought crossed my mind. Could I conjure *someone?* A likeness, perhaps? My mother's face flashed through my consciousness, but I wasn't ready to see her, not here. Not with a dragon lurking in the shadows.

I squeezed my eyes shut.

When I opened them, the likeness of Andrew stood at the far end of the maze. My own creation of him. The hedges pressed close on either side of him, narrowing his path toward me. His hands rested casually in the pockets of his cream-colored pants. He looked different – no easy smile, no boyish glow. Instead, he wore a darker expression – alluring, seductive.

I rose to my feet, my heart quickening.

I wanted him to walk toward me. And so, he did.

He stopped at the center of the clearing.

We stood there, facing off.

Slowly, I stepped toward him. The hummingbird zipped into view, a blur of mauve wings, whipping around me, coaxing me back to my quest. I waved it off. I refocused on Andrew, my mind slipping somewhere forbidden. Memories of my bedroom at home seeped in – where I gave my body to Farley, leaving my soul adrift on the dock. What would it be like to take charge for once, to pursue? I ran toward Andrew like a huntress. A hungry lion. I tackled him onto the plush grass, my hand slipping beneath his head to cradle him. He looked up at me, his familiar face holding me in a penetrative stare. His hands climbed my back, undoing my tunic. I put my lips to his, forgetting the red dragon and the treasure somewhere in this wild plane of thoughts. I had found a new game, another type of dragon to tame. It wasn't how you played the game, but I didn't care.

I awoke in my pod, my skin dripping with sweat. When I exited the dream room, I wanted to slip out unnoticed, but Everly's voice caught me at the door. I pretended I didn't hear her.

"Pip! Pip! Don't forget your purse."

I *had* to stop. My hand hovered on the handle. "Oh. Thanks."

"How was the session?"

I couldn't meet her eyes. Did she know I hadn't found the chest? That the dragon still prowled somewhere in the rafters of my mind? That I'd taken a detour in the maze – and done something…something…

"It was good."

"Great! Should I schedule you for another?"

If Everly could see the guilt on my face, it wasn't evident.

Chapter Thirty-Four

Farley was out with friends when I arrived home late at night.

I found myself standing in front of our bookshelf, pulling out a photo album stuffed in the middle. There was a time we both loved printing out photos. I didn't have a social media presence to organize pictures; my father would have detonated. So, we took comfort in glossy photographs we could flip through like a carousel. A nostalgic tear skated down my cheek as I lingered on younger versions of myself and Farley. I wondered if we would have crossed paths at all if I hadn't been bound to the woods, or he hadn't been the boy fishing in the creek – the one who pulled me from one set of shackles only to replace them with another type. But he was still my Farley. And despite everything, I longed for the friend I loved.

The rift between us was being driven by outside forces pulling us in different directions, but I couldn't let go of Nyxyn. I needed purpose, as did he. I wondered if we could make this work. I thought about calling him, wherever he was, but my head pounded with pain. My mind felt scattered, like it was trying to clean itself up but couldn't find the broom. I wondered if I was being punished for what I did in the maze. I fell asleep swathed in guilt.

Farley slid into bed sometime after midnight, reeking of whiskey and citrus perfume. A red lace bra and matching thong were bunched in his fist. He showed them to me like a cat bringing home a dead mouse. Then, he latched on to me, his lips rough against my neck like a barnacle clinging to a ship. I opened my mouth to tell him I was dead asleep – but I missed him. This was the piece of himself he still gave me. This was what I accepted. What we had become. So, I closed my mouth and slipped into my costume.

"Oh baby. Lie down. Yeah. There you go. Yes. You know what I like."

Afterwards, I pulled my knees back into place, like raising a drawbridge over a dark moat. I lay there, red-faced and red lace over my chest like scarlet cobwebs. I felt hollow, like a machine that had just completed its one job. Once, intimacy between us had been whole – something shared, something equal. Now it felt laborious, mechanical, one-sided. How had we drifted so far away from the old Pip and Farley down by the warm, languid creek, our lines tangled, not a fish caught, too distracted by each other, our mirth and youth too potent to realize the heat of the sun had sent all the fish to the shade? When had I stopped telling him what I needed? When had he become a disgruntled warehouse worker in the night, pilfering what he pleased without restocking the shelves?

"Farley?" I whispered into the void.

"Yeah?" he said, lying beside me in the darkness.

"Look at me."

He turned.

I smiled in the midnight maroon room.

I brought his hand to my cheek, an intimate gesture we'd somehow forgotten.

He pulled away, slippery as a fish wriggling free.

He tapped my hip like he was smacking an old, sturdy table that had been in the family for generations. He got up and headed to the bathroom, leaving the door cracked just enough for a sliver of light to leak through. I listened to the sound of the sink running, picturing him splashing his face – his usual routine before sleep. Then, the water stopped. Pipes rattled in the walls, sending chills up my back.

A strange, heavy static buzzed in my ears. My head felt bloated, dizzy even. I wondered if these were side effects from The Reverie Cloud.

"Touch yourself," his voice murmured, slithering through the darkness like an expanding vine. His voice sounded different. Muffled. Huskier.

I sat up. "What?"

"Touch yourself," he repeated, stronger.

"Seriously?"

Heat spilled through my body. Farley never spoke to me like this. I leaned forward, trying to glimpse him in the bathroom, but all I could see was the pale strip of light seeping through the door.

"Touch yourself, dammit!"

I lay down, playing along, sliding my hand past my chest, down my waist. "Are you going to come out?"

The sink gurgled again, then stopped.

Farley waltzed out, blotting his face with a towel.

When he did, the static quieted, but something inside my mind hiccupped. The room felt different. The air was thinner, lighter, as though something in my mind had just receded.

I lay splayed in the sheets, tracing circles along the most intimate folds of my body.

He stopped, shocked. "Pip, what're you doing?"

I pulled my hand away and sat up. "You said to touch myself."

He laughed. "I did?"

Oh god. I knew I had heard him. Hadn't I? My head spun. I felt dizzy again. A strange feeling of déjà vu suddenly came over me. Farley came to me and held me from behind. His touch felt good, needed, but I stared straight ahead, unable to relax. I couldn't shake the feeling we weren't alone in the room. That, or my father's madness was coming to claim me too.

Chapter Thirty-Five

"I noticed an issue with the *X* button," I said. "It doesn't close right."

Wyatt squinted. "Sorry, the *X* button?"

It took me a moment to remember – I was inside The Reverie Cloud. This wasn't a real conversation. It was my memory, replayed in an Echo Dreampath. Everly had suggested I work through a moment where I'd felt powerless, a chance to exercise my confidence. I knew right away which one to choose: interactions with the Nyxynauts.

"Yeah." I made an *X* with my hands. "You know, it closes the browser out. It's only an issue on computers, not mobile devices."

"Sorry…I don't know what you mean," Wyatt, in the program, said.

Everything played out exactly as I remembered it, only hazier, like a scene unfolding through tinted glass. The cool blue room. The sharp, oppressive eyes on me. The feeling of doom beneath my ribs.

"She means the dismissible *X*, Wyatt," Lyra said, caressing his forearm.

Wyatt burst with laughter. "Ah, okay. Very good." When he got up laughing, the others followed him. I knew what came next. Wyatt would curse in my ear. He'd show me who was in charge.

But not this time. Not here.

Wyatt leaned in. "If you're going to provide feedback, learn the right—" The memory rippled as I shot my hand to his throat and squeezed, breaking my avatar free of the script. I watched the thread of life and death oscillate across his face. Watched him go pink, then blue. The room was suddenly clear and focused.

This probably wasn't what Everly had in mind when she said to build confidence. Maybe she thought I'd practice with words. But this felt good. It felt real.

I let go, shoving Wyatt to the ground, pinning him there. "If you're going to tell me what to do," I said, "earn my fucking respect first."

He opened his mouth to speak, but I punched him. Deliberate and sharp. My knuckles pulled up red. I panted, looking down at his quiet, bloody face. Everly said everything here was PG-13. But this sure wasn't. It was exhilarating though. Empowering. I felt my pulse drum to life, and then I quickly scrambled to my feet.

I ran from the lunchroom and found the Nyxynauts in the hall; it was a scene that straddled memory and fantasy. They were on their way to some party.

"I'm coming!" I shouted at them. A demand.

They turned toward me, the light from the large glass windows crashing over their faces. No longer cold or dismissive, they smiled warmly, as if they'd been waiting for me all along.

"We're going to the Symposium," Ray Cleary said. "Glad you're coming, Pip."

The Symposium was a club I'd heard them talk about in the waking world but never thought I'd be invited to. I was riding some synthetic surge of confidence.

"Meet you there," I said, but suddenly I was planted in the passenger seat of Aunt Vera's blue hybrid.

I'd lost control. Dream leak. It was snowing, thick and syrupy. The car was practically sledding down the road. Vera rambled on about my loose, tattered clothing, but her words came out jumbled and distorted. Motorbikes and trucks skidded into our lane, barely missing us.

"*Stop!*" I shouted. "You're going to kill us!"

Vera slammed the brakes, the car scraping along the guardrail before grinding to a jolting stop. Silence sunk its teeth into the car as I hunted for my grip. I breathed heavily, trying to remind myself this was a dream. Or maybe it had turned into a nightmare.

Vera turned to me, her lips bending into a serene, unsettling smile. "What's wrong, Pip?"

"Everything!" I snapped. "You drive me here and there, and I appreciate it – I really do – but I want control of my own life! I don't want to live behind you anymore. I want to live beside you!"

Her expression remained eerily calm. "Pip, when are you going to take a trip to the department store—"

"I don't know!"

"And why don't you start calling me Mom?"

Her face shifted, morphing into my mother's.

The gray-and-white blanket appeared and wrapped itself around her neck, squeezing the air out of her.

I felt the blood drain from my face.

"That's my good little app tester," she cooed with Vera's tone, her voice oozing with overripe warmth despite her suffocation. "Would you like some more pebbles for your fishbowl?"

"*That's enough!*" I yelled, clamping my eyes shut, speaking into the void, tears welling. "My mom was my world and now she's gone, and I don't even know why. My dad might as well be gone too! A formfitting business suit isn't really a priority for me right now! Can't you understand that!?"

Slowly, I peeled my eyes open. The image of my mother faded, leaving Vera in her place.

Without a word, she pulled the keys from the ignition and slipped them into my hand.

I clutched them, cold and sturdy, and exhaled.

I hated losing control in the program. Dream leaks were the worst.

I circled the car, collecting my breath, and slid into the driver's seat. I had no experience driving, but that didn't matter here. I rolled the window down and let the brisk air sting my arm as I sped down the serpentine road toward the Symposium. I got out of the car to see Ray, Joey, and Lyra waiting outside the club for me. I looked behind me – Vera and her car had vanished.

I turned my attention back to the Nyxynauts.

"Well," I asked. "Are we going in?"

Lyra squirmed uncomfortably, crossing her arms. Her black moon-shaped earrings swayed with each shift, clinking softly like nails on a keyboard. "The boys are. It's a strip club. I'll wait outside."

For a moment, I recognized her hidden ache; she was already placing herself on the sidelines, believing it to be her default position. Whether I was feeling her pain or my own insecurities rising through her image, I couldn't tell.

"No," I said, waltzing up to her, brushing hair from her eyes. "You belong wherever you want to be. We're not tools here, Lyra. Watch."

With a swift motion, I turned to Ray, lifting his sweater to reveal his bare chest. Joey was next, his blond chest curls cascading as I teased his shirt upward. When I looked back at Lyra, she stood frozen, shocked by my impulsive antics. Snow drifted around us, yet the air felt strangely tepid. Her face softened. Her body relaxed. I felt a shift in her, as if her release was my own. She came to me, leaned in, and kissed my cheek through the snowy mist. Then she whispered with her lips on my ear.

"We're not tools in this world," she said.

"No," I said. "We're not."

A smile climbed her face. She reached for my hand.

We walked into the Symposium together, but as soon as we crossed the threshold, Lyra drifted toward the stage, moving on autopilot. She was ready to strip, eager to fall back into her old role. I grabbed her arm and yanked her back.

"Remember what I said. We're *not* objects here. It's their turn."

I snapped my fingers toward Ray and Joey. Without hesitation, they sprinted toward the stage, wrapping their legs around poles, whirling under syncopated lights.

I was in control here.

Every atom bent to my will. Each character was compliant to my desires, my curiosities, my hopes, my dreams. The night moved on or seemed to. Time was elusive. I conjured dancers to the stage, filled the club with music, manifested fireworks. Drinks appeared like magic, each sip more intoxicating than the next. I danced, spouted jokes, reveled in laughter, applause, all of it. I threw the most raucous celebration nobody would ever see.

And then, I grew tired of it.

With the flick of a thought, I swept away every person, each particle, like washing paint from a canvas. The world dissolved into an infinite blank page, leaving me stranded in a sea of white. I waited for inspiration. *What should I conjure next?*

Then, Farley appeared in the distance. He was in a rowboat, one side sinking fast. Color and shapes filled the void – a stormy sea, choppy waves, thunderous skies.

Without warning, I was dropped into water.

"Farley!" I called, suddenly choking on brine.

"Pip!"

Nothing else mattered now. Not Ray or Joey or Lyra or Vera. Just Farley, struggling to stay afloat in the listing boat ahead. He clung to one end as the other tilted high. If I could swim to him, steady the boat, he might make it. Despite his love of water, he wasn't a strong swimmer.

"Pip, there's a hole!" he called over sloshing waves. "I'm sinking! I was fishing, and then this happened."

I hadn't conjured this scene. Another dream leak? I swear I tried to regain control. But couldn't. I wondered if there was a problem with the program. I reminded myself it wasn't real. It was only my worries about Farley seeping through – his drinking, the citrus perfume on his collar, the rifle within reach, his distance.

But logic escaped me. It felt real. My mind convinced me of its verity.

My chest tightened. I had to save him.

I looked around, desperate for the familiar chimes, for Everly's voice to announce the session's end. But nothing came.

Immersed in the freezing cold sea, I swam toward my husband.

I tried to change the scene, but control was long gone.

"Farley!" I shouted, thrashing toward the boat. "Hold on! I'm coming!"

Suddenly, something seized me from below, yanking me under.

Saltwater flooded my throat as I struggled to see through the dark water. Wyatt. His hands clamped around me, dragging me deeper into the cold black depths.

He was drowning me.

My lungs burned, air escaping. Was I feeling this in real life too? It felt too real to be a dream. I thought The Reverie Cloud was supposed to be safe. I could feel myself choking.

Instinct overcame me. I grabbed Wyatt by the neck, twisting, struggling against him as we wrestled like debris in a rushing river's torrent.

"Stay away from Nyxyn," he lashed, acidic bubbles bursting from his mouth. "Stay away from The Reverie Cloud."

I pressed down on his chest with my foot, then his head, using him to push myself upward.

When my chin pierced the surface, I gasped for air. Wyatt was gone.

"Farley," I called weakly, when I reached the boat's edge.

The wood creaked as he leaned over. His hand cupped my face, hot against the callous sea.

For a moment, I thought he'd say something sweet, something to replace the terror. But instead, his voice cracked, warped and raw.

"I have a filthy, filthy heart," he whispered.

Chimes sounded from the sky. I looked up at the white, hot sun. The sea sloshed pleasantly around us. I stared at my husband, wondering why he had said that. *Of all things to say.* The final chime rang, and just like that, Everly pulled me back to reality.

Chapter Thirty-Six

Wyatt came into my fishbowl the next day, radiating petulance.

"Pipsqueak, do you know your Mountainview app notes were incredibly—"

I stood up, cutting him off. "Thorough. Yes."

"What? No! That's not—" he said, looking thrown. "I was going to say—"

His bloody face from last night shot through my mind. My fingers, curled around his throat like rope. My grip on his delicate arterial line. Knowing I'd defeated him in The Reverie Cloud gave me an unexpected smugness.

"Wyatt, Wyatt," I said, measured.

I drifted around my desk toward him, watching him flinch the closer I got. Just a little. Barely noticeable. But I saw it.

"I know this office is called the fishbowl, but just because it's see-through, doesn't mean you're welcome in it without an appointment. I know common courtesy is a hard concept to pick up this late in life, but now you know. Okay?"

"Wait," said Wyatt, tripping over his tongue. "This is— I—"

I moved into his space even more, practically edging him out the door, his tongue unable to form a sentence.

He was unraveling, and I indulged in it like a feast.

I snapped my fingers at him, the same way he'd once done to me. "Hey. I'm moving offices soon, so maybe you can have this one. It'd suit you, Wyatt Fink. The perfect stage. Everyone can walk by and gawk at you. Isn't that what you want? Attention, right? Or is it glory? A place to hawk-eye other people's work and steal it?"

"Pip," he said. "I – don't think you understand—"

"Well," I said, interrupting him with a serrated smile. "This has been *lovely*, but I'm heading to the third floor to see if my new office is ready. Take care now."

I didn't wait for his response. I moved past him and tore through the idea floor, picking up speed until I was out of sight. I breezed up the stairs, panting, my heart floating somewhere outside my body. This was a new Pip Renner. It was all thanks to The Reverie Cloud. I never could have uttered those words otherwise. And even though last night's session went awry – dragging me deeper into my subconscious than I would have liked – I'd take the glitches. I'd take the bad parts of the program just to keep feeling this way. To keep becoming this version of myself.

No way was I coming down from this high anytime soon.

The following night, I returned for another Echo session. This time, I found myself in Nyxyn's kitchen, Andrew at the counter. His back was turned to me as he stirred his coffee slowly. I watched his tight blue shirt quiver like second skin, trying to keep up with his muscular form beneath. He turned, leaning his hips casually against the counter, sweeping hair from his eyes.

"Hi, Pip!"

I bit my lip, staring.

He arched his brow. "Pip?"

"Do you want me?" I said, my voice sinking low.

"Huh?"

I inched closer. "I said, do you want me?"

His bubbly grin faltered, replaced by a handsome, brooding intensity. "God, you have no idea," he said, crooking a finger, his smile turning hungry. "C'mere."

I drifted toward him, stitching the space between us.

His hand found my hip, while his other hand moved through my hair, grabbing me primitively. We sank to the floor, where time seemed to crumble to sand. My thoughts fused with his actions, balancing the fine line of reality and artifice.

Chimes echoed way too soon, just as he sighed my name in my ear.

I left the building with satisfaction coiled in shame.

The Reverie Cloud had sunk its teeth into me. I wasn't sure I could ever stop.

Chapter Thirty-Seven

I got home late, and noticed a couple of trucks in our driveway.

The night air felt too perfect to be real. Laughter and muffled music drifted from our deck in the back, but noises came up distorted, like I was underwater. I wondered if it was that same side effect from the program I felt earlier. Farley's voice rose from the crowd, but it felt filtered and familiar, as though I was retracing my steps somehow. I shook the feeling off, rubbed my ears, and found Farley on the porch with about five work buddies – among them two women I'd never met. They were drinking, flicking bottle caps in some drinking game, passing hand-rolled cigarettes around the firepit. I'd met most of his crew before, but not the women.

I stayed for a bit, slumped into a plastic Adirondack chair, feeling the firelight warm my face. I stared ahead, tracing Farley's trademark pine-soap scent as it chewed through the smoke. Some kind of anchor. Chatter cascaded over me – clients, inside jokes, some country band Farley was eager to see live. A band? I didn't even know he liked concerts. Around them, he was funnier, lighter. And each time he cracked a joke, he'd glance at the blond woman in the low-cut purple shirt to see if she laughed along. The revelation struck me like a cold, heavy slap. Maybe it wasn't just the work that had been keeping him so busy. Maybe it was Purple Shirt all along.

The citrusy perfume she wore twisted the knife in deeper. My life was slipping downstream without me, and I couldn't seem to grab hold of the oar before it drifted out of reach. The other woman next to Purple Shirt kept looking at me, like I was the fool in a joke everyone knew the punchline to except me. I kept my eyes on a leaf about to tumble from a branch.

Farley, oblivious, rolled another cigarette and passed it to Purple Shirt, their fingers brushing, spit mingling on the paper. It could've meant nothing, or it could've meant everything. In that moment, I could understand crimes committed out of passion. The hypocrisy wasn't lost on me. My feelings for Andrew were a stain on my conscience. I wanted to cleanse myself from it, but I wasn't sure how. But the idea of losing Farley, no matter how much we'd drifted lately, felt like death itself. He was my mooring point. I couldn't let Andrew or Purple Shirt tear us apart.

The weight of jealousy pressed against my chest. I excused myself and slipped to the front of the house. I needed a moment to think, to breathe. I noticed the white flag of our lilac-covered mailbox pointing upwards. My pulse quickened. I hadn't noticed it before. I approached the box, and that same strange static filled my ears, like distant radio interference. A nauseous déjà vu feeling consumed me once again. Was I getting sick? I shook it off and opened the lid. Inside was a crumpled note. My father's writing, messy and sloped, covered the page. My breath stalled. *He'd been here?* He'd been here. And that meant he was okay. But how had I missed him? Why hadn't he stayed to see me?

In the ghost-white moonlight, I read the note again and again. His handwriting bled into my mind as though he were speaking the words directly to me. There was only one sentence, scrawled in the middle of the paper:

Prepare for betrayal.

Chapter Thirty-Eight

I stayed home from work, waiting on my father's return.

In the morning, I sat beneath the shade of a spruce out front.

As Vera backed her car out of the connected driveway, she caught sight of me. "Everything all right?" she called.

"I'm useless with this migraine," I lied. "I'll be in tomorrow. Promise."

"You don't want to rest inside?"

I gestured broadly to the trees. "Fresh air."

She waved and drove off. I settled into waiting, watching the lot, the woods – a noise, a glimpse, a shadow, any subtle sign of him. Nothing. By evening, the silence was unbearable. I grabbed my bag and ordered a rideshare to The Reverie Cloud. I needed another session, something to sieve the heaviness flooding inside me.

That night, wind picked up and rattled our windows. The noise jolted me from sleep, and I awoke in a sweat. I went outside to cool off, only to be met with static cling in my ears. The mailbox caught my eye. Its white flag was up again, and something sat inside – a small container with a note affixed. I peeled the paper free and read it in the dim light.

Remember.

I looked around, expecting to see my father lurking in the shadows. But the lot was empty. Silent. An odd peace settled over me, knowing he'd been here again, close enough to leave two messages in a row. The thought of calling the police crossed my mind, but I couldn't risk it. What if an interrogation chased him farther into hiding? No, I needed to catch him myself. Call it superstition or maybe hunter's patience; I felt compelled to lie in wait, careful not to startle the skittish shrew back into hiding.

Slowly, I opened the container he'd left accompanying the note, pulling out a small wooden object. It was too dark to see clearly, so I ran my fingers over its smooth contours, tracing a tiny head, legs, a mane. I smiled once I realized what it was – a horse, complete with a little leather saddle glued to its back.

I brought it to my nose, inhaling softly. The familiar, earthy scent pulled me back to memories of my mother at the stable. This wasn't just any horse sculpture – it was *mine*, a comfort carving I once held close as a child. Immediately after this discovery, I hid the horse away in the coat closet, hoping I could keep a part of him from running away. I lolled his word around – *remember*. Remember. Remember. *Remember what, Dad?*

In the night, Farley came home and stumbled into bed, reeking of perfume and stale beer. The stench made me sick. I splashed water on my face and went back to bed, only to find him already passed out, no explanation. As the moon's murky glow pooled through the window, I stared at him, imagining his hands on Purple Shirt, his breath on her neck. He shot his eyes open suddenly, making me wince beneath the sheets.

"Hey," I whispered. "I thought you were sleeping. Where were you?"

"At the Post," he mumbled. The nearest bar in town.

I wondered what it was like to feel part of a group. To belong. I didn't envy the woman with the citrus scent as much as I envied the fact that he was out, that he belonged somewhere – and I didn't.

"There was something in the bushes out front," he said, rubbing his eyes. "Didn't check. Maybe a raccoon. Damn raccoons."

"I'll go look."

"No, it's late," he slurred. "Come here. Let's cuddle. You're working so late these days. I never see you. I miss you."

His words hit like a punch. "*I'm* out late?"

Foreboding came over me. Hadn't *he* been the one disappearing, night after night? Or was it me? Maybe I was the elusive one, losing myself in The Reverie Cloud. Now that I thought about it, I always came out of my sessions foggy, like time had evaporated, snapping back only when the alarm went off in the morning.

I edged closer, the bitter hint of beer hovering in the space between us. By the time I settled into his arms, he was already snoring, strong as an avalanche. My mind drifted to my father, wandering aimless in the woods, lost in himself. Was he okay? Would he survive? What if that movement in the bushes wasn't just some damn raccoon? What if it was him, leaving another message, right before disappearing into the shadows again?

The thought wouldn't let me go. I couldn't take another disappearance. I needed to know.

Quietly, I slipped from Farley's arms and went to the mailbox.

Chapter Thirty-Nine

Something was jutting out.

I drew a tawny bundle free from the mailbox, holding it up to the moon. Its fibrous feel sparked an odd sense of familiarity. Static whispered in my ears. I was beginning to think I definitely needed to see a doctor. But I ignored it for the sake of another discovery. It was a scroll, rolled tightly, bound by twine.

"Dad," I whispered, my voice scratching in the wind. I stroked the paper.

It was another message from him. Another breadcrumb to let me know he was safe. He was guiding me. Offering me clues. I wasn't alone. I hesitated, trying to angle my neck away from the overcharged static. It didn't work. I untied the twine and unraveled the paper with shaky hands. The words were scrawled sloppily as though he'd written them with his eyes closed.

Stay out of the computer room.

The message was like a strike of ice to my nerves. What did it mean? Why would he say this? What computer room? I put the paper to my chest.

Back in bed, I woke Farley with a kiss along his jawline, bypassing the citrus on his clothes. I wouldn't let Purple Shirt claim him. He was mine.

He stirred softly, eagerly.

I made love to him.

The scroll was an eerie thing to find in the dark – a strange message, but a message nonetheless.

Receiving it brought a peace I hadn't felt in months.

It meant my father hadn't left me completely. He had a plan.

These were all signs of his presence.

Signs of hope. Hope he would come back soon. Hope I could pour into my future, into Farley, into the family we both dreamed of. Things weren't as broken as I thought. Everything was normal. As orderly as my pinecone mandalas.

I gave it all I had.

The tides were changing.

But just like tides, hope could be pulled back into the sea in an instant.

Chapter Forty

Nights later, I lingered at The Reverie Cloud longer than I'd planned.

Time smeared into liquid oblivion. When I finally left, I asked my rideshare driver to drop me off at my father's burnt cabin. I wondered if my father was staying nearby, tucked away in the shed, close enough to leave messages.

The woodshed was dark as ink, guzzling up every shape.

"Dad?" I called. My voice bounced off his old lathe layered in dust. Silence snapped back thick and jarring. Then, the pungent bite of smoke drifted through the slabs. My pulse instantly sped up. I burst from the shed, tearing up the wooded hill, the tragic scent of fire thickening with each step. My worst fears blistered.

Panting, I arrived at the foot of our gravel lot only to witness the in-law suite burning. Our home, covered in rushing flames. Aunt Vera's house remained untouched. Fire feasted on the beams. Familiar heartbreak gnawed at me like wolves tearing into flesh. Firefighters were already nearby, their sirens echoing through the firs. Someone in the woods must've called for help. As they arrived, dousing the flame-slicked bones, I thought of my photo albums, memories erased; of my father's carved wooden horse buried in the coat closet. A talisman of him – gone. I clung to its image, its scent, a tactile feeling in my mind as I stood there in shock, numb beyond belief, unable to form words, shaking, grappling with how this could have happened to our family...again.

Had Farley left the fireplace unattended?

Had Vera done something while I stayed late at The Reverie Cloud?

When Farley stumbled home, buzzed and glassy-eyed, he didn't rush to comfort me, tears staining my cheeks. Instead, he called Purple

Shirt, whatever her name was, to tell her what had happened. Then he turned to his aunt, who was finally coming up the driveway, tires crunching over gravel. She had been out running errands. Just like Farley, neither of them had been answering their phones.

I found it suspicious that they were both absent while our home burned. My father's voice echoed in my mind: *I didn't do this. It was a warning. They're coming for me. For us.*

But why? What dirt was on me? I struggled to piece together the fragments of my life before our move to Snoqualmie Pass. Was there something unspeakable I'd done to deserve this? But how could I know? So many of my memories were murky, painted black.

I peered over my shoulder at Farley and Vera at the top of the lot, where the smoke hadn't reached, embracing and speaking heatedly in the dark. Was I imagining things, or did Vera wear a smirk? And were there smudges of ash on her hands? *She's a plant.* Was Farley guilty by association? But why would he want a child with me then? Perhaps he'd gotten too close to me, and Vera disapproved. She always had sway over him, didn't she? I couldn't believe I was thinking this way. I was losing my grip.

As firefighters continued to battle the flames, I felt myself slipping into a silent, paranoid rage, becoming just...like...him.

I didn't sleep for days afterwards.

I missed work, kept watch on the mailbox, spent my days locked in Vera's spare bedroom.

Once, while everyone was out, I went to The Reverie Cloud and told no one. Not even Andrew.

At night, looking through the spare bedroom's back window, I stared at the charred remnants of our suite. Farley came to see me, but I feigned sleep in the daybed my father once occupied. My husband draped a quilt over me that smelled freshly washed. After he left, I was half-asleep when a hand brushed my cheek in the night. Yet, no one was in the room. I heard a voice call out. It was the same voice I'd heard the night I was with Farley.

"Having fun?" it asked.

"No," I whispered, sliding beneath the covers until the voice vanished.

Chapter Forty-One

In the still of night, I lay awake, unable to sleep, listening.

The rush of wind, leaves against the windowpane, Farley's snoring down the hall. He was confined to his childhood bedroom, a space frozen in time, with a single bed that had been his since his parents' death left him marooned with Vera. I was cooped up in the spare room where a daybed filled the space.

I stared ahead at a hanging ivy plant, its shadows twisting on the wall, and thought of my father who spent nights here after his cabin burned. Did he notice similar intricate shadows before drifting off, or did he lie awake like me, fighting off a voice, wondering about some arsonist's agenda? Turning toward the moonlight decanting through the blinds, I called out to him with my thoughts, my mind netted with frustration. Why did he keep so much hidden from me?

Then I thought of Farley.

After our wedding, we spent time in Leavenworth, a resort town with a cerulean lake, just between city and mountains. During a nature walk, exhaustion hit, and we paused on a fallen log. Farley offered me his last drop of water.

"I can't believe we're married," he had said.

"Are you happy?" I asked, scanning his eyes for reassurance.

He nodded in earnest, grabbing my fingers, threading them with his. "Course I am. You know I've always wanted to marry you, Pip. First time I saw you in the creek, I thought you were an angel." His eyes glistened, lost in the past. "I thought about leaving these woods as soon as I turned eighteen. But when I met you, everything made sense. I knew what I was made for. What my lips were made for. My hands. My heart. Everything. I was made for loving you."

With tenderness, he wiped dirt from my cheek. "I love you, girl. Don't forget it."

I felt devotion in every single word.

There, on the log, like two lion's mane mushrooms sprouting from solid wood, it was inconceivable to imagine our love metamorphosing into anything other than what it was at that moment: steadfast and unbreakable. It's so hard to believe that love will ever change.

Farley's snores continued rumbling from down the hall. I stayed tense and motionless, staring into the shadows, willing the voice not to return. The house groaned low and aching, and the whoosh of wind slapped at the window. Somewhere downstairs, I thought I heard a faint rustle. A chill spread through me. I told myself it was nothing – just the house settling after the wind – but my skin bristled anyway. I slid out of bed and eased into the hall. Farley's door was closed, his snores loud as rolling waves. Vera's door was shut too, a pitch-black strip beneath. For a second, I thought I saw her door shift open a breath, but when I blinked, it was still. I told myself I was seeing things. She must be asleep, too.

I crept downstairs to the kitchen, following the faint aroma of laundry from earlier in the day, but I stopped cold when I spotted a handgun resting on the counter. A sharp gasp escaped my lips. I knew Farley had a shotgun – he used it to ward off mountain animals or for target practice – but I never knew about a handgun. Was it Vera's? But why would it be out?

Suddenly, the voice spoke.

"Grab," it murmured. It was muffled and warped, like it was underwater.

Every hair on my body rose. My chest clamored uncontrollably. I tried to speak, but nothing came out. At last, I swallowed and whispered, "Why?"

It didn't answer.

"Do you want me to hurt myself?" I pressed, trembling.

A low rumble followed. "No."

I couldn't believe it responded. I looked around. No one. Vera had been in the kitchen earlier; the trace scent of detergent still hung in the air.

Had she left the gun here after doing laundry? But why would she even have a gun, let alone leave it out?

"Who do you want me to hurt?" I asked the voice.

"Wyatt," it snarled.

I swiftly grabbed the gun and ran upstairs. The hallway to the spare room felt longer than it should have – like I was moving through a bad dream. But I pushed on, found a shirt, bundled the gun up, and buried it deep in the spare bedroom closet. I replayed the ghostly voice in my mind the rest of the night, staring at the closet door. I looked out the window at our burnt home, my heart throbbing wet and chunky. I pressed my hand to my chest, trying to steady the turbulence, then moved it to my belly, rubbing gentle circles.

I couldn't shake the thought that maybe Farley and I should stop trying. How could I bring a child into this world – a world where a voice urged me toward darkness? And why Wyatt? Sure, he was a bully, but no one deserves death.

The voice was silent the rest of the night.

The next day, I'd only ventured out of the bedroom to use the bathroom and grab a quick bite. It was Saturday. I told Farley I wasn't feeling well, but the truth was, I feared him. I feared Vera. I feared myself and what I might do with that gun the next time I saw Wyatt. I didn't know who to trust, least of all myself. I was in shock by it, the fire, by everything. Confronting them about the gun seemed impossible – what if their answers only deepened my fears or confirmed my suspicions? That they were spies, ordered by whatever force sent my father into hiding. What if I caught them in lies? Or what if I told them about the voice, the gun, and they dismissed me as paranoid, just like we all dismissed my father as crazy. No, I couldn't risk it. I had to figure this out myself. I longed for my mother to show up and sort out the mess. I needed her more than ever. Even her likeness would help. I had to get back to The Reverie Cloud and connect with her in Echo. To seek clarity, to find comfort. I had to do it before someone got hurt.

But then, a memory flashed in my mind – Wyatt cornering me, gripping my chin, cursing in my ear. A chilling thought haunted me.

What if the voice was right…

Chapter Forty-Two

In the thick of night, my mind buckled.

I shivered beneath sheets, my skin paper-thin, as if one wrong turn could rip me in half. Eventually, I surrendered to sleep.

Wyatt met me in my dream. I found myself seated in a small, rugged rowboat – Farley's wooden boat from The Reverie Cloud – this time sinking at the opposite end, with Farley nowhere in sight. Wyatt swam toward me like a deviant sea creature, murder glinting in his eyes. I clung to the rails of the fragile boat as he cut through the muddy water, the silver shine of a gun breaking the surface.

Panic surged as I groped the floorboards until my fingers brushed the cold metal of a handgun. Just as Wyatt aimed for me, I shot him in the head. The blast rang in my ears as he sank beneath me, staining the water crimson.

I woke with a scream. Farley rushed from his room down the hall right to my side.

"Shh, shh," he said, leaning in to cradle my head. "I'm here."

"Farley, I'm not okay," I said, my voice quavering.

He rocked me gently. I could still feel the boat's motion beneath me.

"I'm losing my grip," I said, eyeing the closet door with the gun inside it.

"It's the fire. It's devastating."

"No, I'm losing it."

"I'm here for you."

"I'm losing my grip. I'm losing my grip. I'm losing you."

"No, you're not. I'm here."

"There was a gun," I breathed, staring at the closet door, "on the counter."

I couldn't keep it in. But I didn't want to tell him everything either.

"What gun?"

"I don't know. Was it yours?"

"No. Course not. Mine is locked up. Always is."

"What about Vera?"

He paused. "Not sure."

Our conversation felt like a dream – the kind you only half remember, returning when you least expect it. I couldn't even be sure it happened at all…

In the remains of the incinerated suite the next morning, I wandered beneath cindered beams and over a scorched floor. Farley and Vera were both out early. Farley had a weekend job, and Vera had errands. I crept quietly into the remnants of our fire-ravaged home, desperate to see if my father's wooden horse survived. Wooden beams drooped like black skeletal limbs. Soot coated every surface. I remembered Vera's dirt-streaked hands the night the fire ignited; the very next day, she had scheduled a demolition, her voice sharp with irritation when they couldn't fit us in for weeks.

The closet where I hid my father's carving was now a catacomb of ash and debris. As I wove carefully through the wreckage, I silently apologized to some future child for the strain I was putting on my body, the place they might one day call home. I already felt unqualified to be a mother, and I wasn't even pregnant yet. The air was thick with the scent of smoke and burnt wood. I sank onto a shattered beam, stifling tears in my clammy hands.

I thought back on how I arrived at this point. If only I could remember my life before Snoqualmie Pass, understand why someone would want to burn not one but two homes occupied by the Screed family. If only I knew what had happened to my mother. I left the ashen floorboards and stepped outside onto the burnt gravel. I saw something dark among the rocks. I wiped my tears and brushed aside the debris to uncover the object. My heart sped when I realized what it was – I picked up Wyatt's glasses.

★ ★ ★

I needed to get back to work and interrogate Wyatt. I wasn't afraid of him anymore. I was pissed. The doomsday image of our burnt home twisted my thoughts into snags. My thoughts were so loud, so fast; yet, silence consumed the car on Monday morning as Vera drove us to the office. I fixed my eyes on the winding road ahead, my mind slithering back to the dream I'd had the night before. I didn't tell Vera or Farley about Wyatt's glasses. Not yet. She hadn't believed he stole my Fazzle design; why on earth would she believe he burned our home? Plus, I wanted to pull the truth out of him myself. I wanted to see him squirm. He hated me so much, he had tried to burn me alive. God.

As we drove on, I wondered about the gun on the counter. I opened my mouth to bring it up, but doubt crept in. What if I hadn't seen things correctly? Just like the voice; what if the gun was an illusion too? Everything felt off lately, especially after the fire. Brain fog and déjà vu plagued me more than ever. Days felt out of order – shuffled. Recent events smeared, like a careless finger spiraling through wet paint. I certainly didn't want Vera thinking she had hired some madwoman. I decided to keep my mouth shut until I could get back to the closet and confirm the gun was real – a substantial, physical thing I could hold in my hands.

When we arrived at Nyxyn, cops were parked outside, and officers were scattered throughout the lobby. Upstairs, the idea floor felt somber and was thick with whispers. The Nyxynauts were huddled together by a communal desk, their faces drawn. Lyra leaned into Ray's shoulder, tears spilling down her cheeks. Joey bit his nails, glancing around as if waiting for news. In a corner, Andrew was deep in conversation with a cop. When he spotted me, he approached, his brow furrowed, despair lining his face.

He placed a hand on my shoulder. "I'm not sure if you and Vera had a chance to read your emails yet. I know it's early."

"No, we just got here."

He looked down, then met my eyes, his face weighted with sorrow. "I'm sorry to be the one to tell you this, Pip, but Wyatt Fink was murdered last night."

Chapter Forty-Three

Wyatt was found near his home with a gunshot wound to the head.

Vera unleashed these details to me after wrapping up her questioning with an officer. Soon enough, it was my turn. A man with broad shoulders and whisky-red cheeks approached me, notepad open, pencil poised. I felt like it was just the two of us alone, facing off on the idea floor, with a hot spotlight hanging right over my head.

"Ma'am, can I please get your name?"

"Piper Renner."

"Were you close with Wyatt Fink?"

"Not really. He was my colleague."

"Did you have any recent arguments or disagreements with the victim?"

I hesitated. "No."

"In your opinion, is there anyone who might have had a motive to harm him?"

I could feel guilt clawing in my bones, trying to escape. Sure, I bashed his virtual face in at The Reverie Cloud, but that was only pretend. And the other night, I killed him in my sleep, but that was just a dream. Or was it? Everly once told me that while people experience multiple dreams each night – around six – they only remember about five per cent of them. Could the same be true of reality?

I fought to appear composed although sweat was seeping through my baggy button-up.

"No," I answered.

"Thank you. And can you tell me your whereabouts last night?"

"I went to bed early," I said.

He scanned my frame. "Last question. Do you think there is anything that might be important for us to know about your relationship with the victim or the circumstances surrounding his death?"

Wyatt treated me like trash.

I pulverized him in a virtual sleep therapy program.

I killed him in my dream.

There was a gun in my home. Maybe.

I found his glasses in the ash of my burnt home.

"No, nothing."

"Thank you," the cop said.

I glanced at Vera; she was huddled against Andrew's chest at the far end of Nyxyn's foyer. He rubbed her back up and down slowly. Behind them, a screen in the wall displayed the Fazzle design I had created – the one Wyatt stole from me. My chest twisted. I had to leave before my face betrayed the mayhem coursing through my veins.

There was only one place I thought to go.

Chapter Forty-Four

An alien calm enveloped me as I approached The Reverie Cloud building in the woods.

I told Vera I needed a quick coffee, but the truth was another story – I believed the only way to restore my sanity was to dive back into the program. Just one more time, and I'd be okay. I craved a hit of confidence, a jolt of serenity. But when I arrived, the door was locked. I banged on the leviathan brain-etched door, shaking it violently.

The moment Everly arrived and let me in, my entire body released.

"Pip," she said. "Are you okay, love? We closed early today to do some maintenance on our servers."

"I could really use a session," I said, desperate. "Do you have an opening right now? It's for...market research."

Everly eyed me with concern. She pulled her phone out from her back pocket to check her schedule. "I can squeeze you in in about an hour. Would that work for you?"

An hour? God, I wanted it now.

"Yes," I exhaled. "Yes."

"Perfect. Come in."

I sat in a lobby room down the hall from the dream hub. The marble-covered room was framed with paintings that seemed to be mimicries of life with hints of fantasy – two women in a slick pink convertible, wind tugging at their hair, their car soaring through clouds; a woman carving an apple, dishes floating magically to the sink behind her; a happy family of six eating a holiday feast, their table, with them seated at it, soaring past snow-capped mountaintops, additional guests arriving by flight. I couldn't help but wonder – could *I* fly in The Reverie Cloud? Everly hadn't mentioned it. Moreover, I kept thinking how many of the women in the paintings looked eerily like my mother. One of the paintings depicted a woman standing in a field, horses grazing in the background. How odd.

I stared at the painting curiously until my eyes grew heavy. They opened and shut, sending me into daydreams of flight, until Everly finally appeared, slicing through my thoughts with a blade.

"Ready to go, Pip?"

I nodded eagerly, rising from my seat.

As we walked toward the dream room, Everly turned to me with a barrage of curious looks. "So, Pip, what Dreampath are you thinking of trying today?"

"Echo," I said, resolute.

Everly was quiet. But I caught a slight, crinkled grin, like my visit might align with some unspoken agenda. "Very good."

I followed Everly into the dream room trying to rein in my breath.

This session, I knew, would be unlike any other.

I was going to visit my mother.

I was finally going to pull the truth out from the darkest corners of my mind.

Chapter Forty-Five

In the program, I came upon the ranch where my mother and I used to watch the horses.

It was my comfort. The place she'd take me to when the world became too much. I raised my fingers to my eyes, relieved to find the black patches gone. But where was my mother? I conjured her, but she remained elusive in the cobwebs of my mind.

I paced the perimeter of the fence and spotted the mare cantering with her foul. I was pleased their love survived the trenches of my memories. I sank down into the grass, warmth washing over me like bathwater. Perfect heat. Just the right temperature – how my mother would draw it for me, with my plastic toy ponies scattered around me like a pastel wreath.

A voice cut through my snowdrift thoughts. "Pip."

I looked up.

My mother stood there, the wisps of her braid flowing like a horse's tail in the wind. Her face was perfectly freckled and beautiful, just as I remembered. A flowy white summer dress wrapped around her, her bold smile brightening everything. Strands of strawberry blond danced around her forehead, and her velvet-brown eyes sparkled. She was stunning. She looked so, so real. She reached her hand out to me. I took it as she pulled me to my feet.

"Mom," I whispered. She loomed tall, a protective giant. In her presence, nothing else mattered. No rolling dates on a calendar, no birthdays ticking down to adulthood, to her loss. All that existed was this moment. Mother. Protector.

Questions spun in my mind. What had happened to her? What was Dad hiding? Could she color in my blackened memories? Fix the crushed ceramics of my mind? Please? I knew it wasn't really her – just an algorithmic reflection. But maybe I could unearth some truths from her, from my subconscious. However, as soon as I saw her, my questions fizzled away. When she hugged me, I felt, for the first time, complete. Whole.

"Come, Pip," my mother said. "I want to show you something."

She pulled me along, and we began to run, barefoot as we galloped over the lush grass. My mother led me, swift and free. We reached the far end of the meadow, away from the horses, then she paused, smiling *down* on me. I realized I was a child now, looking up at my warm giant.

"Come on, my girl!" she said, dashing forward once more.

I ran after her, giggling, my voice squeaky and girlish.

All my questions were lost.

"Mom, we're going to run into the fence! Mom! Mom!"

But she just kept going, her laughter ringing out. "Come on, Pip!" she called, glancing back with a smile blanketing her face.

"Mom, the fence! We're going to crash into it!"

"Look up at the sky!"

I trusted her. I kept running, looking up.

I was holding on to her hand so tightly, I thought it might break at the bone.

And yet, she smiled, unbothered. She reveled in her freedom.

"Here we go, Pip," she sang.

With her hand in mine, my heart searching for a place to land, we lifted above the fences and soared over the horses. We flew. Me and my mother, rocketeers in the amber-blue glow. We glided over the mare and her foal, who thundered below, matching our pace. Soon, they vaulted over the fences, and we followed, hovering just above them. The field opened into a vast meadow, wild horses roaming free beneath us. It felt like an eternity, this fleeting moment suspended above the grass, our glorious flight. Me and my mother.

There in the sky, my adult form returned. I saw my hand encased in hers, my fingers growing to match the length of hers.

Now was my chance to question her.

"Mom," I said, my mind whirling. Words and questions escaped me. The wind was too fast, too thick. Here was my mother. My saint. I managed to get my words out, but they were sparse. "What happened to you? What is Dad hiding?"

The joy in her face sunk. "Scarlet," she whispered, and before she could say anything more, I felt the program quiver.

"Please," I pressed. "Can't you tell me more?"

But her form wavered, turned to mist, and the six chimes sung out, ending my session before I could pull the truth out from her. From within.

Chapter Forty-Six

When I arrived back in Snoqualmie Pass, I bolted to the spare bedroom.

I needed to know where my reality ended and the illusions began, driven by a dire urge for sobriety. But when I flung open the closet door, there was no gun. All that remained was the crumpled shirt I'd wrapped it in, or thought I did. I decided I wouldn't bring this up, not to anyone.

In the days following, I returned to The Reverie Cloud every evening. I attempted to conjure my mother again, but she wouldn't come, like a block was on her. Still, I experimented with Echo, Restore, Quest, and Terra, stumbling out of the templelike building, eaten by night, feeling temporarily pleased but hungry for more. I was a vampire, a werewolf, some dark version of myself that couldn't be satiated.

On nights I felt particularly lost, confused, or just plain sick, The Reverie Cloud became an oasis. My church. Sometimes it was the only thing encouraging me to get out of bed in the morning and slog through the day. Within the virtual sanctum of my mind, I shed the shackles of *Piper Renner.* I inhabited an antithetical domain – an opposite world of sorts. Here, I personified everything *Piper Renner* could never be – bold, fierce, strong, confident, explorative, and brave.

I hadn't spoken to Farley in days. Our schedules struggled to align. We became two remote stars in the same galaxy, slipping farther away from one another. I imagined him gossiping about me to Purple Shirt, or maybe I never even came up in their conversations. Maybe it was all physical between them. I thought of bringing it up to him, but something had robbed my will. The euphoria of the program was waning; now, I only went to fulfill an itch, some forced inner duty. But my lips had become glue; my brain, mud. A broken mandala. The simplest words came out like tongue twisters.

I didn't speak to anyone. I did the bare minimum at work before racing to my sleep pod. My thoughts, my existence, my voice only mattered when I was immersed in the program. That was the only time I felt anything resembling sanity. I forgot everything that once mattered to me, everything that weighed on me. The voice in my head had quieted too. I whirled the name *Scarlet* around in my head but came up empty.

One night, emerging from the program, my heart pounding like a drum, I felt compelled to check the mailbox. It had been so long since I'd received a clue, a woodcarving, any sign that my father was still alive. I don't know what I was expecting, but it wasn't this – a crumpled slip of paper. I opened it, pressing my hands to my ears to mute the static and that awful sense of déjà vu. There was only one word on the paper:

Evadere.

In the black of night, I stopped in front of a mirror, trembling like loose tulle in a gale. The reflection staring back was grotesque, a phantasmagoric version of myself warped in the rectangular glass. The hair framing my face was like swamp coral. I pulled it away as though raking back heavy, spider-infested seaweed. The brushing and crackling echoed in my ears. I touched my skin. It felt smooth, but when I looked in the mirror, my face appeared puckered like the stump of a rotting tree. My eyes – sunken deep into my skull – appeared as two large glossy pools of coal.

I stumbled to another mirror, and the same horrific image stared back. Desperate, I tore to the kitchen, slid open the utensil drawer, and confronted my reflection in a spoon. I hurled the silver tool across the room when the same vile troll met me in the ladle. I ran to bed, curled up tight, and didn't move until the next day.

Farley found me in bed at dawn. The outside world was still draped in darkness. He rubbed my back beneath my shirt. He turned me over, but I covered my face.

"Don't look at me!" I cried.

"Pip, what's going on? What's on your face?"

"Don't, Farley."

He moved my hands away, skimming hair off my face.

I expected him to fall back, to cower from my sudden wickedness. He looked at me.

"What?" he said.

"My face."

"What? Your face is beautiful." He massaged my cheek. The scent of leaves. "Is something wrong?"

"No. I saw my face. I know what it is."

He lifted me to my feet and brought me to his childhood bedroom.

"I'm moving your bed in here," he said. "We need to be together until we figure out what to do next. We can't live like this, like little kids in separate rooms. We need our old selves back. You and me. Let's find a new home and become the family we've dreamed of. I miss you. I miss us. The way it was in the creek. Can we get back to us, please?"

He laid me down against a feathered pillow as if I were a sick baby goat, being set beside its mother.

He exhaled. "Maybe it's work. You've been working such long hours lately. I know I have too. I don't know. The fire. Your dad. *Something* happened to us somewhere. We need to fix it. I don't want to lose us."

I lay there looking up at him, the blanket pulled up to the bridge of my nose.

He tiptoed the covers down with his fingers.

"Pip," he said, his voice on the brink of cracking. "Tell me what's going on. Is something going on at work? Are you sick?"

"I think someone is trying to hurt me," I said.

"Who?"

His eyes searched mine.

The door was slightly open.

I felt eyes peering through the darkness.

I sat up. "Who's out there?"

He turned around and then back to me.

"There's no one there. Pip, what's going on?"

I didn't know who was in the hall. I didn't trust whoever it was.

Whatever it was.

"What's on your mind, Pip?" he whispered. "Tell me something. Anything."

I whispered back, "Evadere."

Chapter Forty-Seven

Days later, I couldn't shake what Farley said about becoming a family.

I had always craved a child just as much as he did, longing to pour my love into someone. But how could I do it, really? How could I raise a child, no, a person? I was Pip Renner. Pip Screed. Pip*squeak*.

I touched woodcarvings in the dark, carved by my mad father, and I told no one about it.

I had flashbacks of my childhood that were turbulent and unpieced.

I was unhinged in a virtual sleep therapy program.

I was a lowly app tester addicted to daydreams.

I did unspeakable things in my mind.

I was messy.

My heart was filled with muck.

Farley did not have a filthy, filthy heart.

I did.

A week passed without The Reverie Cloud. Farley insisted I come home early from work. Aunt Vera encouraged it too. But everything felt off as a result. I couldn't work, sleep was foreign, my mouth was parched, words turned to sand once leaving my lips. The gears in my brain were clogged with grime. Farley was gracious, coming home early from work too, tending to me. Baby names rolled out of his mouth like petals in the wind as though that might restore me. I loved that my husband was returning, but I couldn't erase the image of the beast I'd seen in myself. Then the voice returned, cutting through to the bone.

"Finish what we started," it growled.

⋆ ⋆ ⋆

I needed to dive back into the program. It would fix everything, pull me back to center. I would have done anything for another session. Lies clung to me like parasites, their weight no longer unsettling but comforting. I called Farley from work, telling him it'd be a late night with Nyxyn stuff. Then, Andrew dropped me off at The Reverie Cloud.

"I'm having a breakthrough with my app idea," I said, my voice crawling out like dying bees. "A session will help me pull it all together. I'll send you my notes later this week."

"I know you will," he replied. "You're a rock star."

His sleek black car glided to a stop out front where he dropped me off. Then he descended the sloping gravel drive that tunneled beneath the building. Perhaps he had a meeting with someone. I didn't care. I rushed inside.

In the program, I returned to the lagoon that Everly had introduced me to at the very beginning. I lifted my hands, conducting the elements. I conjured a squall of rain, thick and warm against my skin, brushing the drizzle across my face. Time meandered. I dawdled down a lavish green pasture and discovered a lake. I leaned over the water, wondering who I'd see in the reflection. Wondering *what* I'd see.

It was me. The real me. But better. In the wavering water, I was regal. Ethereal. Rosy cheeks, curly lashes – acorn-brown hair like a crown of glory. A spirit of goodness. A goddess staring back. My problems were nonexistent here. Dream leaks were becoming rarer too.

"That's better," I exhaled, feeling weight lift from my chest like a rising pall.

But without warning, flickering erupted from above. The sun – or whatever masqueraded as the sun – blinked like a faulty light. It resembled the same pulse as my fishbowl's once-broken bulb. It warped the landscape's delicate colors to black and maroon. Dark, light, dark, light.

Wyatt's crisp and haunting voice broke the veil.

The mirage of his bullet-wounded face seeped through a cluster of gray clouds.

"Get out!" his voice shouted in multiple layers. His snarled command fused with thunderclaps and lightning cracks, severing every nerve in my body.

"You shouldn't be here!"

His specter-like image hung in the air, and his warped eyes fixed on me like daggers.

A venomous chill climbed my spine.

From the grave, he taunted me. Beyond death, his contempt held me prisoner.

And then the sun stabilized into a halcyon glow. Six chimes rang softly. Tranquil music hummed. Everly's voice pierced the illusion, erasing Wyatt and any speck of him, turning colors soft again.

"You will be leaving The Reverie Cloud momentarily," her voice said. "We hope you enjoyed your dream experience. Come back soon."

My eyes shot open.

Chapter Forty-Eight

It was nightfall in a rideshare, almost home, the woods filing past me like a fever dream.

Images from my experience in The Reverie Cloud clung to me like sap – the hellish sky, the faulty sun, Wyatt's voice oozing through the haze. Why did I keep running into him in the program? I wondered if I should bring it up to Everly or Andrew, but I didn't want to appear suspicious. The circumstances of his murder were still under investigation, with the case far from buttoned up. Rumors swirled that the culprit was someone Wyatt knew – a colleague, perhaps. *It's usually someone you know*, people said.

As a lone car's rain-soaked headlights streaked by, my thoughts drifted to Snoqualmie Pass. The gun on Aunt Vera's countertop flashed in my mind, how I had buried it deep in the closet, or thought I had, how Wyatt died not long after. My thoughts snapped to my father – his paranoia encasing him like an unabating cage, warning me of dangers beyond our cabin. What had he done in The Reverie Cloud? Was it something so terrible, so buried, that he would run off and risk losing me over it?

Maybe the program drew out the worst in its users, amplifying unconscious desires, dark fantasies, primal urges, sex, murder… Maybe it pushed them toward violence, scrubbing the brain clean afterwards. Sympathy for my father seeped in, just as quickly as trust in myself slipped out. He was right about The Reverie Cloud. I should have run. I should have listened to him. Perhaps the program's side effects were much stronger than mild confusion, as Everly had said. What if its side effects were fatal, and the perpetrator was none the wiser – an innocent-minded assassin.

What if *I* killed Wyatt and didn't even realize it?

What if the gun *was* real, but I got rid of it somehow and couldn't even remember doing it?

I had to tell someone about the program's flaws. In the morning, I promised myself I'd go straight to Andrew. We were still planning to enter the program together. I needed to warn him before someone else got hurt, or worse, ended up dead because of me.

Chapter Forty-Nine

Come morning, Ray, Lyra, and Joey intercepted me in the lobby on my way to Andrew's office.

"Hey, Pip," Ray Cleary said, slowing me down.

I fidgeted, anxious to get to Andrew. At the same time, I couldn't believe he wanted to talk. They all did.

"We're all going out after work." Ray's eyes gleamed behind his glasses, clear and focused: an archer set on its target. "You wanna come?"

"Really?" I gasped, avoiding eye contact.

I felt like a sign was written on my forehead: *murderer.*

"Yeah, we need to stick together. What happened to Wyatt is insane. Just want to make sure we're all okay, you know."

I was certain my thoughts were shining over my head like a hologram – my endless nights in the program, my claws around Wyatt's throat, the gun on the counter, his glasses in the ash.

I glanced at Lyra Pierce standing beside him, recalling the way she kissed my cheek in the mist of my dreamscape. Now, she offered me a warm smile, her ice wall crumbling on the cold lobby floor. I looked to Joey Swifton, remembering how I teased his curly blond chest in the program. And Ray himself, legs locked around a stripper's pole. If they knew how I manipulated them like marionettes, their likenesses trapped within the program, exposed to whatever wicked forces lurked there, they'd never forgive me. Worse, what if one of them became my next target?

I had to keep my distance from them. From everyone.

I didn't want to hurt anyone else.

"Um, yeah, insane," I said. "Can you email me about it? I have a meeting I'm late for."

I hurried off, rushing into the nearest open elevator, leaving them behind in a trail of confusion. When I reached Andrew's office, I didn't bother to knock. I burst in, breathless, and found him looking up from his keyboard. I had convinced myself I wasn't drawn to him; I just craved his friendship. But when his aqua eyes locked on to mine, I felt an arrow piercing my chest.

"Pip! Glad you stopped by! How are you?"

"Not great," I said. "I think there are issues with The Reverie Cloud."

His brow creased. "Oh really? That's not good. What do you mean? Something wrong with our latest app concepts?" He snapped his fingers. "I saw your notes earlier. I love the idea of a dream journal. Great idea!"

"Oh, yeah," I said, forcing a smile. "But I think there's something deeper going on with the program itself. It might cause…paranoia, and maybe even forgetfulness. Like the user could black out and not remember things they've done." My voice sank at the end.

He looked at me as though I'd given him a complicated puzzle to solve.

I swallowed hard, knowing I shouldn't mention my father, but maybe it was the only way to break through. "I think my dad may have entered the program before and experienced these side effects."

He leaned forward. "Really? What happened? Maybe I should talk to him?"

"No, that's okay. I…he's not around."

Andrew leaned back, searching my face. "I see. You know the program has extremely safe protocols. They're very close to receiving government funding. We probably shouldn't do anything to sound the alarms."

I nodded, unsure. "Right. Never mind. This was stupid. I should get back to work."

I turned to leave, but then I heard him call my name, rushing after me. He blocked my path in the hall, leaning against the wall, his arm arched over me like a sturdy rail.

"Pip. Let's figure this out together. It's a huge client. I don't want to burn any bridges."

His cozy scent wormed through my nostrils, massaging my brain.

"I-I understand," I stammered. "I won't burn any bridges. I just wanted to warn – *tell* you."

"Let's go into the program together. Tomorrow night. Show me what you're talking about. Let's stop putting off our virtual date."

Date. The word hung between us, electric. His closeness was intoxicating. He brushed an eyelash from my cheek and smiled. When I finally said, "Okay," I wasn't sure if it was truly me or some sedated version of myself, numbed by the familiar scent of lavender and chamomile coming off his collar. As he lumbered back into his office, I did a double take, swearing I saw a plaque on his wall emblazoned with the word *Evadere.* My heart hammered against my ribs. *Evadere.* The word blazed through me like fire – the same word my father mumbled, the one I found in the mailbox. A thread linked my father to Andrew, but how? His door was locked. When I knocked and pounded to get back in, his assistant rushed from the office across the hall, shooing me away with force. Andrew had an important meeting and was no longer available.

Chapter Fifty

At night, Farley was home.

He brought me ice cream and put on a movie, but I craved solitude. I didn't want to hurt him like I hurt Wyatt. How else could I possibly explain Wyatt's death – the gun, his glasses resting in the ash? I remembered Farley's likeness in the program, troubled and sinking. The thought of unknowingly harming him was unbearable, despite his closeness to Purple Shirt. He was still Farley from the creek. My video game partner. My love. Bombarding him with accusations ran through my mind constantly, but I didn't want the truth to further shatter me.

Then, without warning, he dashed out, certain he'd heard a raccoon rummaging through the trash cans outside. I slipped into Aunt Vera's computer room, the word "Evadere" circling my mind like smoke. I needed to dig deeper into my father's latest clue and figure out why the same word, or what I thought I saw, was hanging in Andrew Janess's office. If there was a connection between Andrew and my father, I had to uncover it. But I hesitated when I powered on the computer. I thought of my father's message: *Stay out of the computer room.* Surely he hadn't meant Vera's computer room, had he?

I only wished my father had trusted me more to tell me about The Reverie Cloud, about its effects – addiction, distrust, paranoia… murder. I wanted to find him and tell him I understood now. He didn't have to hide anymore. I was in this with him. We could figure it out together.

I searched for "Evadere," but nothing came up. Just a Latin word meaning escape. I tried "Evadere + Dr. Richard Screed," but all that turned up was an error code. "Evadere + Andrew Janess" also returned nothing. I scrolled endlessly, hunting, hunting. The rain began to fall; its *tic-tac* pattern growing faster and faster – *tica-taca-tica-taca* – until it melded into one relentless stream.

I heard Farley come inside the house, shouting about an exterminator, and in that chaotic moment, I stumbled upon a web page about Evadere and a woman named Scarlet Janess from Seattle. *Scarlet.* My heart raced as I dug into the article.

Seattle-based company Evadere has recently drawn attention for its covert activities, sparking concern in the tech industry. Reports linking Evadere to several residents of the city have further fueled speculation about its objectives, raising questions about ethics. Tragedy struck when Seattle citizen Scarlet…

Before I could read further, the computer shut down with a jarring spark. The house descended into darkness. Lights off. Movie off. Everything black. I called for Farley, but the storm drowned out my voice. I called for Aunt Vera. Nothing. Only violent wind bashing the windowpanes.

I rushed upstairs and locked the door shut behind me to think. I checked the closet again to double-check there was no gun. Nothing. I leaned my head into my palms, wishing I could remember what had happened.

Moments later, creaking footsteps echoed just outside. Slow. Calculated.

The handle jiggled with intensity, making me jump.

"Pip," Aunt Vera called from the hall, her voice sugary sweet, too calm for the situation. "Are you okay? Looks like we had a power surge."

No shit.

"I'm fine. I'm tired. Just going to ride out the storm in here."

The handle rattled again with forceful insistence. "Are you sure? Why don't you come out. Farley and I will take good care of you."

Her tone was unsettlingly calm, as if 'taking care' meant something more sinister than sympathy.

My blood raced; I wondered why she was so relentless.

I forced my words out.

"Thank you, but I'm tired. I'm going to bed."

More footsteps sounded. I sensed Farley's presence behind the door now.

"Pip, you all right in there?" he called from the hall. "It's raining pretty hard. I'm soaked. You okay in there?"

"I'm fine! Just tired."

The door handle shook again.

Then, silence.

I pressed my ear to the door.

I heard Vera whisper, "I'll stand guard."

One set of footsteps faded away. Someone remained just outside the door, waiting.

And then came an unmistakable sound – a *click*.

Chapter Fifty-One

I sank to the floor.

Questions invaded my mind like a rapid infection, barreling after one another, germ atop germ.

Why was Vera keeping guard?

Was that the click of a gun?

What did she want from me?

What if she was trapping me to ensure I didn't hurt anyone else?

Was that why Farley had been so nice lately, treating me like a fragile fugitive?

Or was Vera the murderer…and I, her next victim?

Wyatt hadn't liked Andrew's hire, and Vera had brought him on. *Had an altercation occurred among them that left me in the dark?*

I wanted to leave but couldn't. I was one slab of wood away from a cocked gun. When I heard Vera's footsteps diminish down the hall, I ensured my window was unlocked, just in case the room itself couldn't keep me safe much longer.

I sat cross-legged on the floor, conjuring the woodcarvings from my father in my mind to stay grounded. Each piece illuminated my mind like a flash of lightning in the darkness – the sculpture of my mother, the horse, even his cubes from the shed – all resurfaced in vivid detail.

At some point, I moved to the bed and drifted involuntarily into a dream. I envisioned freeing myself from handcuffs. But I jolted awake, drenched in sweat, craving another clue – anything from my father.

I craved the program too. It was a sickness eating at me.

I knew it was wrong, but I liked the person I was in The Reverie Cloud. When dream leaks stayed quiet, I liked the peace, the control, the feeling that I belonged somewhere. Plus, I didn't have my answers yet. The likeness of my mother had been elusive in recent sessions, denying me access to the buried truths of my subconscious. Maybe my father's likeness would be easier to summon. Perhaps his likeness was the one who held the key to the truth – information about his crimes and a hint at his whereabouts. I needed to find him in the shadows. I needed him with me. I was tired of facing these horrible side effects alone.

I looked toward the window. The night was torrential but filled with possibilities.

All I needed was the courage to escape.

Chapter Fifty-Two

It wasn't quite ten; The Reverie Cloud was still open.

I ordered a rideshare to meet me at the main road, out of the woods. All I had to do was get there. Rain hammered against the glass like angry nails. I opened the window, eyeing the porch roof below. It was wet and slick in the moonlight. If I moved carefully through the sheet of rain, I might make it down without breaking any bones.

With my stomach over the edge of the window, I eased my legs out first, then lowered my hips, chest, and head until I stood upright on the roof. Doubt infiltrated, and I was about to hoist myself back inside when a thunderclap cracked nearby. My fingers lost their grip on the window ledge, and I slid onto the roof's surface. My feet shot out from under me as my face smacked the waterlogged shingles. Soaked to the skin and bleeding from my chin, I slid down the slope, hoping no one in the shadowy home would notice my escape.

I pushed myself away from the house. My chest ached as I cowered from the storm and prepared to tear through the woods toward the main road. The ground beneath me was thick with mud that slowed me down, but I told myself it wasn't holding me back. It was just resistance to overcome. Proof I was awake.

Chapter Fifty-Three

Once I arrived at The Reverie Cloud, Everly hurried me inside, dried me off, and quickly set me up in a sleep pod.

"I was surprised you called," Everly said, placing the halo around my head.

I stayed silent, my hands trembling. When I was in the rideshare, I had called ahead to let her know I was coming. I was lucky she was still there. Still, a voice whispered in the back of my head: *Stay away. You don't have to do this. Go home.* It sounded like my mother's voice. But desperation ignored the warning. I couldn't fight desire propelling me forward..

"Echo, right?"

I nodded, averting my eyes, staring straight ahead at the screen in the wall.

In the program, I found myself standing in front of my father's cabin, calling out for him. Here, in my dreamscape, the cabin was still intact. I walked across the cold, damp floorboards, each creak reminding me of my isolated past there. Beneath the bed I once slept in as a child, I noticed pinecones organized by size, reminding me how I once tried to create order out of calamity. The shucks were out of order though, not how I remembered them. Looking up, I noticed dusty beams and webs drawn like lace wires. I called out again, but my father didn't appear. Even in my dream state, I couldn't convince him I was worthy of his presence.

But then, the cabin darkened. Shuffling noises came from a back room. A raccoon tinkled slow and steady across the floorboards. It hopped onto a shadowy figure's lap I hadn't noticed before. The man sat there, petting the raccoon in a dark corner, his face obscured by shadows. Moonlight shifted through the windows, casting corrugated patterns on his body.

"Dad?"

"You shouldn't be here," he growled.

"Dad, I want to know where you're hiding. Tell me."

"It's not time."

I squinted, trying to catch a glimpse of his face, partially hidden by the unlit headlamp he always wore while carving. He kept stroking the mangy raccoon, ignoring me. I focused, reminding myself I was in control here, that the animal on his lap, his dismissive behavior, it was all just subliminal glitches, dream leaks, leftovers from when Farley left to scare off raccoons earlier. Suddenly, my father let the critter go. It scampered across the wooden floor, drawn to a pile of bones to peck on.

"Shoo," I commanded, desperate for my father's full attention. "Dad, listen. It's time for you to tell me the truth about your past. About Mom's death. I know what the program does to people."

"You don't know, Pip."

"Yes, I do. It messes with their minds, makes them paranoid. It convinces them to do bad things and makes them forget what they've done!"

"You're off."

"I'm not. I know what it does to people."

"Stay…"

"What? Stay where?"

"Away…"

I walked forward. I was on the edge of tears. "Dad, tell me where you're hiding."

He snapped his fingers, and the raccoon reappeared. Another snap. More racoons, feral and fanged, guarding him, hissing.

"Stop it," I said, inching back.

"Stay away!" my father roared.

I had lost control.

"Dad, stop. Tell me where you are! Tell me the truth!"

He remained cloaked in shadows, snapping his fingers as more and more racoons multiplied. They were overpowering me now, hundreds of them. I was slipping, losing even more control. I tried to conjure something, but my mind went blank. I could only think primitively. Fire.

It roared to life in the fireplace beside him, flames shellacking the air, sending raccoons scurrying, fire catching onto the curtains. Yet my father wouldn't budge as the flames magnified and filled the cabin, climbing onto his clothes, his skin. His head remained bent, not looking up.

"*Come out!*" I screamed, my voice cracking.

"Stay..."

"*Come out!*"

"Away..."

"*Come out!*"

"From..."

"*Come out!*"

"The..."

"*Come out!*"

"Computer room."

Finally, my father looked up, and I saw his face burning and blistering through the flames and shadows – Wyatt's face.

Chapter Fifty-Four

Laboring for breath, I stumbled from my sleep pod, heart pounding.

I quit. I was finished with The Reverie Cloud and its suffocating grip. I had tried with all my might to find the answers I craved, but my subconscious had failed me repeatedly. I grabbed my purse and water bottle and tripped over my feet heading for the door.

The night was still thick with thunder, but the building felt sharply lit as I wove through its marbled halls toward the elevator. I inhaled deep and painful breaths as sharp flashes of my father returned to me – his hunched form in the shadows, Wyatt's soldered face on his body, his cabin set ablaze with him inside it, the smell of fire feeding on his skin.

The elevator was taking an eternity to rise to my floor. I pushed and pushed, panic rising. Slamming the heel of my fist into the call button, I realized I didn't need to escape reality anymore; I needed to escape deception. My malicious addiction to the program. I had thought the truth lay within The Reverie Cloud, but each session only dirtied the lake more. The steel elevator chimed harshly and whooshed open in front of me. I would have run right in, but someone was already in there, heading straight toward me.

"Piper Renner," Everly Noon said callously. "Where do you think you're going?"

"My session is over," I said. "I'm going home."

She laughed. "Oh, no you're not."

Chapter Fifty-Five

Sometimes, right before a dream session, Everly Noon felt like my ally.

She'd ask about my work at Nyxyn, about Farley, my favorite music, shows, food – everything that made me who I was. I trusted her and had no reason to think she'd lead me astray. She was my guide. But now, as she pushed me back into the marble hall, dread wrapped its fingers around my lungs, wringing the air from them.

"I have some paperwork for you to fill out," she said, clipped. "Follow me."

"What paperwork?"

Without looking back, she continued, her heels clicking ominously against the slate tile. "Extra forms, since you've been coming here for reasons other than work lately. Your sessions have taken a turn, haven't they? A little...grim, no?"

I trailed behind her and then paused. My stomach was so twisted, I thought I might vomit.

She turned abruptly to me. "You don't want to get me in trouble, do you? My boss would kill me. He's not a forgiving man."

I shook my head, swallowing the burn. I followed her.

We turned a corner into a part of the building I'd never seen. The air felt compact here, a dark and foreboding energy. A covered body was being wheeled out from one of the dream rooms by workers in dark clothing, their faces concealed. We passed a room with a clear window. I peered in, catching sight of the teen boy I shared the elevator with not long ago. He was yelling at the wall, his voice rising frantically, before he dropped to the floor, convulsing. Something was terribly wrong. Every nerve in my body hissed, screaming at me to run. I looked behind me. The elevator was out of sight. If I bolted, what would Everly do?

Would she chase me?

Would I lose my connection to Andrew?

Did I even care anymore?

She paused just outside a beveled door with a blackened windowpane. "Pip..." she said, her expression softening.

"Yes?"

She held a key card, ready to bring it to the door. She skirted her eyes around the hall and then lowered her voice. "Pip, I think you should..."

I searched her eyes. She appeared exhausted, like she'd been up for days, working against her will. She wanted to tell me something but her face quivered, holding in some forbidden truth.

"What's going on?" I asked.

Her watch beeped, and she released a weary sigh. "Forget it. Come on."

I held my ground. I didn't like how she was acting. Senses were firing.

"Everly, I actually need to get home."

In a snap, she gripped my arm. "Sorry, Pip," she said. "I really am." She thrust open the door and shoved me inside. I tried to resist, but a man in dark attire appeared at her side, blocking my escape. Together, they forced me into the room, their combined strength overwhelming. Quickly, I scanned my surroundings – two deep rows of sleep pods filled the room like a small theater. They pushed me backward into one of them, the cold fabric shocking my skin. The door slammed shut behind them, locking me in.

Chapter Fifty-Six

Banging on the door was futile.

A fatal silence pressed in, pierced by a bubbling brook in surround sound. The familiar scent of lavender and chamomile met my nose, more intense than in any prior visit, lulling my senses into submission. I covered my nose, desperate to ward off the encroaching fatigue.

I tried to focus my thoughts on other scents, other feelings – my father's voice thick with rum and honey, Farley fresh from his pine-soap shower, my mother's soft blanket wrapped around my shoulders, the pungent stench of the horse ranch.

But lethargy consumed me, dragging me down in a fog. I slumped into the sleep pod and rummaged through my bag for my phone. My fingers were shaky, my eyelids falling, as I found Farley's number.

There was a text from him. He had sent a link to a house listing in Leavenworth along with a message. *Sorry if this text wakes you. I just can't stop thinking about our next chapter!* the message read. *I love you, Piper…forever, and nothing less. Hope you have a good rest over there, neighbor. Good night.*

He thought I was still in the spare. No one knew where I was right now. When I finished reading, the phone slipped from my fingers, clunking to the floor like a grenade. Sudden pulses radiated from the speakers. The steady, ambient noise seeped into my brain, and I thought I heard words through the cadence – *Stay, sleep, dream. Stay, sleep, dream.*

I just wanted to be home. To fix our marriage. To create a family. I thought about Farley and Leavenworth – our honeymoon spot nestled among the Cascade Mountains, with pillars of pine stretching for miles. But it was too far from Seattle, nowhere near Nyxyn, and not exactly a quick drive for Farley's work either. What would we do? I wasn't sure. Would I even make it home to discuss any of this with him?

As my ballast eyelids fought to stay open, a tear slipped down my cheek. I had to tell him about the program. About Wyatt. Purple Shirt too. I was tired of keeping all these things to myself. He was my partner in life, not my enemy. I mustered every ounce of strength I had and texted him back, *Help me. Reverie C—*

I couldn't get it all out.

Someone was coming into the room.

I thought it might be Farley.

It was the shape of him.

But I was very wrong.

Chapter Fifty-Seven

Andrew Janess barged into the room, but I didn't spare him a glance.

All I noticed was the door ajar behind him. I stood up, ready to make my escape, but he yanked the handle back, locking me in with him. Dizziness overpowered me, and I stumbled back to the chair, fighting to keep the room from spinning.

"Hey!" he chirped. "Ready for our date in The Reverie Cloud?"

"No," I rasped. "I was trying to leave, but Everly and some man locked me in here."

His smile faded. "That's odd. Why would they do that?"

"They said I needed to sign some papers, but they haven't come back."

"Oh, that sounds odd. Should I check with Everly?"

"Yes, please."

"Okay, I'll go get her. Relax. It's okay."

I struggled to sit up. "Andrew, something is wrong. The Reverie Cloud has extreme side effects."

He chuckled. "I've only ever had good outcomes."

"Well, maybe others haven't. I think they're trying to make me fall asleep against my will. Something in this room is doing it. Aren't you tired?"

"No, I'm not."

I couldn't comprehend how I felt so comatose, but Andrew Janess looked chipper as a chickadee. And why was he here so late anyway?

He pulled a water bottle from his work bag and offered it to me with a comforting grin.

"Thirsty?"

"No, Everly already gave me one," I said, panting, looking toward the door.

"Really? It's so hot. You sure you're not thirsty?"

My eyes snapped back on his water bottle. The liquid moved strange and sluggish when he tilted it. How had I not noticed this before?

His ruse was evaporating in front of me just like the beads of his bottle.

"If you're so hot, why don't you drink that water, Andrew?"

Andrew's face waggled in my blurred vision. He wiped his sleeve across his forehead, signaling the heat of the room. In my sluggish state, I imagined him scraping bright paint off his face revealing a layer of gray beneath. The more I focused on him, the more cragged and worn he appeared. He moved forward, as though to touch my knee, but I slithered away. Andrew Janess wanted me to drink more water – *tainted water.* Water that would force me asleep. How had I ever trusted him? Wanted him? Why hadn't I listened to my father and run far from him and the program? Now I could barely rise for the door. My heart was slowing down, preparing me for sleep.

"Let me go," I whispered, hardly able to speak.

"I thought we could go into a session together. You promised."

I pointed at his water bottle. "You've been drugging me."

He looked at me with a laugh. "Pip, it's hot in here, and it's good to stay hydrated inside the program. It's in the guidebook. You know that."

I wondered where his truth started, and his lies began. I lifted myself from the chair, my arms weak as grass blades.

"Where are you going?"

"I'm going home."

I got to my feet but stumbled to the floor.

The taste of carpet stung my lips.

Andrew came to me and rolled me into his arms.

I squinted up at him, his face swaying beneath a saffron light.

"Pip," he said, "you're not well. Let me call a medic."

He pressed the back of his hand to my forehead. For a moment, I felt like a tired child, ready to be cradled by my mother after a long day of sickness, safe at home.

"Pip, you are absolutely burning up."

His face trickled with pity. He reached for his water, dripping some onto my forehead. It fell into my eyes and stung.

"Get your hands off me," I snarled, swatting the bottle away. I spit off any droplets that got near my mouth.

"You feel like you're a hundred and five degrees. I'm going to put you back into the chair and call for help."

"Don't you dare touch me."

He cupped my face. "Pip, I care for you. I don't want anything to happen to you. I am going to help you get through this. You're having a hard time right now."

I locked eyes with him; his pupils were large and open, like portals sucking me in.

I didn't know what to believe.

"I'm going to put you in the chair now."

"Call Farley. My emergency contact."

"Okay, Pip. I'm going to help you." His tone shifted. "I'm going to help all of us. Finally."

Chapter Fifty-Eight

As I slumped in the chair, sleep began its chokehold.

Andrew was nearby; I could hear him shuffling, moving past me, mumbling something about Openfield. *Why wouldn't he just let this go?* All I wanted was to go home. He said he'd call Farley, but I didn't see him leave, grab a phone, or do anything to assure me he was seeking help. I caught glimpses of him in heavy blinks, prepping something on the screen in front of us.

He came near, holding a black object. The room felt oppressive and thick. I thought I might've seen a look of concern on his face, but it was just concentration as he adjusted the halo around my head. The lights dimmed, making the room feel candlelit. I fought to stay awake. The door creaked open, and someone else slipped inside. I couldn't make out who it was; my vision blurred.

"Is she ready?" came a deep, muted voice.

"Just about," Andrew said.

"Andrew," I begged. "Please."

I reached up for him, for anyone. A laugh echoed back.

"Well, thank you," the voice said, and suddenly I felt a grip on my fingers as someone placed black sticky patches on them. "That sure makes it easier."

The halo squeezed tighter. Andrew shuffled past me again, and I felt his fingers brush my cheek, my chin. Maybe he was checking on me after all. I glanced down and noticed a sliver of paper poking out of his pants pocket. I reached for it without him realizing. I unfurled the crinkled piece of paper, a document detailing all my previous visits to The Reverie Cloud – more visits than I realized I'd had or even remembered. I was still scanning the list when Andrew snatched it back, and I slipped into sleep, certain I was headed into the program whether I liked it or not.

Part Four

Delta

Chapter Fifty-Nine

The wind was howling when I opened my eyes.

But all I saw was white. A thick, lacteal fog licked at my skin, concealing the scene around me. The brutal wind seemed to move with intent, hunting me, its coldness drilling straight to the bone. Above, the darkened sky bled through the mist, pluming with explosions of violent light. Thunder cracked so hard it made the ground quake. I'd never done Openfield, but I assumed that's where I was. I could feel its power, its chaos. A grim feeling came over me – I wasn't in control. I was *being* controlled.

I dropped, instinct telling me to stay low. I needed to get my bearings. My hands and knees scraped against the freezing concrete as I crawled forward, nerves flaring with each drag, until something screamed inside me to stop. The fog lifted, almost purposefully, as if revealing the secrets of this place. A ledge lay before me. I was on a rooftop. I peered over the brink as my stomach sunk. I must've been fifty stories up. A chaotic city blared below.

I scrambled back, my breath heaving inside my skull. A skyscraper. They dropped me on a skyscraper. The rooftop suddenly swayed with a sickly groan. My breathing was rapid. I needed to act. I rose and closed my eyes, trying to conjure something – an elevator, a staircase, anything to escape this nightmare. But the scene around me remained unchanged. I tried again. Nothing.

The building growled beneath my feet. It felt moments away from collapse. Could I die here? I wasn't sure. The image of a body being rolled out of a dream room earlier burned through my mind. I shouted into the storm.

"I'm not supposed to be here! Wake me up! Someone – please!"

The building trembled, threatening to snap at the beams. I cried out again, even wishing Wyatt's face would appear. Anything to disrupt this trap.

But there was nothing.

No sign of hope.

Then, Andrew appeared. He came strolling across the shuddering surface, hands in pockets, smiling, whistling a melody. A sharp crack split the floor in front of me, sending chunks of concrete down its mangled spine. I stumbled back as the rupture snaked closer. Andrew didn't flinch. His pace was steady as he leapt to the side of the gaping wound like it was a puddle. He walked the length of it until he reached me, offering a hand. My mind was in pieces. I didn't know what to do. I clutched onto him with a death grip, desperate for security of any kind. He yanked me to the side of the encroaching gash.

When I looked up, Andrew wasn't the worn, stony-faced man I'd seen moments earlier in the waking world.

He was beautiful.

"This building is going down!" I screamed over the wind, eyeing the torn crater growing beside us. "I can't conjure anything to stop it."

He smoothed a hand over my windblown hair, but I ducked away.

"Did you hear me?" I said. "Why aren't you panicking?"

"It's Openfield, Pip! We can do so much here. It's every Dreampath rolled into one! I thought we would start at the top of the world. And guess what, we can visit each other's memories here. Isn't that amazing?"

"But I can't conjure. I tried. Something isn't right."

The ground beneath us shook harder, the building finally ready to crumble.

"You worry too much!" he said, maddeningly relaxed. "Trust me. Trust the program."

The floor split wider, its veins spawning like fractured ice across the foundation. I grabbed his collar as the building caved and pulled us both into the vortex of its hungry mouth. I shut my eyes as the dizzying sensation of gravity consumed me. We toppled downward through a black chasm of dust and debris. Eyes clenched, we plummeted through some forceful drain, the fall stretching and pulling at my skin.

Then, silence. When I opened my eyes, we were in Aunt Vera's spare bedroom. No broken building, no crash, no busted bones. Just a hanging ivy plant and the pleasing scent of fabric softener. Like the fall had never happened.

I looked up.

We weren't alone.

Chapter Sixty

I saw my father standing there, cradling something in his arms like it was a baby.

His face was tense and dripping with sweat. Then I noticed myself – or rather, a memory of me – back turned, motionless, staring at my father. I turned to Andrew beside me, my pulse throbbing.

"What is this?" I whispered.

He leaned in close, whispering back, "We landed in one of your memories."

I looked again. My father's troubled expression. The scent of smoke creeping through the vents. The memory struck me. This was just after the fire. My father's cabin had recently burned. In a few minutes, he would take me to the dark shed to study his wood carvings, right before vanishing.

I lunged forward, desperate to hold him in place, but Andrew pulled me back.

"You can't touch them," he warned, his tone sharp. "The consequences are too severe."

I shook my head in defiance. "But I touched other people in Echo just fine."

"This isn't Echo," Andrew said. "In Echo, you were playing with clay, pulling from imagination, sculpting. It was just daydreaming. There is no harm in fantasy land. In Openfield, we have access to fixed memories. Raw, unprocessed events stored deep in your amygdala and hippocampus. This is real. We're not reconstructing – we're witnessing. You interfere, you break it."

I swallowed. "What happens if we interfere?"

Andrew's eyes bored into mine. "You'd make a false memory. A paradox. Your brain would rewrite its own history to accommodate the change."

I stared at him, skeptical.

He kept going. "Your memories are pinpoints connected to your present self, right?"

I nodded.

"Change one pinpoint, and your mind has to recalibrate everything – your present reshapes your past, or rather, your memory of it – which changes who you are and what you believe about your life. One shift, even slight, and the brain doesn't just edit that one moment. It scrambles to update everything linked to it. The mind craves coherence. Not truth."

I glanced back at my father. He was peeking through the blinds, impatient, haunted. My memory-me stood there, oblivious as to how to help him. I wanted to scream at her, tell her to not let him go. "Wait, can they see or hear us?" I asked.

Andrew shook his head. "No. They're just data. Pictures playing on a loop. But just because they can't see you doesn't mean they can't be affected. If we tamper with them, you could wake up with an entirely different perception of your life."

"What do you mean different perception?"

He hesitated. "Different as in warped. Unrecognizable, depending how much you change. If you mess with a fixed memory, your brain will bend over backward to make sense of it. New rules. New truths. You could lose key parts of yourself. Or gain things that were never real to begin with."

"But you're saying they can feel touch…?"

"It's not quite feeling like you or I feel. Imagine paint on a canvas. The paint can't hear or see, but if it's wet and you push your finger into it, it'll change the look of it, and your brain will readjust your perception of the picture. Memories are like wet paint."

"So, if we touch them…"

"You change the picture," Andrew said.

I nervously eyed my past self. I didn't like that Andrew was here. I didn't like that my life was on display for him. But I wanted answers. "So, what can we do here?"

"Observe. Don't touch."

"Don't touch anything?"

"You can interact with objects that are not central to the memory," he said, batting fronds of the hanging ivy plant. "This is simply sensory filler. Part of the environment. But anything central to the memory? Hands off. Even a small change can have unpredictable consequences. And too many changes? The body simply can't handle it."

I turned back to the scene. My father's eyes twitched, homing in on the plant's slight motion.

"There's nothing here for you to see!" he shouted. "Do you hear me!?"

Chapter Sixty-One

Andrew latched on to my arm with reckless force and yanked me backward from the memory.

The scene changed like sorcery; I found my footing in a shadowy, dark place. No walls, no horizon – just a dense haze of maroon and black, swirling like blood in ink water. The ground was foggy and slick, an ethereal plane mirroring the void around us. Languid lights sparked in the distance, and glowing intersecting lines veered off sporadically into endless directions. It was an ominous, boundless web of dark and light, an astral grid stretching into the ether.

Andrew wouldn't let go of me.

His grip tightened. "We stay together," he said, digging into my arm. "I don't want either of us getting lost or doing anything to fuck things up." It was the first time I'd heard him curse. It prickled my ears. Strange, considering I was the one dragged here against my will. But no, he seemed angered, racing against the clock, his guise shedding like snakeskin.

"Wait," I said, trying to pull away, "how did my dad sense you knock into that plant if it's not *his* memory. If he's just a construct, just data?"

"It was a coincidence," Andrew said, clipped. "A warning he left in real time. He's left dozens. We just tripped over one." He looked back at me, eyes grim. "He knew we'd come."

My father's voice came to me: *They'll find my words.*

I pulled back. My lips shook. My breath thinned. "You do know him."

"We need to focus, Pip. Get what we need and get out before any damage is done."

"What do you mean – *get what we need*?" My voice rose. "How do you know all this? Where is my dad!? Answer my questions!"

He wouldn't speak. I tried to pull away, but he was relentless. He jerked me forward like I was a disobedient child, each step hurtling us both toward the shadows where radiant lights pulsed in the distance.

The lights were alluring, warm, and somehow familiar.

It felt like a trap.

As we neared, I saw the lights were emanating from a massive structure that looked like some interstellar ark – endless rows of shifting images moved along the surface of its framework. Colors collided prismatically in window-like ports, one atop another, an entire mass moving as a living, breathing organism. The images in each window were blurred, yet familiar – a déjà vu sensation crawled over me. I crept closer to the mammoth thing until I could almost feel the static buzz of one of the windows tickling my skin. The images moved within their frames slowly, like colorful vaporized paintings, then shifted suddenly, dissolving into something new. Each port contained a moment, a scene. My memories.

Sounds oozed from the windows as the images changed: crying, laughing, splashing, thwacking, talking, running, buzzing, carving, brittle leaves crunching. Even closer now, my body felt its power – the structure radiated sorrow, joy, longing, grief, love, each image blending into the next. It was like standing in front of an infinite wall of televisions, each broadcasting a different channel of my life. Some screens were smeared in black ink, as though someone had blotted them out entirely.

I saw myself – every age, every phase. The sparkle in my eyes waxed and waned. Smiles came and went. It was a gallery of my life, every moment blinking and shining like holiday lights. And there was Farley, grinning beside me, swathed in sun by the creek when we were teens. He appeared in window after window. Laughter in every shot. Smiling, holding hands, kissing, warmth. And then, there he was, in our maroon room, silent. Distant.

Andrew came beside me, jolting me, his face lit by the structure's glow. "We call it the memory carousel," he said, his voice almost reverent. "As you can see, each window contains a memory. Much like the one we just came from."

I turned to him. "You mean the one with my dad just now?"

He nodded, seemingly interested in discussing the carousel, leaving my previous questions to rot.

I pointed toward the images. "You mean, it came from in there?"

"That's correct." He motioned toward one of the windows. "You can enter any memory you want."

I raised an eyebrow. "Just right in there?"

"Yes," he said, straddling the line of impatience and amusement. "You walk right through. It tingles a little."

I reached out, my hand hovering near one of the windows that was slightly taller than I was. I could feel its magnet pull, hear its machinelike hum. The memory itself wanted to suck me in. I yanked my hand back before it could claim me. Panting, I centered my breath. "And how do you get out of one?"

"Simple," he said. "You just walk away from the scene. Toward the shadows. Like we did moments ago. It'll bring you back here." He opened his arms and spun around slowly. "We call this place the tarmac. Think of it like an airport terminal."

I faced him, arms crossed. "You keep saying *we*. Tell me who *we* is!"

He scratched his chin. "I'm still learning how to relocate my own memory carousel once you exit a memory, but isn't it beautiful?"

"Hey, did you hear me?" I said, boiling. "Why did you bring me here? I didn't sign up for any of this."

Andrew turned to me, reaching for my hand. I pulled it away. "Actually, you did. In all that fancy documents Everly had you sign. Anyway, I thought we could experience this together," he said, more relaxed, yet desperation rising. "You're standing at the edge of something phenomenal. Don't you want to be on the frontier of science and technology?"

It was hard to look away from him.

His conviction was strong.

He believed every word.

"What's your favorite memory, Pip? Something when you were a child maybe. I bet you were the cutest kid."

"I don't want you in my memories, Andrew."

We stood in silence watching the carousel shift and glide. Images of my mother caught my eye. Her smile glowed through the murk. Details of her face changed with each glance I took – a laugh line thicker here, eyes softer there. No memory ever stayed exactly the same. The carousel seemed to know this, reshaping the images slightly with each passing look, like a potter molding clay on a wheel, slightly different with every spin.

"Pip, over here!" Andrew called, chasing one of the windows. "There you are as a kid. Let's go in. We have to go in together. When you have two players in this Dreampath, you have to stick together. Rules."

"No." My voice stayed fierce; my eyes fixed on an image of my mother at the horse ranch. Her form was smeared in cloudy colors. Terribly haunting. Terribly beautiful. "You're not welcome in my memories, Andrew."

As the words left my mouth, I sensed the air tighten. He was coming for me. He was going to force me into a memory, and I had seconds to act. Farley's face, darkened by shadows, appeared in one of the windows, just about to change into some new scene. Without hesitation, I lunged into the postern, leaving Andrew behind. A tingling surge passed over me as I pierced the memory's threshold, clinging to my skin like it was alive, pulling me into the past with brutal force.

Chapter Sixty-Two

I entered the memory like a bullet and instinctively dropped to the floor.

I had a feral desire to stay low until I knew it was safe. I lifted my head, scanning the scene. Maroon walls. A pile of clothes on the floor. A blanket-crinkled bed. Farley and me tangled together amid sheets and pillows, sweating, making love in our dark bedroom.

I crawled closer, a voyeur into my past. From this view, we appeared divine. Energy radiated from our skin. Their skin. My knees dug into the floor as I watched. I was mesmerized by how Farley moved. His entire body, every muscle, pulled tight, perspiring. His work hoodie was bunched on the floor, reeking of body odor, a twelve-hour shift that day. But now, his gaze was tight, searching, no – *worshipping*, my past self.

I felt a quiet ache.

Back then, I'd felt hollow, like a worn piece of furniture.

But here, now, I saw it differently.

In my eyes – her eyes – there was desire.

In his, devotion.

I studied his face. There was something raw there, something I'd missed the first time around. This wasn't how I remembered it at all. It hadn't felt romantic then. Certainly not intimate. How could it? I was hiding The Reverie Cloud from him. My emerging addiction. My quiet despair. How could intimacy exist in the same room as deception?

And by the look of his clenched jaw, the mist in his eyes, he was hiding his own misery. But what? He wasn't just seeking pleasure through whatever sadness ate at him; he was struggling for connection, for intimacy in the only way he knew how. Every movement felt onerous, like he was scraping for a sliver of normalcy in a day that had chewed him up and spat him out. An empty bottle of rum was beside his night table. I hadn't noticed that in the waking world.

I wanted to reach forward, to soothe these old, delicate versions of us. Seeing the memory left me confused; it didn't match the script I had replayed in my head so many times. Back then, I felt like a metallic carousel horse in a cheap mall, endlessly spinning through the motions. But from this vantage point, I saw us as one, moving in tandem, connected, in love, in pain.

It made me wonder – did the memory change, or had I simply missed the nuances the first time around? Back then, I'd felt hollow. That part was true. But now I saw Farley more clearly. His distance wasn't apathy; it was distress. Something was eating him alive. I could tell by the lines of ache on his face. Some unspoken hurt. Maybe I ended up here for a reason – to see more of the picture, not just my part in it. To understand we were both struggling, just in different ways.

Farley got up, heading to the bathroom. My memory-me lay back, her eyes following him. I sunk deeper into the shadows, hoping to hide from Andrew and wait out the session. But as I reached the room's edge, a warbled, distorted voice broke the ether.

"Pip, I'm here."

It was Andrew. A silver, translucent gash split the center of the room, shimmering like an incandescent wound. His hand reached through the rift, fingers mauling for something tangible. I whipped my head toward my past self on the bed; she didn't react, her eyes locked on the bathroom light, trying to catch a glimpse of Farley.

"Touch me," Andrew demanded, his voice slipping through the thin, wavering portal. "It's the only way I can have access."

"No," I spat.

"Pip, you can't leave me out here like this. We have to stay together."

"I don't believe anything you say anymore."

The portal fizzled and snapped, threatening to close. "Pip, we could die if we don't stay together."

"What are you talking about?"

"Godammit, Pip! You weren't supposed to go into a memory *without* me. This wasn't part of the plan."

"What plan?"

Andrew gasped for air as the portal shifted, sliding to another part of the room. His voice followed, booming louder, sending ripples through the memory. My memory-me stirred, her eyes drifting toward the walls as if sensing the disturbance there. This wasn't supposed to happen – she wasn't meant to notice anything. The integrity of the memory was becoming compromised.

"If we get separated," Andrew continued, his tone frantic, "our minds could get trapped in your memories. We'd be stuck – permanently. We are stronger together."

"Andrew, she heard you," I said. "I thought you said they couldn't hear us."

"They can't," he snapped, trying to lower his voice. "Not if I'm *inside* the memory. The firewall activates once I'm fully in the memory window and the portal window closes. But I'm between worlds and you're keeping me out. If she noticed sound, it's the memory trying to rewire itself around some new input audio coming from the tarmac – me." He lowered his voice even deeper. "You're not playing by the rules, and it's messing things up. They won't save us if we fuck this up."

"Tell me for the last time. Who is *they*?"

"The ones controlling this world, Pip! The ones in the Circadian Room."

"*The what?*"

"The Reverie Cloud control room."

"Tell me who they are, and I'll pull you in."

He hesitated.

I curled my lips. "Tell me."

"They're called Evadere."

Evadere.

"I can't believe you don't remember," he huffed. "Your parents really did a number on you, huh? Now, grab on to me. The memory carousel is shifting. If I lose the portal, I lose you. I'm the only one who knows this program, Pip. I'm the only one who can get us out."

"Everly will get me out."

"Everly can't help you."

I didn't know what the truth was, and I sure as hell didn't understand this mode. I grabbed on to his fingers through the portal. "How do I pull you in?"

"Just hold on to me as best you can."

"Okay."

Then, like a gun blast into the void, Andrew yelled, "Touch yourself!"

I stared at him, frozen, my chest twisting.

"I said touch yourself!"

My hand floundered as I clung to him through the gateway. I didn't know what he meant – touch myself. Where? My heart? My head?"

"Touch yourself, dammit!"

He was too loud. I knew my memory-me heard him. She'd felt it, which meant it was part of me now. His voice ripping through the portal would be embedded like a seed, and my mind would rewrite itself with some false narrative to make sense of the anomaly. A voice speaking to her. Even if it wasn't real, it would root itself in her mind. My mind. Forever.

Finally, Andrew's grip tightened on my hand, as I placed a trembling hand on my heart. I wasn't sure if I was doing it right, but it was enough. The portal snapped open wider, and Andrew pulled himself through before it sealed shut.

He collapsed onto me in the bedroom, searching for his breath. Before he could orient himself, I grabbed his face, forcing him to look away from the vulnerable figure of my memory-self lying on the bed.

"Don't," I growled.

Without a word, we bolted for the door. Beyond the memory, murk stretched onward in undulating coils. No sign of light. No sign of breaking free from Andrew and his labyrinthine grip.

Chapter Sixty-Three

Andrew seemed lost as he tugged me onward through the shadows.

The darkness clung to us like tar. We moved cautiously through the abyss that seemed to have a pulse of its own. Above, sparks of light flared like firing neurons, then sizzled into vapor. While Andrew hunted for the memory carousel, he warned me about staying together.

"We are not real here, Pip. Do you understand that?"

I stumbled, trying to keep his pace, following the deep cuts of his voice. "What are you getting at?"

"We are not flesh and bone. We only think we are. We feel things. We sense things. But it's all wired." He glanced back at me, his sternness illuminated by a sudden spark.

"Yes, I know."

He trudged through the darkness and loomed over me. "No, I don't think you do, otherwise you wouldn't have gone into a memory without me. We're just data – avatars made of code. Our presence is simulated. Do you get that?"

"Of course I do, but so what if I—"

"Listen," he said, grabbing on to my arms, rubbing his thumbs up and down. "Touch is our anchor. It helps our avatars stay connected and synchronized with each other as we move through memories."

I tried to wrench free.

He held me tighter. "We're both asleep right now. That's reality. That's the truth. Us, here right now? We're just signals moving through neural pathways. Think of us as two tiny dots on a giant highway in your brain. If we lose connection, Pip, we lose everything. It's very easy to get lost in memories. Don't get cocky with this simulated body of yours, thinking you can do whatever you want. You are nothing but a speck in a massive universe here. Do not go into another memory without me. You could get lost. Forever."

"Andrew, I am not going into any memory with you ever again. I am waiting until our waking window arrives. Then I'm quitting Nyxyn and filing a lawsuit."

I finally managed to slip out of his arms and plant myself on the ground.

Andrew sighed theatrically and dropped to my level. "Pip, I know how strange this might be for you. I'm so sorry. Maybe if you knew the truth, you would want to go into a memory with me. You might even thank me."

"What the hell does that mean?"

Before he could answer, his face lit up with fevered hope. "There it is. Your memory carousel. We're close. Come on."

Reluctantly, I followed, heeding his warning. As we walked on, the tarmac's fog rolled over us like a restless tide. Light from the carousel flashed in the distance.

I couldn't stop wondering about his connection to my father.

I shouted after him. "How do you know my dad, Andrew?"

He didn't look back, his eyes fixed on the carousel ahead. "We're all more connected than you realize. You just don't remember."

His cryptic response boiled my blood. How was it that Wyatt and Andrew seemed to know more about my past than I did?

I skipped a step to catch up to him.

But the closer we got, the stranger the carousel appeared.

The swirling images were wrong, unfamiliar.

They weren't mine.

"Fuck!" Andrew spat.

He was visibly upset by the carousel.

As a young, fresh-faced young boy whirred by in one of the windows, I knew why.

My stomach twisted.

This wasn't my memory carousel.

It was his.

Chapter Sixty-Four

Andrew's memory carousel was less vibrant than mine.

Many of its windows revealed sickly beige walls and tombstone-gray furniture – the kind you'd expect in a cold, corporate tech lab. Sunlight, it seemed, was rare, except for memories where he marveled at skyscrapers. His life whooshed by in fragments: a kid slouched over a computer, his face lit by the cold blue beam of a monitor. In other windows, he appeared isolated, wired by electrodes, while a man – his father, I guessed – loomed in the background. Sometimes his mother flashed by – a brief flare of love breaking the cold, clinical moments of his life.

Andrew yanked at my arm.

"Let's move," he said. "We don't have time for my carousel. We need yours."

But I couldn't look away. One of his memory windows stirred with something familiar. A lilac-covered mailbox. The gravel lot, surrounded by trees. The dark beams of our A-frame. The home Farley and I shared before the fire. The image was vivid. But Andrew had never been to our house before. My pulse hammered.

He saw it too and pulled me harder. "Forget it. Let's go."

"No." I planted my heels, eyes cemented on his window. "How do you have a memory of this?"

"Jesus, Pip. This isn't the time."

"Answer me."

He exhaled, eyes wild, surveying the void around us. Then he leaned in close. "Listen to me. Openfield doesn't work like other Dreampaths. There are six spaced-out chimes, unlike other modes where they all come at the end. Think of these like pre-chimes – a clock ticking down.

Warnings. After the sixth one, there's no room left for grace. Then come *six more* chimes – quicker, closer together. That's the end."

"So, twelve total."

"Yes, but those six final ones are the ultimate wake-up call. You must be on the tarmac, fully present, to wake up. Miss it, and you're stuck in a memory. Permanently. Dead. We need to get to your carousel, then straight back to the tarmac. Do you understand now?"

I didn't budge. "Why do you have a memory of my house?"

"I said forget it!"

"No, I can't forget it. Tell me."

He gritted his teeth. "You're going to kill us, I swear. You don't know who we're dealing with. You think they'll wake me up if I don't get what they need? No! They'll let me die here. Both of us."

The dull, gray light from his carousel reflected in his eyes. It hummed mechanically as images cantered with talking, shouting, keyboard clicks, electric zaps. I wondered if he was a victim here just like I was.

"Andrew, let's solve this like two rational adults."

"Yes, that's what I want to do. To do that, we need to leave my carousel and go to yours."

"No. To solve this problem, I need to know the truth."

With that, I shoved his hand to his chest, put my hand to mine, grabbed his free hand, and heaved us backward into his memory with all the force I had left.

Chapter Sixty-Five

We stumbled into Andrew's memory of the in-law suite with the grace of a gut punch.

The sky was a damp blood orange. We stood on the gravel lot, the one that severed Aunt Vera's house from our A-frame. I wracked my brain: *Why was this built into Andrew's memory?*

The house stood there with its wooded backdrop, pre-fire, unscarred, blind to its fate. Magenta zinnias, my favorite, paraded themselves in perfect little rows out front. Freshly planted. A few stragglers sat in black crates beside an empty bag of mulch, waiting their burial turn. I'd never noticed them before. And that meant one thing – this was moments before the fire. Was Aunt Vera out shopping for more supplies when the flames started? The revelation stung like a slap. It explained where she'd been when our house turned into an inferno.

She was no *plant*; she was planting flowers for me, just trying to finish the job.

A peace offering after our tense car ride that one day.

But that didn't solve the larger mystery – why Andrew had this memory hosted in his brain. Then I saw Memory-Andrew round the bend, headed toward the suite, and he wasn't alone.

Wyatt Fink.

I sensed a sudden presence. Andrew's hand fastened around my arm, trying to tug me back to the shadows, but I twisted free.

"Why are you so stubborn?" he shouted.

"Me?" I snapped, pointing at his former self. "Why were you at my house with Wyatt?"

"It's irrelevant," he said, eyes darting to the memory versions of himself and Wyatt.

"Like hell it is!" I ran toward the past version of him, betting he wouldn't dare risk touching his own memory data...I hoped.

Memory-Andrew was in Wyatt's face now, their voices raised in a heated conversation.

"I know you think you're doing something noble here, Wyatt," Memory-Andrew said, vexed, "but you're about to destroy everything our parents built. Think of my mother. Think of *your* father. *Her* father. This isn't some little experiment; this is extending the work of our bloodlines."

Wyatt's face creased with exasperation. "They've got you so brainwashed, it's pathetic. I came here to tell Pip the truth. You're using her as a pawn."

"She's the only key to Screed," Memory-Andrew said. "Evadere needs his work. This is bigger than us."

"Evadere's a monster," Wyatt struck back. "Why do you think they can't go publicly by that name anymore? Why do you think they moved to Issaquah, hiding out in the woods no less? Their lies have been exposed. The ones with morals? They've all left. Evadere might hide behind the name Reverie Cloud now, but it's a lousy cover-up. Pip deserves to know that."

Memory-Andrew's face darkened, spit flying. "You're calling our fathers monsters? My mother? She was a goddamn genius!"

"Yeah. I am," Wyatt said. "They *killed* your mother. Dr. Screed killed your mother."

The air thinned. Memory-Andrew began pacing, fists clenched.

My eyes hooked on to Andrew, my heart pecking at my chest. He was quietly maneuvering toward me, careful not to shatter the memory's integrity. But I kept my distance, calculating each step.

Memory-Andrew was practically growling. "She died in the name of scientific progress. Even more reason for making this program work to its full potential."

Wyatt didn't flinch. "You're wrong. The full potential of this program is death. It's one thing to let users have unique virtual experiences. It's another to manipulate their memories – or worse, delete them, their entire sense of self gone. Your mother and Screed knew the danger the second they wrote that death code. But he used her as the guinea pig anyway. And she died for it."

"Harsh, Fink. Also untrue," Memory-Andrew said. "The code doesn't delete or manipulate memories. It removes pathways to painful ones and integrates them with something more positive. Dr. Screed and my mother believed it could help people heal, replace their pain with something better. You know that."

"Placing fake memories on top of real ones is psychotic. It's immoral."

"It's brilliant."

"You're delusional. It's a death code."

Memory-Andrew's face burned red. "My mother was a hero. The *Requiem* just needs fine-tuning. Once I have it, I'll perfect it. Evadere is counting on me."

"Evadere is counting on government dark ops paying to use it as a weapon," Wyatt said. "Why are you messing with this kind of manipulative darkness, Andrew?"

"I said it's not manipulation. And anyway – Dr. Screed signed the contract and ran off like a coward before handing over the schematic. He moved off-grid, but we found him. He ignores the promises he made."

"Maybe so, but he has a conscience. He's not going to give it to you. Not after what happened to your mom. You, of all people, should know better."

"No, he's not. That's why we burned his cabin. To make it clear just how serious we are about him holding up his end of the bargain."

"You're sick, man."

"The contract had consequences. He knew that. Evadere let him off the hook for years. No one had the guts to find him until I did. It was the only way to keep my mother's work alive."

Wyatt's shoulders stiffened. "I thought I'd escaped this Evadere bullshit when I started at Nyxyn. Just because my dad is a founder doesn't mean I want anything to do with it anymore. But then you slithered back into my life."

"It's not my fault Screed's daughter ended up there," Memory-Andrew said, shrugging. "I would have followed her anywhere."

"You and Evadere stalked her. You told me so yourself. Then, you manipulated Vera Renner into hiring you. As soon as you found a connection, you attacked immediately."

Memory-Andrew's eyes were ablaze. "Maybe it's fate. Once I extract the schematic from Pip's mind, you, me, and her – we'll rebuild the founders' legacy. We'll rise like a phoenix."

Wyatt let out a hollow laugh. "What makes you sure she even has the *Requiem* in her mind?"

Memory-Andrew smirked. "She saw it. When she was a kid, in Screed's computer room. Right before he wiped it. She probably doesn't remember, but her mind does."

"How could you possibly know that?"

He didn't answer right away. When he did, his voice was quieter. "Her parents looked after me once, after my mother died. Pip and I were in Screed's computer room together, right before her father deleted the *Requiem*. I didn't look at the screen – what did I know back then? But I saw her look. She might not have known what she was looking at, but once I gain access to the right memory, I can capture an image of the *Requiem* schematic from her mind and be on my way."

"Andrew—" he paused, practically speechless, "—that's madness. It's a breach of privacy. And you have no clue how her brain processed that image. For all you know, it's a jumbled mess."

"It's worth a shot," Memory-Andrew said. "Even if it's a blurry image, we can use intelligence to fill in the gaps."

"Why do you have to invade the poor girl's mind? Get someone else from Evadere to recreate the schematic and do your dirty work for you."

Memory-Andrew rolled his eyes. "You think we haven't tried? We've come close. But Screed wasn't just a genius – he was paranoid. He built a privacy mechanism into the program. Any attempt to fully access or recreate the schematic without his specific codes renders it completely useless. I think he embedded the codes into the schematic blueprint itself. Sure, we could try building the entire thing from scratch, get whole new machines and come up with our own codes, but that would take decades.

The Reverie Cloud is a lifetime of work, and Screed made damn sure no one could tamper with his masterpiece."

"You can't use Pip like she's a hard drive."

"Wyatt," Memory-Andrew said soberly. "This program has the potential to change everything. It could end wars, cure diseases, reshape society. We need those codes and that schematic."

"It could also *start* wars, *start* diseases, and *end* society," Wyatt said. "But whatever, man. I'm doing everything I can to keep you out of Pip's head. Don't forget – my father *still* works at Evadere or whatever you want to call it these days. He let me inside the other day…"

Memory-Andrew's expression blackened. "*What did you do?*"

Wyatt's face shifted into that familiar, cocky smirk I knew so well. "We placed a disruption code in Pip's files," he said, inching closer. "My face. My voice. It'll pop up every time the program detects a rise in cortisol. I'm making her life a living hell at work and in the program too. Anything I can do to scare her away from The Reverie Cloud, away from Nyxyn, away from you."

"You're a deadweight."

"And you're deluded. This obsession has turned you into a monster just like them."

"You're halting progress, just like your father."

"Fuck you, man," Wyatt said, turning toward my house. Maybe he was planning to wait on my doorstep for me; I couldn't be certain. "You've lost it."

As Memory-Andrew reached into his coat pocket and pulled out a gun, I ducked, forgetting this was a memory.

He fired.

The gunshot tore through the memory, warping the scene as it ripped past. The explosion echoed off Aunt Vera's pristine siding and the polished metal of Andrew's car out front of our suite. The bullet found the back of Wyatt's head, sending his glasses flying to the gravel. His blood soaked the zinnias.

I blinked back tears, my chest closing in on itself.

Wyatt, dead.

Andrew, a killer.

And my father – a grizzled woodsman who spent half my childhood buried in his work and the other half preaching the dangers of technology – was *Evadere.*

He was *The Reverie Cloud.*

And worse, he'd created something called the *Requiem.*

A *death code*, as Wyatt called it.

A code Andrew believed he could pull from my mind.

Chapter Sixty-Six

Suffocating silence.

I stood frozen, stunned, shaking, witnessing Memory-Andrew hoist Wyatt's limp body and dump him unceremoniously into his trunk.

I turned to Andrew several feet away, my voice trembling. "You're a murderer."

He moved toward me slowly, closing the gap between us. "Pip, let me explain."

"There's nothing to explain. I saw everything."

He conjured a gun in his hand like it was a card trick. "Pip, let's leave this memory and go on a quest." He grinned, accelerating his steps. "What about the maze with the hedges? Remember that? I saw it all. I know what you want. I want it too."

"Wyatt was right about you," I said, bile rising in my throat. "You're sick."

I couldn't take my eyes off the gun, even though it wasn't real. We were just dots on a neural highway. But fear gripped me, removing logic. I couldn't afford to take anything for granted. Desperately, I tried to conjure something, anything.

I clenched my fists, forcing my words out. "Why can you conjure, but I can't?"

"They've put certain firewalls on you," he said, deceptively calm. "You're not playing by the rules, Pip. Neither are they. But come with me, and everything will be fine."

His gun clicked. I struggled to breathe. Then, like an erratic phantom, Memory-Andrew surged forward, passing clean through his present self. It made Andrew stumble, dropping his gun. Memory-Andrew plowed through me next, causing my ribs to squeeze. I felt brittle, like glass under pressure, ready to shatter. I steadied myself, watching Memory-Andrew stop at the blood-splattered gravel, panic flooding his face. "Oh god, oh god," he muttered to himself. He bolted toward the back of the suite, and I followed him, hungry for more information. Present-Andrew's footsteps were thick behind me.

Memory-Andrew was frantic now, his hands digging at dry leaves and an old newspaper from the deck table. His movements were jerky, spasmodic. Desperate and delusional. He piled the dry materials against the wooden beams of our house.

"What are you doing?" I screamed at the memory, even though he couldn't hear me.

Andrew watched his past self quickly unravel, then turned to me. His eyes pleaded. "I didn't mean for it to go this far. I swear."

My voice ruptured. "You set my house on fire to hide your crime?"

"Your father is to blame. He owed us that schematic."

Memory-Andrew fumbled the box of matches Farley had left out, his hands shaking. He struck a match. The flame waggled in the heavy air. He hesitated, then threw the lit match onto the leaves. Flames climbed hungrily up the house.

"No!" I screamed, feeling the heat of the rising fire.

Andrew took a step toward me. "Pip, we need to leave this memory. Please, I'm begging you."

I backed away from him. "You killed Wyatt and then burned my home to…*what*? Cover your tracks? Teach my dad a lesson?"

"Pip, listen to me. We can still fix this. We can still—"

"There's nothing to fix!" I shouted. "What's done is done."

The flames grew bolder. The crackling of splintered wood filled the air. I could feel the heat intensifying, and I knew I had to get out of the memory before it consumed me too.

Memory-Andrew moved rapidly, rounding the house. His shadow sunk into the dark as he slammed the trunk on Wyatt's body. He'd ditch it later, I realized, where no one would connect the dots. Leaving the body in the fire would've pointed too easily to me. He needed me available, desperate, clinging to The Reverie Cloud. I realized how deep his depravity was to get inside my memories, desperate to reach the work of my father, Dr. Richard Screed. The man who built a monster and then left me in the same room as it. But no matter how angered I was by his secretive life, I wouldn't let Andrew win. I didn't have time to seethe. I needed to wake up.

"Goodbye, Andrew," I said, turning away from both versions of him.

Chapter Sixty-Seven

When I punctured the shadows, landing back on the tarmac, Andrew was right behind me.

There was no time to escape.

No time to catch my breath.

The only escape was inward – my own memories.

My carousel hovered there like an ethereal ship in a black sea. One of the memory windows felt familiar, comfortable; a gravitational pull so alluring I immediately jumped in. I landed clumsily in a memory not far from the fire. Aunt Vera's spare room. Night. The air was soaked in silence. I saw my memory-me draped on the daybed. Shadowed lines of sleep stained her face. She looked so small, so fragile lying there in the moonlight. A girl haunted by the past, fearful of the future, stuck in the present.

I moved closer, a mother checking on her child. The scent of linens rose from her pillow, creamy soap and muted florals. I hadn't noticed it back then, but now it hit me: someone had washed them for me. Someone had cared. The proof was there. It was in the details, some small invisible kindness.

I knew the rules – don't touch. But the boundary between past and present tilted on its axis. She wasn't my child, and yet, she was. A former self, exposed and unguarded. Something protective gathered silently inside me. I reached out, my finger brushing her cheek, light as lace. Her body twitched, and I shifted back regretfully.

Without warning, a silver scar sliced the fabric of the room. Andrew. He'd found me. He tore through the memory like a madman, forcing open a hole in the room with his bare hands. He couldn't fully enter without me, but his eyes landed on me. He grinned.

"Having fun?" he growled, razor-sharp. I slid backward, away from him, away from the memory, but I didn't land on the tarmac. I found myself in a new memory. I wasn't sure how I'd arrived; I only knew the familiar scent of fresh linens was still salient.

In this memory, Aunt Vera's house stretched out in darkness. The scent of laundered clothes clung to every grain. My memory-me drifted close, moving toward the kitchen.

Andrew found me again. He was relentless, clawing a new incision into the memory. "Grab me," he slurred, straining through the rip. I reached the kitchen, my eyes landing on a handgun resting on the counter. My memory-me sidled near; her eyes wide on the gun too.

The silver line of the portal pulsed beside me, glinting like liquid metal. "Grab—" Andrew choked out again. I swatted at him, shoving his head backward.

"Who else have you killed?" I asked, fighting him, my teeth clenched. "My mother?"

"No," he said, his face glitching like a hiccup.

"Then who?"

"Wyatt," he said, just as the rip sealed shut. His voice was muffled behind the closed seam. "Only Wyatt," he murmured, his face appearing again through a new fissure.

Only, like he should receive a gold star.

Behind me, rustling. A chill ran the length of my spine. There was a presence in the shadows, movement in my periphery. Who, though? I'd been alone when this memory first played out. No witnesses. No shadows. Maybe this was someone – or something – roosted in the cobwebs of my subconscious, or worse, someone watching now. Either way, I had no time to find out. I needed to stay hidden, far from Andrew and the minions in the Circadian Room. I was too vulnerable here. I needed to move.

★ ★ ★

I slunk into the shadows and entered the tarmac. My carousel was there, waiting. I hunted for a memory to enter. The mailbox messages came to mind; the cryptic clues my father left behind. Maybe the program could show me some detail I'd missed. Some small mark in my subconscious, a breadcrumb in my periphery. Maybe it could tell me where he'd gone.

Andrew was lost somewhere inside the program. It was my one advantage. For all his talk, he couldn't navigate the tarmac very well. It didn't come naturally to him. Maybe it was a mental block, the idea that his own unreliable memories didn't serve him well. As for me, my memory carousel seemed to be waiting like a loyal steed.

I moved into a memory window where I thought I'd find traces of my father at the mailbox but accidentally got pulled into a vortex of arbitrary ones instead. My body forced me into new memory rooms, one after another, flashing me with images I thought I'd forgotten: plunging down a soapy slide as a kid in summer, standing at a sudsy sink with my mother, pizza sauce smeared across my lips; Vera's meticulous collection of soaps in a basket, an engagement gift; the steamy cocoon of a bubble bath after work.

Andrew found me in the last one. He tried to penetrate it. "Finish what we started," he growled into the rip. The air was ripe with soap, and suddenly, it clicked: soap had been a common thread through each memory I'd just barreled through. Olfactory memories. I could whip through memories at a blistering speed by recalling scent memories. With that realization, I focused on Farley's pine-soap shoulders – a scent memory right before finding one of my father's messages. I closed my eyes, steeped in his sharp, earthy odor, and I opened my eyes to a new scene.

It was evening. Laughter buzzed from the suite deck. Farley's friends were gathered, laughing, smoking around the firepit. I stood among them, the scene playing out before me. It was right before my memory-me would run off, disturbed by Farley's lustful looks he saved for Purple Shirt. But I squinted, confused. I recalled Farley being super close to her, but he wasn't. Far from it. He was near my memory-me. Eyes on her. Hands on her. Devoted. Connected. Concerned. Suddenly, my memory-me stood up and stumbled away from the deck. I ran ahead of her, knowing she was headed toward a message from my father.

I made it to the lilac-covered mailbox in front of the suite and waited. My memory-me was coming close, head down, eyes raking the dirt. I scanned the woods around me. Could my father be out there, hidden behind a tree, crouched low behind some brush pile or mound of earth?

No sign of him.

I knew that as soon as my memory-me reached the mailbox she would find a letter from him in there. I was so anxious to see her find it, to feel that surge of hope again. Even though I remembered the note being ominous – *prepare for betrayal* – it still gave me assurance he was out there. My silent guide.

When my memory-me wasn't looking, I lifted the lid, just to confirm what I already knew. But the box was empty. I slammed it shut before I might alter any data. *Where was the letter?* I felt my body dissolving. My avatar was loose and unstable. Images in front of me stretched horizontally, everything smearing as an abstract painting. I was being ripped away from the memory against my will. The truth hammered down: my father never delivered a letter. My memory-me would open the lid and see a hollow box. Everything I thought I knew – lies.

Chapter Sixty-Eight

It was cold in the tarmac.

Shadows churned around me, squirming like smoke in this sullen, liminal space of my mind. But it wasn't just my mind, my plane. Andrew and I shared it, two cerebral nomads crashing into each other's subconscious.

Arcane noises grinded in the distance.

I wondered if it was him.

I closed my eyes and felt his presence.

A connection.

Could he feel me too?

Even after everything – Wyatt's murder, the fire consuming my home, the cold click of Andrew's gun – I didn't sense malice from him. No nefarious aura, no villainous intent. I couldn't quite pinpoint it, but I sensed fear. An unrest. And that's what adrenalized me. I wasn't leaning on him. Wasn't leaning on anyone. It was on me. It wasn't just a matter of defeating Andrew. It was about rising above him to crush the powers controlling both of us. I needed to get us both out of the program, but I needed to know the truth about my father and his mysterious messages, or rather, their aching absence.

I stood in the dark, listening to my breath drift in and out like waves. My memory carousel loomed near, creating a comforting hum. It took me a while to find a good window to enter. I finally pierced through, finding myself in the suite.

The room I entered was shrouded in darkness. A static cling enveloped me as my memory-me passed by, brushing into me. I felt instantly tethered to her, glued. In fact, I wondered if it was a glitch – my brain struggling to understand which vantage point to focus on. My movements became hers, or maybe hers became mine. I couldn't tell. As she walked, I walked. She paused in front of the mirror, and there we were: two faces vying for control of a single reflection, a singular truth.

Her face. My face. Our face.

Distorted, monstrous.

The mirror perverted under the burden of two timelines colliding. Past and present twisting, bending. I wanted to tell her – no, tell myself – that it wasn't a flaw. This distortion wasn't a sign of ugliness but proof of resilience. We weren't broken. We were layered and complex. Time had molded us into something stronger. Something shocking, but also magnificent. Something I never could have conceived. Something powerful.

My memory-me raised a hand to her face – our face. Her fingers were warm, tinged with garlic and musty book pages, with dirt and wood. I could smell it all, and it told a story more profound than any reflection ever could.

She stepped into the kitchen and lifted a silver spoon to examine our warped image again. The deformed reflection stared back, and in a burst of frustration, she hurled the spoon across the room. The clang broke the fuse. I felt the bond between us snap.

I blundered backward, peeling away from her, and fumbled back into the tarmac.

Andrew was waiting, his silhouette standing beside my carousel. His presence shook me, but I didn't falter. I lunged into the nearest memory window, narrowly escaping his grip.

Chapter Sixty-Nine

I stumbled into a new memory.

It was from the night I left my bed, driven by a maddening hope I'd find another sign from my father. A lifeline. Proof he was out there, watching me.

Caring. Protecting. Guiding.

I knew what was supposed to be in the mailbox. The note that said *remember.* The wooden horse, carved by hands I thought were looking out for me. Its musty saddle finely placed. Back then, it meant everything. A reason to keep moving forward.

But when I lifted the lid, the mailbox was empty.

No message. No horse.

Just a hollow space echoing back.

I closed the lid, my heart racing, the truth hitting like a punch. The memory had been so clear. So vivid. I remembered the weight of the wooden horse in my palm, its imperfect grains running down its mane. But had it only been a mirage? How could I remember something that felt so real if it never even existed?

Aching questions burned through me: Had I invented the mailbox messages just to survive? To believe I had a father who cared enough to leave behind clues? Was I the architect of my own deceptions…or was someone else?

The images around me began to warp as my memory-me drew close. The program wouldn't let me have the answers I craved. I was thrust into the shadows, the force brutal and indifferent.

★ ★ ★

Back on the tarmac, a chime rang out. My memory carousel glistened, its windows shining like the surface of a summer pool. Then, it began to drift. Slow at first, then faster, like it was on a mission. I sprinted to keep up, but it moved farther away, as if it had developed a mind of its own. I'd lost control of it. I wondered if a chaotic memory carousel was the result of tampered data. How could you hold on to your past if it was always rearranging its memories? Like a broken part sent off to some distant factory for repair.

Soon, it was gone. Swallowed by the tarmac's darkness.

I stood there, alone in the funereal shadows. That's when Andrew's carousel slithered into view. I ignored it, longing for my own. But as it drifted closer, one window caught my eye – Andrew and Wyatt, standing outside my suite again, arguing. But when I looked closer, I saw *myself* in the scene watching them. It wasn't his original memory. It was new. A memory inside a memory, born moments ago when Andrew and I entered his carousel.

Something was wrong.

The window glitched. The scene blared in a janky loop. But behind the repetition, beyond their feverish argument, there was a faint blur of motion, something layered behind their images. The more I focused, the more artificial the scene appeared – like it was trying to cover up something.

Andrew's voice cut through the shadows until he came beside me.

I needed the truth.

I deserved the truth.

I pulled Andrew into his memory portal again.

Chapter Seventy

The familiar blood orange sun hung over the gravel driveaway, its low disc casting marred shadows.

The scene played out as before, only skewed: Memory-Andrew and Wyatt faced off, arguing, pacing, their images signaling in and out like busted holograms. Andrew, surprisingly co-operative, stood beside me; it seemed he craved the truth about this memory even more than me. *Why was it so glitchy? What was that shadowy image in the background?*

Ahead, I spotted my memory-me. She hovered near the action, skittish and horrified. But something was off. She didn't look like me – not quite. Her skin was pristine, acne scars erased, her hair darker, fuller. Even her figure was different, chiseled by Andrew's projection of me. The love handles I'd agonized over were either gone or, somehow, inviting. It was disorienting, seeing myself through someone else's lens, one that glossed over stains I seemed to magnify.

"Look," I said, nudging Andrew. "Oh god. Oh god."

Together, we watched as Memory-Andrew raised a gun toward Wyatt, the barrel's outline misfiring in and out.

I talked low. "I don't remember it so…spotty."

Andrew grabbed his head and then kicked at the gravel like it had personally offended him. "They embedded me. Sons of bitches."

I eyed him, waiting for him to reveal more. But there was no time. Memory-Andrew pulled the trigger on Wyatt. The sequence repeated the same actions as earlier, only malformed, like a bad dream. Their faces appeared disturbingly morphed, features half-present. The gun choked out a distorted, fragmented bullet, making colors in the air smudge like watercolor. I turned my head, unable to stomach the sight of Wyatt collapsing all over again.

The gravel below my feet suddenly undulated, and the woods around us lost pigment, morphing into something of a crude sketch. I moved toward the edge of the memory to center my balance, and that's where I noticed activity just behind a shadowy veil.

"Andrew," I called, gesturing toward it.

He followed, flustered.

Together, we pushed through the hazy shroud, its film dissolving like scentless smoke over our forms. On the other side, the driveway stretched out before us, eerily identical but changed. A mob of men in dark weathered coats filled the space. Some of them circled Wyatt and another man – older, but unmistakably tied to him. Same dark hair, same sharp face, a quiet authority. Others emerged from the suite, trampling past the threshold, crushing the leftover zinnias without a care. It was clear they had just ransacked the place, probably hunting for any trace of my father. All their focus turned to Wyatt and the man beside him.

"Who's that next to Wyatt?" I asked, even though I was certain I knew.

"That's his dad," Andrew whispered. He was shoulder to shoulder with me now. "Stanley Fink."

"And who are all those men?"

"Evadere."

Among them stood a man who seemed to steal Andrew's breath. "And that's my father."

The man Andrew called father lifted a gun – clear and solid – and leveled it at Stanley Fink. His sleek flaxen moustache was sharp, and his ice-cold, calculating eyes sent a winter chill up my spine. His tense shoulders were stilted beneath the frayed fibers of a pointed charcoal coat. He tilted his head mechanically, as though considering his shot. From the fringes, Memory-Andrew spilled in.

"Don't do this," Memory-Andrew begged. "Wyatt is my friend. Mr. Fink is your partner."

Andrew's father shot him a glacial, dismissive look, then pulled the trigger. Stanley Fink crumpled, blood flowering across his chest. Wyatt dropped to his knees beside his father, eyes ripe with shock. Before he could act or speak, Andrew's father gave a head jerk and another Evadere member stepped forward, raising his gun. The second shot was prompt, bereft of mercy. Wyatt slumped beside his father, their blood melding and blending into the gravel beneath them.

The Evadere mob shifted their attention to my house, ready to burn it down.

Another message to my father.

I looked to Andrew. He appeared pallid, blood syphoning from his face.

My voice shook. "Why would they do that to Wyatt and his dad?"

Andrew spoke as if the answer had been locked away until now. "My father thought Stanley had become an obstacle," he said. "He'd been stalling progress. Wyatt was encouraging him to stop parts of the program. They came to stop the fire. To warn you."

We stepped out of the memory, falling back onto the tarmac. Andrew's memory carousel hovered where we'd left it, humming steadily. He stared at the window we just exited – the image of his gun raised, glitching wildly, aimed at Wyatt, the light playing on their faces. It played on repeat, each cycle more blighted than the last. The real memory lurked behind the static.

"This is why they crave your father's knowledge," Andrew said, struggling to get his words out but seemingly comforted by the truth. "They wanted me to believe I murdered Wyatt. They embedded me with that lie, that false memory." His posture lengthened. "But they couldn't erase the truth. Not completely. Without your father's *Requiem* schematic, they can't completely overwrite the original memory. If they had it...if they triggered *Requiem*...I'd never have remembered this. It would've been gone forever."

"Embed. *Requiem*. Stop speaking in code! Spit it out."

Andrew gripped me, but I recoiled. "Embed means implanting an artificial memory so real, so vivid, it becomes part of who you are," he explained. "All the user has to do is enter a memory room, imagine a different outcome, and suddenly, it's not just a daydream – it's reality. It's conjuring pushed to the extreme. They must've lured me into the memory of Wyatt's murder, whispered into my unconscious, and twisted some old argument we had, making me believe I drew blood and fire. But you..." His eyes burned into me. "You helped me uncover the truth. I've been carrying guilt for something I didn't do."

I studied his face, searching for scars in his truth.

Andrew spoke quickly, like he was running out of time. Another chime rang out. We were.

"Evadere needs your father's *Requiem* schematic – the one he destroyed himself – to perfect the embedding process. I can remember the truth now because it's still buried beneath the fake memory. In time, I would have naturally remembered the truth, but you never know how long that takes. But if they had his schematic, his codes, they could erase the original memory entirely. I'd never be able to remember the truth. Poof."

"Slow down. *Requiem* schematic. Explain."

Andrew exhaled, his voice curdling in the darkness. "*Requiem* schematic – think of it as a blueprint. A step-by-step pictorial on how to permanently erase a memory. Requiem, like a farewell. If Evadere gets it back, they could wipe memories so clean it'd be like they never existed. Not that memories are fixed things – it's not like deleting a file from a computer. But it would stop the user from being able to reconstruct a memory. That's all memories are anyway – reconstructions. Imagination rebuilt over time. The *Requiem* schematic shows programmers exactly how to sever the brain's ability to reconstruct a specific memory. Back in the day, they'd use seedy drugs to block memories – recall the memory, inject the drug, block the connection. It was faulty at best. Your father figured out how to do it better – how to do it virtually. No injections. Just code and electrical activity. Disruption of neural impulses. Rewiring the brain."

An image of my father, barefoot, beard wild, in the dim shed flashed through my mind.

Andrew continued. "He wrote his notes down nice and tidy, until he decided to delete it, wiping it off the servers. He left no trace. Evadere wants it back. They've been offered more money than you can imagine, Pip. We're playing a game we can't win."

I shook my head, confused. "Get what back exactly? His notes?"

Andrew sighed. "Pretty much. And his codes. The *Requiem* schematic is a visual framework, like a neural map. It shows which memory nodes to target, using Screed's proprietary codes, and which neural pathways to follow to cut a memory connection without causing major damage to the user's brain."

My mind spun.

"Your father was an artist," he said. "The way he codified the process, the way he visualized it – it was beyond genius. I never saw it myself, but my father *envied* it. Can you imagine? Isolating a memory and cutting off the brain's ability to rebuild it, like it never existed. Revolutionary."

I put my hands to my head, processing his words. "My father created a system that erases memories? And then he made a visual map to show programmers how to do it themselves?"

Andrew nodded. "In a nutshell. He co-created the whole thing with my mother. And now, the *Requiem* schematic is my father's holy grail."

"And Evadere thinks they can pull this schematic from my head? That's ludicrous."

Andrew's eyes were intense and unsparing, like he could see something inside me that I couldn't. "You hold the key, Pip," he said. "It might be buried. But it's there."

I remembered him telling Wyatt he'd been in my father's computer room with me. I'd wanted to interrogate him about it, but I'd been too busy trying to avoid his madness.

Then, the memory hit like a hammer all on its own: the computer room, my mother, my father typing feverishly on a keyboard, a quiet, sad boy there too…

"Drew," I whispered.

I tried to picture his face as a boy but the memory was blurry. It was so long ago. But slowly, the pieces slid into place. Yes, now I remembered a boy whose mother had just died. My mother felt so, so sorry for him. She had told me about him in the dark during a storm.

"Yep, Drew," Andrew said. "My nickname when I was a kid. I was hoping you'd remember."

Chapter Seventy-One

Andrew's memory carousel began to flit away like a dying moth.

Mine wasn't anywhere nearby either. I sensed him moving in on me. I eased into the thick shadows before he could touch me.

"They'll find you," he called. "No matter what."

I paused. "I'll wake up before then. I don't mind waiting in the darkness. I'm used to it."

"You don't understand," he said, measured. "They don't care if you wake up at all. They want me to drag you into the memory of your father's computer room, and they'll do whatever it takes to get you there."

I stepped out of the shadows. Slowly. "And what happens if you don't succeed?"

He walked toward me. "They'll do to me what they did to Wyatt. And you?" He paused. "They'll freeze your brain. Use a neuro-decoding method to find the schematic. Memory extraction on an extreme level. Basically, targeting and imprinting all your memories into their databases like a stamp. They might find it. They might not. But you most certainly will not survive it. They'll do whatever it takes. Following their orders is the only way to survive."

I swallowed. "You're lying."

"I wish I was."

"But your father – he's Evadere. He wouldn't hurt you."

Andrew laughed. "I call him 'Dad' but it's just a word. He's not my father. Not really. He married my mother, sure, but he never wanted me. I was an inconvenience. The bumbling son of his beautiful, new wife."

His eyes clouded. He looked away. "He loved my mother. His precious Scarlet."

Scarlet.

"But me?" he continued. "Oh, he hated me. Always in the way, always a disappointment. Until he found a use for me. I became his lab rat." He paused. "Hey, did you like that skyscraper scene? I helped him test it. Can't tell you how many times I fell through that thing. Always loved skyscrapers as a kid. When you're up that high, it's like you're away from everything."

He looked misty-eyed. For a moment, I considered reaching out to him. Almost. But I stopped myself.

"You said you were in the computer room with me," I said. "Why can't they get the memory from *your* mind?"

"Because I never looked at your father's screen. But you did. I saw you do it. You seemed entranced by it."

"Okay, then what about your father's mind – your stepfather, I mean."

"I still call him Dad. It's complicated."

"Well, you're telling me he's seen the schematic already. So, it's in his own mind. Experiment on him!"

"He'd never risk it. Too proud."

"Okay, anyone else from Evadere then!"

"Anyone who has seen it is a programmer. Why would he risk losing his moneymakers?"

"No one thought to copy it down at the time?"

"No. Your father was extremely protective of it. It was his secret."

I tried to buy time until the waking chimes. "I still can't wrap my head around this. Why would our parents want to erase memories?"

"Their intentions were good, I promise. They thought it could replace traumatic memories. They never intended for it to get out of hand."

I shook my head. "My dad always said memories make us who we are. Why would he want to mess with someone's memory?"

Andrew's eyes relaxed. "Unless some memories are really just too painful, too damaging to move forward. Our parents believed it could give people a chance at a better life."

I closed my eyes, trying to understand my father in this new light. "But doesn't that change the person?"

"Maybe," Andrew said. "But they hoped it would be a change for the better. They believed in giving people a chance to rebuild their lives without being haunted by their worst experiences. It was never about altering someone's identity. It was always about healing. They never predicted others would want it for the wrong reasons."

"But now you're trying to exploit it."

"I still see its potential, Pip."

I scanned him, trying to understand whether his intentions were pure or stained with broken, mired hopes.

He sighed. "I shouldn't have told you all that. They might intercept if they think I'm not doing my job. Just believe me, if you help me get this schematic, I'll fight to ensure it's used for good. I promise."

I laughed, cold. "Your promises don't mean a damn thing to me."

Chapter Seventy-Two

I saw my memory carousel flickering in the distance.

Andrew lit up with a spark. He was hell-bent on getting me into the memory of my father's computer room. I wondered if I should give in. Just walk into the memory and let Evadere rip the schematic right out of my skull. Clean and simple, like yanking a rotten tooth. But just as Andrew couldn't turn a blind eye to his mother's vision, I couldn't abandon my father's convictions either. Even though he was the one who created the *Requiem*, he was also the one who destroyed it. He was the one who left everything behind, who abandoned his own identity, just to let the *Requiem* settle in the dust. If it was important enough for him, I shouldn't give up the fight that easily.

"Over here, Pip," Andrew said, waving me toward a row of my memories. "This is the age I remember you at. Come on."

I traced Andrew's steps, but at the last second, I slipped away, sinking into another memory window without him. I wouldn't be caught dead in the same memory room with him. I would keep running to protect the schematic, even if it killed me. But survival wasn't enough for me. I wanted answers. Where was my father now if he wasn't roaming the woods leaving me letters? Was he alive or dead? And why had I been so certain those memories were real? How could my mind betray me? Yet, every memory I sunk into left me more and more confounded, until one thing became bitterly clear: the more I hunted the truth, the farther I slipped from waking up.

Chapter Seventy-Three

When Andrew found me back in the shadows of the tarmac, he looked unhinged.

He grabbed me hard, pressing his fingers deep in to my arm.

"Stop running off without me," he shouted, holding me tight. "Another chime came. That's barely enough time to find the right memory, pull the schematic, and get back here to wake up."

His words sailed past me as I strained against him, trying to tear free.

I wasn't after the schematic.

I wasn't even thinking about survival.

I was coming apart.

All I could think about was my mind deceiving me – the fine line between memory and madness – and how easily I had crossed it without even knowing.

I didn't know who I could trust anymore.

Not Andrew.

Not myself.

Not even my own memories that once felt like lifelines after my father vanished.

Something in me must have shifted, sagging inward, because Andrew loosened his grip.

He must have seen it, felt it – the way my will was seeping out of me.

Finally, he let go and began to pace, his rattled steps matching his jagged voice. "If we get stuck in a memory, we'll miss the final chime. I told you – we could die in your memories."

"I don't know what to believe. I don't even know if *this* is real."

"This is real, Pip. And I'm trying to tell you the truth. If we miss the waking window, it's over. Sure, they might try to keep our bodies alive, but our consciousnesses won't make it back. It's what happened to my mother. Your father embedded her and then used the *Requiem* to erase her authentic memory. She never made it home."

I thought back on all the times my father was shut away in his computer room, lost inside code and glowing blue screens, swallowed by business trips. All that time, he'd been crafting something that blurred the lines between salvation and destruction.

"I'm not saying your father is a criminal," Andrew continued. "My mother consented. She knew the risks. But she became a victim of her own invention. She went into the program to test her memory, to see if it was truly erased. Well, it worked. Too well. Her original memory path was gone – and she got so disoriented entering a void space, maybe even distracted, that she missed the waking chimes. The incident report has since been destroyed, but I remember what it said. I was certain to review every line. Turns out she visited a memory of my biological dad before he died. She was so entranced by it that she stayed there. Forever."

"I am sorry that happened. I really am. But you need to forget the *Requiem*. You said yourself it could fall into the wrong hands."

"Pip, there is no way to win here." His face twisted painfully. "You think I want to do this? You think I like doing this to you? Of course not. I like you, Pip. But if I don't get the schematic safely from your memory, they'll kill you. And me?" He turned away, unable to finish.

I flinched, imagining the back of Wyatt's mangled head.

Andrew sighed, retreating into himself with silence.

I wasn't sure if he was giving up, but maybe Evadere sensed he was.

A sudden wave of heat came from the shadows. I felt it slice my nerves. Hot, boiling pain. Then came a screech. High-pitched. Splintering. The sound burrowed into the meat of my brain like slow, stabbing needles. I grabbed my head, but there was no escape.

"Fuck," Andrew said.

I looked up. A red-tinted shadow bled over the tarmac's dark horizon. The shadow bore the shape of a dragon, but not the whimsical version from Quest. This one was ghoulish and grotesque, born from some tortured corner of my subconscious. It was there and not there, like a hallucinatory nightmare. Its shadow stretched against my memory carousel, its form contorting as it crept closer.

Andrew's face drained alabaster. "You see something, don't you?"

"Yes, don't you?"

He didn't answer.

The creature seemed to twist and expand, growing viler with each movement. The beast opened its jaws, spilling translucent heat. I knew I was nothing but an avatar, but the pain was scathing and true. I screamed as agony ripped through me.

I wanted to believe I could outrun it, but it wasn't just chasing me – it was *everywhere*. The air around me seared with blistering heat; it felt sentient, like it was hunting me, hounding every step. No matter where I turned, the heat followed, scalding the very ground beneath me. I had a sinking, gut-churning feeling that it wouldn't stop until I was burnt to oblivion.

Chapter Seventy-Four

The beast lingered by the fray of my carousel, half shadow, half rot, hunting memories, its fangs cutting through the dark.

A thread of fire streaked the void, an arc of warning, narrowly skimming me. I fell to my face, my teeth cracking the cold, blackened ground. Skin peeled from bone, dragging behind me like loose threads of a worn mop. This wasn't real – none of it was real. *You're in a pod. Asleep*, I told myself.

But the pain didn't care. The heat was a scalpel, slicing me open, pouring in molten lava. My insides churned, liquefying. What were they doing to me?

Andrew's words echoed – a firewall was placed on my ability to conjure. But there, on the ground, suffering, I fought against its limitations. I tried to summon a shield. A weapon. Anything. Nothing came. The heat blistered my skin, making it pop like boiled soup, and it dragged my mind back to my father's woodshed. How I sat on the floor with him, engulfed in night's darkness, the scent of smoke still bonded to the air, as he placed wooden trinkets in my hands. What a silly thing for my him to do, I could cry.

My existence was evaporating, my brain matter sifting like sand. I would die here, at the claws of a chimera. And yet, in the face of this illusory death, my mind shifted to my father's wooden pieces – a grounding act, his stalwart lesson. *The darkness may not ask permission first. But you'll know what to do.* I remembered losing time in the shed, memorizing the feel, scent, and shape of each carved item. I closed my eyes, fighting the pull of death.

When I opened them, one of my father's wooden cubes was resting in my palm.

I stared at it.

Frozen.

I had conjured.

Another torrent of heat rippled the tarmac. My scream came loose and guttural. I gripped the cube tightly, latching on to its promise. Questions stabbed at me: *How had I conjured? How had I broken through the firewall?*

My father's voice surfaced – *Isn't it amazing, Pip, how memories are stored in different parts of the brain. Sights in one place, sounds in another, and scents and feelings elsewhere. But all together, they create the road map of who we are.*

I thought of other items from my father's shed – the butter-smooth cube, the ridged block like a choppy sea, the solid square that weighed like an anchor. I focused, summoning each from memory, enchanting them into existence one at a time. The pieces appeared from nothing, landing before me like children's blocks. I toyed with their forms, stretching and enlarging, testing their limits. A realization struck – sensory memories. The firewall kept me from conjuring sight memories, but tactile ones were fair game.

My body lay broken and burnt. Still, my palms rose, quivering against the enclosing heat. I clenched my eyes, clinging to the feeling of my father's carvings, his meticulous work pressed hard into my memory. And when the pieces materialized, they grew with a life of their own, multiplying like a rising flood. Block by block, a fortress assembled. The fire struck it, a predatory blast, but the wall I created persisted, swallowing the dragon's wrath.

Andrew stumbled to my side, breathless. "What's hunting you?"

"A dragon," I said, shocked he'd even ask. "You can't see it?"

"No. I see my own monsters," he said, jaw clenched. "But Evadere is stronger than your wall. It won't hold. Just show me where to look, Pip. A row, a window – anything. I can find your memory of the schematic myself if you just give me a starting point."

My carousel churned beside us, each frame shifting like fragile pages in an ancient tome. "I don't know," I said, trembling on the ground by his feet. "My memories are a blur. I don't even know which ones are real anymore." I shook my head, fighting back tears. "I thought my father left me messages…but he didn't. I made it all up. And if he didn't leave me those signs, it means he's not okay. It means he's…he's…"

"Pip, listen. We don't have fucking time. All that matters is finding the schematic—"

"*Fuck* the schematic, Andrew. My father could be dead."

Fire splintered the wall. I cradled my head, but it came for Andrew, sliding skin off his bone. Parts of his skull protruded from his face, but he kept speaking, ignorant to the beast devouring him. "He's alive!" he yelled, his voice mangled. "He's in confinement."

I felt my own skin skating down my cheek. I touched a calloused bone beneath my eye. "In confinement where?"

"In the undercroft of this building. There. Is that enough for you?"

"No," I said. "It's not."

Without thinking, without a plan, I crawled forward into my closest memory window, not even seeing which memory it was. I just wanted to get away from Andrew and the heat pulling at my skin.

As the memory's force sucked me in, I realized that memories in the program weren't always linear. Everything existed in fragments, scattered across chambers but connected as a whole, impossible to chart.

I landed ungracefully inside a memory that felt soft. Colors, scents, and feelings suddenly lifted weight off my chest. It was just an ordinary day back in Seattle, my quaint childhood home. A kitchen flooded with sun. Then, I saw her. Me. Five years old. Shaping horses out of brown clay, a table draped with plastic. Little-me pressed her tiny fingers into clay, giggling at an orange puppet on the small countertop television. Andrew punched through the memory, shouting into the silver gash. He must have had some way of tracking me, a method I didn't understand and couldn't escape. The girl, the little girl who had been me, turned. Her face wrinkled with fear. I moved to protect her, but my actions betrayed us both. Her body fell with the clay, convulsing, as my mother flew into the room. I left her behind – little-me, shaking in the kitchen, her clay horse trembling between her fingers. I backed away, quick and quiet, the villain of my own story.

★ ★ ★

The bitter scent of clay stayed with me, its olfactory power catapulting me toward something new. *Senses open doors.* The memory shifted, pulling me into a sunlit meadow. It was a picnic with my mother, simple and bright. Hummus, carrots, cheap plastic bubble wands that left sticky trails across the blanket. The sun was warm. It was safe inside this memory. Little-me rose from the blanket and pulled the hardened horse from her pocket, proud as anything, showing it off to my mother as though proof of her worth. My mother smiled at it, at her, and then Andrew ripped another hole into the memory, shouting at me to come out. Little-me shattered. She shook. She cried. She asked who was yelling.

"Help," my mother called. "My daughter needs help!"

I wanted to stay. I wanted to hold them both. But I couldn't. Andrew was chasing me, dragging me deeper into the abyss of my own mind. As he did, he distorted my memories, adding more convulsion episodes to my childhood. I knew it would make it impossible to ever tell which memories were real and which had been twisted by him, if I ever woke up at all. I touched my memory-mother's shoulder briefly, remembering her jasmine scent like it was the last thing I'd ever do. It didn't damage the memory I was in, but it flung me into another one, one I wasn't ready to face.

★ ★ ★

I stumbled into a new memory like a pebble flailing down a drainpipe. My parents' bedroom in Seattle. Morning. Little-me was sleeping in their bed, curled and cozy, oblivious to what came next. Down the hall, my mother's voice called out, rousing me from a fuzz of dreams.

"Pip! Come here, Pip. We have a visitor."

I knew she was calling out from my father's computer room.

The last time I ever saw her.

Here I was.

Exactly where Andrew had been leading me all along.

Chapter Seventy-Five

The memory unfolded quietly.

It was morning after losing power in our Seattle home. The clocks blinked the wrong time on the night table. I remembered how I had climbed into my parents' bed the night before, burrowed between their warm shoulders. The thunder couldn't reach me there. But now the bed was empty, their warmth removed.

I reached for my face where skin sagged from the bone. I ignored it. What mattered was her. Little-me. I wished I could keep her safe, tucked away forever. It might just change everything. She looked so peaceful, her toes poking through the sheets as though testing the limits of her tiny world. I wanted to hold her there, to freeze time, to protect her from everything she didn't yet know. *Stay here*, I thought. *Stay safe, tucked in this warm bed. Delay what's coming. Delay what's already been written.*

Little-me stirred, her ears straining, chin perked toward the voices down the hall. She plopped her head back down, cocooning herself, the sleepy girl. I let out a long sigh, scanning the exit. As much as I wanted to stay, to see my mother one last time, to know what happened in that computer room, I couldn't willingly lower the castle door. They were mercilessly hunting the *Requiem*, and I was the gate. I ran to the edge of the memory but was thrust back in. I could feel the cold hand of Evadere locking me in.

Curiosity crept its way toward little-me. She slipped out of bed, her tiny feet padding against the wooden floor. I felt it in my gut – a steel kink. Dread whispering: *This is where it starts*. I followed in her wake. Something else felt off – something I couldn't quite place. Someone else was here with me. I could feel it – a presence, a static cling in the air. I thought I'd left Andrew behind on the tarmac. But no. Andrew had a loophole. He had wormed his way into this memory, guided by the imprint of his younger self. That was his trick. This wasn't my memory alone. It was *ours*.

"I'm waiting, Pip," Andrew called out from the computer room. His voice was sharp and grim. I followed little-me like I was her keepwarden.

Whatever lay ahead, I had to face it.

The truth. The fight. All of it.

Chapter Seventy-Six

The light in the computer room was unkind, as though my father's monitors were sucking up all the joy.

When little-me entered, my mother looked up. She was kneeling beside a young boy slouched on a leather chair in the corner. A touch of somber honey was in her voice. "Good morning," she said. "This is Drew – the boy I told you about. He's visiting for the day."

As she spoke, her eyes met little-me's. It was a quiet, heavy look. A look that said: *this is the boy we made the blanket for. The one who is sad.*

It hit me then – something I hadn't fully understood before. All this time, I remembered the night we stayed up late during the blackout, knitting a blanket, as a special bond between me and my mother. A small world we made for ourselves by the glow of candlelight. But the memory had blurred the truth, which suddenly came rushing back. My mother had suggested we make a blanket for a child of one their colleagues. "A boy who is very sad." A boy who needed something soft to hold on to. I was too young to understand what that meant – that the boy's mother had died.

And now I realized her death was tied to my father's doing. The *Requiem.*

I followed little-me's gaze to the boy. Drew sat hunched and silent, his unbrushed hair making it look like he woke up in a field. He looked up slow. His familiar ocean eyes were rimmed red. The look of a grieving boy.

And then there was Andrew, standing in the memory like a crack in a cured pot. He was leaning against the wall, smirking.

"Cute, aren't I?" he said, nudging his head toward his childhood self.

The air compressed between us. I held my tongue, witnessing the memory unfurl around us.

"Pip, do you want to get Drew his gift?" my mother asked with broken kindness. She knelt beside him, checking constantly, watching him like a mother robin.

My father was at the computer, tinkering, oblivious.

I watched helplessly as little-me walked past him and his glowing screen toward a closet. I held my breath waiting for her to turn her head to his monitor. But she passed by, blind to it. Relief swept over me, but it was temporary. This wasn't over. Evadere was just waiting for the right moment to capture the *Requiem* schematic.

Little-me remained fixed on her task, her small hands fumbling with the bulky gift as she came and knelt beside Drew. "Here you go," little-me said, still sticky with sleep. The present was clumsy in her small hands as she transferred it onto Drew's lap. "Me and my mom made this for you," she said, bright-eyed.

Drew unwrapped the present slowly like it might bite him. Inside dollar-store paper was a hand-knit blanket, gray and white, soft as a chinchilla. He barely glanced at it, his fingers wandering the yarn absently.

"Thanks," he mumbled, his loss too fresh for anything more.

From his chair by the dim glare of the screen, my father cleared his throat. "I'm done, Cove," he said, not even turning to look. "I'm getting rid of it. You think that's the right thing, don't you?"

Cove – my mother – lifted her eyes from the blanket. "Yes," she said. "Delete it. It's not worth the money. Delete the schematic. The codes. Everything. And never look back. Do it for Scarlet. Contract or not, it's yours. We can't risk something like this ever happening again."

He nodded slowly, letting out a heavy breath. "Delete it. And never look back. Wise words. For Scarlet."

My mother glanced at Drew, her face supple with empathy. Supple with guilt.

Andrew lunged toward my father's computer like he wanted to swallow it. Something stopped him cold. An invisible shackle kept him bound to the limits of Drew's memory. He stumbled back, cursing under his breath, his eyes violent with frustration. No matter how hard he pushed, he couldn't escape the cage of the boy he once was – like he wasn't ready to see the memory from any other perspective. Meanwhile, little-me knelt beside Drew, her small fingers prying a loose thread on the blanket resting on his lap. The two children were knit there by the soft blanket between them, their fingers tracing its velvety fibers.

"Look up!" Andrew hollered at little-me. He turned to me, his face folding with fury, his loose skin rippling over exposed bone like gills straining for air. "She looked at the screen," he said, pacing. "I remember it. Why isn't she looking?"

His hands hovered near little-me's head. A threat.

"Leave her alone," I said, nearly growling.

He turned to me, demented. "I bet *everything* on her looking at your father's computer screen. Did you change this memory?"

"No. Maybe you're the one with faulty memories. Anyway, she's not looking up because she's busy empathizing with you, Andrew. Can't you see?"

He spun to face her. Little-me's small hands were threading through holes of the blanket, finding Drew's trembling hands there, a fragile smile cracking his face.

"No," Andrew said. "This is not what I remember. You have no idea what this costs. What's at stake."

"Mom, I feel fainty," little-me said, her fingers slipping through the blanket.

"You can't change the past," I bit back. "I don't know what to tell you."

Little-me flopped to the ground.

"Yes," Andrew said, walking toward her. "You can."

Chapter Seventy-Seven

Andrew was supposed to let the bones of the past lie still.

Touching was forbidden. Tampering was off limits. Altering a memory was too great a risk. Yet, he charged forward, taking advantage of little-me's state, grabbing her head like it was a joystick. He twisted her neck toward the humming light of the computer screen.

"Stop, Andrew!" I shouted. "You're not supposed to touch."

I rushed toward him as little-me jerked, her small frame convulsing. My mother reached for her, cradling her, trying to keep her head from striking the floor.

Yet, Andrew's hands on little-me broke something deep within. A wave of disorientation crashed over me. The room shuddered. Edges of the memory blurred. Everything felt erratic and half-formed. Memories churned like water in a whirlpool, rearranging themselves, breaking apart, rising to the surface. I hit the floor as images surged forward like flocks of birds pushing past a brutal storm. Memories that had been concealed now flooded my mind. One after another. In them, I saw glimpses of a past I'd somehow crafted without knowing it. I saw myself inside The Reverie Cloud, leaving messages in the mailbox – scenes I hadn't truly lived but had conjured: a note, a wood-carved horse, a scroll. Breadcrumbs, hastily scattered, perhaps to offer clues and warnings. Although all they ever did was bring me hope in the waking world. My eyes fluttered as I processed this revelation.

The memories were planted. By me.

I was my own messenger.

My own guide.

For so long, I'd believed my father was out there somewhere, watching over me, leaving signs in the dark to help me find my way. But it wasn't him. It never had been. The signs were mine.

But questions gnawed at me: How could I have forgotten embedding those messages? Was I so starved for my father's guidance that I spun lies – that it was him – to fill the void? When really, I was my own savior. And if Andrew wasn't lying – if my father truly was locked away in the lower level of the Reverie Cloud building – what then?

I forced myself to breathe, to stay focused on the details.

"Pip! Oh my god! Rich, help!" my mother cried out.

"Hold on, Cove. I'm deleting it now," my father said, barely turning.

"Forget the computer," she said, jagged. "Look at your daughter. She's having one of her episodes!"

"I'm deleting it."

"*No!*" Andrew shouted, his grip tightening on little-me as she squirmed. "Look at the screen."

Little-me struggled against his invisible force, her eyes rolling white with terror.

Finally, my father turned.

Andrew was invisible to my parents. They didn't see his hands on little-me. All they saw was her trembling body. I couldn't tell if she was shaking because of Andrew or if she was having an episode on her own, with him taking advantage of her in that fragile moment. Maybe both. I only knew I hated the way he was trying to manipulate my memory like it was some defective gear he was forcing back into place.

"Leave her alone!" I shouted.

I grabbed at Andrew, pulling, clawing, but he was an immovable boulder. An untouchable beast who could not hear, see, or reason with me.

I staggered back into the shadows but didn't leave entirely. I opened a rip between the memory and the tarmac, dropping the firewall so little-me could hear me. Color and light from the tarmac breathed through the tear.

"Pip," I called to her. "You're going to be fine. I'll stop this, I promise. Just close your eyes. Trust me. Close them until it's over."

She turned toward me. Pale. Drained. And somehow, she saw me near the rip in the memory. Behind me, shadows of the tarmac swirled with the radiant glow of my carousel – prismatic reds, vibrant greens, canary yellows, inky maroons, every particle of my life's memories sewn together, time intersecting. She looked at me, and for that split second, she seemed at peace. She closed her eyes.

Andrew shoved little-me, sending her small body crashing to the floor. The sight of it broke me. Without thinking, I stepped forward, sealing the rip behind me, and launched myself at him. He tried to ward me off, but our bodies locked in an ugly struggle. Andrew's knee caught my chin, and the bitter sting of blood filled my mouth.

Over by the desk, my father was a rushwind of movement. He placed an old, clunky BCI around little-me's head. It was an old model with more nodes and wires than I was used to; wires spilled across little-me's face like black veins. He plugged them into his computer, firing up a program on his second screen.

"Grab a pillow, Cove," he instructed, moving with precision. "Put it under her head. I'll link her to the program. Then you can connect me to her. I'll figure it out. It's my fault. All of it. I shouldn't have let her into any of those trials. I swear to God, I didn't think this would happen. We should have stopped experimenting the very first time she had an episode."

"We're both to blame," my mother said, her voice full of ache, clutching little-me's hand. "But I'm the only one who can help her now. Connect me instead. I'll go in. Give me the solution – through the veins. It'll be quicker. Load the horse ranch sequence – it's listed under Terra Protocol, Dreampath Six."

My mother's hands blanketed little-me, a cover of strength but heavy with guilt.

Now I understood – the convulsions weren't some lifelong mystery, but a direct consequence of my parents' experiments on me. They had done this to me. I was a beta tester to The Reverie Cloud, just like Andrew. Maybe they had wiped my mind clean of their trials, of Evadere. Or perhaps those moments weren't fully erased, no *Requiem* triggered, but instead buried deep inside, waiting the day I might uncover them. I couldn't be sure.

This realization didn't change the fact that Andrew was exploiting little-me's vulnerability. That he'd already tampered with so many of my memories. That when I woke – if I woke – I'd have to face the damage. That my memories would be a cruel patchwork – pieces of painful reality stitched together with fabricated moments, conversations, and scenes, my brain scrambling to recalibrate in response to corrupted recollections. Tampered memories disguising themselves as linear truth. And the worst part? I might never untangle the two to separate fact from fiction. The thought left me feeling completely alone and shelled out.

My father fumbled with a needle, with wires. So many wires.

It was too much. I closed my eyes and focused on the memory of my mother's touch.

Soft as summer.

When I opened them, she wasn't just a memory anymore.

Another version of her appeared beside me – one who saw me. Truly saw me.

Chapter Seventy-Eight

When my mother entered the memory – or some version of her – it was like light breaking through.

She wore a milky white sundress that draped around her body with a regal sweep. She stood quietly, as though she had always been there, waiting for the right moment to appear. I wanted to believe in her, but I knew better. She wasn't real – she was a construct, part memory, part artificial intelligence, scripted by some unseen author in my mind. I'd conjured her by recalling a tactile memory of her. The real her was slumped beside little-me in the memory room, laced with wires from her BCI, unconscious from whatever potion my father had injected. And the truest version of her was gone, lost in a grave my father never showed me.

Her eyes moved to Andrew, sharp and exact, before settling on me.

"Is he the disturbance?" she asked.

I hesitated, torn between hope and doubt.

"Pip? Sweetheart."

"Y-yes," I stammered. "He's looking for the *Requiem* schematic here in this memory."

Andrew moved in on little-me again, but the projection of my mother blocked him. "System breach detected," she said, holding him back like an immovable mountain.

In that moment, it didn't matter if she was a projection or some phantom of my imagination. She was here to protect me. That was all I needed to know. I glanced at the memory of my father, hunched over the computer, typing furiously, neural patterns flashing across his screen. On the far side of the room, Drew fidgeted, clutching the torn wrapping paper from his gift. His eyes shifted to little-me, unconscious on the ground. I'm sure the sight weighed heavy on him, so soon after losing his own mother to the same program. He swallowed hard, and then stood, shaky, preparing to leave.

As Drew crossed the room, Andrew began to fade. He couldn't stay in the memory without him. His voice was garbled, firing in uneven sparks. "Make...her...look...at...the...screen. Please. For my mother," he said.

I studied his glitching face as he reached for little-me. His outstretched hand wavered in and out, and his face – one I had once been drawn to – was crumbling. Not just physically, but emotionally. His rawness was wet in the air. He wasn't a monster. He was tragic. A man blinded by grief. In that moment, I saw him clearly. His pain. His conviction. His need to make his mother's vision live on. Perhaps it was like bringing her back to life.

And in that, I could understand him.

"Your mother was brilliant," I said. "But she wouldn't want you to suffer for her."

He snarled. "You don't understand."

I looked at the projection of my mother, then back at him. "Andrew, please," I whispered, tears forming. "I understand more than you think I do." I felt myself breaking apart, the weight of everything pressing on me. I lifted my hand, and my fingers broke at the seams, falling to the floor like blocks. I remembered what Everly said about losing control. I tried to reclaim my power, but I couldn't. I tucked my other hand away, desperate to keep it safe. It was all too much – seeing little-me convulse on the floor, my mother's lifeless form beside her, my father's frantic keystrokes, trying to save me with codes and sequences; their secret experiments on me, the ones that broke me. And the ache of missing him – my father as he was in the present – hurt deeper than I thought possible.

"Andrew," I pleaded, trying to reach him before he vanished completely. "Tell me the truth. All of it. I've seen myself in memories I don't even remember. What is this? How do I wake up?"

"Pip," he said. "You've been in this simulation many times before. You just don't remember. We've been watching you. Learning you. We know you better than you know yourself." His eyes glistened. His body phased, momentarily lost to static before reappearing.

"What?" My voice quivered, and when I spoke, my teeth shattered, falling from my mouth like broken glass. I felt my lips pucker, dry as clay in the sun. But I didn't care. I needed to know more. "When? What do you mean?"

"We've gone through this same pattern countless times," he said, low and unraveling. "This is just a replay to bring you back to the same point. Perhaps this time, we might succeed and get the schematic, but only if you cooperate." His eyes sizzled like dying stars and caught on to mine. "Close your eyes. Touch me. Maybe I can give you the rest."

He stumbled close, his glitching palm cupping what was left of my hand.

When my eyes shut, it came flooding back. I saw it all – those nights spent in The Reverie Cloud long past my allotted time, slipping into hypnosis against my will. I had been here before. The skyscraper. The tarmac. The carousel of memories moving with minds of their own. Wyatt's death. This room. Every moment folded into the next. Andrew had always been there, trying to pull the memory of my father's computer room into focus. And I had always resisted, pushing him back, delaying progress, tampering with memories in the process. Each time, I learned the rules of this place. I learned how to navigate memories, manipulate them, embed new ones. I had been leaving myself messages in different memory rooms all along, bypassing the firewall, conjuring by other means.

I was a clever thing, walking into vulnerable memories, ones that felt fragile, easy to rewrite, and I'd imagine something new in its place. And each time, I awoke from the program, forgetting what I'd done entirely. I'd walk out in a haze, the entire session buried in my mind. Until now.

"Of course, you realize," Andrew said, interrupting my vision, "if I had access to the *Requiem* schematic, you wouldn't have been able to recall the truth just now. Those memories would be gone, forever. You'd live in peace. No more chaos. Don't you see how important this is?"

I closed my eyes, sifting through the rubble of my mind. The Reverie Cloud. All those long hours trapped in its grip, floating through its digital landscapes, blissfully unaware of the truth. And Andrew – pulling me back to this same place. Over and over again.

My voice caught in my throat. "Peace? I will never know peace. Every moment of my life feels like it's been tampered with. My parents lied to me. You lied to me. I don't know what's real."

Andrew tilted his head, his expression near pity. "We were all test subjects, Pip. You, me, Wyatt. But they handled you differently. They cleaned up your memory afterwards – the wires, the needles, the endless failed sessions. They left you with beautiful experiences like the horse ranch sequence, erasing all the trauma it took to get you there. I'm sure your sessions just feel like organic memories to you at this point. They gave you that, pure and clean, without the reality of what it took to create it."

He paused, his tone sharpening. "They didn't do that for me. Or Wyatt. I remember everything. Every single session. The pain. The confusion. The terror."

I stared at his flickering form.

"Don't you get it, Pip? This world is ours. We *are* The Reverie Cloud. This program wouldn't exist without us, without our pain. But it came with a price – a price you've been spared from fully remembering. You only remember the beautiful parts. Consider yourself lucky."

Andrew's body pulsed in and out.

I turned to the memory – little-me on the floor, my mother beside her, my father caught between them and his machine. My head throbbed.

"Why are you telling me all this now?"

"You know what they say: insanity is doing the same thing over and over again and expecting different results," he said. "Every prior session, we wiped your mind clean, a temporary block. It should come back to you with time. But this time, I thought you might be ready for the truth. Maybe it'd make you compliant. And…maybe you deserved to know."

I tried to breathe, but it felt more like drowning.

Andrew's voice dragged on with a hollow, malfunctioning whir. "We're so close, Pip. Every time we reach this room, the programmers capture partial impressions of the schematic from your subconscious – fragments, patterns, shapes, symbols. Never the whole thing. But this time? This is supposed to be it. If it's not, they'll extract everything, no matter the risks. These sessions are draining their resources. They can't afford to keep trying."

I couldn't find my breath. "Subconscious?"

"Yes," he rasped. "It holds more than you think. You must have seen the schematic more than once, even if you don't remember it. Something about this memory room draws it out. When you're here, it provokes something buried. You've given us a lot to work with already."

"No," I said, gasping. "You can't do this."

"You had parents who cared about you," he said. "They would've done anything for you. I can see that. Some of us have to pay for our parents' glory. It's just how it is. Don't hate me for it."

With that, Andrew rushed at little-me, grabbed her chin, and pried her eyelids open – as if his fortune lay in the whites of her eyes, as if this were the final trigger to peel me open. But her eyes saw nothing and held nothing. They were lost between worlds.

And then, little Drew left the room, a silent gush of terror written on his face. His exit was enough to break Andrew's connection, forcing him out of the memory.

My father leaned over little-me, holding her still, trying to fix something he had broken repeatedly. As little-me trembled, I felt it in my own bones. The memory was warping, already too fractured by Andrew's intrusion.

My knees buckled. I felt weak.

I hit the ground.

I was stretched across too many overlapping realms: my real body, asleep in the pod; little-me, convulsing on the floor; and my avatar, stranded in this shattered memory room.

I couldn't hold it all. My mind split under the pressure.

The projection of my mother appeared beside me, her presence a tender light in the maelstrom.

I felt her. I knew she was there.

I knew I needed to leave.

But I couldn't.

I was stuck.

Chapter Seventy-Nine

My projection-mother cradled my neck like I might break.

Light poured out of her face like she was built from the sun. Her hair was fair and lush. She felt so real, I forgot she wasn't. I wanted her to fix me. To restore my face, my hands, my heart. Around us, the memory of little-me in the computer room dulled, a blur of gray and white, making my projection-mother stand out.

"Mom," I managed. "Can you hold me a little while longer? I'm falling apart."

"Of course," she said, reeling me into her warm breast.

I let my body go slack against her, a rag doll, awaiting death.

It hurt to speak, but I drove my words out. "There were four chimes already," I said.

Her face twisted.

I could feel her fear.

"What is it?" I asked.

Her arms wrapped tight around my tired body. "We need to leave," she said. "This program isn't safe. You're running out of time."

"But, Mom…" My words came out blanched. I was delirious. "This program is amazing. I flew with you. I painted a lagoon. I—"

She shook her head, her glow dimming. "There are beautiful things here, yes, but the risks are too great."

"Like the dragon."

Her face dried pale as the moon. "You've seen a dragon?"

"Yes. It melted my skin. Can't you see my skull poking through?"

"No, Pip," she said. "It didn't melt your skin. That was an illusion."

"Did you and Dad make the dragon?"

"No. That's Victor's work." She looked past me as though planning our escape. "That thing will be waiting for you on the tarmac. We need to think of something."

A tendril of black smoke corkscrewed into the room, making me cough.

"It's trying to breach this memory now," she said, prodding me back to life. "We need to go."

I didn't move. My eyes drifted toward the nebulous vision of my father, still hunched at his desk in the midst of the memory.

"Is it true?" I asked. "Did you and Dad experiment on me? Did it make me sick?"

The smoke hardened, spooling closer, but she didn't look away. "Yes," she finally said. "I'm sorry. He thought he could fix it by putting you back into the program where you felt comfortable. You were always so relaxed there. One more time in the program, just one more time. He always thought cures were a keystroke away."

My eyes moved to little-me, hooked to wires, her small body limp as brain activity fired on my father's monitor.

"But he didn't fix me," I said, finally understanding the weight of this memory. "I got lost in the program. And you went in to pull me out. But you got stuck there." I paused, holding back tears. "You never made it out."

She didn't say anything, only squeezed my hands tighter.

Again, I forgot who she was. What she was.

"Mom," I said. "If you come to the tarmac with me, could we both wake up together?"

"Don't get confused," she said. "I'm only a reflection of her. But that doesn't mean I don't love you. You must stay strong now, Pip."

The smoke closed in, sizzling.

"That wasn't a dragon chasing you either," she said. "It was an extraction process – a tool Victor uses to rip memories out and transfer them onto his machines. It manifests as whatever the user's subconscious fear is, even if it's something buried deep from childhood. For you, it chose a dragon."

"Dragons," I said, remembering. "I had a fear of them when I was a kid, didn't I?"

"For a time, yes. But whatever the extraction masquerades as, it makes the user numb. It suppresses cognitive resistance, making it easier to harvest data. It'll kill you if we let it, Pip. And it'll be here any second."

Chapter Eighty

I wanted to lie beside little-me.

She looked so calm, so serene. Safe asleep with her mother beside her.

My projection-mother spoke, her words muddled.

"You need to get up now, sweetheart. You need to get up before the extraction occurs, before the dragon comes."

I didn't want to. I couldn't.

"I thought the dragon couldn't find me in my memories."

"It can't access your *core* memories," she said. "Ones you remember completely."

I couldn't focus.

Couldn't hold my head up.

I let myself sink deeper, eyes closed.

"Stay alert, Pip," she said. "You need to get us out of this room. This is a vulnerable memory."

Blistering winds coiled in, sharp as fangs. Searing. Burning hot. It came from the edge of the memory, carrying the scent of something charred. My hand – or what was left of it – lifted, a bony stump dissolving into a breeze of particles. The dragon – no, the extraction – was clawing its way in, vaporizing me. Its barnacled nail, black and monstrous, sliced a rip into the memory. A screech from the tarmac tunneled into my ears, and I swore I felt blood oozing down my neck.

I couldn't fight the heat, the pain.

It slithered up my nostrils, severing nerves like pigheaded weeds.

I was dying. I felt it. Every beat of it.

My father's voice broke through. "Core memory," he said. He typed urgently, his words entering the program through his keyboard. "Get her into a core memory and force eject her from the program."

He was speaking to my mother of the past, but his words felt just as urgent now. My projection-mother leaned close, her face blocking the hot smoke that rolled in surges from the beast's mouth. "Remember how you moved to memories through scent? Through touch? Take us somewhere," she said. "Think of something special. Something that makes you happy."

"I'm too tired," I said. The words trudged slowly up my throat. The room faded to gray, dense with the dragon's breath.

"Comfort carvings," my father muttered to himself, his hands rummaging through a cluttered shelf. "She needs to remember the horse ranch. It didn't load in the sequence. She has to bring it on herself."

I closed my eyes and slipped into a dark realm. The dragon was there. It flashed in the void, its flames punching through.

"Keep your eyes open!" my projection-mother shouted, shaking me.

I forced my lids open.

Through the smog, I saw my father in the memory room. He placed a wooden horse in little-me's hand, its brown leather saddle glinting faintly. A sculpture of my mother arrived in her other hand. And then jasmine. A scent as shocking as sudden gold in a bleak mine. It seeped through the smoke – frail, delicate, sweet.

I felt it. I remembered. The carvings. The ranch.

"Feel them," my father whispered to little-me. "Smell them. Go to the horse ranch. Remember."

Chapter Eighty-One

I forced my eyes open.

Light shimmered hot and golden, soaking into my skin. An endless sapphire sky wrapped around me. My projection-mother stood beside me, her presence grounding me as I took in the scene.

The smell hit me first – pungent leather, sunbaked hay. It anchored me in a way I couldn't quite explain, pulling me into the moment.

We were at the horse ranch. My core memory. The moment a foal labored to walk.

I realized now, this was a simulated environment, a program in The Reverie Cloud. A beta Dreampath, designed for peace and contemplation. But it was still my memory. It belonged to me.

My projection-mother took my hand, and we moved forward. But something caught our attention. Ahead, two figures stood at the wooden gate that enclosed the horses – my mother and little-me.

We watched what held their gaze.

On the other side of the gate, a foal lay nestled in yellow-green grass beside its mother.

The foal tried to stand, wobbly and unsure of her legs.

After several attempts, its little legs strengthened, and she took off clumsy and wild. Little-me clapped and cheered. I smiled at first, but then her laughter pierced my heart. I understood something profound about this memory. Something new. This moment wasn't spontaneous. My parents had crafted it. An unnatural scene, inspired by nature. They wanted me to see the foal's struggle. To watch her stand, shaky at first, but steadfast. They wanted me to learn something from her. To understand that sometimes, things take time. They wanted to inspire me, to leave something permanent in my mind. It was beautiful and terrible all at once.

My projection-mother and I walked closer, nearing the marrow of the memory. I watched my mother – the past version of her – swirl her hand gently against little-me's back, tracing an infinity loop.

"What do you think my mother was thinking here?"

My projection-mother hesitated. "I was thinking about time."

I paused. The word *I*. I remembered who she was. She wasn't real. Just data and light. A projection. But her façade was breaking; she was taking this role to heart.

"That I wasn't sure I could ever be this happy. Just being here with you."

I studied her face, wondering how much of my real mother was built into this version.

She paused, her eyes sobering up. "Pip, there's something I need to tell you about this particular memory."

I stiffened. The shift in her tone told me I needed to focus.

"Core memories like this – they're comforting, but they're also dangerous," she said.

"What do you mean?"

"They're encoded so deeply, they're almost impossible to rewrite. They make up who we are. They're like beams holding up a house. So strong that the mind reactivates them constantly, strengthening them. But this reactivation creates temporal feedback – a loop. It can feel endless and alluring. It can trap you."

I stayed quiet, processing her words. I reminded myself, she wasn't my mother. Just a projection programmed from the scraps of her I carried in my subconscious.

But the way she spoke, the compassion in her voice – it felt so authentic. Was there a part of my real mother in her? Something embedded in the code? Or was she just playing a character, feeding me what I needed to hear to help me survive?

"So," I said slowly, "if we don't leave this memory, we could stay here forever. Or what feels like forever."

"Yes," she said. Her voice tensed. "You would never hear the chimes from here. Stay alert. I need to teach you how to defeat the extraction. The dragon. Once you understand, you can leave this memory and finally wake up."

Chapter Eighty-Two

My projection-mother tried to pull me away from the gate, but I lingered.

The horses dipped their heads at the trough. Not a worry. Little-me stood by my mother, her back turned slightly, watching, waiting, safe.

I didn't want to leave.

My projection-mother said core memories were inviting.

They were. I felt the tug. The warmth.

If I stayed, I might live forever. Or at least believe I had. I might never wake. Never feel the ache of being away from her. Never face the stalk of death.

I turned to her. "So, if we stay…?"

"Life would go on just like this," she said. "Forever. Everything else would be forgotten."

I looked around. I listened. The soft creak of stable slats. The sound of hooves grinding against dirt. Grass bending under a steady wind. Somewhere in the distance, a nightingale's song.

"It seems nice here," I said.

She looked back at the memory, at the versions of us caught there, standing at the gate. Silent. I wondered if she felt it too, the pull to stay. She was some rendering of my mother, wasn't she? Built to care for me. Surely, she felt it too.

She held my hands. "I know this place feels safe. But you need to leave while you can. As much as I love you, I want you to live a full life. I can't be selfish. I can't keep you here."

My eyes swelled. "But Mom," I said. "You won't be there when I wake up."

She seemed to be holding back tears of her own. She didn't answer.

"It's not fair," I said. "Let's both leave."

"I can't," she said gently. "I only exist here. But you – you still have a chance. You said there were two chimes left?"

I nodded.

"And I'm sure another's already passed. There's not much time."

"What do I do?" I asked, breaking. "I can't – I can't just leave you here."

I glanced at the past. At little-me holding my mother's hand, the two of them running wild through the tall grass, laughing like they were horses themselves.

"I'd love nothing more than to wake up with you," my projection-mother said, her voice blurring the line between what she was and who she claimed to be. "To watch you grow, to be there for you. But I *am* with you. I promise. You might not see me, but you know me – my touch, my smile, my heart. You know what I would say, what I would do, how I'd laugh. You remember me holding you, lifting you up, talking to you. I'm imprinted within you, Pip. I am part of the code that makes up who you are. I am always, always with you."

Tears finally came, pooling in my eyes, gliding down my cheeks.

"But if the extractor takes everything," she said, "neither of us stands a chance."

"This is all my fault. I shouldn't have taken that job. I shouldn't have gone into the program. Dad warned me. I'm such an idiot. I'm sorry, Mom."

"Shh," she said, pulling me into a hug. "This isn't your fault. Some rides we're just meant to take. And besides, I can move through the memories we share. Yours and mine – they're one. Like you said, you've learned how to travel between them. So can I. There's nowhere else I'd rather be."

She took a long, deep breath and stood back, taking me in. "Hold my hands. Close your eyes. I'll show you."

I shut my eyes, and the world vanished. For a moment, Andrew came to mind. Had he reached the tarmac? Escaped the program? Was he awake now, sitting beside me as I lay sleeping? Or had he entered the Circadian Room, readying the dragon?

"Feel," my mother said. "Remember." Her hand grazed my arm.

I remembered what it was like to feel her.

Her touch, warm.

Her stroke, kind.

I opened my eyes, and I was on my mother's lap, snow falling out the window.

Her fingers, brushing my arm.

Me, seven.

Her, holding me on the rocking chair while my tooth hung by a thread.

"This is where I'll be," she said. "Close your eyes again."

I did, and when I opened them, I was a baby snug in her arms.

"And here," she said. "Close your eyes again."

I opened my eyes again and again, each moment flickering like the shutter of a camera. Each scene showing something special between us – splashing in a cyan pool, digging for sand crabs, laughing at cereal commercials, her hands tickling my belly, her lips pressing kisses to my cheek, showing off my Halloween pail stuffed with candy, the gleam of a new bike beneath a tinsel-covered tree, her proud smile on Christmas morning.

She paused at a memory of a dandelion field, an Easter egg hunt taking place.

I pulled us into it. The memory stretched all around us.

"I'm in every one of these memories," she said. "And you are too."

"But I—"

"If you live, I live."

"Mom…" I whispered, my breath hitching as the rush of memories swept through me.

My words didn't make it out. Fire came, blazing and unforgiving, sizzling across the sky like a red nebula. It scalded my skin. I hid my face behind my palms, the heat chewing at my knuckles. "I thought the dragon couldn't enter core memories!"

"This must be another vulnerable one," she said. "They're usually ones you can't remember too well."

"Take us somewhere else then!"

"I can't, Pip. That's up to you," she said. "I live in these memories, but I don't control them. You do. Only you can take us somewhere safe."

"But you've been moving us!"

"I've been showing you visions. What we share. But stepping into another memory room? That's you. You're the driver, and you have to do it now."

Children ran past us, clutching rainbow-colored buckets as they searched for eggs in the tufts of grass and at the foot of bushes. Another rush of fire came from the shadows, unseen by anyone but me. It knocked me to my knees. I looked up and saw my projection-mother's charred face. I lifted my hands to my own blistering skin.

"Take us somewhere!" she said.

"I can't," I said. "I'm burning. You are too."

"You're not burning," she said sharply. "Neither am I. That's the extractor. It's trying to take your memories. That's the pain you feel. Now, take us to a core memory where I can tell you how to defeat this thing."

I tried. I tried so hard. "I can't. I lost the feeling."

"There's no time. I'll explain now. Do you remember when you were a child, your grandmother told you the story about the Sword of Choice?"

I searched my mind, but the memory was half-formed.

No time.

I collapsed

with the weight

of everything

into her arms.

Chapter Eighty-Three

I felt skin sliding off the bone.

Above, the dragon blotted out the blue sky, its form writhing, appearing more like smoke than flesh. One moment it was a shadow, snaking through air. The next, its face emerged from smog, grotesque and shifting, boiling like tar. Its eyes burned into me, two pits of blood-soaked veins.

The pain came down heavy and fast. My skull splintered, driving serrated pieces deep into my brain. I heard the cracking, the popping, the gushing inside my head. It was pulling my memories, splitting them apart like wishbones. I screamed and shut my eyes, as though that might do something.

It was useless. My head was liquid.

Then came a voice. My projection-mother was singing.

Let's take a joyride, darling, past the county line, where clocks are broke, and no one talks 'bout getting back in time.

Her hand was in mine. Her voice was solid, cutting through the pain. The melody rooted at something deep inside me. I latched on to the notes, scanned them, held them – I remembered. A song from years ago – a car ride with my mother when we sang along to a radio song, my hand resting in hers like it was my compass.

The heat paused.

My burning skin cooled.

I opened my eyes.

I was in the passenger seat of a moving car, sitting next to the memory of my mother. She couldn't see me. Couldn't sense me. Her hands rested easy on the wheel as she drove down an open highway. A crisp, cerulean sky lay ahead, endless.

I realized it then: I could travel by way of auditory memories too.

"I wasn't talking about a real sword, Pip," my projection-mother said.

I turned. She was in the back seat, sitting next to little-me.

"It's a story my mother told me when I was a child. And she told it to you too, right before she passed. Do you remember the warrior princess? The one with the Sword of Choice? She carried it in her heart, Pip. That's where her power came from."

The car moved on, tires billowing over asphalt, calm and metered.

I looked out the window. Sunlight sparkled across the glass as we passed a creek. In the driver's seat, my mother reached back, her hand hooking on to little-me's small fingers.

"I can't really remember it," I said, low.

"Hold my hand," my projection-mother said. "I'll try to transfer it to you."

I reached back, my fingers folding into hers. She held on to me tight as though to say everything would be okay. Little-me held on to my mother at the same time, their arms crossing with ours. Wind swept through the car, carrying the loamy scent of the creek.

I closed my eyes.

My projection-mother's story flooded into my mind. A dam busting open.

The story of the Sword of Choice, long entombed, came rushing in.

Chapter Eighty-Four

In my mind's eye, my grandmother's house murmured into being.

Her parlor was warm. Heat snapped from the fireplace, and the air was ripe with cinnamon and ginger, so thick it clung to my skin. A bookshelf in the corner leaned precariously, its spines worn and gritty. Gingerbread cookies rested on a side table, half-eaten. Little-me, barely five, sat nearby on a faded red love seat, her legs dangling over the edge, secretly slipping cookies into her mouth. Beside her, my mother sipped lemon tea from a steaming mug.

My grandmother sat hunched across from them in her old, frayed armchair. Her hands, wrinkled and soft, rested on her lap as she spoke. The memory felt flimsy, like silk caught in the wind. It hurt a little too: the ache of pulling something ancient and buried out of the dust.

"A long time ago," my grandmother began, her voice crackling like an old fire log, "there was a young warrior princess. She was alone. Her family was gone, swept away in the swell of a terrible war."

I watched the vision unfold, fading in and out like steam. I saw myself, a little girl, perched wide-eyed on the worn sofa, clinging to every word that tumbled from my grandmother's lips. My mother looked uneasy, as though the story might be too much for little-me.

My grandmother continued anyway. "But before her world crumbled," she said, "her parents gave her a sword. They called it the Sword of Choice. When fear found the girl, the sword gave her strength. When a charming thief tempted her, the sword led her away. When trouble stirred in her heart, the Sword of Choice brought her comfort. And when her mind whispered lies, the sword silenced it. It cut through the illusions of the world and showed her the truth. That *choice* was her greatest power, always there, never fading. Even on the most perilous paths, it would never leave her. The Sword of Choice was her strength, her guide. All she had to do was look within. And it was there."

The parlor began to warp, its warmth elapsing. The edges of the memory burned like flames to paper. Open air raced in, snapping wind through my hair.

I was in the car again.

But the sky had lost its blue.

It was smothered in gray. Thick with smoke.

★ ★ ★

Back in the memory of my mother's car, I looked out the window. The sky was peeling apart, like flakes of old paint washed away in a storm. I turned to look at my projection-mother in the back seat. She seemed uncertain too.

We were moving away from the core memory now, slipping toward an unknown place. The road stretched out ahead. It was strange. Foreign. Was this a repressed memory? Heat filled the car slowly. The dragon was near, lingering above, its effects invading the crevices in between, making me squirm. Little-me shifted in her booster in the back seat and muttered, "Is that a deer?"

The car swayed violently, avoiding the deer just as the dragon's claws carved into the roof.

"The Sword of Choice is inside you, Pip!" my projection-mother yelled as we spun. "You choose your thoughts!"

The memory of my mother fought to control the wheel, swerving until we spun and grated a guardrail – some accident I must've buried. I looked back. Little-me was okay, just shaken. I stumbled out of the car, stunned. The dragon slithered through the sky like black smoke. It warped from haze to flesh and back again, a massive, scaled face – monstrous and mesmerizing – surfacing between each shift. I felt myself slipping, my body burning. But I couldn't look away. The beast in the sky was pulling at me, draining me, killing me.

"Take us somewhere, Pip!" my projection-mother cried, coming out of the car, shaking me. "Smell it. Feel it. Hear it. You're in control! Take us to a core memory!"

But all I could feel was the demon's smoldering breath.

It was everywhere.

I could taste it.

Smoke. Fire. Ash.

Smoke. Fire. Ash.

I closed my eyes.

Remember, remember.

The crisp scent of burning leaves.

Soot smothering the air.

Sadness eating me alive.

I gasped and opened my eyes.

We were in a new memory. The woods, just outside my father's burning cabin in Snoqualmie Pass.

Core memories could be as brutal as they are beautiful.

The dragon was gone. But a fire remained.

My projection-mother and I watched the cabin's flames lick the night sky red.

"I'm sorry this happened to you both," she said quietly, meaning me and my father. "I'm sorry I couldn't protect you."

I leaned into her as the crackling of the flames filled the silence. And then I broke. I collapsed against her.

She held me, rubbing quiet circles on my arms. "The Sword of Choice is inside you," she whispered, reminding me. "It's the way to wake up without harm. The dragon, the extraction – it'll be waiting on the tarmac. But that's the only place you can wake, so you must confront it. When the final chime rings, you'll face the heat. The sword will ground you and remind you of the truth – that the dragon isn't real. The power is yours. This is your mind, and no one else's."

My voice frayed. I felt small. "I don't want to face that thing ever again."

Her hand came to rest over my heart. "I know, but it's the only way to wake up."

"You mean an actual sword?" I was grasping at the concept, desperate to understand. It was like trying to hold rushing water in my hands.

She kept her palm steady on my chest. "The sword is here."

"I don't get it," I admitted, my breath shaky. "I want to learn, I do. But I don't know what you mean." My chest rose and fell, but I tried to calm myself. I didn't want her to see me like this.

"Maybe holding something real will help," she said.

I kicked at the ground. "What about a stick? Should I use one of those?"

Her smile was patient. "We can do better than that. Close your eyes. There's another way to conjure. Not with scent. Not with touch. But with your heart. Feel it. Don't just hear my words – let them move through you. Find your inherent truth."

I shook my head. "I can't. I just can't. I'm tired of fighting this program. I'm tired of everything. Let's go back to the horse ranch. I don't care about the chimes. I don't care about waking up."

She leaned in, pressing her forehead to mine. "Close your eyes. Listen to my words. Feel my love, Pip. Here's the truth. Your father and I carved a sword once."

My eyes were clenched. I breathed in and out.

"We carved it from oak," she said, "the strongest oak we could find. Strong as the Earth's core. As strong as my love for you. The handle? It was a heart. Can you see it?"

I nodded.

"A reminder that love is always at the root of every choice. Keep your eyes closed now."

My eyes stayed clamped. But right then, it was hard to envision my parents doing anything except hooking wires into me, placing me in the program. Did I even know what I was doing back then? Did I agree to it? Or did they bribe me? Force me? Or was I just a kid who thought I was playing a game?

"We kept this sword with us," she went on, "from the time you were in my womb to every kiss planted on you. Sometimes we forgot the sword was with us, I'll admit. But it always returned. The sword is special like that. Once you know you have it, it'll always be there."

Fleeting images came to me. Camping with my father, picnics with my mother, holidays and quiet days, a listening ear when the dragon felt too real. I could uncover the whole truth, couldn't I? And still choose love as the leading force?

"I'm giving it to you now," my projection-mother said, "to know the worth and power of your own choices. Can you see it? It's there. The sword is waiting for you."

I reflected on her words. From oak. Love. Yes. Love was the root. The foundation. My mind, my heart, my choice. I could feel it now – growing, branching.

"Look at your hands," my projection-mother whispered.

I opened my eyes and gazed down.

My fingers, strong and whole, wrapped around the handle of a wooden sword.

Chapter Eighty-Five

The sword felt alive.

It was heavier than I expected. I ran my fingers along its fine, knotted grooves, admiring the wood that spiraled in on itself like an intricate fingerprint.

My projection-mother stepped ahead of me. "Come this way," she said urgently. "It's time to wake up."

The cabin's flames faded into shadows as we moved toward the tarmac. The air congealed with black fog, rolling over us like wind. My memory carousel was there, mysterious and vast. I turned and saw myself – my memory-me – reflected in one of its panes. She appeared as an obscure figure by the lilac-covered mailbox, concentrating, imagining, focusing until the image shifted, morphing into memory-me finding a message in the mailbox. The image stuttered, shaking with static – the unmistakable sign of an implanted memory.

Which nights had I planted each of these messages? After seducing Andrew in the hedges? After Wyatt's face met my fist? The timeline twisted and bent so much in my head, I wasn't sure I'd ever iron it out. It was a catacomb of dispersed realities tugging on my sanity. Andrew's words about the *Requiem* surfaced unwanted. Wouldn't it be nice to know peace? To erase it all and move on in ignorant bliss?

I stopped dead when I heard the snap of flames. The dragon had pierced the endless darkness of the tarmac, its body wreathed in smoke. Its jaw was sharp and lined with thorns. Its eyes were hollow, churning with waves of blood. I raised the sword, cowering from its surprising weight. I prepared for fire. For heat. But the dragon didn't breathe out – it consumed, pulling me in. I couldn't breathe. I was aspirating, scraping for air. My projection-mother thought I was ready for this. She was wrong.

"Raise it!" my projection-mother shouted. "The dragon isn't real, Pip. You can send it away. You have the choice to vanquish the thought!"

But I couldn't even breathe let alone tame my thoughts. Even with a righteous sword in my hands, I was powerless against death. It was too real for me to dismiss it as an illusion.

"I'm not ready," I said, wheezing. "I need to go back to the ranch."

The dragon inhaled, unbreakable and mighty as gravity's pull. My heels slid across the floor, my skin stretching toward the dragon's mouth. My projection-mother came forward, touching my shoulder. Her touch was a gravitational force all on its own, some final bolt keeping me together. I sensed her. Remembered my real mother. Her familiar, saccharine scent. I let my eyes fall shut. When I opened them, we were back in the field, hands clasped, knees pressed into the dirt. The sword stayed with me.

I gasped for air.

"Sorry," I heaved. "I couldn't do it."

Nearby, there was laughter. It sounded like fresh rain. I looked up. Little-me was cheering as the little foal ran free. Oh, how I knew this place. I knew it so well.

I turned to my projection-mother and took a full breath. "Let me just stay. It's safe here. For both of us."

"Safe," she said, stroking my face, "isn't always where you find your strength."

"Mom…" I begged. "Please."

She smiled knowingly and then pointed toward the edge of the memory. "Besides," she said, "they need you."

Her hand guided my chin toward the horizon.

I squinted as two figures walked through the light, something fierce blooming inside me.

Chapter Eighty-Six

My heart sank as I watched the figures move across the horizon, backlit by a sinking sun.

At first, they were nothing but shadows, just dark shapes moving languidly through dying light. But then, as the light shifted, their shapes became clearer. One of them was unmistakable with his tall, broad frame – Farley. His woolly hair caught the sun's last gilded rays. He walked with someone smaller, holding their hand. I tried to place the other figure. I thought it might be his friend from work – the one I dubbed Purple Shirt. But no…the figure was too small. As they got closer, my chest twisted. It wasn't a woman at all. It was a child.

I swallowed a gasp and turned to my projection-mother. "Who is that?"

The last trace of light danced on her face, sad and serene all at once. "Go to them," she said.

I shook my head. "I can't."

"You can."

"I'm not ready."

She put her hands over mine. "Tell her about the sword someday."

Her.

"But the dragon—"

"The dragon's power is a lie," she said. "It only has the strength you give it. Realize your power, and it will vanish. Remember the choice inside you."

I held on to her. "I can't do this without you."

"Live fully, for us both," she said. "I'm right here, safe and happy. I love you."

Her kiss was gentle, and her hug was deep. A goodbye.

Then, she let me go.

★ ★ ★

I walked forward, gaining distance. Ahead, the child drew me in; a visceral and protective compulsion overcame me. I turned back to see my mother. She stood among the horses. She was still waving goodbye, her arm moving soft and measured like ellipses on a page, something not quite finished. I thought of running back to her. But I snapped back around, only to find the child was gone. Only Farley remained. The space between us felt painful. I ran. My lungs blistered, but I didn't stop. Somewhere behind me, my mother faded deeper into my memory. I felt the squeeze of her settle there like a warm, content seed.

As the sun dipped, the field around me began to blur, and the landscape shifted, peeling back more of the truth. My projection-mother must've shown me a vision – of him, of the girl – inside the memory. But now I saw it clearly: he wasn't inside the memory at all. He was beyond it, near the shadows that led back to the tarmac, caught behind some veil as though the program had glitched and didn't know where to put him.

"Farley!" I called as I neared, my cry echoing against the translucent veil separating us. Its texture felt like a strange filmy membrane – warped and damp, almost alive.

His eyes widened, disoriented from the other side. He pressed his palms to the unbreakable film. I dropped the sword and tried to reach through, but the veil resisted, hardening at my touch. I tried again, then again. With each attempt, it softened slightly, warming to me. As if it was realizing I wasn't an invader. As though it knew me.

I pushed my arm through until I felt Farley's trembling fingers close around mine. I pulled gently, but the veil tightened like skin. Still, the more we persisted, the more it began to yield, stretching open and slowly allowing him through. He screamed as the oily material gurgled over his skin. When his body was finally free, he spilled into my arms, and we clasped like magnets, engulfing one another, drinking each other up. His breath came unsteady, his chest heavy against mine. Around us, the in-between space hung suspended, a half-formed place of shifting light and fog.

He pulled back to take me in. "I came. I got your message. Are you okay?"

I wanted to answer, but the words didn't come. Was he real? Or just another projection, some new illusion the program had concocted?

"Your text – it wasn't clear," he said, speaking quickly. "Then I realized you weren't in your room. I – I saw the open window. I called Cassandra right away. Her wife – Cybil – she helped me track this place down. You remember them, right?"

Cassandra. Cybil. The names floated around me like strange, uneven winds.

I searched his face. "Who is Cassandra?" I blinked, embarrassed; maybe I should've known. "Cybil, who?"

"You met them. They came over and hung out on the deck that one time. Cassandra. You know. From work."

Purple Shirt flashed into my vision.

I paused. "Wait. You said *her wife*?"

"Yes, Cybil. The cop. Remember? She helped us after the fire. It doesn't matter now. I'm here."

No, I didn't remember. The lines between real memories and the program's distortions blurred together, with some blotted out completely. What was real? What had been tampered with? But one thing felt certain: this was Farley. The way he held me, touched me, the concern in his voice – it was him. And yet, of all things to say and with time slipping away, my piddling qualms bubbled to the surface.

"I thought you might be having an affair with Cassandra."

Farley cracked a smile, and then he steadied himself.

"Is that funny?" I asked, prickly.

"Only a little," he said, softer now, apologetic. "I'm sorry if I ever gave you that impression, Pip. I really am. I would never hurt you."

"But you were gone at night. And you came home smelling like perfume."

He exhaled, running a hand through his honey hair. "The bars in Snoqualmie Pass are sardine cans. Perfume clings to everything. And yeah, I went out a lot. Too much." He hesitated, pawing at the crook of his neck. "But you were gone too, Pip. You stayed at work so long I thought you might move in there. You came home silent, like a zombie. I felt like I didn't know how to help you anymore. So, I didn't. I stopped. I stopped trying. I'm not proud." His voice tremored slightly. "I'm not saying I did the right thing at all. I let myself get lazy. Not from loving you, but from trying to fix things. I thought maybe if I ignored how bad our distance had become, that maybe it would just…go away."

My eyes widened. "Why didn't you tell me you felt this way?"

He looked down, his face coming up raw. "I didn't want to make things even worse. I didn't want to admit we had drifted. I thought if I didn't bring it up, it wouldn't be real. I do that sometimes," he said. He swallowed. I could tell this was hard for him. "After my parents died, I used to tell myself they were just on vacation. Coming back any day now. If I didn't say out loud that they'd died, then it wasn't true. I'd sit at the window every day, just waiting to hear their tires crunch over the gravel. I'd rake leaves endlessly just to be outside to catch them come home."

I grabbed his hands.

His eyes were honest. "I guess I started doing the same with you. I didn't want to lose you. But I think I pushed you away even more."

My throat ached. "I thought you were running from me."

"Never. I'm sorry. I didn't know how to fix things, so I pretended nothing was broken."

I stepped in closer. My chin found his shoulder. "I don't need you to fix anything. I just want you with me."

His fingers twined with mine. "I want that too."

I pulled back. "Farley, it's not just that. I got carried away with this program. I did terrible things. I'm sorry, I—"

"It's okay," he said. "Whatever it is, it's okay. You're my home, Pip. Always have been."

I smiled. "You're my home too."

"So we're both home now."

I leaned against his shoulder. While I enjoyed talking so openly with him – something maybe I needed to do more of – we both needed to get out of the program quickly. Maybe he sensed the same.

"I came here ahead of Cybil," he continued. "I knocked forever. I practically bashed the door in until someone finally came. Some woman. She rushed me in. I saw you. You were sleeping in a chair. They told me you were lost in some sleep program. It happened so fast. They told me: 'Get her to the tarmac.' I drank something, and the next thing I knew, I was here. There was a little girl with me, but she ran off."

He looked down, his eyes landing on the sword at my feet. "What is that?"

He could see it too. We were connected cerebrally.

I held it up but felt hope waning. How could I tame an illusion? Even though I had the weapon secure in my hand, I doubted my ability to wield it. You can arm yourself with all the weapons and armor in the world, but until hope is planted within, the battle is already lost.

Speaking of lost, I didn't like the young girl roaming rudderless in this terrifying world.

I held my belly, a strange instinct telling me who she was.

She was part of me. I wasn't just Farley's home. I was *her* home. She was growing inside me. I could feel it. I was going to be a mother.

And when I realized this, something shifted. The sword in my hand no longer felt like an impossible burden. It felt like a bridge from my past to my future. It wasn't just carved wood. It was everything. My choice. My will. A way to wake up and face whatever waited for us on the tarmac. This time, I wouldn't run. I would face it head-on. I would wield the sword. For us. For her.

"Come on," I said, moving us away from the veil, toward the shadows that led to the tarmac. "Let's wake up, together."

Chapter Eighty-Seven

Farley and I moved through the shadows.

On the other side, our feet hit the coal-black tarmac. The dragon crouched there, waiting, but it wasn't alone. The tarmac was crawling with wraiths, hundreds of them hissing like a fleet of snakes – dark, warped shadows that barely resembled human form. They moved like smoke, their eyes radiating a relentless blood-red glow. They came for us, clawing at the air, blind with insatiable violence. From the churning darkness, one emerged – large, fast, and putrid. It swung a feral sword of flames. The blade came down with a roar; the heat of it burned through my skin. I barely blocked it in time, the impact disorienting me.

Farley lunged in before I could fully recover. "I won't let them touch you."

But he was suddenly jerked away, fending off a creature I couldn't even see. He punched and slashed at nothing, his body writhing. His monsters were invisible to me. It hit me – we were in the same program, facing entirely different battles. If we stayed close, maybe we could get through this. I struggled my way back to him.

"We need to get back inside the memory carousel," I rasped, swinging at a wraith, cutting it off at the neck. "It's safer there." I kicked a wraith in the throat, but more importantly, I thought of the sword. My choice, my power. The wraith shrieked, turning to vapor.

I looked up and saw the obscure shadow of the little girl again. She raised a hand, pointing toward a carousel hovering in the distance, its lights approaching ominously.

"*In the what?*" Farley said.

"Come on, Farley. Give me your hand!"

A phantom charged at us, but we both ran toward the carousel before it reached us – Farley's carousel.

Chapter Eighty-Eight

We fell into Farley's memories.

But it was far from smooth. The program was faltering. Time was ticking down. Walls were crumbling to pulp. Maybe there were too many users activated. Too much pressure. Farley's panicked eyes met mine as the floor beneath us groaned.

"Is this…our bedroom?" he said. His voice trembled as we both took in our maroon room with its scattered mounds of clothes and piles of books amid the program's decay.

I tried to speak, but debris rained down on us. "Farley, this is your memory. But we can't stay here. I just needed a place to tell you something. Those things on the tarmac – they're not real. They're illusions. Don't give in to them."

He looked at me with a fear I'd not seen in him before.

"Think of a sword in your heart…"

His face twisted with confusion.

It sounded better coming from my grandmother.

A sudden column of rubble slammed down between us. We both hit the floor, coughing, crawling. Our hands fumbled through the soot until we found each other again. For a second, the room was silent, save for the whine of the walls about to collapse. And then came a noise. Panting. Low, soft, and rhythmic, coming from the bed. Farley snapped up.

"Oh my god," he said. "That's…that's us."

"Farley. I know this is confusing, but you need to focus. The sword…"

But he didn't hear me. He was too busy watching his past self rise from the bed after making love to my memory-me, leaving her behind. He raised his hands out of frustration. "Go back to her, dumbass! She's not done." He turned back to me. "*I* wouldn't have left her, you know."

I wanted to smirk, but time was chewing through the memory. The program was wearing thin, shedding layers like dried-up blood, and I could feel the heat of the dragon getting close.

I reached for his hand and pulled him close to me as dust swirled. "Since this is your memory, that means only you have the power to shape it or go to another one. Focus on something that grounds you – a scent, a touch, maybe. We can get out of here if you concentrate on it."

He looked at me like I'd sprouted twelve heads. But then he leaned forward, touching his forehead to mine. He reached for my hands and closed his eyes. I did the same.

When we opened them again, the chaos had vanished, replaced by a cool, quiet night. We were on the suite's deck, the firepit crackling low. Farley's friends sat around it, stained with dirt and sweat, their voices lively as they shared beers and cigarettes. The scent of smoke was thick in the air.

Cassandra and Cybil were there too, their hands clasped. I realized their names now, their connection. And there was my memory-me, slouched in an Adirondack chair, staring into the distance, disconnected, eyes fixed on the swaying leaves above. I must've just come from a mind-sucking Reverie Cloud session. Memory-Farley stood, walking over to her – *to me*. He placed his hands on memory-me's shoulders, massaging gently, like he might be able to pull her back to reality with his touch.

Cassandra leaned forward, seeming to notice memory-me's disassociation. Her voice cut through the tension. "Pip, what kind of music do *you* like?"

She was trying to loop me into their world, but I didn't answer. Didn't even acknowledge her. I wasn't there, not really. My body was present, but my mind was scooped hollow from a Reverie Cloud session, leaving Farley to pick up the pieces. I watched memory-me gape at the tree beyond the rail, watched her regard a leaf dropping from a branch as though it were a grand spectacle.

Cassandra stared at memory-me's vacant face, and then she offered empathetic eyes toward Farley.

Everything went quiet on the patio, except for the static twang of country music coming from a radio.

Farley's hand slipped into mine. Together, we watched as memory-me rose from her seat, sluggish and strange, drifting past Cassandra, mumbling something about The Reverie Cloud. Memory-Farley followed her, eyes full of worry, and then he came back to his coworkers with a forced smile. "I think she's just having some stress at work," he said. "We should probably call it a night."

The Farley beside me squeezed my hand, and I turned to him with a heavy heart. "You were trying to break through to me," I said.

"I thought you were angry with me that night. I didn't know what was wrong or how to help."

"You did help. Your touch. Your eyes on me. That was help. I just didn't see it then. I was...lost."

Farley half smiled, his lips quivering like he wasn't sure if he was allowed to say what came next. "You were lost *here*. In this program. It was draining you. I see that now. And I just stood around, pretending nothing was happening to my wife. You said someone was trying to hurt you, and I didn't do anything about it. I'm so sorry. I wish I could go back in time and be there for you."

I squeezed his hand back. "But you're helping now. You found me."

Farley had always been a rock. It wasn't something he acknowledged, or even something he believed about himself. But it was something I saw in him: the way he carried himself, the way he brought his friends together that night. Maybe he wanted community. Maybe he just needed support and didn't know how to ask. And I had chosen this memory to rewrite, to send myself a message about the program. But the rewrite came with side effects; it filled in the gaps with subconscious fears and amplified insecurities. All the while, Farley lived the moment in a completely different light.

He kissed me on the lips, and a cascade of his memories came to me in visions – Farley, alone in the woods, a bottle in his cold, gloved hand, the stillness of night against his warm, silent tears. The crack of gunfire as he practiced target shooting with no audience but a grove of oaks. The quiet drip of the woods as he stood over his parents' graves, coated in leaves, dusting dirt off their names. All this time, I'd thought his silence was a strength. I hadn't known it was a struggle.

The memory shifted. The floor turned to mud, and when I opened my eyes, we stood in the shallow part of the creek between my father's cabin and the hill leading up to our suite. The water rushed past my knees. Laughter bubbled ahead. I looked down at my hand. I was still holding the sword.

"Pip! Look at us," Farley said, deep with longing, spotting our past selves in a deeper part of the creek. "Look how young we are."

We'd landed in one of his older memories, the creek where we'd spent so many afternoons. In this memory, we were teens, tangled in fishing wire, laughing so hard that I could almost feel the ache in my gut again – how light and in love we were. Farley had brought us here, maybe without meaning to, but it had hypnotized him all the same.

He lumbered toward the figures in the distance as though under some spell. But as he moved through the water, his body began to fade. His outline shimmered like smoke from a wick just blown.

Behind me, the shadows of the memory wall curled inward, withering in on itself like burnt paper.

Time was waning, and with it, our chance to escape.

"Farley, we need to go!" I called, struggling through the water after him. My legs fought the brisk current, each step heavier than the next. "If we stay, we'll get lost here forever."

His figure wavered, the glimmer of the creek piercing straight through his torso. "I'm not lost," he said, pushing even more, keeping his head pointed toward our former selves. "I know this place. Let's stay here, Pip. Just a little longer. I want to feel this memory again."

"Sorry, we can't. We have to leave. Now."

"I just want a closer look."

"Please, Farley. You don't understand this program."

He didn't answer, eyes locked ahead, moving deeper still. "Oh, we're so in love here, Pip."

He trudged farther into the creek, as the waterline slurped at his waist.

Tears burned the crease of my eyes. "We're still in love," I called, wading after him. "Even more now."

He turned his head to me then, but I stayed planted, trying to be strong for him, for both of us. I couldn't blame him. I'd wanted to lose myself in my own memories too.

"Sure, we had butterflies back then," I called out in a plea, water gushing up to my hips, as I kept my sword above the current. "But that's not all love is. Love is walking into the unknown, knowing it might not be perfect, it might be hard, but you still choose to stay every day. I choose you, Farley. I choose to walk into new memory rooms with you. Even if they're thorny. Even if they're dark. Even if we don't know what's coming next. I want to do that with you. Always."

Just then, memory-Farley hoisted memory-me by the waist and carried her to the deepest part of the water, laughter bouncing off rocks and the arc of trees. They settled in the water there, belly-high, quieting each other with a kiss so full of life the air seemed to hum.

Farley – real Farley – reached out toward them. His hand stretched forward, desperate, but then it started to fade. He pulled it back quickly. "Pip!" he called. The water around him surged, threatening to pull him under.

Behind me, the fragile shadows leading back to the tarmac were disintegrating like ash. The landscape was filling in, artificially mirroring the woods and creek all around, trapping us in the memory.

My heart thundered. We were going to be left to die.

They'd connected Farley for this reason – knowing he would come for me, knowing I'd follow him if he got lost. If they couldn't get the schematic from my memory, then they wanted me dead so they could scrape what they needed. My projection-mother would never let me idle away in a memory like this. But Farley was new here. He didn't know. His memories were a comfort to him. They knew my mind, my memories. They knew I wouldn't leave him. That I loved him.

But they didn't know my strength.

I pushed against the water, moving in the opposite direction to him.

I sloshed back toward the remaining shadow, the water climbing all around me until I was shin-deep again. I needed to keep the gate open. But my foot snagged on a root hidden by the depths of the creek. I went down fast, smacking face-first into a mossy boulder. Everything went numb and white with pain. Blood dripped onto the rock, but I pushed myself up, reminding myself there was no blood, no pain. If I could keep the portal open, even just barely, I could secure our escape and then go back and get Farley. But the shadow was diminishing even quicker now, and as it did, something strange occurred. My body tingled with an almost euphoric sensation. I felt peace. Love. Perhaps Farley was right about staying a bit longer.

The sounds of our younger selves reverberated like a chorus in a canyon. My head lifted one last time. I saw the shadow – our escape – shrunk down to the size of a fist. There was no chance now. Feeble, broken, I let my face rest against the creek boulder. I felt its wet moss, its cold stone. The portal closed, inch by inch, and I waited.

This was it.

The joyous sounds of our past selves swirled together, crashing like cymbals, until all that remained was the calm sweep of water.

I closed my eyes.

Everything fell silent. I couldn't move. Couldn't speak. Couldn't even think.

But then, there came a lingering thought. The little girl. *My* little girl. Small as a bean, not fully formed but alive somewhere inside me. Maybe her image was crafted by my mind, created the same way my projection-mother came to be. I couldn't say. But I couldn't give up either, not with her wandering alone here. I couldn't let her become trapped before her life even began.

I opened my eyes.

A wet hand, strong and stable, landed on my shoulder. Farley.

His breath was jagged.

"Through thorns. Through darkness," he said, extending his arm toward me.

I slithered off the rock with Farley's help. He pulled me up, and I met his sage-brushed eyes. "Through roses and light too," I added.

We kissed, and then I pulled back. "There might still be time."

We moved through the creek together, pressing toward the small shadow. When we reached it, I moved my hand into the gray portal and immediately felt seething hot pain bite me from the other side. I yanked it back out.

Farley tried next, his jaw tight. The pain had found him too.

I gripped the sword, my knuckles taut, and reached for him with my free hand. "Let's try together."

We linked our fingers together and pushed into the shrinking shadow. The pain hit instantly.

"Look at me!" I shouted to Farley. "It's you and me, against whatever's out there."

With every ounce of strength, I snaked the sword into the portal's murk, lancing it open farther. As I cut, I thought about the sword in my grip. It wasn't some fanciful, childish thing, but something ancient, handed down through inherited memories.

The Sword of Choice had been my mother's story once, her salve, and before that, my grandmother's. Women who found their greatest power forged within. Now I carried it. And I'd pass it on to my daughter, too, with Farley beside me.

The shadow widened. Behind us, the memory began to fade, suturing itself up like a scar. I looked at Farley one last time.

"Thank you for coming back," I said.

There was his clumsy smile I adored so much. "You can always count on me," he said.

"All right," I said.

Together, we stepped onto the tarmac. It felt like walking into hell itself.

Chapter Eighty-Nine

Farley and I entered the tarmac side by side.

The wraiths seized at once, twisting and pulling at us, whispering, hissing, trying to force us back into the past. I looked at Farley. His jaw was slack, and his face was deformed from the scratch of their claws – a nightmare version of him my mind created to signal his pain.

A vast and final chime rang out. It vibrated up my spine like a bell of death.

Both our carousels were on either side of us, their towering frames and ark-like presence closing us in. Our windows shifted, showing memories of pain and love, dark and light. But when the chime struck, our carousel windows cracked and splintered, raining down memory shards that shattered like broken glass.

And then came the dragon. I shoved Farley sideways. "Watch out!" Fire rained down from the dragon's maw. Its bony, black-feathered wings flapped above us with a hollow rattle, and its teeth dripped down globs of something vile. The creature circled back and landed in a pool of flames on the far side of the tarmac. It stared at us. It knew us. It smacked its drool-soaked teeth, ready to feast. Beside me, Farley was breaking. His face was melting like hot wax, tortured by wraiths I couldn't even see. I couldn't even be certain what they were doing to him. I locked arms with him as he writhed.

The dragon clicked its teeth open, the slow scrape of stone on stone grating on my ears. I lifted my sword and looked the beast right in its blood-drenched eyes. My stance was firm, ready. But I noticed something strange – a sickly trail of dust was swirling into the creature, soaking into its primordial pores. I followed the dust with my eyes and realized it was coming from my own memory carousel. My memories were feeding it:

silent tears, raw, unheard screams, solitude. This energy was funneling straight into the dragon like gasoline. And the dragon guzzled it up; as a result, it became stronger, fatter, more powerful.

The dragon opened its jaws fully, showing off its terrible, infinite throat, and then its fire came. It boiled out thick and foamy, making the tarmac tremble like jelly. Farley tried to dive in front of me, but I raised my sword first, blocking the flames before they could touch either of us. Fire ricocheted off my sword, parting flames left and right, landing directly into our respective memory windows. Images and color spilled out of the windows like molten lava, hissing as they broke, landing at our feet.

The dragon screeched madly, and I saw its truth. Its power leeched on my memories – my pain. Evadere thought they could break me. Make me small. But a lie only works when you believe it. "I'm in control of you," I said. "And now, you die."

I centered my focus, severing the dragon's supply with nothing but my mind. The creature trembled, its body burning from within until it burst at the seams. It convulsed once, twice. Then, combusted, imploding into a mushroom cloud of black snow. The wraiths went with it, dissolving into the abyss, leaving behind nothing but silence.

From that silence came applause.

Part Five

Nocturne

Chapter Ninety

A cloaked man emerged from the shadows.

He walked forward, purposeful, shuffling through the dragon's ashen ruins. The man had no face. Just darkness.

"I won't be surprised if you don't remember me," he said. His words unfurled slow and measured. "But I know you."

I gripped the sword.

The man stopped several yards away from me. He tilted his head until it cracked. "I'm Victor Janess." He paused, letting the name soak in. "We've crossed paths before. You were just a child then. Bright-eyed. Beautiful. It's okay if you don't recall. Memories…they can be tricky sometimes."

His face appeared in pieces. I couldn't place him in my own memory. Only Andrew's. Victor Janess, one of Evadere's founders. I flinched as an image of him shooting down Wyatt's father flashed through my mind. Slowly, the shadow over his face dissolved, revealing angled, cunning features, the image of him now available to me. His wheaten mustache whittled to a point, and his dark coat billowed behind him like the sleek wings of a raven.

Victor strutted forward. I thought he might barrel right into me. My knuckles ached from pressure as I clenched the sword tighter. He moved closer, until he was barely an arm's length away. His presence was suffocating. My throat dried up; it ached to swallow.

"Back up," I snarled.

Victor's expression widened, revealing malicious blue eyes that appeared strangely beguiled. "You look just like your mother up close. It's the eyes, I think."

"Keep her out of this."

Victor paused and then smiled. "You share more than looks with her, you know. You share her mind. She was gifted. More than they ever gave her credit for. Maybe even more than your father knew." He brushed dust from his coat. "Losing her was regrettable."

"Stop it."

Farley stepped in front of me. "Back up. Now."

Victor's eyes burned right through him. "Oh, don't be stupid," he snapped.

I pulled Farley back to me. He didn't know what this man was capable of.

Farley shifted, tense and unyielding beside me, ready to strike.

But Victor stepped closer. The sword in my grip meant nothing to him. He pushed it aside like it was a flimsy tavern door. "Yes, your mother was one of our brightest, but you, Piper Screed – you are something else. A genius like your father. A natural at navigating this program. You have the best of them both in you."

Victor circled me, his eyes dripping over me like syrup. "I've never seen anyone manipulate memories like you, implanting them with such gusto, such...precision. Your imagination is otherworldly. And isn't that how one embeds memories? Through imagination? Far beyond what my stepson – my son – could ever achieve. He lacks the necessary creativity for this program – only does what he's told."

His sharp steps filled in each pause. "I've enjoyed watching you throughout the course of your sessions, Piper. More than you know. The things you've done in The Reverie Cloud, your potential...it's astonishing. Of course, we couldn't capture the entire *Requiem*, but that's why I applauded you. I've never seen someone weave through this program like you. Someone who puts up such a fight. I assume after I convince you to join my team, we'll be able to capture the last remaining particles of the schematic and your father's codes with ease, and with your consent and partnership this time. I'm sure there are many other memories we could explore that hold the answers we need."

I backed up, frantic, my breath wild. My eyes darted for a way out. "Where are the final waking chimes!?"

Victor huffed. "Piper, I'm paying you a compliment."

Farley stepped forward, fists clenched. "I said get away from her."

Victor snapped his fingers, and Farley was propelled across the tarmac as though jolted by an invisible force, crashing down with a sickening thud.

"Farley!" I cried.

My legs moved to chase him, but Victor lifted a hand.

My body locked in place. I was frozen.

Farley moaned in the distance, his body curling in on itself.

"He'll live," Victor said snidely. "For now."

Victor dropped his hand, releasing me.

I centered myself, my chest burning. "What do you want from me?"

Victor came close and drilled into my eyes. "First off, thank you, Piper. You've taken us far – so close now to completing your father's schematic. I debated another sequence, leading you back into the program, the computer room, the whole tired routine. But no." His voice eased, as though he were offering a charitable gift. "I wanted to talk to you directly. Personally."

I narrowed my eyes at him.

He smiled. It felt like poison. "I don't normally enter the program," he said. "Not anymore. But for you, I made an exception. I thought my words might hold more weight here. I no longer consider you a client or a tool to access your father's brilliance. I consider you a *partner*. I hope you might see it that way soon enough."

He came behind me and breathed over my shoulder. "I've been watching you a long time now, studying you. You've done remarkable things here, but I think you can do more." He moved my chin toward Farley across the way. "I've seen your memories too. *He* doesn't get you. Doesn't see your gifts like I do. He's a drag."

"You don't know what you're talking about."

His mouth twitched in amusement. "Oh, come on, Piper. We both know you'll remain a caged bird going back to your old life. Don't forget how isolated he made you feel. He's either at work, with friends, or off alone in the woods doing who knows what. Just eager for the next second to leave you alone…to rot."

"You're twisting the truth."

"Don't fool yourself. Work with me, and you'll soar."

"Never."

Victor's smirk faded. "Never? Really? Hmm." He looked over his shoulder at Farley, who was squirming on the ground, clutching his ribs. "Look at that poor little boy. Are you ready to watch him die? Because that's what's going to happen if you refuse my partnership. Both of you will die here. Him first, then you."

"I don't believe you."

"Your father didn't believe me either when I gave him an ultimatum."

I clenched my teeth. "What did you do to him? Where is he?"

Victor shrugged. "Dead, I assume. I lost track. He's useless to me now."

"You abducted him."

"He left us no other choice. We tried to access his memories, same as you. But unlike you, he had a firewall on any mention of the *Requiem*. Too many of our attempts left him a piddling fool. Last I saw him, he was a babbling madman. He didn't even remember who *you* were. So foolish of him to refuse to meet his end of the bargain."

I swung my sword sharp and furious at him and felt a snag. He shifted before I could catch him fully, but I cut something. My blade fumbled to the ground with a *clank*. I stumbled, steadying my footing. Victor regained composure cooly, wiping a bloody hand on his coat.

"You'll regret that," he said, licking his wound.

I stared at his smeared hand and reminded myself he was only an avatar here. Avatars don't bleed; they only *think* they do. As the thought struck me, the blood on his hand vanished. But he kept cleaning his hand, oblivious to the illusion. I chose to keep this observation to myself.

"You're a genius when it comes to some aspects of this program, but others you barely grasp," he said. "In many ways, Piper, you and I are alike. We both crave knowledge. We both want the truth. But there are stark differences between us. You're playing the game, but I wrote the rules."

His fingers spread slowly, then pressed together with dreadful pressure. I gasped as my throat tightened. His knuckles clenched, crushing my airway. He seemed to take pleasure in it. My lungs were scalding, crumpling like paper.

Farley's voice came from afar, broken and bruised. "Pip, I'm coming."

My vision blurred white. Death, a knock away.

Victor was getting to me.

I swung my sword clumsily but missed. His vicious cackle was going to be the last thing I ever heard. The air was thinning around me as the light died out. Darkness rolled in like a wave as my throat gave up.

And then he released me.

I fell to the ground, straining for air.

His boots clopped close, invading my space. He crouched down and used two fingers to casually snuff out my sword like it was a wavering candle flame. It evaporated into wood chips.

"Oh, Piper."

"I'll never help you," I wheezed, breathless. I slowly climbed to my feet.

No sword. No shield. Just me.

"Then I can't help you either," he said, smooth as stone. "You asked about the waking chimes. They are near, yes. But not for you. For me and Andrew. You and your husband – you can choose any memory you'd like to die in. Take your pick." His hand waved toward our broken carousels. "His or hers?"

I glared at him with disgust.

"Can't decide?" His smile tapered. "I could select for you. I could let you free in the memory of your father's disappearance, where you'll spend eternity searching for him. That could be exciting. Or maybe the suite fire?" He stepped closer. "Your own tailored hell."

I searched for Farley. He lay broken on the tarmac, folded over in pain, trying to lift himself. If I could hold my ground, maybe we could wake together. We could break free of Victor's threats, his cruel game. He was only an avatar, an intruder in my mind, feeding off what I gave him.

I thought of the dragon – how it lived because I believed in it. Victor was no different. But his conviction made him feel real, stronger.

Victor raised his hand, and suddenly I was stunned, rising from the ground. My feet dangled, gravity defunct. Farley levitated too, helpless across the tarmac. Victor's eyes burned with pompous glory – he was going to hurl us into one of my memories and leave us there forever.

But just then came a low and jarring chime. Unlike the six before it, this tone was deeper, more discordant. The remaining six chimes were upon us. The final countdown before waking or death. Victor faltered and dropped us both. Perhaps he hadn't anticipated the timing. He recovered quickly, his smirk returning. "Ah, good. That's my signal." He snapped his head to the void, looking around feverishly. Then he bellowed, "Goddammit, Andrew! Where the hell are you? Everly! Locate him – now. The fool isn't here."

A second chime struck.

Chapter Ninety-One

Everly Noon's voice seeped into the program like the voice of God.

"Andrew is showing signs of neural dissociation, Mr. Janess." Her soft, clinical voice reverberated in the void. Yet, her image was nowhere to be seen. She was awake, speaking into the program from the Circadian Room.

"Vitals are stable," she said. "However, he has yet to return to the tarmac."

"I can see that!" Victor barked.

"He appears to have drifted," Everly continued, unfazed. "Cognitive activity suggests a significant detour. He's stuck in a loop. I...I can't get him back."

A third chime.

Shadows danced across Victor's face like dark, roving tentacles. For a fleeting second, he appeared concerned for his boy. Then he turned with a sharp snap of his coattails. "Pity. Same as his mother. Weak minds always wander."

He clicked his fingers. At once, wraiths frothed into being, driving Farley and me toward our carousels. I strained to reach my husband, watching as he fought off the shadows, his hand outstretched for mine.

Victor pivoted at the edge of shadows. "What a waste, Piper Screed. You almost stood beside me. Almost."

He vanished into the darkness, his boots crunching over broken pieces of our carousels – an afterthought. I noticed a shard on the ground that his foot barely missed; some broken remnant glinting with light inside it. A memory. Movement danced across the glass-like scrap. I rushed to it and stooped to the ground to investigate. I gasped. There in the shard was the moving image of a young boy. Small, docile, back turned. The muted voice of a woman called to him – *Drew*. I froze. Andrew's figure overlaid the boy, a spectral outline, as though the two were one and the same, past and present coalesced. Andrew was trapped in a memory of his childhood. His beautiful mother Scarlet – coal-black hair, coral-red lips, sea-green eyes – was beside him.

Our carousels were damaged. Mine. Farley's. His. Entire sections were shattered by the dragon's inferno and the program's collapse. Andrew's carousel, like ours, had lost parts of itself. Slivers of his mind were scattered amid the wreckage. Rogue memories lay on the cold floor like iridescent stone. Andrew's memory, once held in place like a perfect mortice, now lay exposed and vulnerable.

The phantoms raked at me, but with Victor's back turned, I reminded myself: they were intruders. *He* was an intruder. I made the rules in my house. I didn't need a sword – I *was* the sword. It lived within me, deep and ancient. I called it forth – not the blade, but the idea of it – and the phantoms dropped, dense and lifeless like wingless flies.

I cradled Andrew's memory shard in my palms. He was going to die in there with his mother, and maybe he should. He loved her. Why should I stop it? What did I owe him? He was the one who got lost there. He did terrible things. Lured me, manipulated me. His regard for my life was threadbare. Then I looked ahead at the shell of the man he called father. Victor wouldn't just let Farley and me die – he'd let his son die too. A trickle of sorrow spilled through my veins.

"Andrew," I whispered, leaning close to the shard. I touched the glass, and it quivered beneath my finger. It created a tiny rip. I spoke his name again, quieter, as its ripples absorbed my voice. I hoped Victor wouldn't hear. Meanwhile, Farley was nearby fighting wraiths, unaware of the powers of his mind, but steadfast in his brute strength, nonetheless.

The boy in the shard froze. I could feel him. His fear, his confusion.

I focused harder, pressing deeper into the rip. I felt it give, hoping I wouldn't crush it.

"Come back, Andrew," I said. "Walk toward the shadows. It's time to wake up."

The boy in the shard turned, and I met his fearful eyes. For a moment, I thought Andrew wouldn't respond, that he was too deep into the memory, his grown form almost consumed entirely by the boy's. But then, the shape of him began to shift. The child fell away and there was Andrew, mature and solid in the shard. His face was pale, eyes full of shame, but he was whole.

"I'm sorry," he whispered, his voice echoing. "I got lost."

"You don't have time," I said. "And neither do I. Come back."

Fourth chime.

★ ★ ★

I held the shard in my hands, squinting into the simulacrum. The image of Andrew was gone now. Swirls of dark smoke distorted any clear sign of him. I looked up. Victor lingered in the far shadows. I wondered what he was waiting for, what came next. His coat shone with carousel residue; memory mites landed on him, caught in some cerebral wind. It struck me – like it or not, he and I were connected. Here. Now.

I looked back down at Andrew's shard. Dark as magma now.

He was lost. Gone. Swallowed by his memory.

Five chimes.

The tarmac began to tremble.

Ash fell from the vacuum above.

Fire sprouted from the foundation, licking at my heels. At first, it seared. My flesh burned.

But I let it pass through me. I thought of the sword.

They were simulating a fire, frightening us off the tarmac, herding us into our carousels.

"Farley!"

My voice rotted off into the smoke, a tinny bleep next to the roar of fire. I moved through a cloud of ash until I found Farley halfway between the tarmac and a memory. The wraiths were there, unseen to me, but I felt them – they were pulling and pushing him into his carousel.

"They're not there!" I yelled, yanking at him. "Farley, please!"

The memory was eating him whole. The suction of it was too powerful. His body warped and twisted, losing form.

"Pip," came a voice from the murk.

The voice startled me. I turned. Andrew.

He stepped through the darkness, threading his eyes into mine. "I did what you said. I walked toward the shadows. Thank you."

I grunted as I pulled Farley back with everything I had. "Your father…was going to let you…die there," I said in spurts, keeping my hands and eyes on Farley.

He looked toward Victor. "He's not my father."

The sixth chime was imminent.

The memory window became a vortex – a mouth of swirling color – pulling in whatever energy source got close.

Farley was slipping into it. My hands pulled at him, useless.

I was going to lose him.

Andrew stepped beside me. He didn't speak. He reached. We both pulled at Farley, battling smoke and brimstone from the tarmac, and towed him out like some root stuck in the grips of hell. Farley fell onto me as we landed in a stream of fire. Farley was about to scream, but I grabbed his face and kissed him.

"The fire is not real," I said against his lips.

He breathed heavy and fearful into my face, scrunching his brow.

When the sixth chime came, the tarmac began to crack.

Everly's serene voice fell from above. "You will be leaving The Reverie Cloud momentarily. We hope you enjoyed your dream experience—"

It was over. We were going to wake up. We made it.

"*Stop!*" Victor roared. "Restart the program. Get them in their carousel cages. Do not let them wake up."

Everly's voice returned. "Mr. Janess, are you certain?"

"*Do it!*"

I concentrated on Victor through the flames, opposite me on the tarmac. He was waiting in the shadows, away from the fire, to watch us die, to ensure I either joined him or wandered off to my death. From there, he'd scrape whatever he could from my mind. I wondered if he let his wife, Scarlet, die this way too. But no. He'd loved her, or so Andrew had said.

Flaming timbers fell from delusory wooden arches above. Another illusion – this time, a bizarre replica of my father's burning cabin. Victor was using my mind against me, my fears, convincing me of its realism. But I saw him now for what he was. Small. A man afraid of losing. Too meek to walk through the very flames he created. A man who didn't even know his weaknesses were on display. A delicate bird. He had called *me* caged, but I wondered, what if he was the imprisoned one instead?

What made one mind more powerful than the other? The ability to cut through illusions. I saw us both in our true states – asleep in pods, connected by wires linking our minds. If he could maul into my thoughts, I could worm into his.

I remembered the wires connecting me to my mother – thick, leathery, stinking of burnt rubber. I could feel them now. See them. That's all the mind is: imagination built from data pulled from the waking world. And I had all the data I needed. My senses, my tools. I understood now why my father wanted me to harness them all.

I closed my eyes and thought of the wires. My mother's wires.

Slowly, a faint blue specter of wire materialized. I extended it with my mind; its ghostly shape snaked toward Victor. It curled around his head, forming a cage-like halo, a visual anchor I could use to take control. The collapsing program oscillated between his shouts to Everly and the eroding world around us. I tugged the wire taut, feeling its pull meld us – our minds pressing together like resin settling into the grains of wood.

Victor felt it. He fought against the connection, jerking as though he could sever it. I didn't let him. I dragged him onto the fire-scorched tarmac, reveling as he stumbled against his will.

From the void, Everly's voice cut through. "Mr. Janess, what would you like me to do now?"

Chapter Ninety-Two

Victor flailed, his hands clawing at the air.

I felt his fear as I pulled the wire tighter, moving him toward me. He was losing control, and he knew it.

"Initiate waking sequence," I mouthed.

Victor's mouth moved without his consent, the words leaking out of him. He blinked, angered by the sound of his own voice forsaking him.

"NO!" Victor cried, fighting his words. "Don't!"

Everly's placid voice interjected. "Mr. Janess, can you please confirm? I'm getting mixed communications, and we're running out of time."

I pulled harder. "Initiate waking."

"Thank you. I will now initiate waking," Everly said. "Please ready yourselves on the tarmac."

"Farley!" I called. "Stand by me. We're waking up."

Farley stood shaking, a hand outstretched for me, for my belly. Did he assume the little girl we saw was ours? The thought warmed me, but it caused me to break focus. Victor seized on that tiny, minuscule slip. Nausea flooded through me as the world flashed white. I was hurled toward my carousel, crashing to the ground.

I blinked my eyes open slowly. Victor was coming toward me fast.

"Prepare for waking," Everly called from above.

Victor moved in and hovered over me. "You think you have control, Screed," he said, "but this is *my* program!"

My back was against my memory carousel. There was nowhere to run. Victor's eyes radiated venom. Farley ran to me, Andrew too, but suddenly, Victor raised his hand and parts of my carousel shattered down at the pull of his hand. It broke like glass, my past turning to crystal, raining down on me my sins, my shame, my pain, my longing, my love, burying me alive.

"STOP IT!" I shouted, brushing debris off my body.

But he didn't stop. He was relentless.

"Launching..." Everly said.

Victor lunged for my neck. Farley came beside me, fighting him off, an ocean breeze against his vile storm. Andrew came too, pulling at him as though evil could be plucked like a splinter. The four of us became entangled. Four dots on a neural highway.

"Thank you for visiting," Everly's voice echoed, calm and detached. "You will now be exiting The Reverie Cloud."

The tarmac flashed white as Victor shoved me into a memory portal. I grabbed hold of him. If I was going to die here, he was coming with me. I fell backward, atomizing into my memory, pulling him along. I just didn't expect Farley and Andrew to follow.

Chapter Ninety-Three

When the light struck my eyes, it took a moment to adjust.

Horses stirred in the distance. The quiet thrum of crickets came from the grasss. The horse ranch – my core memory. The simulated haven my parents created. I'd been here countless times throughout my childhood, though some of those visits were in hard-to-reach places of my mind or suppressed entirely.

But something was different this time. Sure, I was learning memories never stand still. They shift like sand. Move like water. Bend like grass. They're not paintings fixed to a wall, the same each visit. They're redrawn each time you enter the room, the lines and colors never quite the same. Something always a little strange, a little different. But always familiar. Yet this version, this rendering, was completely new to me.

My memory-mother stood ahead near the gate. She looked different here. Frantic. I wanted to move closer, to pull the curtain back on what I'd forgotten. But I remembered the vulture beside me.

Victor blinked into the light, disoriented, a foreigner here. His face contorted as he took in the scene. "What the hell is this?" He turned in a panicked circle, scanning for something familiar, something he could control. There was nothing. The open expanse offered no screens, no console. Only infinite grass and sky.

"It's my memory, Victor. My world."

Victor's head snapped back at me. "Your world?" he sneered. "Your world? No, no. This is not your world. This is a fucking tomb!" he spat. "This cannot be happening. It can't be—" He cut himself off, pacing like a caged tiger. He breathed heavily, scanning the field for answers. "My god. You have no fucking idea what you've just done. You trapped us. You killed us. All of us!"

"I didn't trap us," I said calmly. "You did."

His lip curled. He was about to move on me, but he stopped himself and turned to Andrew, pointing a trembling finger. "You have a back door. Tell me you do. Tell me you've got an escape plan."

Andrew stared at him, motionless, his face drained. "You said it was your program," he muttered, cold.

Victor lunged, gripping Andrew's collar with a knuckled grip. "How the fuck is there no override after what happened to Scarlet and Cove? What have I been paying everyone for? There should be a forced exit – some command sequence if your avatar hasn't made it to the tarmac. My life's work should not be this vulnerable!"

Andrew ripped himself free. "Well, you killed the person who could've built a back door. Stanley Fink was working on an escape mechanism. But you silenced his voice. And by the way, you almost let me die in the program too."

Victor was shaking. "*Fuck!*"

Andrew exhaled sharply. "Listen, I don't want to die here either. I'll look for an irregularity. Some kind of crack in the framework. But don't expect much."

Victor's face twisted. "I cannot believe this!" he shouted. "Everly!"

Andrew angled downward, rounding a slope. Mountains loomed in the distance, blue and white brushstrokes smudged against an eternal sky. The shadow of a hawk swooped over the grass, seeming to guide Andrew's way. Victor moved to follow, but Andrew was too quick, fading down the hill, leaving Victor stranded. He clawed at his hair, pacing frenetically.

"Everly!" he howled, but we were alone now.

He screamed an unholy roar, and a small host of sparrows rose from the grass. Then he turned his rage on me; he and every ounce of his fury came barreling toward me. Farley moved in front of me, landing a meticulous uppercut when Victor got near, a beautifully cruel punch, staining him crimson in our minds. Victor staggered back, touching his face. He smeared his blood absently with a shaky hand. Then he laughed, crazed and wild, a sound that didn't belong in this place. "You're children," he spat, still laughing. "Just children." His laugh grew darker, his grin twisting. His voice descended into a near-growl. "*Stupid* children. I pity you. I do. Go ahead. Die here. You don't know the way out. I do. So long, Screed. Enjoy eternity."

He stumbled off belligerently. Farley eyed him. I knew what he was thinking.

"He's bluffing," I said.

"He said he knows the way out."

"No, he doesn't. The way out is right here."

His eyes clouded, searching my face for answers. "What do you mean?"

I pointed to my memory-mother in the distance by the ranch gate. "She knows the way out. I know this memory. It's coming back to me."

"What is it?"

"It's the place where my mom showed me how to wake up. She knew an escape hatch. It's where she lost her life in the process."

Chapter Ninety-Four

There, beyond the wooden gate, in the amber light, stood the mother horse and her foal.

And there too, across the slats of knotted wood, was the girl I once was, her mother brushing tears from her face. Farley and I moved toward the pen, slow and soundless. Little-me slouched crestfallen beside the gate.

"That's you?" he said.

I nodded.

He took my hand and squeezed it firm.

This place had been reshaped so many times, molded and corrugated like clay. It was a synthetic environment, one they used to create worlds that would eventually become templates for The Reverie Cloud. And yet, this place was also my refuge. A comfortable lie. It was a space built to soothe, shield, and hold me whenever the program or life became too much.

My heart was torn.

My mother was kind. My father, brilliant.

I loved them. They loved me.

But love is flawed.

They shouldn't have used me for their gain.

Should I be angry at them for experimenting on me? For pushing me farther than they should have? Part of me might always hold that grudge. But anger shouldn't write the whole story. And neither should blame. They were people, not gods. They were part of my story. Part of me. Accepting what happened might help me move forward. Even love, with its cracks and scars, is still worth holding on to.

The memory swam into focus. Little-me sat weeping. She was lost. Confused. Perhaps she forgot how to walk toward the shadows. My mother knelt beside her. She had come into this program, into my mind, to rouse me. To pull me out. To force eject me.

Her freckled face bunched as she whispered something to little-me, too low for me to decipher. Then she moved, turning in a way I hadn't expected. She took little-me by the shoulders and forced her down, head to earth. A large rock waited there. My mother pressed little-me's forehead into the cold stone. "I'm going to hurt you," she whispered, "but it's the only way."

I heard her words perfectly, as if she spoke them right into my ear just then. I was connected to the memory. The pain came upon me too. The pressure was mild at first, but then it spread like brushfire, intensifying.

Farley stiffened beside me. "What is she doing?"

At first, I didn't know. But then came understanding. This wasn't cruelty; she was breaking through the program's control. She was using pain as a forced override. Her last-ditch effort to save me from the prison of my mind.

"It's pain," I whispered. "That's the back door. It's how you wake up if you miss the waking window."

Farley tightened. "I don't understand. I felt pain on the tarmac. More than you can imagine. Why didn't I wake up then?"

I looked at him, and for a moment I felt the hurt he carried.

We both winced as little-me interrupted us, crying out, her voice bigger than it should be. An open wound. "Because in the tarmac and in memories," I said, "there are certain protections. The program lets you feel pain, but it's only simulated. It never actually reaches the body. That's how they keep you asleep." I stared ahead at the scene unfolding. "But not this one. This one is raw. My dad must have done something from the outside to allow physical pain through." I looked at Farley, then at my memory-mother in the distance. "Because if pain can cross over – if the body feels it too – that breaks the barrier between worlds. It wakes you up. My mom must have known that. She knew pain would force me awake." Still, I wondered: *Why didn't they tell Victor?* Maybe it was something new they were only just testing. Or maybe they knew him too well. Knew he'd use a tool like this for torture – not escape.

In the memory, little-me wailed, and I doubled over inside. My mother's hand trembled on her nape, but she didn't stop pushing her head into the rock.

Farley gasped. "Pip, she's hurting you."

"No," I cried, a tear skating down my cheek. "She's saving me."

I understood now.

This was the escape.

This was how you woke up.

Pain.

At least here – in this memory room, where my father removed protection.

Little-me thrashed, trying to flail her off. "I can't, Mom! Let go of me!"

"We're running out of time. If I don't make it back," my mother shouted, unsteady, "I'll leave a piece of myself inside you. You won't be alone. I'll be there, in another form. A projection of me. But only if you consent."

"Mom," I whispered to myself. "It was you. Part of you."

Farley shuffled. "What does that mean?"

"I will always be with you," my memory-mother said. "But you have to agree. It's your choice."

Little-me turned to face my memory-mother, her sobs quieter now, as she understood the cost of what was being asked. The pain was still there, but I felt a strange comfort. I knew it then, as I knew it now: I couldn't let her go. Her form didn't matter.

I watched the scene blossom, my heart hulking. This was it. The moment I'd forgotten. The moment that shaped everything that came after.

I watched as little-me whispered, "I accept. But please try to wake up too."

"I'll try," my memory-mother said. "I'll try my best."

The memory began to dissolve. I was waking. Waking then, waking now.

Farley gripped my hand. "Pip, you're disappearing."

"Pain," I said, hearing myself from far away. "You have to let it move through you. It's the way out."

"Don't leave me!" he cried.

At that moment, Andrew came beside us and knelt. "There's no back door," he said, breathless. Then, he flinched. "Pip, you're fading."

I took his hand, Farley's hand. I held them both.

"There *is* a back door," I said. "It's right here. It's pain. This isn't your memory, so I don't know how this might affect you. But maybe if you hold on to me, we might be able to keep our connection intact and wake up."

"Pip," Farley whispered, trying to hold my glitching form in place. "Oh god, you're barely there. I love you."

"Don't let go of me," I said. "Press. Feel. Don't run from the pain. Let it pass."

As I spoke, the memory around us began to fade, its colors of wheat and jade bled into one another until it was just the three of us knitted in a muddled, blurry field. I lowered my head to the earth slowly, pressing it into the dirt. Farley and Andrew imitated my movements. And then I lifted my head up and smashed it back down again with force.

Part Six

Dawn

Chapter Ninety-Five

When I woke up gasping for air, the first thing I thought of was the girl.

Was she real? Was any of it real? The visions. The dragon. The sword. My mother.

I tried to move but quickly realized I was strapped down. The room ached with bright light and was filled with a throbbing alarm. It blared from the screens, drilling into my head that already hurt from my painful awakening. Farley jerked beside me, his panic mirroring mine. I wanted to reach for him but couldn't; the straps groaned in my ear.

Andrew stirred on the far end, craning his neck to see Victor behind us. I hadn't noticed he was there at first. In my periphery, the old man lay still as stone, eyes shut. My heart pounded at the sight of him. Then an image of him wandering a barren field flashed through my consciousness. How long would it be until he figured out the secret, that pain awakens? Until then, I could feel some parasitic trace of him roving the folds of my mind. I could sense his frustration, his revenge.

The room whirled with Evadere operatives, their faces obscured by black masks. They moved slick and precise. Fast shadows. Checking vitals. Checking Victor. My head throbbed. Silver specks swam through my vision.

"Pip," Farley slurred from his pod. "Are you okay?"

"Yes," I breathed. "We made it out."

My fingers were trembling when I lifted them. The black patches were there. Proof of reality. I tried to move again, but a cold, gloved hand shoved my chest back down.

They weren't done with us.

But they *were* distracted.

They hovered over Victor's silent body, their lord, oblivious to a sudden banging at the door. The thud grew harsh and urgent, blending into the hellish beeping. They didn't look up. Didn't waver. Not until a bullet struck, bursting the hinges clean off.

"Move him to the back!" a voice shouted.

A woman in dark tactical gear barged in, her boot slamming the door open with brutal force. A gun glinted in her gloved grip. I couldn't place her at first. "Everyone down! Now!" Her voice was sharp enough to score glass.

I squinted at her name tag. Officer Cybil Hayes. The cop Farley had mentioned. Cassandra's wife. Cassandra stumbled in behind her – Purple Shirt – clutching a gun with far less confidence, trying to mirror her wife's ironclad focus. This wasn't sanctioned. They weren't here under orders. This was personal. This was a rescue.

And then Aunt Vera stepped in, calculated and composed. A gun rested in her steady hand. Her eyes swept the room, calm as a millpond, yet protective – a mother bear ready to strike.

I couldn't see the chaos behind me, but I heard it. A low and desperate shuffle to save Victor's body. A gunshot fired from behind me, and the women ducked.

"Call for backup!" Cybil shouted, storming farther in, firing.

Evadere scattered into the bleak edges of the room, dragging Victor's limp body, their boots scuffling coarsely against the sterile floor. They slipped through an exit I'd been too blind to notice before. Then Aunt Vera moved like a falcon. She knelt to me, cutting my straps with a pocketknife. My mind screamed as the halo tore free, like ancient glue ripping from my skull. My head pounded as reality settled in. She didn't pause – Farley was next. But then came a shot. A rogue bullet dug into Vera's shoulder. She fell to the floor with a hard thump.

I dragged myself to her, my legs like seaweed. My shirt came off without a second thought, revealing a bra beneath, and I pressed it to her wound. The fabric soaked up red. Vera lay still, her eyes losing light.

"Hold on," I murmured. "Please."

She had always been a mystery, this woman who saved me more times than I deserved. I burned with shame how I'd made her a villain – someone trying to replace my mother, someone I thought meant me harm. But I was wrong. She wasn't a threat. She was just Vera – flesh and bone, bruises and battles, a carousel of stories I'd never see. And all along, her love had been there ready and raw. It was in her quiet actions, her sidelined safekeeping. Now, as she lay there bleeding, I held her hand, a cavernous ache swelling inside me. I couldn't lose her. Not another mother. I wouldn't survive it.

Cybil and Cassandra were at Vera's side in seconds. Cybil, sturdy and compact, scanned for danger, while Cassandra, lean as a willow, knelt over Vera like a medic.

"I'll call an ambulance," Cassandra said, already moving for her phone.

Officer Cybil stood, eyes sharp. "I need to find their location before backup arrives," she said. "We can't risk them swarming the moment we move. Cass, watch my back. Pip, keep Vera comfortable."

They each offered me a quick glance before sweeping into the hall, leaving a false sense of comfort in their wake.

I exhaled for the first time since waking up.

But it didn't last.

The back door opened.

Then – *click.*

A gun cocked behind me.

Chapter Ninety-Six

Everly Noon held the gun steady.

Her sunny hair was pinned back in a tight twist, sweaty strands clinging to her temples. Sleek Reverie Cloud-branded clothing gave her a polished look that clashed with her unraveling expression. Too many hours spent in the Circadian Room, executing Victor's commands, must have left her brittle.

"We don't want trouble," I said. "My aunt was shot. She's bleeding. Please, help."

I hadn't realized Andrew was free until now. He leaned into Everly, balancing himself as he worked his way to consciousness, his hand familiar against her waist. They were together. I felt no jealousy, only shame that I'd ever trusted him.

"I can't let any of you leave," Everly said. "Victor would have my head."

My own head pounded. The hint of him still in there.

"He tried to kill us!" I pleaded. "How can you follow someone like that?"

I caught Andrew's eyes. For a moment, I thought he'd slip free of her, detach at the seams. Didn't we both just witness his stepfather's cruelty? But instead, he tightened his arm around her, a clear choice. I was clinging to false hope. Evadere was his family. The Reverie Cloud, his religion. Disobedience was out of the question, even if Victor's love was unattainable. But I knew he was the only way to get out.

"Andrew," I said, fraying. "You know me. You know who I am. We were kids together—"

Everly's voice cut through mine as she locked both hands over her gun now. "He was playing a role to get what we needed," she said. Her eyes flashed with panic, looking to Andrew for backup. "You know Victor would never approve letting her go after all this. She needs further testing. Further sessions. More—"

"Enough!" I shouted, pressing harder against Vera's wound. "Victor isn't waking up! He's going to die. Just like our mothers – lost in a memory. *My* memory."

Everly fired impulsively. The bullet hissed past my ear, so close I felt its heat. Vera moved before I could register what she was doing. With a quick shrug of her unwounded shoulder, she fired her gun and then slumped back down. I looked down at her with shock.

"Where do you think Farley learned to shoot?" she muttered with a defiant smirk, then she winced in pain.

Everly shrieked as the bullet clipped the back of her hand. Her gun skidded across the floor, forgotten, as she dropped to her knees, clutching the wound. Andrew darted to a drawer to find a bandage, his eyes meeting mine. "Go," he mouthed, as blood pooled down Everly's arm.

Meanwhile, Farley came to my side, helping me haul Vera to her feet. We staggered for the door, each step a battle, pain pounding in my ear.

We were free of The Reverie Cloud.

Almost.

There was one stop I needed to make first.

The basement.

Chapter Ninety-Seven

In the hall, Farley and I steadied Aunt Vera between us.

Cassandra and Cybil found us there. They took my place, ensuring Vera was stable. They spoke to me, but their words spiraled past my ears. The pain of waking still clung to me, my mind trapped in fog. Displaced memories came to the surface only to sputter and die before they had the chance to burn bright. I imagined them broken, in messy piles, waiting to be swept away. And the thought of my father – somewhere in this archaic, stone building, dead or alive – devoured any sliver of focus.

I pressed on without thinking. The elevators were dead, but a stairwell gawked open. Its walls were lined with exposed stone. A slim metal rail guided me down a cold set of stairs. Dim, recessed bulbs provided little help, casting haunting shadows as I descended. My footsteps were sharp against the concrete, but my thoughts were clogged with white noise. I pushed forward, leaving them all behind. The angular spiral of stairs seemed to lurch on. Then – footsteps. Aunt Vera's voice echoed. "Wait! We're not leaving you! We're sticking together." I stopped, looking up the gray shaft of stairs. Vera didn't need more battles to conquer; she needed rest. I climbed back to them, panting, forcing my mind to think straight. How could I leave her like this? I was hell-bent on finding him. That's why. I was so close.

"I don't want to hold anyone up," I said, eyeing Vera. My chest clamped at the sight of her wound, still bound by my shirt. "Especially you. My god. But I need to find my dad. I know he's down here somewhere. Please, go without me."

"I believe you, Pip," Aunt Vera said. Her voice was weakening by the minute. "Farley, help me down these stairs. Let's stay together."

It seemed she expected Farley to offer an arm, but instead, he swept her up into his capable arms, cradling her like a child. Without hesitation, he carried her down the stairwell.

A basement corridor came upon us. A dead end. Uneven stone walls seemed to ricochet any sign of light. The air was damp and earthy here. There was a single door at the end of the corridor, but its weathered, iron door was sealed shut. I kicked at it and banged, hoping someone inside would hear me. "*Dad*," I shouted. "*Dad!*"

"Stand back," Cybil said. She shot at the door, but the bullet clattered against the hinges, dropping down like sloppy nails. I wondered what secrets Evadere was keeping in there. What were they protecting so fiercely? Only a bomb, it seemed, would pry the door open.

I moved down the passageway, my feet clicking against stone. My eyes hunted every shadow for a clue – any sign of my father. A narrow stairwell came upon me quickly, gaping downward. At the bottom, heavy wooden double doors sat slightly ajar, buried in cobwebs, buzzing with an ancient aura. They screamed *do not enter*, as though they once guarded crypts, long before Evadere ever claimed this building. I shoved them open. Cold air rushed in. The space revealed itself – a vast concrete parking lot drowning in darkness with only a few flickering bulbs overhead. Stone pillars held up the weight, casting oblique shadows on the cracked foundation.

Cybil fired into the hollow space. Her bullets rattled like coins as they dropped. Gunsmoke hung in the air as I stepped into the empty lot. The cold nipped at my bare shoulders, and the pressure of everything slammed into me at once, making it difficult to catch my breath.

"Here," Cassandra whispered. She sidled beside me and slipped something soft into my hands. I looked down – it was her crumpled, lavender sweater. The sight of it startled me. I pulled it over my shoulders. "Thank you," I muttered.

We all moved farther into the space. My eyes adjusted to the low light. I noticed a few scattered cars and rusted pipes hissing overhead. The place was deserted. I bolted forward, running between cars and pillars. "*Dad!*" I cried. "Are you in here!?"

"Pip!" Cybil's voice broke the darkness. "Vera's getting cold. She could crash out. We need to leave *now*."

I stopped dead and hurried back to them.

"It's just a graze," Vera said, trying to sound convincing. But her face was pallid and sweat crowned her brow. "I'm lucky. It missed anything important."

Officer Cybil wasn't buying it. "Honey, it doesn't look good. We should go."

Vera caught my eye. Her smile was genuine but weak. "We've come this far, Pip. Find him."

"We're losing time, and so is she," Cybil said straight out.

"Let's leave," I said.

But suddenly, an overhead door groaned open on the other side of the lot. High beams flashed bright, nearly blinding my retinas. A massive SUV spilled down the driveway from the outside world and passed through the open metal door. The midnight-black vehicle roared with life. Its tires drilled through the darkness. I was certain it was going to crash right into us. But then, it screeched to a halt, squealing as it slid sideways, stopping inches from us in a brute display of power.

The side door slid open, and Andrew stepped out.

In the front seat, Everly sat slumped, her bandaged hand pressed to her chest, soaked through the wrap. Beside her, some masked driver gripped the wheel, waiting impatiently.

"You're making a mistake!" Everly shouted. "Think twice, Andrew."

Cybil and Cassandra squared their guns on him.

"Wait!" I said, lifting a hand to them.

Farley called out from the shadows, Vera firm in his grasp. "Pip, stay away from him."

"It's okay," I said. "I can handle this."

I didn't trust him. I never would again. But without closure, he'd keep finding ways to make my life hell.

I met Andrew where the hum of the car's white lights spilled a thick, synthetic glow. He stood there disoriented yet staunch. I wondered if his mind felt just as broken as mine. There were parts from our Reverie Cloud experience I remembered, and parts I just couldn't place. They were gone. Snuffed out by Victor.

One of the headlights on the SUV flickered, then sizzled out. Andrew turned his head to the dead light and then gave me a crooked grin. "Looks like I'm the one with the bad bulb now."

I looked him over, every version of him crowding the same body. Who stood before me now? Was it the slick, smiling Andrew from Nyxyn? Or was it the one from the program – manipulative and cutthroat? Or could I be looking at the little boy, Drew, who just wanted to see his mother one more time?

I chose to see the little boy.

"I'd help you fix your light," I said. "But I don't think you want that. You want to keep things just as they are."

He hung his head low. "I know you may not understand, but I *still* see the program's potential. Maybe you might see it too, someday."

I looked past him and saw Victor's limp body through the open door in the back seat of the vehicle. He was hooked to tubes and wires, some breathing machine shooting air into his lungs. An Evadere assistant labored over him, keeping him steady. A horrid sensation grabbed at me when I saw him – a pull, almost physical; it scratched at my mind, shrieking like nails over glass. I pressed my fingers to my temples, forcing it away.

"I hope this isn't goodbye," Andrew said, unaware of my struggle. "I hope we come to a middle ground. The program's in you as much as it's in me. I hope someday you'll see that. Until then, you deserve peace."

He dug into his pocket and drew out a small chain of jangling metal keys. He removed one from the bunch and placed it in my palm.

"Over there," he said, nodding in the direction the headlight was facing. "Storage room."

I turned and saw a weathered metal door in the near distance caught faintly in the light. It was old, with a rusted handle, nearly swallowed by the expansive lot.

"Pip, that's enough," Farley called.

As Andrew walked back to his vehicle, Everly droned a litany of accusations at him, lecturing him on his disobedience. Andrew ignored her and then shot me a look.

"Told you it was life-changing," he said with a smirk.

* * *

I watched Andrew's truck peel off into the distance. They stormed out the door, up the driveway, and into the world beyond. The overhead door slammed back down like a guillotine. I wondered if they were gone for good. I turned my attention back to the key Andrew gave me. It felt warm and willful in my hand. I ran for the storage room.

The lock resisted like clenched teeth but soon sunk into place with satisfaction. The door flung open like an open wound. I felt around for the lights and flipped them on. Light slopped in hard and heavy. There he was. My father was hunched in the corner like some underfed, feeble animal. He flinched from the light, then turned back to his task – plucking paint chips off a table leg, scattering them like dried leaves on the dirty floor. I hardly recognized this man carved down to the bone. I ran to him, my throat turned to sand, my words barely coming up.

"Dad. Dad. Are you okay? Are you okay?"

I hugged him, picked up his drooping face, felt his heart, his forehead.

"Hmm?" he mumbled. "No more. No more tests. That's enough for today."

"Come on, Dad. Time to go home."

Home. What was home to him now?

His shed? Vera's home?

His truck.

No.

Me. I was his home.

I tried to pull him off the floor, but he thrashed at me.

Victor's words came to me. *A madman.* That he didn't even know who I was anymore. What did they do to him? I could kill them all. How dare I tell Cassandra and Cybil to lower their guns.

Then I looked at what he was doing with the paint chips. He was making art out of them. Some mosaic of a girl, a woman. Maybe of my mother. Maybe me. I realized he'd been working only by touch and the subtle glow of the EXIT sign above the door. I couldn't help but draw similarities: how I created mandalas with pinecones when my father first moved us to Snoqualmie Pass. Something to keep the brain wet.

He turned his head to me and searched my eyes. I wondered if he might ask for water or food. Maybe he assumed I was his warden, some basement keeper. The room reeked of mildew and rust, with a small bed tucked in the corner. Trails of footprints marked the floor, leading to the door. They kept him here, then moved him upstairs whenever they needed to scrape his brain. I must've passed him every time I visited. "Dad," I whispered. "It's me, Pip." He stared vacantly. He looked smaller than I ever thought possible.

Cybil's voice came low from the door. "Backup is on the way." I didn't look at her.

I kept my eyes focused on him, wondering where his mind was. His eyes slumped deep in his head, and his damp wheeze told a cruel story. He looked like he had only a few hours of life left in him. *What did Victor do to you?*

Chapter Ninety-Eight

When Cybil's officers arrived, my father curled up like an armadillo.

He mumbled indecipherably until it turned to weeping. Between garbled syllables, I caught slices – "Please. Please. No more." His words morphed into a coughing fit as though the pressure of it might break his ribs in half. I couldn't stand to see him like this. I combed my hand over his head and tried to calm him. His silver beard was so long now, sagging down his chest like a bib.

The officers, four of them, struggled to get him to his feet. He clawed at them like a feral cat. He must've thought they were there to do bad things to him. His cough came on again, sounding like branches breaking, pausing only when dark blood pooled up from his throat and splattered down his beard. He doubled over like an old goose about to die.

"Lord, have mercy," one officer said, looking to me like I had an answer. I didn't.

Cybil's radio crackled from her belt – *ambulance almost here.* The sound of her boots trailed away. Meanwhile, my father sat there, bleeding from his cracked lips, staring ahead at nothing. I could have cried, but I was a hawk from too much adrenaline. I stayed beside him on the cold floor as the officers questioned Farley and checked on Vera, their voices muted like they were in a far room.

I tried to remember my father as he once was. But memories were hard to bring into focus. I knew they were there, sitting in piles of glass, but I couldn't pull them out of the shuffle. Couldn't lift them. They weren't organized or whole. I sank into darkness behind closed eyes, searching for something meaningful, anything. And then I found a memory perched on the tip of my brain, some warm petal waiting to be plucked. It sat like a canister, some forgotten centerpiece on a barren table in my mind, ready to be poured out.

It went like this:

When I was a kid, he took me and my mother camping once, to Snoqualmie Pass. It was night, and it was raining. I was small, curled up in the corner of the tent beside my mother, afraid. My father was soaked through his clothes, tipping pools of rainwater from the ceiling of the tent with a stick. Thunder crashed so loudly, I felt it shake the ground below me. I fell asleep to the chaos, my cheek pressed into my mother's breast.

And then it was morning. I awoke inside the damp blue tent, sunlight sifting through the nylon walls. My father sat across from me, cross-legged, holding a paper plate full of pancakes. Beyond the tent, a robin sang.

"Morning, sweetheart," he had said.

His voice was young then. Full of life.

"Did the thunder get us?" I asked, still groggy.

He smiled. "Nope. I scared it off."

I blinked at him, sitting up in my sleeping bag. "What do you mean?"

"I didn't let it near our tent," he said, leaning in conspiratorially. "I went outside, jumped around like a monkey, and screamed until it disappeared. That thunder took one look at me and thought, *that guy is crazy*. It was like, *I'm outta here*. Didn't you know? I'm a storm tamer."

I couldn't contain the smile that crept across my lips.

"I'm serious!" he said, laughing. "You were sleeping so soundly, though. I think your snoring might've scared it off too."

"Nuh-uh!"

He shuffled over our clustered nest of sleeping bags, the plate of pancakes steady in his hand, and set it beside me. He brushed my dark messy hair from my eyes and kissed my forehead.

"Mom and I kept watch over you all night. You were safe. Everything's okay now. The storm is gone. And these pancakes are delicious."

I stared at him in earnest. "But...how did you do all those things to make the storm go away? And I didn't even see you do it?"

At the time, it was unthinkable that something so extraordinary could happen outside my sight, beyond my knowing.

"Sometimes," he said, "the most important things are the ones you don't see. That's just how life is. That's how love works too. It's always there, even when you can't see it."

The dull groan of doors snapped me back to the room, followed by the buzz of an engine. Cybil had figured out a way to let the ambulance into the lot. A stretcher rattled into the room as EMTs rushed in. One EMT went to Vera, her face pale as oats. Three of them moved in on my father. But he swung wildly at them when they got close. The EMTs stood back, mumbling softly about their restraint plan. My father returned to the paint chips, speaking quietly to no one. The lights in the room were a sickening white, making everything feel bleached. I thought of something.

"Turn the lights off!" I shouted. "I have an idea. If he can hear my voice in the darkness, he might be more compliant. He might remember me."

The EMTs exchanged curious looks before one of them, a woman with a stern voice, stepped forward. "We can't do that, ma'am," she said. "We need to assess his condition."

Another EMT chimed in. "Turning off the lights could be dangerous, especially if he becomes violent again," he said.

They were polite, but their refusal was firm. "I'm sorry," the first EMT added. "We understand you're trying to help, but we need to stay safe. Safety is rule number one."

I was past rules. "I know my father. Turn the damn lights off!"

Farley walked toward the light switch as though it was just him and me in the living room, and I'd asked him to complete a simple task. *Click.* The room flushed with darkness.

"Everyone quiet, please," I said.

I reached for my father's cold, flimsy hand. He flinched at first, but then he stilled between my fingers. "Dad," I whispered. "I'm scared of this storm."

No one moved. No one said a word. I could hear their breath rising and falling behind me, like rain tinkling on the tent.

"Dad, can you make the storm go away?"

I closed my eyes. I tried to harness more memories, more ideas to stir my father to life, but none came. They were hidden in nooks, placed on the wrong shelf, jammed in a grate.

"Dad, please." My voice broke. Tears fell, hidden by darkness. My shoulders shook. Someone shifted toward the light switch. They'd had enough of my nonsense. Maybe they were right. Victor was right too. My father was gone. He didn't know who I was. And it would require crude force to get him onto the stretcher.

"Dad.

"Dad.

"Please," I said again, so soft even I couldn't hear myself. "Please. The storm."

I slipped my hand away and brought it to my face to wipe my tears.

I couldn't place all my memories.

And neither could he.

But you don't need memories to understand love.

I felt his hand search for mine, landing soft in my palm.

"Don't worry, Pip," my father whispered. "That's what storm tamers are for."

Chapter Ninety-Nine

Nine Months Later…

There were days during my pregnancy I thought I'd never get my father back. He clung to the window like some old house cat. Sunlight bled through the glass and stained his face amber as he stretched his toes out like a lazy Maine coon. Sometimes he wouldn't say a word. Whole days passed with nothing from him.

Aunt Vera's house was cramped with all of us there. But she was kind. She'd pull him from the window after his sun sessions and settle him on the sofa like a fallen soldier and launch a comedy on the old TV for him. She brought treats on trays for the both of us – croissants, peppermint tea, small squares of chocolate. It was then I saw her clearly. She wasn't a saint; she was more. A mother figure. Not a replacement though. Just a reminder that family, even when carved from scraps, can still form something strong. Something beautiful.

Slowly, my father's mumblings turned to words, and soon he started calling us by name. And on the day that I gave birth to my daughter, it was like he was born all over again. We all were.

Vera brought him to the hospital. He ambled in steadily and stood over me where I rested. The baby, swathed in a white blanket, lay snug on my chest. He looked down at her, eyes wide, as though the sight of her had turned a key inside his head.

"What's her name?" he asked.

The baby squirmed, rooting for milk. The nurses said she was clever already, and I believed them. I wondered then if my mother's heart had felt this way once – like steel and lace. Like you'd do anything to keep this tiny soul safe, but one small sob from her could crush you to pieces.

I thought of my mother often; mainly, I wondered if she was here now, somewhere nearby, watching us.

"A name? Well." I looked to Farley. He shifted beside me on the hospital chair that had become his second home.

"We have a few ideas," he said. "But we haven't picked one yet."

There was silence in the room. The precious girl lay calm on my breast. I felt her little heart gallop against mine. Her scent was so peaceful and pure. And then, from nowhere, a name came, so clear it might have been spoken aloud – *Chloe.*

"What was that?"

Farley gave me a look. "What was what?"

"You didn't hear that?"

He peeked over his shoulder. "The heater, maybe?"

My father looked puzzled too. No one had heard the voice. Only me.

I half smiled. "Yeah. The heater." I paused, then regained momentum, thinking about the voice I just heard. I knew it belonged to my mother.

"What about the name Chloe?" I suggested.

"That's cute," Farley said. "I like it. How did we miss that one?"

But my father? He pulled back in surprise. "Chloe. Cove loved that name. We almost named…" He stopped and shook his head, eyes glassy. But he smiled, really smiled, for the first time in so long. "It's a beautiful name."

It was strange. I'd never even considered the name. But it had struck something deep inside my father, making him remember something, remember her. He'd not spoken my mother's name in so long. But I knew the truth. The name came from her. She was with me. After all this time. I was certain.

I cradled my baby, holding her tight, when hope suddenly plummeted. If a part of my mother still lived inside me, then so did *he.*

Two years later…

Farley warmed milk from the fridge and threaded honey in like an alchemist. Chloe watched him, her marble-green eyes wide with wonder.

Seeing Farley like this, a father, watered my soul so deliciously. He was gentle, protective. A caring father and husband.

Our girl lit up whenever he walked in the room. She'd become our universe. And after everything we lost to The Reverie Cloud, getting here felt like a small miracle. We didn't take anything for granted. However, my memories were still plagued with holes. Full pages were torn from the book. Farley fared better, though he had his moments. We both did. In fact, if I were to write a memoir, it would begin here. Just the last year. Therapy taught me that: begin where you are. Say it out loud, write it down, give it shape. On days my father was most lucid, he promised he'd try therapy too. But that was a thin promise so far.

My baby girl had just finished her food, her messy hands whopping against the tray of the highchair. "Here, baby," Farley said to her, setting her bottle in front of her. "Warm milk." It was Saturday. Farley had the day off. He had his own landscaping business now – a small crew of men and a reliable truck with the company's name painted on the side. It wasn't much, but it was enough.

We'd moved to Leavenworth. Farley found clients here, good neighbors in need of well-tamed yards. He made the work his own, and so did I. On his jobs, he'd cross-sell my woodwork – small things I crafted by hand. It had taken me two years to learn the skill. My father taught me everything he knew.

Carving had become a sort of redemption for me. My father too. On days he forgot things – names, memories – his hands remembered the wood. His voice softened when he showed me what to do, how to cradle the knife, how to listen to the grain. I made spoons, boxes, mailboxes and signs, candle holders, and garden figures. Things people wanted.

Farley and I called ourselves Renner Landscaping and Wood Artistry. We made it ours.

Our new home was modest, one might say cramped, but the land around it was voluptuous. A creek ran alongside our chestnut-brown home, its waterway always in motion. Evergreens rose tall around us carrying a holiday scent in the breeze. Beyond them, there were plenty of neighbors, and right outside our community there was a school just waiting for Chloe to grow into.

For months, my father lived with us. It wouldn't have been possible without woodcarving. It was his medicine. My salve. It was slow getting into a rhythm, but soon it became a ritual for him, for us. Farley built a shed in the yard that turned into our studio. There, I listened to my father's lessons – basswood was best for beginners, walnut had a rich color value, and cherry was meant for finer details.

But after a few months, I could sense loneliness brewing inside him. Some gap I couldn't fill. He'd linger at the table long after his coffee was sipped. There were no words left in him, no more lessons for the day, just time for staring and tracing the rim of his mug. Then one afternoon Aunt Vera visited. She brought a casserole and bread with her, and I saw him blush at the sight of her. His posture seemed to lengthen, and his eyes stirred with life. He even tried some jokes. They landed crooked, but it didn't matter. For the moment, he was whole. And it was then I knew I couldn't keep him with me forever.

She started coming by more often. Meanwhile, memories began returning to him; he remembered the fire. It angered and saddened him. He wanted to rebuild. I didn't like the idea. He was still too vulnerable. Oh, he pestered me about it, begged me with tears.

I spoke to Vera alone.

"He comes alive when he talks about the cabin," she said, close and hushed. It was true. He was getting better by the day, and Vera and the cabin were fueling him with purpose. Lately, it was only when the journalists came or the police knocked on the door, questioning him about The Reverie Cloud, that he would he slip back into that fragile, manic state, deflecting their questions.

"I know, Aunt Vera, but—" I said.

"You don't understand. I feel alive when I'm around him too."

There was a twinkle in her eye. She was persistent. She...*liked him.*

"What if he stays at my place," she said, "while he rebuilds? I'll feed him. Make sure he has someone to talk to. It'll give you and Farley some time with Chloe."

Something shifted when I met her eyes. Maybe it was the way she looked so genuine, or maybe it was the realization that she wasn't taking my mother's place. She was simply Aunt Vera, offering what she could. I nodded, not because she or I had it all figured out, but because I knew I could accept change without losing that which was most precious to me.

And Vera had always been there, hadn't she? Even during my sessions in The Reverie Cloud, she'd been watching out for us. I thought back to shortly after she'd been released from the hospital, her bullet wound still healing. We were all staying at her place at the time – Farley and my father camped out in the living room, absorbed by some show. Vera had pulled me into the kitchen. She offered me mint tea, steam rising between us as we sat on high stools at the counter. I remembered then – it was the same counter where, once, I'd seen a rogue gun. The memory was hazy, like the view in a hurricane. But something was there.

"I have to tell you something, Pip," Vera said quietly. "I've known Officer Cybil and Cassandra longer than you think. Before Farley ever worked with Cassandra."

I blinked. "How?"

"We met years ago, in a target practice class." She hesitated, cautious. "I know this last year has been confusing. The program did things to your memory. I'm sorry if this upsets you, but there were nights you came home acting…strange. Like you weren't really there. And then I started seeing men – on our land, lurking. Like they were looking for something, or someone.

"One time I walked right up to one of them and asked them what they wanted. They mentioned Dr. Screed's old paperwork. Then they asked about *you*. If you knew anything." She shook her head. "I didn't like that. It didn't sit right with me. I asked Cybil to keep an eye out on the neighborhood. She told me to keep a gun on hand, just in case.

"I didn't tell you then because I didn't know how serious it all was, and I didn't want to worry you. I thought you needed space, to figure things out for yourself. But, Pip…" Her voice trailed off. "I regret it. I should've paid closer attention."

I felt the ground move beneath me.

"I took my gun out of the safe," she went on. "One night, I was so stupid – I left it out on the counter while I went to change a load of laundry. You saw it. It was a night you seemed really off. Just swaying there, staring at it, something strange in your eyes." Her eyes welled up. "God, Pip, I'm just so glad nothing bad happened. I'm just so glad you're okay."

She glanced at my father, still laughing at the television in the other room, a sound so rare it felt like we'd unearthed a long-lost ruby.

Vera smiled and then turned to me softly. "He has a great laugh, doesn't he?"

I reached for her hand. "Thank you," I whispered. "For everything."

Chapter One Hundred

One Year Later…

On Halloween day, Chloe wore a red crocheted hat freckled with white dots. My little mushroom was almost four. She was tall for her age, always on the go. And today, her mission was clear: chocolate. "Come on, fairy!" she hollered, waving me along in my slapdash winged costume. She was faster than I could keep up with, darting down the leaf-scattered sidewalk, her linen bag swinging as she collected candy from every door that opened for her.

The smell of smoke laced the crisp air. Farley, dressed as a gnome, reached for my hand as we followed her. At the end of a cozy block, a bonfire crackled in someone's yard, drawing us in. A sign hung on the fence: *Enter if you dare! Treats inside.* It was a house we'd seen before but never thought too much about. The black metal gate squealed open as we pushed through. Inside, it seemed the whole town of Leavenworth was gathered. I recognized some families from Chloe's school, and one of my clients as well. "Hey, Pip! I'm in love with my new candle holders." The air was rich with mulled cider and roasted marshmallows, and the hum of conversation and children's laughter wrapped around us.

A shrill cackle torched the air. A witch drifted from child to child, offering candies from her swaying seed bag, an apple etched into the canvas. Her hat was black and crumpled, her nose warted and plastic, and the white wool of her hair puffed out like smoke.

She came to us, hunched over in character, offering Chloe some plastic-wrapped fruity candy. Chloe drew back, pouting her lips.

"Oh, don't be scared. I'm a nice witch," the witch said.

"I only like chocolate," Chloe said assertively. "Not that."

The witch laughed. It was no longer a cackle, but something real. She rose to meet me and Farley eye-to-eye. "Here I thought I was scary, but she just knows what she wants. I like that." Then, she paused, her smile fading. She looked hard at me. "Pip?"

I squinted past her green makeup and fake bumpy nose. "Lyra Pierce."

Her face brightened, and the red on her lips stretched as she smiled. "It's been years. Wow. Are you in Leavenworth now?"

"Yes," I said, still processing the sight of her. "This is my daughter, Chloe. And my husband, Farley."

"Nice to meet you," Farley said, slightly tipping his burgundy gnome hat, trying to keep up with everything.

Lyra chuckled, digging into her bag. "Hold on." She puttered around until she found a mini chocolate bar. She bent low, dropping back to her sorcerous rasp. "Here you are, Chloe. One chocolate bar, *full of worms. He he he!*"

Lyra straightened, tucking the bag back under her arm with a wink. "It's funny," she said, turning her attention to me. "When we moved out here, everyone said tech folks are fleeing to Leavenworth. You know, with all the remote work and those layoffs last year. A chunk of Seattle and Issaquah seems to be out here now, working from their cabins. But I never expected to actually see someone I knew."

Tech folk. I once would have felt honored to wear the title, but now it felt like a curse.

Chloe inspected her chocolate bar as though it might wiggle away from her. She squinted at Lyra suspiciously. "Are there really worms in here?"

"Oh, oops!" Lyra laughed. "No."

I smiled. "It's a joke, Clo."

Chloe giggled, understanding the ruse at play.

"Honestly, she probably would've eaten it regardless," Farley said. "Chocolate is gold around our house."

"My little guy's the same way," Lyra said.

"Oh, you have a son," I said.

"Yeah, he's probably the same age as Chloe." She pointed toward a man with clear glasses, dressed as a shiny, silver robot near the bonfire. "Ray's his dad." Ray Cleary was handing out marshmallows and sticks to a group of kids. His easy, natural smile made it look like he belonged there more than any old copy machine.

I felt my stomach drop. Ray Cleary. Lyra Pierce. The memory of Nyxyn clawed back to me, their voices once booming as gods, their shadows eating up entire rooms. And now here they were, grounded, real, handing my daughter a chocolate bar.

"I want a marshmallow!" Chloe piped.

"I'll take her," Farley said, his hand slipping into hers.

As the two of them sauntered toward the firepit, Lyra leaned into me, pulling her witch nose down. "Hey, I never knew why you left Nyxyn. Vera Renner was tightlipped about it. I never wanted to pry. I hope you're doing good now?"

I thought back to the day I found my father in the storage room. I was in shreds afterwards. A shell of myself. I couldn't function, let alone look at a computer screen. I didn't want to be anywhere near them. I craved reality. The woods were safer. Real. You can trust the air, the leaves. The way they sway above you, giving you breath. It might've looked like a nervous breakdown from the outside. A crack. But I called it a reset.

I had told Aunt Vera that leaving my father didn't sit right. I was ready to focus on family. Nyxyn was out of the question. She understood. There were days I thirsted for a normal routine – coffee in a tumbler, the buzz of an office, a reason to look put together and not like I'd just tumbled out of bed. It was Snoqualmie Pass all over again, that same feeling of being stuck in a world I didn't know how to escape. But other days, the world slimmed down to a block of wood and a sharp knife. Something I could control and shape. Something I could hold still for a while.

"I work with my husband now," I said. "Nyxyn feels like a world away. You and the Nyxynauts were always so inventive."

"Us?" Lyra said. "You were the inventive one. You know that Fazzle design you made? We raved about it for years. It became the gold standard. I'm not there anymore, but I bet they still talk about it."

I blinked. "I didn't know anyone knew I made it."

Lyra shrugged. "Andrew Janess never came back either. His disappearance was stranger than yours. But one day, out of the blue, he sent this letter to the company. No return address."

"What did it say?"

She leaned in and lowered her voice. "It said Wyatt got shot during a robbery. Andrew wrote that he wanted to give us some closure, that he missed us all. But the weirdest part? There was no obit in the papers. So, I'm not sure how he knew about Wyatt, or why no one else did. We all sort of dropped it after a while – got bogged down with work, and I guess we just moved on. Anyway, in the last paragraph, he gave you full credit for the Fazzle design."

"He did?"

"Yeah. You ever hear from him?"

"No."

"Me neither. Ray's still there. I've moved on."

"That must be far for Ray."

"Remote work. Goes in for client meetings."

"Ah. And what about you?"

"I'll show you. Stay right here!" She darted inside, leaving me on the lawn. Little monsters and goblins hurried past, the fire snapping in the distance. Chloe stood at the bonfire, marshmallow in hand. I glanced at Ray, who was talking to Farley – casual and familiar – two men who had no reason to speak before now. Ray caught my eye and gave me a smile. His look seemed to say, *I'll meet up with you in a second!*

Lyra burst back out, handing me her business card.

"Pierce Point," she said. "I started my own development company. It's small right now. Just a few of us. But I'd love to work with you someday, Pip, if you're ever looking for something new. You always did your own thing at Nyxyn, and I admired that."

She held out her card, and I took it. Lyra Pierce, once untouchable, now standing here offering me a job and my daughter chocolate as if we were old friends.

"Thank you," I said. "I'll think about it."

I felt the pull of her offer. The quiet return to a digital life. But before I could fully process it, my eye caught movement beyond the black gate, past the candy-corn lights and skulls strung like garland. It was my father wandering down the block looking rumpled and lost. My breath stalled in my chest.

Chapter One Hundred One

When I found my father outside the gate, he was rattling off words, fast and broken.

He clutched a stack of messy papers in both hands. The wind lifted his silver hair, making him appear undone. I knew he and Vera were visiting, but not until dinner. And certainly not like this – wandering the streets, muttering like he was in mid-argument with himself.

When he saw me, he gestured at the stack – hundreds of pages haphazardly aligned. His face was gaunt and bewildered, as if holding his papers hurt more than he could possibly ever explain. A low buzz rose in my head, like static waiting to burst. I pressed it back.

Through the gate slits, I saw Farley searching for me, Chloe's red hat bobbing like a flag. I felt the urge to collect them both and go home. But my father turned, staring at the smoke rising from the bonfire. "Come on. We can burn these in there."

He darted for the gate, moving like a wave about to crash to shore. I caught him by the arm and pulled him into a hug, the papers crumpling between us like leaves. For a moment, his body stilled, and the anxiety seeped out of him.

"What's going on?" I whispered into his ear.

"I was cleaning out the foundation." I knew he meant the cabin. The one he and Vera had started to rebuild. "And I found something. Something buried." He paused, swallowing hard. "It was a chest. Full of drawings."

I pulled back. "What kind of drawings?"

"*Mama!?*"

Chloe's voice shattered the moment. I turned to see her bright red hat moving swiftly through the slats. I needed to go to her. But I stayed one second longer with my father there.

He looked down at the papers. "I…I can't remember what these are. I should. But I can't." He touched his temple, pressing his fingers deep as though to activate the memory. "They feel important. Dangerous. But it's gone. I can't explain it. The feeling is there; but the reason for it isn't."

His voice shook. "I need to get rid of them, Pip. If I don't, I feel that something bad will happen. Something evil." He looked at me with desperation. "I thought maybe you'd know."

"Can I?" I asked. I eased the papers from his grip.

"*Mama!?*"

His grip trembled as he let go. I held the stack close. Chloe's voice rang out again from behind the gate, until she burst onto the sidewalk, bobbing up and down in her mushroom suit. Farley followed close behind.

"Mama! Granddad!" Chloe shouted, jumping in place.

My father's face softened. Whatever tension ate at him melted away like wax at the sight of her. He beamed like a child, and with a soft chuckle, he followed her into the yard without a second thought.

"Well, I guess we're going back in," I said to Farley.

"I didn't know where you went," he said. "I was nervous."

"Sorry. My dad was on the move."

"He's early."

"Yeah, I just hope he's not regressing."

Farley planted a warm kiss on my cheek. "I'll keep an eye on him. Catch up with your friends."

"Thank you," I said, exhaling. "Then we should all get him home. Looks like he walked here."

"Okay, I'll bring the car around after."

"That's okay," I said with a faint smile. "I'll drive."

I watched Farley, my father, and Chloe get pulled into some Halloween scavenger hunt game. Lyra stood off to the side, smiling proudly as kids searched for orange paper-cut pumpkins scattered around the yard as clues. I moved toward the warm bosom of the bonfire. I had wanted to catch up with Ray, but he was tangled up in the game too. I stood alone, my father's papers heavy in my hands. He seemed to forget about them for the time being. The fire crackled, and I thought of throwing them in. They would burn quickly. No one was watching. No one would ever know.

But something held me back. I flipped through the pages, slow at first. But then, my heart began to pound. Schematic after schematic. Diagrams, notes, and codes, all marked with *Evadere* on them. It felt like I was prying open a sealed tomb.

Then, I came upon a page that felt verboten.

"My god," I whispered.

The *Requiem* schematic. The one Andrew and Victor had hunted. There it was, effortless in my hands, lines scored in permanent ink. I stared. A map traced a brain, pathways like snarled vines. Nodes dotted in my father's codes. It looked familiar and foreign at the same time. It was beautiful, just like Andrew had said it would be. *Incredible*, I thought. But we had moved on from this. All of us. And my father wanted this burned. I glanced up to make sure no one was looking, ready to toss the stack in the flames.

My wrist was in position when I heard a voice. *His* voice.

Stop.

The word pounded down on me like an iron fist. My head filled with static. The voice reverberated inside my skull.

Don't burn them.

Look at them.

Look.

Keep them safe.

I closed my eyes, but the voice rose to a shout.

Look!

My hands began to tremble, as the fire's heat swam across my face. I opened my eyes, feeling the flames reflected in them. I couldn't let go of the schematic, nor look away from it either, as though it had a pulse of its own.

"*Mama!*"

With a sharp gasp, I finally broke eye contact. The papers slipped from my hands, but I caught them just before they scattered. I rolled the stack tight, my fingers moving fast, like I was being watched. I slipped the bundle into the side pocket of my coat, pressing it close to my body.

My little mushroom ran to me. “Mama! I found five pumpkins!”

“Good girl,” I said, taking her hand, pulling her away from the fire. “Good girl.”

A pulse of energy prickled behind my eyes.

Yes.

Good girl.

Chapter One Hundred Two

Months Later…

Chloe was four now, and the doctor said it was a little early to lose her first tooth, but not unheard of. She was not taking it well. It was dusk, and some doom had taken up rent inside her mind. The concept of losing some physical part of herself was unimaginable. A kind of death, though she could never name it that way. The world had indeed ended. We walked hand in hand to her bedroom where a cozy rocking chair sat waiting.

I invited her onto my lap. I tried not to speak too much. The tooth fairy could not fix this. Neither could money. Instead, I listened to her small voice and followed the undulating hills of her emotions. I didn't have an answer for her grief. I knew what my mother would say though; and in that moment, I heard her. *It's part of life*, she said. *To live is to let go*.

In recent years, it had been a battle. There were two voices inside me. My mother's – loving and steadfast, guiding me through trouble. And then there was Victor's – contemptuous, driven by power lust and self-preservation. My mother's voice, I was certain, kept him at bay. When he rose to the surface, her words would sprout mighty, sweeping him away like dust. And then there was my own voice, naked and raw, still growing, still trying. It was different than both of theirs. It didn't always comfort. Didn't always control. Didn't push. It just was.

I thought about Victor sometimes. Whether his body lay somewhere, preserved like frozen meat. Whether someone might dare risk bringing him back someday, in some form, some way.

On the rocker, Chloe clutched my finger.

"I don't want it to go away," she said.

I kissed the top of her head. "I know. It's okay to be sad about it. I'm here for you."

"Will it grow back?"

"A new one will take its place."

"Will that one go away too?"

I thought for a moment, and decided on, "No."

"Can I keep my tooth?"

"If you like."

Her small sobs came on like a dripping faucet.

I thought of telling her that a new tooth will be strong, that we can have a tooth celebration – some sort of ritual for each tooth to fall! But it wasn't right. Not then. Maybe later once the feelings settled, once we got through this tunnel of sadness together. I didn't want to placate the truth either. That loss is part of life. That we need to wiggle out joy while we're at it. That everyone, everyone, experiences this.

I didn't say anything.

I closed my eyes and thought of my mother holding me when my own tooth was ready to tumble out and when the dragon story scared me. I couldn't remember what she had told me then. I just knew she was there.

She was there.

Later, when Chloe was fed and smiling, we walked as a family into the woods. Golden leaves lay at our feet, and the sky glowed blue through a canopy of trees. Farley tottered through a mountain of leaves, shuffling them into the air. Chloe was close behind, laughing, confetti everywhere. I stood still, breathing in the reality around me. It was enough. It was everything. Sure, there were days I thought of other paths, like when I looked at Lyra Pierce's business card and contemplated calling her. Or when I thought about taking my father's drawings out of hiding. But mainly, I enjoyed creating memories. Rock-solid ones. For Chloe. Maybe this would be part of her carousel someday – the breath of shuffled leaves, our laughter mingled with the wind. I moved playfully into the leaves with them both.

Chapter One Hundred Three

Farley called out while I was on the phone with Lyra.

"Package for you!"

"Can I call you back later tonight?" I asked.

"Of course," Lyra said.

Click.

I stepped into the living room as Farley brought a package inside from the stoop. Chloe burst in; her face lit up. "Is it a present for me?"

"What could it be?" Farley asked, setting it down on the coffee table.

"I have no idea. I'm not expecting anything. You?"

He shook his head. We knelt around the package. I let Chloe open it, ripping past cardboard and bubble wrap. I helped her a little.

"Is this mine?" she asked, pulling out something soft and familiar. It was gray and white, worn with time – the hand-knit blanket my mother and I made the night the power failed. The memory returned in flashes – us sitting together in the dim glow, knitting the blanket by the tap of rain. I hadn't thought of it in years, but running my hands over the fleecy fabric connected me to that time and place, and to my mother, in such a profound way, I felt a gentle sorrow settle in the pit of me. A small note fell out, tucked between the folds.

This should really belong to you. We'll meet again. AJ.

"What is it?" Chloe asked.

"It's something I knit a long time ago. And now, somehow, it's come back."

I tried not to let my expression falter as I stared at the note and wondered: *How does he know my new address?* I gulped it down. Because all that mattered was the way Chloe's face shone when she discovered something I once lost found its way home.

Epilogue

I sat across from my therapist. Silence spread between us as she watched me with patient eyes.

"Let's try this again, Pip," she said gently. "We've talked about your confusion in the program – how not all the pieces are there for you. You're not sure which memories are authentic, and which ones are the result of…*memory tampering*, as you called it. And we've talked about the voices – your mother's, Victor's. But I want to know about *your* voice. Not theirs. Can you tell me what it sounds like to you?"

My hands fidgeted in my lap. The air conditioner blared suddenly, loosening my focus. I closed my eyes and breathed in, trying to ground myself. I thought of my comfort carvings, especially the new one I had just made of my mother, how I brought it to my father's old hands in the dark, telling him to feel. *Feel.*

I opened my eyes.

"Don't force it," she said. "It's in there somewhere. Reach past the noise."

I exhaled. "My voice? My voice. I once heard my voice ring out loud as church bells… It was my mine, but it was also beyond me – I don't know if I believe in higher selves, but perhaps it was something like that. Like something telling me: *I'm here. I've always been here.*"

The therapist sat still for a moment. Listening. Waiting. Then she leaned forward, her face catching a soft ray of light from the window. "Pip, you've survived things no one should have to go through. The people who were supposed to keep you safe didn't. Your memories were stolen and twisted. And yet, you're still here, trying to find your balance – your voice. That's something. That takes strength."

I felt my chest relax, but my throat tightened as I suppressed tears. "I just don't know how to fix it."

"You don't have to fix everything today," she said. "Not for yourself, and not for anyone else. But you can let yourself live – even with the questions, even with scars. You are not broken. You are *becoming.*"

Her voice was a steady heartbeat. "Sometimes healing isn't about returning to the person you once were. Sometimes, it's about stepping into the person you are now. That voice you heard? That higher self? It's not something far, far away. It's not accessed by a program or hidden in code. It's *you.* And it's pulling you toward something new – something waiting on the other side of pain. Are you ready to let her in?"

My tears broke free, as I let out a flimsy breath. "Yes," I said.

She studied me a moment. "Will you let the voices rest, Pip? And let *yourself* lead the way now?"

But *his* voice was still there – Victor's. Scratching at the surface, prowling in the hollows like a phantom that refused to die. And behind him, matted up in the noise, I felt *her* too – my mother's voice. She was quiet but unyielding, whispering lovely things between his roars. I'm sure she didn't mean for it to get this way, but the two of them coiled together like ivy wrapped around a pole, inseparable. To let go of one, I had to let go of both.

I swallowed hard. I heard a hiss.

Find Andrew. Bring me back.

"No," I whispered, shoving him back down. There wasn't space for him. Just like in the program, I could snuff him out by choice alone. Yet, it felt like betrayal to quiet my mother too.

But I'd known too much loss to let this game continue. I knew what it was like to drift from Farley, to lose my mother, an ache as constant as the creek beside our home, to see Chloe move like a shadow in the program, fragile and out of my control, knowing I couldn't hold her forever. I was losing my father too – slowly, sadly, and surely – like sand slipping through my fingers no matter how tightly I cupped them.

But I wouldn't lose myself in the process. For my sake. For Chloe's.

I closed my eyes and whispered a promise inside my mind: "I'm quieting the voices now. It's going to hurt. But it's the only way."

Acknowledgments

Huge thanks to Patrick Vincent Welsh for reading the early pages of this novel and helping me see where scenes could open up through dialogue – and for introducing me to Larry Forberg, whose thoughtful direction arrived at just the right time. To my son, Felix, and husband, Mike, who unknowingly sparked the idea for this book while we checked out virtual goggles at the computer store. To my mom, who listened patiently as I rattled off this complex concept while we floated in the pool, and who suggested that Andrew might need a redemption arc. Finally, thank you to Don D'Auria and the team at Flame Tree Press for giving me the room to imagine freely. Writing about The Reverie Cloud became my own Reverie Cloud, a space where anything could happen.

About the Author

Elizabeth Anne Martins is a Philadelphia-based writer who studied English and Publishing at Rosemont College. Her writing often explores resilience, identity, and survival, blending speculative elements with deeply human stories.

Her debut novel, *Dry Lands*, is a post-apocalyptic story of motherhood and survival set in a world reshaped by water. The book was named a 2024 Great Group Reads pick by the Women's National Book Association and has resonated with readers who connect with its themes of hope and endurance.

When she's not writing, Elizabeth can usually be found at the piano, composing something new or playing a duet with her son or husband. Music, like storytelling, is her way of making sense of the world – one note or word at a time.

FLAME TREE PRESS
FICTION WITHOUT FRONTIERS
Award-Winning Authors & Original Voices

Flame Tree Press is the trade fiction imprint of Flame Tree Publishing, focusing on excellent writing in horror and the supernatural, crime and mystery, science fiction and fantasy. Our aim is to explore beyond the boundaries of the everyday, with tales from both award-winning authors and original voices.

•

Other titles by Elizabeth Anne Martins:
Dry Lands

The Sentient by Nadia Afifi
Junction by Daniel M. Bensen
Keeper of Sorrows by Rachel Fikes
Silent Key by Laurel Hightower
The Widening Gyre by Michael R. Johnston
The Heart of Winter by Shona Kinsella
The Sky Woman by J.D. Moyer
The Guardian by J.D. Moyer
Brittle by Beth Overmyer
Tempered Glass by Beth Overmyer
The Goblets Immortal by Beth Overmyer
One Eye Opened in That Other Place by Christi Nogle
The Last Feather by Shameez Patel Papathanasiou
Tinderbox by W.A. Simpson
Tarotmancer by W.A. Simpson
The Hatter's Daughter by W.A. Simpson
A Killing Fire by Faye Snowden
A Killing Rain by Faye Snowden
A Sword of Bronze and Ashes by Anna Smith Spark
Stars Like Us by Stephen K. Stanford
Idolatry by Aditya Sudarshan
The Roamers by Francesco Verso
Whisperwood by Alex Woodroe
Of Kings, Queens & Colonies by Johnny Worthen

•